Lucy King spent her adoles[cence in a] glamorous and exciting wor[ld] when she really ought to have been paying attention to her teachers. As she couldn't live in a dream world for ever, she eventually acquired a degree in languages and an eclectic collection of jobs. After a decade in southwest Spain, Lucy now lives with her young family in Wiltshire, England. When not writing, or trying to think up new and innovative things to do with mince, she spends her time reading, failing to finish cryptic crosswords and dreaming of the golden beaches of Andalusia.

Millie Adams is the very dramatic pseudonym of *New York Times* bestselling author Maisey Yates. Happiest surrounded by yarn, her family and the small woodland creatures she calls pets, she lives in a small house on the edge of the woods, which allows her to escape in the way she loves best— in the pages of a book. She loves intense alpha heroes and the women who dare to go toe to toe with them.

Also by Lucy King

Heirs to a Greek Empire miniseries

Virgin's Night with the Greek
A Christmas Consequence for the Greek
The Flaw in His Rio Revenge
Expecting the Greek's Heir

Also by Millie Adams

Italian's Christmas Acquisition
His Highness's Diamond Decree
After-Hours Heir

Work Wives to Billionaires' Wives collection

Billionaire's Bride Bargain

Discover more at millsandboon.co.uk.

WITH HIS RING...

LUCY KING

MILLIE ADAMS

MILLS & BOON

First published in Great Britain 2025
by Mills & Boon, an imprint of HarperCollins*Publishers* Ltd,
1 London Bridge Street, London, SE1 9GF

www.harpercollins.co.uk

HarperCollins*Publishers*, Macken House, 39/40 Mayor Street Upper, Dublin 1, D01 C9W8, Ireland

With His Ring… © 2025 Harlequin Enterprises ULC

King's Emergency Wife © 2025 Lucy King

Dragos's Broken Vows © 2025 Millie Adams

ISBN: 978-0-263-34480-6

09/25

MIX
Paper | Supporting
responsible forestry
FSC™ C007454

KING'S EMERGENCY WIFE

LUCY KING

MILLS & BOON

CHAPTER ONE

THE TINY YET prosperous kingdom of Montemare shared a border with northeast Italy, Slovenia and Croatia. Home to half a million inhabitants, its forest-covered hills in the north sloped and curved around the Gulf of Ficanza, the glittering capital city built on the coast facing west. To the south lay the region of vineyards, the nation's largest port and countless Roman ruins.

On a promontory, just outside the capital, stood the two-hundred-year-old castellated palace, and in its first-floor, exquisitely panelled private dining room the current King sat alone at the table, frowning at the empty chair that thirty seconds ago had been occupied by the last candidate on his list of suitable brides-to-be.

The country's constitution required the monarch to marry before the age of thirty-five or else abdicate in favour of someone who had, or would. At thirty-four and a half, Ivo Maximiliano had been aware for a while now that time was running out. But up until a couple of months ago he'd given it precious little thought. He'd spent the last three years devoted to building on his father's unimpeachable four-decade legacy and quashing the small but ever-undulating tide of republicanism.

With the regular sixteen-hour days that the job required, he'd had neither the time nor the headspace to waste on what he considered to be a simple, easy-to-arrange, box-ticking exercise. There'd been cross-continent trade deals to secure. International treaties to approve. Not to mention the development and implementation of domestic policies designed to increase the prosperity of his subjects so that they could see first hand the benefit of an absolute monarchy.

Therefore, finding a wife had been right at the bottom of his long list of priorities. Especially since he didn't even want one. Besides, his thirty-fifth birthday had always felt comfortably some distance in the future.

But it wasn't. Somehow, it had crept alarmingly close. And, as his mother and various courtiers kept reminding him, he had to address the situation as a matter of urgency.

No longer could he ignore the pressing reality of his situation. He would not allow the crown to pass to his feckless, much younger second cousin, who'd made it his life's mission to career around Europe, lining the pockets of the continent's most exclusive casinos, trashing every nightclub that naively allowed him access and leaving a trail of broken hearts in his wake. He'd worked too hard to capitalise on his father's success and make it his own.

Not while he drew breath would all that unravel.

Under no conceivable circumstance would he stand back and watch the monarchy that had survived for five hundred years topple and fall, as had very nearly happened under his grandfather's reckless stewardship.

So, to be able to continue his work, to ensure stability and secure the line of succession and to end the incessant speculation about how he was going to proceed, he would marry. In six weeks' time.

Operation Trapdoor—the code name given to the plans for the royal nuptials—had been in place since the day he'd turned eighteen. With one quick phone call, the palace machine would kick into action. The only missing piece of the puzzle had been the identity of the bride. To that end, he'd had his advisors draw up a list of eligible candidates and invite them to lunch for inspection, one a day for the last fortnight.

Ivo had not anticipated a problem with this. Yes, the time frame was tight, but he was the ruler of a rich and powerful nation. Being also intelligent, healthy and—so he'd been told—devastatingly handsome, he was highly eligible himself. In all honesty, he'd assumed he'd have his pick of the crop.

Yet to his astonishment, he'd been repeatedly turned down. Day after day, his dining companions had risen from the table at the end of a five-course gastronomic extravaganza and politely told him, thank you, but no. This afternoon's contender hadn't even waited until dessert.

'You don't want a living, breathing woman,' Princess Amalia had remarked in response to the requirements he'd laid out once the remnants of a chateaubriand had been cleared away. 'You want a robot.'

Amalia was wrong, Ivo reflected as he sat there in bafflement, unaccountably stung by the accusation. What he needed, he'd come to accept—grudgingly—was a partner. Someone with whom to share the burden of rule. Someone to provide him with support and bear his heirs. And quite frankly, he couldn't understand why finding one was proving so hard. It wasn't as if he were demanding the moon. The requisite skill set was entirely reasonable. His bride-to-be and the future Queen of Montemare had to be a woman who understood duty and the value of hard work. She would recognise the responsibilities of such a role and be well able to withstand the pressure of public scrutiny. She would be dependable, discreet and super cool in a crisis. Attractive enough that the wedding night and further efforts to produce children were just about tolerable.

Love wouldn't come into the equation, of course, as he'd had to clarify on Tuesday, when the Marchioness of Maasstadt had asked what she would receive in return for 'such a sacrifice'—unbelievably, her actual words. Nothing would distract him from the brutally tough business of running a country. His grandfather had married for love, and within six months the Council of Ministers had had to step in to see off a military coup, which, in his newly wedded bliss, the King had failed to notice brewing.

The repercussions of that had lasted years. The forced abdication had rocked the nation and the resulting regency had been so tumultuous that the country had become an international disgrace. The subsequent stress placed on his father, who'd had to step into the position far too young, at the age of eighteen, had been immense, and there was no doubt in Ivo's mind that it had contributed to his premature death, which had left him—his son and heir—grief-stricken, rudderless and angry.

Ivo couldn't imagine indulging in such monumental selfishness. His blood ran cold at the thought of such appalling weakness. Only once had he felt something approximating it himself. He'd been twenty-four and a mere crown prince at the time, but nevertheless he should have known better than to become so entranced by a

Portuguese countess that he'd very nearly proposed. If he hadn't caught her wrapped round someone else at a party on Lake Como, he might have been stuck with her deceit and disloyalty for life.

Never again, he'd sworn then and ever since.

Never *ever* again.

Every decision he'd taken from that moment on had been made with his head, with duty his top priority, and not just because his father had drilled into him how important that was. Convinced that it was safer to remain emotionally alone than risk another assault on his heart, he'd realised that the relationship to emulate was not his grandparents' but his parents'. *Their* marriage had been a diplomatic arrangement in which love had played no part. It had been solid and stable, free from volatile emotion and untainted by drama. His mother had been tireless in her support of her husband, and Ivo couldn't recall them ever sharing a cross word. It was the ideal framework for rule, the definitive blueprint for success, and he'd always vowed that when the time came, his union would be no different.

So he would not fall at the first hurdle, he thought, as he rose abruptly from the table and stalked back to his study. He would not be thwarted in his endeavour to find a wife. There was still time. No need for alarm just yet. He'd instruct his advisors to widen the net and conduct the interviews not just over lunch but at breakfast and dinner too. He'd have his Communications Secretary orchestrate an emergency marketing blitz to highlight the attractions of the country and extol his own virtues so that no one at any point would be making 'a sacrifice'.

Filled with fresh resolve and absolutely refusing to

countenance failure, Ivo sat down at his desk and pressed a button on the console in front of him to summon her. Three minutes later there was a light knock on the door. Armed with her customary notebook and pen, Sofia Romero entered the room and tapped her way across the polished oak floor before taking her usual seat on the opposite side of the desk.

This was the sort of woman he was after, he thought, as he watched her arrange her legs and adjust her jacket in the neatly efficient way she had. Unflappable. Loyal. As hard-working and as driven by duty as he was. Sofia wasn't prone to drama. She'd never toss aside her napkin and flounce out of a room. She was cool-headed and dependable, and she understood the need to preserve the monarchy because it was her job. She'd be the ideal candidate.

So perhaps he ought to add her to the list.

There was nothing in the constitution to prevent him from marrying whoever he chose. He liked and respected her. Sleeping with her would be no chore. With her blond hair, above average height and willowy figure she was reasonably attractive, he supposed, not that he'd ever given it any consideration before. She'd been working at the palace for what, six years now, directly for him for just over one, and he'd never seen any evidence of a boyfriend, which suggested she was as uninterested in love and romance as he was and aligned nicely with his view of a purely expedient marriage.

In fact, she could take the number one spot. And really, why bother with anyone else? Why expend time and effort on interviews and a marketing blitz when what he needed was right here under his nose?

These thoughts had begun to enter Ivo's head in a mildly amused, vaguely hypothetical sort of a way. But by the time he'd reached the end of them, the amusement had vanished. He'd gone very still. His mouth was bone-dry. Every sense he possessed was on high alert and his rapidly accelerating pulse now thundered in his ears, because what if this latest brain wave of his *wasn't* hypothetical? What if he *did* marry Sofia? Wouldn't that be the perfect solution to an unexpectedly troublesome problem?

As bulb after bulb lit up in his head, such a plan increasingly made sense. They worked well together. She understood him. Frequently, she knew what he wanted before he did. If she could successfully handle his second cousin's idiotic antics, she could handle anything.

And now he was looking a little more closely, he realised that she was more than just passably attractive. She was actually remarkably striking. Her eyes were the colour of the sea where it approached the beach—a light, clear jade. Her hair was more golden brown than blond. It reminded him of the cornfields to the north at harvest time. And how had he never noticed the luscious appeal of her mouth before?

'Is something wrong? Do I have parsley stuck in my teeth?'

Her voice jolted Ivo out of his trance. He wrenched his gaze from her mouth to her eyes and stamped out the unexpected flare of heat that surged through his body. Nothing was wrong. Everything was suddenly very right indeed. He could scarcely believe he hadn't thought of her before, since she fit the bill in every respect. She was exactly the asset he required. What luck he'd realised it in time.

He cleared his throat and pulled himself together. 'No,' he said, determined to do whatever it took to secure her agreement, because he was on a deadline and could not afford such a prize to slip through his fingers. 'You're perfect.'

'I'm sorry?' Her eyebrows lifted a fraction but that was her only response to the observation that was perhaps a little more personal than usual. She was composed and poised at all times. She was exemplary.

'I'd like you to draft an announcement regarding the imminent change to my marital status.'

If she was startled by his request, she didn't show it. She barely even blinked. Bombproof. That was what she was. 'Have you finally made your choice?'

He nodded shortly. 'I have.'

'I understood none of the current candidates was deemed to be suitable.'

'That's correct,' he said, deciding to gloss over the disagreeable fact that it was actually he who hadn't appealed. In light of his eureka moment, it wasn't relevant anyway. 'I had to think laterally. Outside the box. It turned out to be an excellent move.'

'Then may I be the first to offer you my congratulations?'

'You may.'

'The palace will breathe a sigh of relief.'

'I can almost hear it now.'

'I'll draft the announcement immediately and email it to you for approval,' she said, glancing down briefly to jot something in her notebook. 'It will be sent to all major news outlets within the hour.'

'Good.'

'The people will be ecstatic.'

'I certainly hope so.'

'Just one thing…'

'Yes?'

She lifted her gaze back to his, her smile faint, her expression quizzical. 'Who's the lucky lady?'

'You are.'

CHAPTER TWO

WHEN THE KING'S call had come through earlier, Sofia had felt the usual rush of exhilaration and the familiar leap of her pulse, swiftly followed by the inevitable torrent of despair and the urge to bang her head against the nearest wall.

She ought to have resigned months ago, she'd told herself for what had to be the billionth time as she'd picked up her pen and notebook and left her office for his. At the very least she should have requested a transfer when, eight weeks into the job, she'd realised she was not just crushing on her boss but madly in love with him instead.

But had she?

No.

Because apparently, she'd lost her head along with her heart. Apparently, she was a sucker for punishment.

Every time she sat down to draft an email in which she quit, her fingers froze. On the rare occasion she drummed up the courage to speak to him directly, the words dried on her tongue. No matter how agonising the torment of knowing her feelings were unreturned—and most likely always would be—she simply could not give him up. She was an addict who craved a regular fix. She was her own worst enemy, and there didn't seem to be a thing she could do about it.

Her only comfort was knowing she'd always concealed how she felt about him. Her career required her to project confidence and calm, even when on the inside she was anything but, and she'd developed a poker face that had failed her not once in a decade.

Right now, with Ivo's astonishing pronouncement hanging between them over the vast mahogany partners desk, with the only sound in the room the heavy tick of the grandfather clock behind her and the thundering of her blood in her ears, she'd never appreciated it more.

Outwardly, she barely moved a muscle, but beneath the surface, shock ricocheted through her. Her head spun and it was taking every drop of strength she possessed to remain upright. She'd heard on the grapevine that Princess Amalia had left lunch early, and it was understandable if he therefore bordered on desperate, but had he gone completely and utterly mad?

'Are you feeling quite well?' she said in the cool even tone that came to her as naturally as breathing. 'Should I send for the physician?'

'I've never felt better.'

'You cannot be serious.'

Ivo's eyebrows shot up. A muscle jumped in his jaw. He was unaccustomed to being challenged, and honestly, she couldn't recall the last time she'd had cause to do so. But if ever a situation needed questioning, this was it.

'It's hardly something I'd joke about,' he said flatly. 'I am in urgent need of a wife, and I choose you.'

Sofia stared at him. Her mouth dried. Her pulse raced. He meant it, she realised, noting his resolve as her stomach gave a ridiculous little leap. He actually meant it. 'Why?'

'Because you fulfil my every requirement. You share my values. The monarchy seems to mean almost as much to you as it does to me. You're level-headed and dedicated. Pragmatic and a realist. Nothing rattles you. We get on well. We make a good team. The skills you possess will be a useful asset when it comes to facing the public and the press. In short, you're the perfect candidate for the job.'

Ah.

Of course.

Be still her beating heart.

'And when did this epiphany strike?' she asked, thinking that he was wrong. Dead wrong. He rattled her all the time, and never more so that at this precise moment.

'Two minutes ago. When you came in and sat down.'

In other words, when he was all out of options and clutching at straws. 'I see.'

'Excellent.' He nodded briefly and flashed her a smile. 'I'll inform the team so they can get things moving.'

Excellent? It wasn't excellent in the slightest. It was deranged, and she was the biggest fool in the world for imagining, even for a *nano*second, that he might feel the same way about her as she did him.

Marrying the King was something Sofia had often fantasised about over the last twelve months or so. Alone at night in her bland rented city centre flat, she regularly closed her eyes and drifted off into various scenes in which he swept her into his arms and declared that he couldn't live without her. She'd never imagined those dreams becoming reality. And if she had, reality certainly wouldn't have looked like this. A marriage of convenience that suited him alone? Because time was running out and she was available? No, thank you very much. She might be in love with him, but she did have *some* sense of self-preservation.

'I'm honoured by your proposal, of course,' she said, before he could reach for the phone, 'but I'm afraid I'm going to have to respectfully decline.'

He stilled and frowned. His penetrating gaze collided with hers. That muscle ticked harder. 'You *decline*?'

She nodded. 'I do.'

'Why?'

Because this was madness. He wasn't thinking straight. And even if this *was* an actual proposal, there was no way she'd marry him when her feelings were so obviously unrequited. They'd eat away at her constantly. She'd wind up scrabbling around for crumbs of affection and jettison her dignity in the process. And from there, how long would it be before love and longing turned into bitterness and resentment? She'd managed to hide how she felt about him for over a year but the strain of having to do so up close and personal for decades would likely destroy her.

So the thrills of excitement that were shooting through her like a meteor shower could get lost. As much as she'd been dreading the day he took a wife, at least it would draw a line under her impossible infatuation. At least it would obliterate the absurd hope that he might suddenly, miraculously, see her in a different light. However painful, however much she loved her job, she needed to move on, and she'd marked his wedding day as the moment that would happen. 'I have other plans.'

'What other plans?' he asked, with the innate arrogance that came from being the most powerful man in the land, if not the continent.

'I'm not sure that's any of your business.'

He scowled at that. 'It's your job to protect the monarchy.'

'My job, yes, but not my life.'

'Am I displeasing to you?'

Lord, no. Quite the opposite. He was the most devastatingly attractive man she'd ever come across. He was built like a god. Or maybe a warrior. All broad shoulders and virile strength, he would be as suited to armour and a sword as he was to a jacket and tie. At six foot four he towered over her, and she was by no means short. He had thick dark hair she longed to plough her fingers through. Deep brown eyes that threatened her thought processes every time she gazed into them, and since she'd had a poster of him pinned to her wall the minute he'd stepped into the limelight as a sixteen-year-old hunk she'd been gazing into them a long time.

But it wasn't just his staggering looks and powerful physique she'd fallen for. When she'd started working directly for him and gained further insight into his character, she'd swooned even more. His dedication to duty was unshakable. His integrity ran deep. He inspired trust and loyalty and gave both in return. She'd grown up in a household filled with confrontation and discord, her parents at one another's throats pretty much constantly, even more so towards the end, and his ice-cool composure and steadfastness was like a balm to her soul. She hadn't seen him lose his temper once. He rarely even raised his voice. She couldn't imagine him ever throwing something in a rage. He epitomised everything she valued, everything she admired, everything she'd ever wanted in a man.

'No, of course not,' she said, clamping down hard on her roiling emotions and biting back the appalling urge to confess just how pleasing she found him. 'But that's not the point.'

'Then what is the point? I like you. I have enormous respect for your abilities. Many marriages are based on less. Certainly royal ones. Is there someone else?'

Someone else? Ha. As if that was a possibility when he dominated her thoughts and owned her heart. 'There's no one else.'

'So what objection could you possibly have?'

Apart from the shock and inappropriateness of this gear change in their relationship? 'Well, what about what *I* want?'

His brows snapped together. Confusion shot across the handsome planes of his face. Evidently her role in this scenario had been to simply agree, but he was nothing if not adept at altering his strategy to achieve his goal. 'What *do* you want?' he asked, a glint of ruthlessness lighting his eyes. 'Name it and it's yours.'

If only.

'It's not that simple.'

'Materially, you will want for nothing.'

'Materially, I want for nothing now. You pay me extremely well.'

He regarded her thoughtfully for a moment. Then he leaned forward, giving her the worrying impression that he was about to bring out the big guns.

'I can offer you security,' he said, as if he could see into her soul. 'Loyalty. Support. Companionship. Children. Not love, I'm afraid. I haven't the time for that and can't afford the distraction. Nor am I remotely interested in the drama it can cause. I'm not interested in drama full stop. But I would give you everything else that's within my power. You and I would be a partnership of equals, Sofia. We would rule together. Side by side. In harmony. A united front to secure the future of the monarchy. You could continue to work, if that is what you wish. Beyond the requirements of the role, you could do anything you please. I am aware that this is a sudden decision, and one born out of necessity, but I'm nevertheless convinced it's the right approach. I believe we would do very well together. I have to spend the rest of my life with someone, and I'd like it to be you.'

Ivo stopped and sat back. Sofia reeled, her chest so tight she was barely able to breathe. Well, that was deeply unfair. How was she supposed to keep her head when he promised her so many of the things she craved? And how had he known which buttons to push when, before today, their interactions had always remained strictly professional? A crystal ball? A lucky guess?

Whatever it was, it was badly shaking her resolve. He painted an alluring picture of a full and fascinating life. Alarmingly, she was beginning to think that she could do a lot worse than a drama-free partnership based on mutual respect and common interests. How he might go about giving her those children was certainly sending her imagination into overdrive. She could practically feel his mouth on hers. The thought of his hands slowly stroking over her skin as they explored her body electrified every nerve ending she possessed.

So, could what he offered be enough? Was she content to enter into such a one-sided relationship just to be with the man she adored?

No.

Absolutely not.

What was she *thinking*?

Everything about this was ludicrous. Her brain had gone so awry that she ought to be getting up right now and walking away before she lost what was left of her marbles.

Potential sexual fireworks aside, marrying him would be a disaster. A one-way ticket to misery. Although, to be honest, she'd been feeling pretty wretched recently anyway. She'd always recognised the need for his marriage—from his perspective as well as hers—but she hadn't liked it. Whenever she thought of some other woman sharing his bed, she seethed with jealousy. Her heart physically ached at the bleak reality of resigning and never seeing him again in person.

But now, in light of this frankly bizarre conversation, none of that need happen. If she accepted his proposal, she would no longer have to worship him from afar. Wistfulness and pining would be a thing of the past. *She* could be the one in his bed and in his life. She could have it all.

Well, nearly.

She'd have to keep how she felt about him to herself, of course. Presumably, unrequited love was exactly the sort of drama he strove to avoid. But it wouldn't necessarily turn into bitterness and resentment. It would be up to her to manage that. And despite his assertion to the contrary, who was to say that over time he wouldn't develop some sort of feelings for her? Her parents might have more or less ignored her, preferring to indulge their toxic feelings for each other instead, but that didn't mean she was completely unlovable, did it?

So perhaps she was being a tad overdramatic about this. She did value the monarchy—he was right about that. She cared about it deeply. She'd been fascinated by the mystique and glamour of the royal family for as long as she could remember. Daydreaming about what life in the palace might be like and putting herself right in the middle of it had provided a mental escape from the emotional turmoil of home. She'd been so enthralled by the idea of it that when she left school and embarked on a career in PR, she'd done so in the hope that one day she'd end up there, which she had. The day she'd started working directly for Ivo—both the man and the King— had been the most thrilling of her life.

Did she really want to be responsible for the collapse of an institution that had survived for five hundred years? Its future hung in the balance. Time was running out so fast for him that he'd sounded as though he was very close to begging. She knew how he felt about his second cousin taking the crown, and even though she couldn't understand why he hadn't set about finding a wife sooner, she loved him too much to let him down. He'd worked so very hard to keep the peace and build on everything his father had achieved. And so had she with her unerring support. She couldn't allow her self-centredness to cause him—*them*—to fail, for all that immense effort to come to nothing. She just couldn't.

And then there were the children he was promising. She'd always wanted those. They could make a start on the line of succession right away and within five years or so, assuming all went well, she could have the happy family she'd longed for ever since she'd realised how dysfunctional her own was.

It was funny how life could turn on a sixpence, she thought a little dizzily, as what remained of her resistance and her brain crumbled to dust, and excitement swooped back in. Twenty minutes ago, she'd been mentally sticking pins into Princess Amalia. Yet now, here she was, unbelievably about to agree to take her place, positioning herself at the very heart of the royal family, where she'd always dreamed of being, married to the man she worshipped. It was more than she'd ever thought possible.

But it wouldn't do to throw caution *completely* to the wind before diving in headfirst. This partnership couldn't just be about what *he* deemed important. Thanks to her parents' tumultuous relationship she had her own list of requirements, designed to guard a heart that was all too easily broken. The risk of that happening seemed even greater when he did not feel the same way about her as she did about him. Therefore, she had to take extra care to protect herself—and any offspring they might produce, because no child of hers would *ever* suffer the way she had.

'You're asking me to give up my freedom,' she said, channelling a cool sort of thoughtfulness, as if her pulse wasn't thundering and her emotions weren't whipping around inside her like a tornado.

He nodded. 'Some of it, yes.'

'My life would never be the same again.'

'That's true,' he agreed. 'But it could be better.'

Yes, well, she'd do everything in her power to make it so, starting with giving herself a fighting chance of levelling the playing field. 'I'd need some things in return.'

His jaw lost its rigidity and a spark of triumphant relief lit the depths of his mesmerising eyes. 'Such as?'

'Fidelity.'

'You'd have it.'

'Communication.'

'Not a problem.'

'Conflict must be avoided at all costs. I'm not a fan of arguing. Any disagreements will be dealt with in a civilised fashion, and in private. Always.'

'Agreed.'

Good.

Right.

So what next?

There was more she should demand. Sofia was sure of it. The devil was always in the detail. But she was damned if she could think of anything else. The sheer force of her emotions was obliterating the contents of her brain. And so this was it. The moment she either stepped back from the cliff edge or threw herself into the void. The moment she had to choose between the security blanket of the known and the wild unpredictability of the unknown.

In the deafening silence that had fallen, the voice of reason implored her to see sense. If they married and it all went wrong, she could get badly hurt and there'd be no escape. The constitution prohibited divorce so she'd be tied to him and misery until her dying breath, and she knew from experience how devastating the fallout of that could be.

But despite her very real concerns, reason didn't stand a chance against the thrilling possibility that on the other hand, if she took the risk, she would have *him*. A family. A calm, steady, grown-up relationship, free from the selfish passion and explosive chaos that would eventually destroy it.

How on earth could she give that up?

She couldn't.

And it wasn't as if she'd be going into this with her eyes closed. Ivo could not have been clearer about what their marriage would and wouldn't involve. However much she might yearn for his love there was no guarantee she'd have it. She had to accept that being by his side to enable him to continue to do his duty might have to be enough. Her head would have to rule her heart. She must never forget that this was all about convenience and fall into the trap of believing it was real. She must never want more than what he offered.

At least she was used to being put second. For nineteen years her parents had prioritised their corrosive relationship over the emotional needs of their child. She'd cared too much, they'd broken her heart and she'd sworn it would never happen again. As long as she kept her position in the hierarchy at the forefront of her mind at all times and kept a firm lid on her feelings, she could do it. She knew she could.

'All right, then,' she said, nevertheless hoping to God that she wasn't making the biggest mistake of her life, that she was opening herself up to the bright shiny future she'd dreamed of and not decades of heartbreak, trauma and despair. 'For the sake of the monarchy, I accept.'

CHAPTER THREE

IVO DIDN'T MUCH care for whose sake Sofia had agreed to marry him. The point was, she had, and the problem that had been causing him such grief had instantly gone away—at exceptionally little cost.

Fidelity posed no problem. He'd never screwed around. His experience with Carolina, the Countess of Vila Real a decade ago had made him wary and mistrustful and as a result, his liaisons were infrequent and casual and ultimately, inconsequential. He enjoyed sex as much as the next man, but it didn't—and never would—govern his life. Such distraction was unthinkable. The possibility of it developing into something deeper, something that might render him powerless, exposed and open to exploitation once again was to be avoided like the plague.

Nor did he foresee trouble with communication, which was, after all, the basis of their working relationship and would, he imagined, naturally transfer to their marriage. It hadn't caused an issue before, and he saw no reason why it should now. And when it came to conflict, they were both so even-keeled and emotionally restrained he couldn't envisage either of them losing control even if such a situation did arise. The very thought of it was laughable.

The press had leapt on the announcement like a pack

of rabid wolves, of course. Ever since the news had been released a week ago, the story had dominated the headlines. No one could be under any illusion that theirs was anything other than a marriage of convenience, but the interest in Sofia was nevertheless rampant.

Within the palace walls, his choice of bride was considered excellently pragmatic. Beyond them, ridiculous notions of a highly unlikely romance swirled. The fact that she'd worked for him this past year had escaped no one's notice. According to some, it must have been a thrilling slow-burn affair. For others, a last-minute *coup de foudre* must have struck. His people appeared to have collectively turned to sentimental mush, and he could only hope the affliction was temporary.

Ivo had intended to stay out of the proceedings as much as possible. 'Never explain, never complain' had been the mantra of his family for generations, and he'd had no intention of diverging from a policy that had served them so well.

Sofia, however, had other ideas.

'Controlling the narrative is crucial,' she'd told him over the phone yesterday lunchtime. 'Because I'm such an out-of-the-blue choice, speculation in some of the more hostile quarters is rife and lurid enough to become a problem if allowed to continue unfettered.'

'You've handled worse,' he'd replied, slightly perturbed by the way her voice now seemed to lift the tiny hairs at the back of his neck.

'True, but you bringing the wedding forward by a fortnight hasn't made it any easier.'

'We're embarking on a three-week tour of the country in lieu of a honeymoon, and I want it over and done with so I can get back to business as quickly as possible. Besides, I couldn't risk you getting cold feet or some other delay.'

'Why *did* you leave it so late?'

He'd shifted in his seat and given her the same reason he gave himself. 'I was too busy focusing on the job to watch the clock.'

'Such a lapse feels very uncharacteristic.'

'I'm not superhuman,' he'd observed, stifling a dart of irritation. 'I can't bend time.'

Silence fell for a moment, then came an astonished, 'Wow.'

'What?'

'I don't think I've ever heard you confess to a weakness.'

No, well, why would he when he did everything in his power to prevent such a thing? When any sort of vulnerability could bring about not the destruction of the monarchy he lived for but also, quite possibly, himself? 'Aren't we getting sidetracked?'

'Maybe… Where was I…?' There'd followed what had sounded like a shuffle of papers. 'Ah, yes. Because of the truncated time frame there are rumours of a shotgun wedding, which need to be nipped in the bud. Plus the anti-monarchists are taking advantage of this spotlight on you to renew their calls for your abolition.'

'You can put a stop to that immediately,' he'd said, the chill that had run down his spine obliterating his discomfort at the images a shotgun wedding brought up. 'And anything else that threatens my position or integrity.'

'My thoughts exactly. Which is why I've set up an interview with the nation's favourite chat show host so we can knock this all on the head and spin the situation the way we want. Ten o'clock tomorrow morning. Your private sitting room. Don't be late.'

Now, running a finger around the inside of his shirt collar to ease the pressure on his windpipe, Ivo sat beside Sofia on one of the two large sofas that framed a coffee table before the fireplace in a space he'd always considered his sanctuary. He'd rather face down a roomful of international despots than undergo this. He could defend the monarchy any day of the week but if the conversation strayed into the topic of romance, or worse, *feelings*, he'd be completely at a loss. So far out of his comfort zone he might as well be on another planet. In the disconcerting position of having to rely on Sofia to cover any awkward moments as he'd never had to before.

And then there were the memories of his ex that this whole damn setup was battering him with. Less than twenty-four hours after he'd told her to get out of his sight, Carolina had scurried to the press. The lurid details of their relationship would have been splashed around the world had the palace not gained an injunction just in time and then paid her a hefty sum in return for her silence.

The thought of how close he'd come to both stalling his father's progress and wrecking his own future as King still made him shudder. Quite apart from the personally painful double betrayal, he'd have been cannon fodder for anyone with a grudge against the monarchy. Another member of the royal family weakened by a woman. He'd never have lived down the hideous comparisons with his grandfather. He'd had a staggeringly lucky escape, and it was an experience he had no intention of repeating on any level at all.

However, it wasn't just the nature of the imminent interview that was causing him such grief. Or the unpleasant memories of how dangerously naive and reckless he'd once been. With the exception of a handful of phone calls, he'd barely had any contact with his betrothed since she'd agreed to become his wife. He'd had a trilateral aerospace deal to sign off, and she'd gone into full on PR mode, holing up with advisors to discuss logistics and issuing press releases left right and centre.

In itself, this passing like ships in the night wasn't a problem, even though it was the longest they'd gone without much in the way of communication. Because Sofia generally accompanied him on overseas trips and rarely took a day off, he'd become used to her being around at all times. Like a part of the furniture. However, now, the only piece of furniture she reminded him of was a bed. Even more so when he was in his. Realising how attractive she was had triggered an awareness in him that had become frustratingly impossible to ignore. He dreamed of her every night and invariably woke up in such a state he would have been in danger of developing a repetitive strain injury in his wrist had he allowed himself the pleasure.

Hot on the tail of a week of fractured sleep and unwelcome desire, therefore, this morning was turning out to be more of a trial than Ivo could ever have imagined. They'd never been in such proximity. They'd never even touched before. Yet currently, his thigh was a mere inch from hers. He could feel the heat of her body. Every time she moved, the scent of her shampoo, of *her*, drifted up his nose and into his head. His lightweight navy suit felt impossibly tight and heavy and the tiny shivers of electricity that darted though him had brought him out in a rash of goose bumps.

But while he battled the urge to strip her of the yellow dress she wore and flatten her against the soft feather cushions, she, on the other hand, remained as cool as Lake Superiore in winter. There was no need to dab the shine from *her* brow, he thought darkly, trying not to grit his teeth against the disturbing impact of her nearness. *Her* muscles weren't taut and aching with tension.

'This will go a lot more easily if you smile,' she murmured, leaning in as the hair and make-up artists and lighting technicians darted about the room.

'I'll bear that in mind,' he murmured back, shifting a fraction to his left to restore the gap between them.

Evidently noting his move, her eyes narrowed and she frowned. 'I thought you agreed that this was an excellent idea.'

'I did.'

'So what's wrong?'

'Nothing's wrong,' he said, irritation at being so transparent sharpening his tone. 'Why would you think it was?'

'You seem… I don't know…a little *unnerved*.'

That had to be the understatement of the century. He was more than a *little* unnerved. He'd never experienced such an intense response to anyone, and he liked it as much as he knew what to make of it—in other words, not at all.

Until now, his body had always remained firmly under his control, and the fact that it seemed to be going rogue was both bewildering and concerning. It made him wonder if taking Sofia as his bride wouldn't prove to be a colossal mistake, if she wasn't somehow dangerous. He found himself increasingly preoccupied with why she'd agreed to marry him when everyone else he'd asked had refused. In fact, he thought about her far more than was necessary, which was frustrating as hell when work required his full focus. Even the diamond ring that adorned the third finger of her right hand and flashed at him whenever it caught the light felt like some sort of an omen.

This engagement of theirs had the potential to be far more complex than the straightforward arrangement he'd envisaged. However, it was too late to back out now. The die was cast. So he'd just *have* to regain command of himself. How hard could it be? Two years in the army had taught him self-discipline. His willpower was formidable. After all, it wasn't as if he could simply permit the attraction to develop. No matter how much he might enjoy letting go physically—and it would certainly be a bonus to do so with the woman he was marrying—such self-indulgence was an anathema. That sort of distraction was for the weak. The reckless. And he, who had duty and responsibility embedded in his DNA, who lived, breathed and slept for his country, would allow none of it.

'Don't be ridiculous,' he said, pulling himself together and forcing the tension from his body. 'Of course I'm not unnerved. I've done hundreds of these things over the years.'

'None quite like this, though.'

'It's uncharted territory for you too.'

'But it's my job.'

'And also mine, don't forget. I'll do whatever it takes to protect the monarchy. My country. The future. Nothing else matters.'

A flicker of emotion darted across her face but it came and went before he could even think to identify it. 'Talking of forgetting, do you remember the plan?' she said so coolly he figured he must have imagined it anyway.

The plan she'd first emailed yesterday afternoon and

then followed up with a thirty-minute call? Of course he remembered. 'The last royal wedding—my parents'— was thirty-eight years ago,' he recited. 'Times have changed. An absolute monarchy is something of a rarity these days. A throwback to the past. Aloofness and mystery no longer works. We must be open. Relatable. Relevant. Competent and diligent but at the same time anodyne and uncontroversial.'

'Exactly. See? Simple.'

Evidently, their understanding of *simple* differed. Ivo suspected the next hour was going to be one of the most stressful of recent years. But at least he was to have respite immediately afterwards. From here, he was travelling straight to Paris for a two-day conference on artificial intelligence—on his own for once, since Sofia was needed here. And although he had no doubt that, with effort, he *would* conquer his desire for her, and despite the fact that he preferred to confront difficulties head-on, it felt like a much-needed escape.

Swept up in a whirlwind of activity, Sofia had barely had time to breathe since her engagement to Ivo had been announced. Not everything could be delegated to her highly competent team of four. They continued to handle the day-to-day running of the department, but she was the one who had to find time for dress fittings and a trip to the Jewel House to pick up the rings and tiara she'd been assigned. Only she could sit beside him on that sofa, smile in all the right places and talk about how excited she was about the wedding and how she hoped she'd do a good job of serving King and country. His mother's advice about the role of the Queen and managing expectations were for her ears alone, and no one else but her could pose with him for the official engagement photos.

Sofia knew when Ivo was due to return from Paris—the trip was detailed in the tightly packed schedule—but she didn't see him until the doors onto the terrace flung open on the dot of eleven and he strode through them. He'd only been away for two days but, judging by the wave of longing that swept through her as he headed for the wisteria-clad summer house in front of which she stood while the photographer tested the lighting, it might as well have been two months.

Oh, how she'd missed him, she thought, battling back a wide smile that would be far too giddy for the occasion and perilously revealing as a result. Absence really did make the heart grow fonder.

But evidently the only heart thus affected by forty-eight hours apart was hers. Because as he approached, making short work of the immaculately mown lawn with his long purposeful strides, she noticed that his jaw was tight. His face was dark and his deep brown eyes seemed oddly flinty. Despite the warmth of the mid-morning sun, he emanated an ice-cold steeliness she'd never seen in him before, as if he were all hard planes and sharp edges, as if he were someone not to be crossed. He spared no words for the team. He had no smile for anyone. He seemed ruthlessly focused—and utterly different.

At this wholly unexpected version of a man she thought she knew inside out, Sofia's head spun and a shiver of apprehension rippled down her spine. What could have caused such a dramatic change to his demeanour? Had the conference not gone well? Surely she would have heard.

'Hello,' she said, plastering her easiest, most professional smile to her face as he came to an abrupt stop in front of her and the photographer moved to a discreet distance.

'Good morning.'

'How are you?'

'Fine. You?'

That was an interesting question. Actually, she was all over the place. Her body temperature was sky-high. Her heart was beating at twice its usual rate. And as if that wasn't enough, in response to the clipped frostiness of his voice her skin was prickling and she felt a little light-headed. 'All good,' she said, one hundred percent certain that, despite the mess she was inside, outwardly she projected nothing but serenity. 'And Paris?'

'Constructive.'

'Anything I need to be aware of?'

'Like what?' He fastened the button of his jacket, then reached up into the sleeves to tug down the cuffs of his shirt, an unexpectedly sexy move that would have derailed her focus if she'd let it.

'I have no idea,' she said, lifting her gaze from his wrists to his face, a route that took in the enticing wedge of chest revealed by the collar that was open at the neck. 'News that needs promoting or a problem that needs handling, perhaps?'

'If there was, you'd be the first to know.'

Right. That was true. Clearly, then, the conference wasn't the issue. So what was? More pertinently, what did it mean? She'd never seen this side to him before. She'd never considered him...*dangerous*. What if he possessed other characteristics that lay hidden? What were the implications for their marriage if he wasn't the man she believed him to be? Might she have made a mistake in accepting his proposal?

'Sofia?'

The sharpness of his voice jolted her out of her head. 'Sorry,' she said, parking the many clamouring questions for later analysis and pulling herself together. Now was not the time to tumble down that particular rabbit hole. Or to imagine stepping in close and undoing a few more of his shirt buttons. Who knew what the camera might capture in an unguarded moment? 'I was miles away.'

'That's a first,' he said with a frown. 'Is there something *I* should know about?'

Definitely not. 'No.'

'Sure?'

'Absolutely. I was simply wondering why you look like thunder.'

'Do I?'

'Yes. So much so that I fear for the photos.'

'It's nothing.'

'It doesn't seem like nothing.'

For a moment, he continued to glower at her. But then the frown lifted and his jaw unclenched. He released a breath and his shoulders relaxed—and, ah yes, there was the man she recognised once again. 'Is that better?'

Hmm. She didn't know about *better.* Quite honestly, she was even more confused because now she could add *mercurial* to *steely* and *dangerous.* But at least he no longer gave the impression he was about to march into battle, guns blazing. 'Somewhat.'

'Good. So what *has* been going on in my absence?'

'Mainly, yet more dress fittings,' she said, stamping

out the rogue flare of heat she felt when his gaze flickered over hers. 'The latest poll, taken after the interview, shows a 5 percent jump in your popularity, which is an excellent result. And yesterday afternoon, your mother and I had a long chat over tea. That was illuminating.'

'In what way?'

In the 'don't ever forget what this is about' kind of a way. Having shared a mountain of practical advice, Elenor, the Dowager Queen, had certainly hammered *that* point home. She'd intimated that she'd held out for love for the entirety of her marriage to Ivo's father but to no avail. He'd been so preoccupied with restoring the monarchy and then running the country it sounded as though he'd had little time to woo his wife. The tips she'd passed on were to have children asap. More than one if nature cooperated, which sadly it hadn't with her. To keep busy. And most importantly, to remember that the job would always come first.

'I never realised hers was a marriage of convenience too,' Sofia said, thinking of the disappointment and regret that had tinged her future mother-in-law's guidance and vowing that, whatever the future held, she would do her utmost to avoid the same fate. She would prioritise her head over heart at all times and keep her feelings for her fiancé firmly under control. Unlike Elenor, she would never make the mistake of wanting her husband to put her first. She would never set herself up for such crushing devastation. She had no interest in the pain that could cause. 'She and your father always seemed so...together.'

'They were skilled politicians. My mother still is. But they did have a lot of respect for each other and they did get on well. I like to think they were friends. As a team they were unparalleled. They devoted thirty-five selfless years to duty. Not once did they fail to present a united front to the public. They kept it up even in private. I don't remember them ever arguing.'

Now that sounded like utter bliss. Sofia couldn't remember her parents ever *not* arguing in private. Both highly volatile people, they'd let rip over the slightest of slights. A misread look here, a point to be scored there. She'd invariably got caught in the cross-fire, not that they'd ever noticed. Their passion was so wholly selfish that for years she'd felt unloved and unlovable, which was why she now abhorred and feared it in equal measure. Could passion and love coexist within a relationship? Not in her experience, and if she had to forgo the former to achieve the latter, that was fine with her. She wanted chaos and implosion like a hole in the head.

'We have huge shoes to fill, but I have no doubt that fill them we will.'

'Mine are killing me,' she said, leaving the trauma of her upbringing in the past and focusing on the considerably less distressing present. 'I've been on my feet for hours.'

'Then let's get things moving.'

Ivo summoned the production crew with a barely perceptible nod of his head and almost immediately they were being dabbed and brushed and tweaked. Finally, they moved into position. At the photographer's suggestion Ivo stood behind her, just to her left. The pulse at her temples pounded so hard she could hardly hear what was being said, but a moment later he placed his right hand on her right shoulder, at which point her brain disintegrated.

It was the first time he'd touched her, and even though

the move was utterly impersonal, for the camera alone, Sofia felt it like a brand. Her breath caught in her throat and every cell of her body froze. She'd never been so aware of anyone in her life. The urge to spin round and press herself up against him, to find out if reality lived up to her dreams, burned so fiercely it hurt.

The stress of the interview was nothing compared with this, she thought as she frantically willed herself to calm down. Then, she'd had to fight the temptation to lean into him and snuggle, but at least she'd had a script to stick to. At least she'd been kept on her toes fielding questions about the royal family's relevancy in this day and age. Now she had nothing to distract her from the brush of his body against hers apart from the occasional instruction of the photographer. All she had to do was smile and pose and try to suppress the intoxicating heat that swept through her.

But she had no intention of acting on the impulse to hurl herself at him. She did still possess *some* dignity. So, drawing on every professional instinct she had, Sofia stayed right where she was, on fire—thanks to his hand searing through the thin fabric of her dress—her heart galloping like a racehorse in the final furlong and riddled with envy at his ice-cold composure.

When the torment was finally over, after a half hour that felt like a decade, she ducked away from him. She flashed him a super bright smile and said, 'Right. Well. Good to have that out of the way. I'd better get going. There's still lots to do. I guess I'll see you next at the rehearsal.'

And then, just about clinging onto the remnants of her self-control, she turned on her heel and left.

CHAPTER FOUR

THE NEXT FEW days sped by in a blur of logistics and protocol. But whenever Sofia had a moment of calm, she took the opportunity to address the concerns she hadn't had time for at the photo shoot and soon realised that she'd badly overreacted. She hadn't slept well. She'd skipped breakfast. She'd been running on fumes that morning, which was obviously why she'd succumbed to such appalling theatrics.

Of course Ivo wasn't *dangerous*, she told herself with a mental eye-roll every time a vision of him striding across that lawn entered her head. He was hardly the mafia type. Nor was he mercurial. On the contrary, he was the most steadfast, honourable, honest man she'd ever met. He was exactly who she thought he was. And so what if he *did* possess a steely side? Wasn't that proof of his iron-clad control? Didn't it demonstrate the supremacy of stoicism over emotion?

Something had clearly been bothering him but he'd kept it contained, and that was a trait to be celebrated. Which she did. Because if only her parents had exhibited even a modicum of such self-discipline, her upbringing could have been a whole lot calmer and infinitely easier than it had been. She might now embrace passion rather

than fear it. She might not feel such a strong need to protect herself from pain that it prevented her from risking
her heart. She might even believe herself worthy of being
put first, of mattering to someone above all else.

As for the enormous shoes she and Ivo had to fill, she
understood what was required of her. Not only had he
made it very clear on numerous occasions, but she'd also
ruminated on the conversation she'd had with his mother
at such length it was imprinted on her memory for ever.
And she got it. She really did. The chances of him ever returning her feelings were so vanishingly small they were
virtually non-existent. If there was any danger of her heart
getting the better of her head—any danger *at all*—she
ought to back out now and save herself a whole world of
pain. Except she wouldn't. Because firstly, there wasn't,
and secondly, she'd already signed the marriage contract.

She'd been presented with the twenty-three-page doc-
ument a week ago, while he'd been in Paris. It had taken
forty minutes to read from beginning to end. The clauses
about not bringing the royal family into disrepute and
compulsory attendance at various ceremonial events had
been easy enough to follow. It was the four-hundred-year-
old stipulation that their marriage be consummated by
the midnight of the wedding day to ensure the legitimacy
of the union and any future heirs that had derailed her
thoughts to such an extent that the words had blurred on
the page. She'd often dreamed about what sleeping with
him would be like—the agonising tension, the fireworks,
the pleasure. Many a night she'd woken up hot and aching,
desperate for his touch. The realisation that it was actually
going to happen, and soon, played havoc with her control.

But she kept it reined in. She kept *everything* reined

in, particularly her imagination, and reminded herself over and over again how much she and Ivo both abhorred drama. Which was how she got through the rehearsal. With ruthless detachment. By focusing on the procedural details and not the fact that she was marrying the man she loved. Or that once she had, she would be his queen, the mother of his heirs, and her life would be irrevocably changed.

However, when it came to the day itself, detachment proved impossible. The weather was glorious. Joy rippled through the country. Bunting strung from every vertical support, and according to reports, over ten thousand street parties had been organised.

Inside the palace, Sofia stood in the Chamber of the Robes while a pair of ladies-in-waiting bustled around her, one fitting the tiara and veil, the other tackling the three hundred tiny pearl buttons at the back of the dress. There was a crackle of electricity and a buzz of excitement in the air. How could she *not* respond to it? She was excited, terrified, overwhelmed—a bundle of nerves. And not just because of the ceremony, which was of course daunting, but also, because of what came after.

She couldn't stop thinking about the past and what the future might hold. She'd been on her own for so long. It had been fourteen years since her parents had died, but even before then they'd been so self-absorbed, so wrapped up in their growing hatred for each other, that she'd had no one to rely on but herself. She was used to complete independence. But after today she wasn't going to have that. She'd become public property, with expectations put upon her that she couldn't begin to imagine.

What if she wasn't up to the job?

Ivo clearly thought she was but he'd been born into the

role. He wouldn't understand the enormity of such an undertaking for a novice. And she couldn't discuss her sudden flurry of insecurity with him because he'd chosen her for her composure and level-headedness. He'd be appalled by this sort of a wobble. She certainly was. Right now, she'd never felt less composed or level-headed, and if she didn't get a grip on her rampaging emotions pretty damn quick, they could spin wildly out of control. What chance would she have of keeping everything together then?

Through sheer force of will Sofia managed to steady herself enough to descend the stairs and climb into the carriage. But these were such immense and overpowering thoughts that when she stood at the entrance to the cathedral, enveloped by the heady scent of the jasmine that trailed from the arrangements dotted about the place, she took in the sight, sweeping her gaze over the majestically soaring arches and the vast glittering dome beneath which stood a thousand guests, and for a moment wanted to turn on her heel and run.

Was she really ready for everything that was about to happen? Was she strong enough to weather whatever her new life threw at her? What if she did in fact forget that this was a purely practical arrangement and started to believe the fairy tale? What if she ended up hoping he'd put her first? How long would it be before everything she valued came crashing down around her?

But then her gaze collided with Ivo's and the storm inside her quietened. Standing at the other end of the aisle, he looked so devastatingly handsome in his military regalia he took her breath away. A shaft of sunlight anointed him with a soft shimmering glow. The epaulettes, the medals and the gold braid gleamed. He gave her a nod, perhaps somehow sensing her uncertainty. Filled with relief that he wasn't bothered by a wobble after all, that everything was going to be fine, she found herself walking towards him as if on the end of a rope he was slowly pulling in.

Drawn by his calm confidence and solid reassurance, she barely noticed the congregation. She spent the rest of the service—the singing, the vows, the exchanging of rings—in a dreamy sort of daze. Nothing about any of it seemed real, although her signature in the centuries-old register confirmed that it was.

And then came the only moment they hadn't practised in the rehearsal.

With the archbishop's 'You may now kiss the bride' ringing in her ears, Sofia felt a hand on her waist, and she first jumped, then turned to her brand-new husband, her heart thudding wildly. How he felt about it was anyone's guess. He was looking straight at her but his eyes were dark and, like the Sphinx, his expression gave nothing away. She, on the other hand, was doing her best to contain her excitement.

Leaning in a little, her breath hitching, Sofia lifted her face as he lowered his. With her surroundings disappearing from view, with his spicy masculine scent enveloping and befuddling her, and with time gliding to a halt, their mouths met.

It was meant to be a perfunctory touching of lips. A move designed to delight the people watching across the country and to soften the heart of the staunchest republican. But less than one second into it, something went wrong. On contact, her senses reeled and her brain fell apart. Desire slammed into her with the force of a freight train, sending her temperature through the roof and her head into a spin. The strength drained from her limbs so fast she had to clutch his arm before she collapsed in a heap at his feet.

Every soft inch of her was suddenly pressed against every unyielding inch of him, their mouths not brushing against each other lightly but crushed together hard. For one heart-stopping moment the world froze. His arm around her waist seemed to tighten minutely. She thought she heard him groan.

But she must have been mistaken because a split second later he jerked back, his jaw tight, a tiny muscle hammering his cheek. His dark gaze drilled into hers, flickering briefly with what looked like horror before clearing of all emotion. Then he let her go and turned back to the archbishop, his expression utterly impassive, as if there was nothing untoward about what had just happened at all.

Somehow, Sofia maintained her composure for the rest of the ceremony. She waved and smiled from the gilded open-topped carriage that bore them from the cathedral back to the palace along streets lined with people. She watched from the balcony as six jets passed overhead in V formation, trailing red, white and green smoke to the whoops and cheers of the crowds below.

But beneath the surface, her emotions churned like a tempest.

How could she have lost control like that? And what lay behind his appalled response to it? Could she have revealed how she felt about him? Did she physically revolt him? Was he suffering from buyer's remorse?

Whatever it was, it had major implications for tonight.

She'd been anticipating the consummation of their marriage with very mixed feelings. On the one hand, it was something she'd dreamed of for months, and whenever she thought about it, hot thrills of excitement darted through her. But on the other, the circumstances were very much not the stuff of dreams, and whenever she thought about *those* the thrills evaporated.

It didn't help that she hadn't a clue how Ivo felt about it. Would he make the most of the experience or simply grin and bear it? She rather suspected that, despite her wildly oscillating thoughts on the subject, she'd want to do anything *but* grin and bear it, which was a concern. What if she got so swept up by desire that she threw caution to the wind? She couldn't risk revealing she was in love with him through her actions. Or accidentally blurting it out in the throes of ecstasy.

This arrangement was one-sided enough already, and if he ever discovered how she truly felt, he might think her a sentimental fool. He might lose respect for her, and right now that was all she had. So she must not disrupt the deal or put her emotions in further danger by recklessly lowering her guard again.

Unfortunately, she could not plead a headache or request a delay. She had a legal obligation to fulfil. But how hard could it be to disengage from the proceedings? she wondered as she did precisely that during the photos. She'd spent a year keeping her feelings for him to herself. And yes, continuing to do so when he was on top of her, beneath her, moving inside her might present a challenge, but she'd grown adept at shutting down her emotions when it came to certain things. Blocking out her parents' constant rowing had been the only way to deal with it.

So it would be fine. She indulged her love for Ivo because some bizarre masochistic part of her craved the torment, the buzz that made her feel so alive, but she could not afford to indulge the attraction.

Therefore, she vowed with steely resolve as, back in the Chamber of the Robes, she stepped out of the wedding dress and into something more suitable for the reception, no matter how fantastic he was in bed, no matter how much she wanted him and how great the temptation to give in to pleasure was, she would resist doing so with everything she had.

By the time the last of the guests had left, at around about eleven, Ivo was running on fumes. The internal battle he'd been waging since five o'clock this afternoon had completely sapped him of strength.

Up until that point, he'd been doing an excellent job of controlling his unacceptably dramatic reaction to Sofia. He'd spent the two days in Paris reminding himself of the dangers of weakness and fortifying his defences, and so effective had this strategy been that the photo shoot had presented no problem at all. The rehearsal had been a breeze. He hadn't batted an eye when she'd appeared at the door to the cathedral this afternoon, wearing a long fitted white dress that somehow managed to simultaneously convey modesty, extravagance and sexiness. Because he'd bullet-proofed himself so successfully he had not experienced a minor earthquake at the sight of her, looking more beautiful than he could ever have imagined but also curiously and achingly alone. He'd paid no attention whatsoever to the sudden clamouring urge to meet her halfway down the aisle and take her hand in his, and not once during the first hour and a half of the ceremony had he lost focus. He'd mastered his desire for her so skilfully—he'd believed—that he'd no qualms at all about kissing her at the altar.

It was only when their mouths met that he realised how very wrong he'd been.

When she'd grabbed his arm as if it were a lifeline, seeming to melt into him on a soft breathy sigh, the burst of heat that had shot through him had nearly taken out his knees. Suddenly racked with overwhelming need, he'd been on the point of wrapping her in his arms and kissing her properly when a low clearing of the throat from beside him had pierced the thundering desire and snapped him out of his daze.

That had very nearly become a kiss that was for anything but show, he'd thought grimly as he'd fought for the control that had momentarily deserted him. If the archbishop hadn't brought him up short, he might well have had Sofia flat against a pillar within seconds, her with her skirts around her waist and him beneath them. In full view of the congregation. The clergy. His mother. In a cathedral. Without a thought for the scandal. Or the sacrilege.

So much for assuming he had his response to her in hand. He'd been right to suspect she might be dangerous. She threatened his equilibrium. She made him want to forget all about his obligations and his priorities, and the irony of the situation was not lost on him. He'd specifically selected her to be his bride because she understood the requirements of the role. He'd banged on about them enough. Yet it seemed that *he* was the one in need of a lecture on the importance of duty and commitment. *He* was the one in jeopardy of putting his needs before those of his country. And what appallingly primitive needs they were. The reception had been torture. He'd strengthened alliances and paved the way for lucrative new trade deals, but all the while he'd been agonisingly aware of her—every second of every minute of every hour. During dinner, the speeches, the dancing.

His mother's passing comment about the heat of the kiss—which he'd been trying to forget—hadn't helped. She'd admitted to being envious, but she had no business being envious. Royalty didn't have the luxury of such self-centred emotion, so what on earth had she been thinking?

And then there'd been the unpleasant encounter with his dissolute second cousin, who'd rudely interrupted a conversation he'd been having with Finland's ambassador shortly after the speeches.

'Congratulations,' Tommaso had said boozily, giving him a slap on the back that had nearly knocked him into the Finn. 'And thanks for saving me from a fate worse than death. Phew. Just in time, right? All that responsibility. Marriage. Kids. Jeez. Where's the fun in that?' His unfocused gaze had landed on Sofia then, and his grin had turned disgustingly predatory. 'Mind you,' he'd added, oblivious to the mine-strewn territory he was entering, 'if I'd had to marry her it might have not been so bad. She's hotter than the sun. Let me know when you're done with her, cuz. We could have good times.'

Ivo had never thought he possessed either a protective or a violent streak but in that moment, in response to such unfathomable disrespect, he'd experienced both. A red mist had clouded his vision. His pulse had pounded so hard at his temples that he'd felt as if his head were about to explode. He'd wanted to rip Tommaso's throat out and feed it to the sharks in the aquarium on the other side of the city.

Somehow he'd managed to resist the temptation to slam his fist into his cousin's jaw, but the roaring surge of emotion had thrown him further. He'd never felt so unhinged. It had taken him a good half an hour to calm down. He still wasn't entirely himself. And he would shortly have to take his brand-new wife to bed, which would test his control like it had never been tested before.

But he would prevail, he vowed as, having retired to his suite, he toed off his shoes, stripped off his clothes and headed for the shower. He would not lose his head and the monarchy because of a woman. The attraction he'd shared with the Countess Carolina had led him to very nearly miss his investiture as Grand Duke of Ficanza. A search party had eventually tracked him down to her hotel suite and he'd never been so shaken up, so mortified and ashamed. But had that put him off? No. Astoundingly, he'd fancied himself in love with her. So in love with her, in fact, that he'd been blind to the treacherous nature that had not only concealed her faithlessness but also her loyalty.

When he thought about what could have happened had he actually married her, he felt physically sick. At some point she'd have revealed her true colours and he'd have been destroyed, unable to focus and dangerously preoccupied. There'd have been no unity. Stability and security would have been compromised. He'd have been no better than his grandfather, and once again the country would have suffered because of the selfishness of its rulers.

As a result of that horrendous experience, he'd promised himself that he would never let anyone down again, least of all himself. Like his father before him, duty and responsibility would always be his number one priority. And right now, that meant suppressing everything but the need to consummate the marriage as per the clause in the constitution designed to legitimise the union and his heirs. As quickly and efficiently as possible.

So why, he wondered with a frown, having emerged from the bathroom and donned a robe a good thirty minutes after he went in, was he stalling? Why was he stalking to the drinks cabinet and pouring himself an enormous whisky? He'd never needed Dutch courage. He'd never shied away from doing what was necessary, however much he might want to. So why now, when only half an hour remained for him to fulfil his obligations, was he procrastinating—again?

The delay in finding a bride had been one hundred percent down to work, but on this occasion the trouble was Sofia still messing with his head. And such a situation was as ridiculous as it was unacceptable, he thought grimly as he downed the drink in one and felt the heat of alcohol burn its way through his body. He had to stamp out these appalling...*jitters*...and get a grip. He could not continue to allow himself to be derailed like this. He was the King, for God's sake. He ran a country. He negotiated multibillion-dollar deals on a daily basis. He crushed insurgents. He wasn't weak. He wasn't vulnerable. He was invincible.

And so he would not, he vowed as he slammed down his glass and braced himself, be felled by a wife.

CHAPTER FIVE

WHERE ON EARTH could he be?

Sofia stood at the floor-to-ceiling sash window staring out into the dark night, uncertainty knotting her stomach. She and Ivo had left the reception and parted company nearly an hour ago, he to his suite, she to hers. Doing her best to contain the thrills of anticipation and reminding herself that she would *not* give herself away, that she *would* remain unmoved, she'd taken a quick shower and changed into a cream satin slip and robe and then sat down at the dressing table to wait for what she'd assumed would not be long.

She'd been preparing for this moment all evening. Outwardly, she'd spent the reception and then the dinner following the schedule and chatting to the guests. Inwardly, however, she'd worked on her control until she could look at him without reacting. Until she could think of what was to come and not feel even the hint of a shiver.

But not once had it occurred to her that he simply wouldn't show up.

As the nerves twisted harder and her throat tightened, her composure fractured a little more with every minute that ticked agonisingly by. What was keeping him? The likelihood of a matter of state claiming his attention at midnight on his wedding day was virtually zero, so could it be her? Was the idea of sleeping with her so unappealing he was putting it off for as long as he could? Was he planning to defy the constitution and forgo his duty entirely? Just how far down his list of priorities was she?

She knew he wasn't interested in her as a woman. He'd made it exceptionally clear that his sole focus was protecting the monarchy and she accepted that. But a stab of hurt nevertheless struck her square in the chest. Her feminine pride stung. She was no supermodel, obviously, and yes, she lacked the breeding of the few aristocratic women he'd dated in the past, but surely she wasn't *that* unattractive.

Deeply frustrated by the pointless whirling of her thoughts, Sofia was contemplating tracking him down to remind him of his responsibilities—possibly in the hope that the negligée would succeed where she had evidently failed—when there was a sharp knock on the door that separated their suites.

She jumped and spun round, her heart giving a great crash against her ribs. The door flung back and Ivo stood in the space, wearing nothing but a black robe that hung open to the belt that was tied loosely at his waist and finished half way down his long muscled calves. The light behind him gave him a sort of corona that made him look like even more of a god than he usually did, and as her pulse spiked, her mouth dried.

'May I come in?'

His expression was unreadable but he sounded as if he were going to the gallows, and her confidence plunged. 'I assume that's a rhetorical question,' she said, drumming up a smile that she hoped disguised how vulnerable she suddenly felt. 'What took you so long?'

He advanced into the room, running his dark, flat gaze over her as he did so, and came to a stop behind a red velvet armchair that stood in front of the rococo fireplace. 'I had some loose ends to tie up,' he said, resting one large hand on the back of it as a muscle flickered in his cheek.

In response to his clinical inspection of her body, a flurry of hot shivers raced down her spine. 'What ends?'

'Ones that unfortunately couldn't wait. Today went well, I thought.'

He slid his other hand into the pocket of his robe, the epitome of steely control and cool authority. Despite his indifference, she was so relieved that he'd shown up, she wanted to run across the room and throw herself into his arms. To express her embarrassingly pathetic gratitude for not rejecting her after all by pushing aside his lapels and exploring what looked like a hard-muscled chest with her mouth. But, horrified by her lack of self-respect, she remained where she was, her guard up, the smile on her face as practised as it had ever been. 'It couldn't have gone better,' she replied. 'It was faultless from start to finish.'

Apart from the kiss, of course. But she was hardly going to raise that when it had been such a disaster. Nor, it seemed, was he, thank God. 'The reception was certainly productive.'

'I particularly enjoyed the quail.'

'You dance well.'

'So do you.'

'Lessons as a teenager,' he said with a wry twist of his mouth. 'Loathed at the time, but it's turned out to be a surprisingly useful skill to have.'

'All those balls, I imagine. Dangerous for the toes of the unprepared.'

'Quite.'

'For me, it was a coping mechanism,' she said. 'I spent a lot of time in my bedroom as a teenager listening to music with my headphones in, the volume turned up to max to blot out my parents' arguments. Dancing became an outlet for the stress of it.'

'Did they argue a lot?'

'All the time. They called it passion but really it was hate. Especially towards the end.'

'The end?'

'Their car went over a cliff when I was nineteen. They were on their way to consult a divorce lawyer.'

He frowned. 'I'm sorry,' he said gruffly. 'I didn't know that.'

'You never asked.'

'That seems remiss.'

'Yes, well, we have decades to catch up on each other's life story.'

'It'll have to wait until the morning.'

'Because the moment has come to consummate the marriage,' she said with a nod of acknowledgement, a surge of heat and a fresh twist of nerves. 'As required by the constitution and stated in the contract.'

'Right.'

'I must say, though, once again, you're cutting it fine.' She cast a pointed glance at the clock on the mantelpiece, which was striking a quarter to midnight.

'Perhaps I like living on the edge.'

Him? Was he serious? 'I've never met anyone who likes living on the edge less,' she said, aiming for lightness and absolutely nailing it. 'If you *did*, however, I might be tempted to point out that if we didn't actually go through with it, who would ever know? I mean, it's not as if it's witnessed these days, is it?'

A moment of stunned silence followed that. Shock rippled across the strong planes of his handsome face. '*I* would know,' he said, his obvious consternation indicating that he could not be further from the edge if he tried. 'I'm surprised you'd even *think* it, let alone suggest it.'

'I was joking.'

'It's not a laughing matter.'

'I apologise. I'm a little nervous.'

'Why?' His brows snapped together. 'Haven't you done this before?'

'I've done this several times before,' she assured him, thinking for a moment of the few unmemorable experiences she'd had in the past. 'But not for a while, not as a wife and never with you.'

Some unidentifiable emotion flitted across his face and his jaw clenched. 'I'll do my best to minimise the ordeal.'

'I know you will.'

'What makes you so sure?'

'Because you have integrity. You're honourable and upstanding. I've always admired that about you.'

'Anything else?'

Well, there were his spectacular looks and his powerful physique, but hell would freeze over before she admitted how weak she went at the knees every time she looked at him. This arrangement would become even more one-sided than it already was. 'Your sense of duty and responsibility and your equanimity.'

'Is that why you agreed to marry me? Because you admired me?'

'That and a strong desire to save the crown from your

cousin,' she said, determined to keep her love for him firmly to herself for the safety of her heart.

'How flattering.'

The dryness of his tone lifted her eyebrows. These were traits to value. How did he not see that? 'Do you *want* flattery?'

'What I want is irrelevant,' he said, not quite answering her question, she noticed. 'But forget it. This conversation is over. We have a constitutional obligation to fulfil, and as you observed, time is marching.'

Sofia took a deep breath and braced herself for fifteen minutes of complete and utter torment made worse by the knowledge that he'd be operating under duress. 'OK, then,' she said, swallowing hard as she undid the belt of her robe and slipped it through the loops. 'Let's get it over and done with.'

Despite his best efforts to remain ruthlessly unaffected by everything that happened here tonight, Ivo's eyes nearly fell out of their sockets when Sofia shimmied out of her nightwear and sidled over to the vast mahogany *lit-en-bateau* in all her nearly naked glory.

Not that he'd been doing a particularly good job of detachment before then.

He'd been clinging onto his control by a thread ever since he'd opened the door to her room. At the sight of her standing by the window he'd nearly swallowed his tongue. The vision of ethereal loveliness that had walked down the aisle had long gone. So too had the white high-necked, low-backed evening gown she'd changed into for the reception. The cream slinky column of a slip overlaid with a matching robe clung to her curves and seemed to move like liquid in the moonlight. Her hair, which he'd never seen down before, tumbled over her shoulders as if she'd just got out of bed.

It had struck him then like a blow to the head that the woman in front of him—his queen, his *wife*—was about as far from his uber-efficient Communications Secretary, who favoured sober suits and never-a-hair-out-of-place updos, as it was possible to get. He'd been gripped by the urge to stride across the room and haul her into his arms. To take her right there up against the wall. But with superhuman effort he'd banked it. He had to start as he meant to go on.

With that uppermost in his mind, he'd resolved to keep his eyes on her face and off her body. But her features were so exquisite—how he could ever have considered her 'passably attractive' he had no idea—he'd had to avert his gaze just to stop himself staring at her like a drooling adolescent. As if magnetised, his eyes had automatically landed on the rest of her, lingering on her lush curves and intriguing dips, and that hadn't helped his resolve at all.

She, on the other hand, simply admired his *character*. His integrity, honour and his sense of duty and responsibility. Which piqued his vanity, and that annoyed him because he hadn't thought he had any. If he'd been asked, he'd have said that character trumped looks any day of the week. But now, frustratingly, he found himself wondering what was wrong with him physically.

Of even further irritation was the fact that the equanimity she also lauded seemed to be so under threat he'd actually—for the first time in his life—fished for a compliment. For reassurance. And all that had come on top of, not only the realisation that once again he'd found himself delaying the inevitable by asking her about her parents but also the strangely fierce and faintly disturbing surge of primitive satisfaction he'd experienced when she'd observed that this would be the first time she'd have sex as a wife. *His* wife.

This evening was not going as he'd anticipated. He didn't recognise himself and he didn't like it. He was rapidly reaching the end of his tether, and now, to add insult to injury, she wanted the consummation 'over and done with' as quickly as possible.

Were those really her feelings on the subject?

Was this simply a chore to be borne?

Well, he wasn't having that, he thought, his pulse thudding hard and fast as she climbed beneath the covers and pulled them up to her chin. Forget that he too had once considered what was about to happen in those terms. He'd changed his mind. This would no longer be a purely perfunctory coupling. He was going all in. He would do his utmost to reduce her to a puddle of need within minutes. He'd dispel her nerves and shatter her cool and she'd be writhing and panting in his arms, gasping his name when she came, way before midnight.

And then, after the clock struck twelve, he'd do it all over again, only slower. And again and again, until dawn. Ruthlessly. Dispassionately. Not for himself. *Never* for himself. But to secure the line of succession. To ensure stability. For the sake of the monarchy, he would have her at his mercy, crying out with pleasure and begging for release while he remained totally in control—unmoved, focused, invincible.

Relieved beyond belief to be finally back on track by

deploying the pragmatic approach he swore by, Ivo shed his dressing gown and stalked to the bed.

With every step he took, Sofia's eyes dropped a little bit lower and widened a little bit more. A flush hit her cheeks and he thought he caught the sound of soft gasp, which meant she was *not* immune to him, and his integrity and sense of duty *weren't* the only things she admired about him, thank God. He didn't repulse her at all, and he could work with that.

She would find this no chore, he swore to himself as he threw back the covers and stretched out beside her. By the time he was done with her she'd be limp, sated and boneless with satisfaction. He might not have played the field all that much over the years but he'd always valued quality over quantity and he'd make sure this was an experience she'd never forget.

'Could you turn off the lights?' she said breathlessly as he ran his gaze over the stunning length of her and assessed where he was going to start.

'No.'

'You promised to minimise the ordeal.'

'I know,' he said, rolling over to spear his fingers through her hair and setting his mouth to the soft, warm, fragrant skin of her neck. 'But I lied.'

Sofia's fifteen minutes of torment had started the second Ivo dispensed with his robe. She'd often fantasised about the body beneath the suits but her imagination had been woefully inadequate on that front. He belonged in a museum. She'd never seen such perfect proportions. And where on earth he found the time to keep all those muscles in such good shape she had no idea.

But whether or not she'd be able to accommodate his impressive erection, which lent a whole new meaning to the word *upstanding*, wasn't what had set alarm bells off in her head. That would have been the determination etched into his expression and the wolfish gleam in his eyes, which had given her the impression that he intended to gobble her up. And she'd been right to be alarmed by that because he'd *lied*? What did he mean by that? What in God's name did he intend to do to her?

'You're very tense,' he murmured, his warm breath feathering over her feverish skin and leaving a rash of goose bumps in its wake.

Well, of course she was tense, she thought, closing her eyes in the hope that not looking at him might make this easier to bear. She hadn't been near a gym in years. She had cellulite. The faint trace of alcohol on his breath suggested he'd needed fortification to go through with this. Plus, he was all over her and not responding to his electrifying touch was taking every drop of self-control she possessed. 'It's been a long day.'

'Relax.'

Relax? Had anyone in the history of the world ever relaxed simply because they'd been told to? Besides, she couldn't afford to relax. She couldn't afford to let her guard drop for a single second.

But, as he placed his hand on her waist and slid it up her ribcage to her breast, she could feel it slipping. This was what she'd dreamed of for so long. Was it any wonder she was melting like butter in the sun? How on earth was she going to protect herself against him? How was her armour to withstand such an assault? The strategies she'd used in the past to block out feelings she'd rather not have didn't seem to be working now.

Maybe the best form of defence was to go on the attack, she thought dazedly as he rubbed his thumb over her achingly tight nipple and she fought back a whimper. Maybe if she focused on getting *him* to lose control, she'd hold on to her own. It didn't feel like the most robust of arguments, but with the imminent collapse of her brain it was all she had.

And she would not be passive in this, dammit. She was his wife, the Queen, and contrary to her earlier concerns, he *did* seem to want her right now, which went some way to restore her battered self-esteem. No doubt he thought he was in charge here—the lights were still on, after all—but he wasn't. She simply couldn't allow it.

Steeling herself, Sofia shifted into him, lifting a hand to his shoulder and wrapping a leg around his hips. She crushed her breasts to his rock-hard chest, pressed her pelvis into his and felt the tremor that gripped her rip through him too.

But if she thought such a move would give her the power she sought and the opportunity to explore his magnificent form, she was sorely mistaken. It was as though she'd lit a wildfire. In a flash, she was once again on her back, pinned to the mattress by the heavy weight of his body, and she'd barely had time to catch her breath or gather her wits before his mouth crashed down on hers.

He kissed her as if he intended to imprint himself on her, and her head emptied of everything but him, because this surpassed her wildest dreams and they'd been pretty wild. But while she'd frequently imagined the heat and skill of his tongue in her mouth, she'd never considered the specifics. She'd never imagined that his lips would mould to hers as if they'd been designed to do so. Or that he'd instinctively know how to make her writhe beneath him and sigh and gasp for more.

Which he gave her.

After wreaking devastation on her with his kisses, he turned his attention to her breasts, first with his hands, then his mouth, and she lost what was left of her reason. When, precisely, she succumbed to the clamouring needs of her body she had no idea, but within moments she was so addled with desire that she barely noticed him removing her underwear. It was only when he thrust his fingers into her slippery heat and she nearly jackknifed off the bed that she came to her senses.

What was she doing?

She was falling at the first hurdle. She ought to be switching positions—putting him on his back and her hands on him—not swooning in surrender. Yet she collapsed as if she had no strength in her limbs. She simply couldn't help it.

Fixing her gaze on the ceiling and frantically trying to figure out which myth the fresco up there depicted, Sofia grappled for control. But his fingers were too clever, his mouth tormenting everywhere it landed, and despairingly, she knew it was a battle she was losing. She wanted him too much. Her defences lay in ruins. She had no protection. She'd been naïve to think she did.

She shattered beneath him with embarrassing speed, the pleasure spinning through her like the fireworks she'd imagined, only faster, higher, stronger. Trembling, catching her breath as the stars behind her eyes faded, she filled with fury, directed at herself for being so weak and him for being so good. And she vowed then that if she was going down, she was taking him with her.

So when, as the clock began to chime midnight, he pushed into her, filling her so fully she could feel him everywhere, she resisted his attempts to take charge of the situation by holding her still. Just about managing to stave off both the stunning disbelief and the blissful delirium of actually having him inside her, she wrapped her arms around his neck and her legs round his hips, angling her pelvis to take him in deeper.

He emitted a harsh groan and began to move. She ran her hands all over his shoulders, his back, his buttocks, pulling him in even further, and met every one of his powerful thrusts with demands of her own. She needed him to lose control the way she had. She had to level the playing field and prevent herself from confessing she loved him by focusing on the physical.

So she told him how good he felt and how good what he was doing to her was. She did nothing to hold back the sighs and the moans that emerged instinctively from her mouth. She kissed him as fiercely as he kissed her and clenched her inner muscles around him with all her strength, until his movements lost their restraint.

He pounded into her with increasing intensity. He started to shake. His muscles strained. There was a wildness about him, a sense of desperation that triggered in her a sharp surge of triumph and a wave of relief. And then, as she flew headlong into heart-stopping oblivion once again, he let out a roar, buried himself as deep inside her as he could get and erupted.

CHAPTER SIX

Royal Tour in Trouble?

Less than forty-eight hours after an unnecessarily lavish event, which cost the country millions that would have been better spent elsewhere, it looks as though the honeymoon is over for King Ivo and his brand-new consort, Queen Sofia.

Tension was high during today's visit to Livigno, where Their Majesties were treated to a spectacular show in the town square involving towering human pyramids and death-defying acrobatics. Despite bestowing many a smile upon those who had gathered to hand them flowers and wish them well, they had none for each other. Barely even able to look at one another, the impression they gave was one of newly wedded blues rather than newly wedded bliss.

Is this fair to anyone? Is there really a place for an absolute monarchy in today's world? To paraphrase Winston Churchill, democracy is the worst form of government but it's the best there is, and we, the citizens of Montemare, deserve the best. So isn't it time to lay this antiquated, out-of-touch institution to rest once and for all?

ON BOARD THE Royal Train as it meandered south among the towering pines of the Great Forest, Ivo scrolled through the rest of the blog post, his frown as deep as the valley they'd just traversed.

Ninety-nine percent of the press coverage of this tour so far had been positive, and so it should be when the royal correspondents, the photographers and camera crews had been carefully selected for their favourable opinion of the monarchy.

The remaining 1 percent, however, concerned him. This report—and others in the same vein—were few and far between, but every 'like' they attracted was one too many for his comfort. These days, the smallest wave of dissent could gain momentum before anyone was even aware of it. From there it could spiral out of control in the blink of an eye. It had taken six months for the anti-monarchy movement to galvanise sixty years ago. Today, it would take weeks, possibly even less.

He'd dedicated his entire life to maintaining the stability and security of his country, and he'd vowed long ago that nothing would ever jeopardise that, least of all himself. Yet, if what he'd just read was to be believed, that was precisely what was happening. Those who lived to brief against him had spied an opportunity to further their agenda. And because he'd taken his eye off the ball, which had allowed the opportunity to arise in the first place, he only had himself to blame.

Distance between himself and Sofia in private was one thing, he thought, as he moved on to the comments and his frown became a scowl. In public, however, it was quite another, and if he'd known in advance how the last couple of days were going to pan out he'd have addressed it at the time. But he hadn't anticipated distance. He hadn't anticipated a lot of things, it seemed.

Consummating the marriage had not gone as he'd intended. To prove to himself that he was in complete control of their relationship, that it would present zero threat to his work, he'd planned to destroy Sofia's defences and ensure her surrender. He had not expected to be challenged. He had not expected a battle.

However, a battle was precisely what he'd encountered, and it was one he'd lost pretty much the minute she started it. She'd twined herself around him like a vine and with the ferocious immediacy of a match to a touchpaper he'd gone up in flames.

Admittedly, it hadn't taken much. Her scent and taste had already intoxicated him to a dizzying degree. He'd never felt such soft skin. The strength of her reaction to his touch had been mind-blowing. He couldn't recall ever having been on the receiving end of anything like it. He'd felt as if he could conquer the world. Like some sort of superhero. Little wonder, then, that between the first and twelfth chimes of the clock he'd utterly forgotten who he was.

When he'd recovered, he'd been so shaken by the experience, so horrified by the total reverse of his plan as well as the complete collapse of his control that he hadn't stuck around for further annihilation. Feeling anything but invincible and badly needing to regroup, he'd lifted himself off her and snatched up his robe. Then, after muttering something about their early start and the importance of rest, he'd disappeared through the door.

It hadn't been his finest move, even if it had been one borne out of self-preservation. But much to his amazement, Sofia had not called him on it. In fact, they'd barely spoken since, unless to discuss the tour. Breakfast the morning after had been a monosyllabic affair. She'd spent most of the subsequent train journey along the coast to Livigno with her head buried in her laptop. And twice now she'd bidden him goodnight after dinner and headed to her carriage alone.

Because this had suited him, Ivo hadn't questioned it. He'd been angry with himself for such appalling weakness, and angry with her for having such a hold on him. Even now, two days since that night and with much royal-related business to occupy his mind, every time he so much as glanced in her direction he had a flashback of her, head back, crying out his name as she came for a second time. His body invariably responded with frustrating predictability. The last thing he needed was that to become a permanent affliction so he'd avoided contact as much as possible.

But thanks to the negative press the tour was garnering he could now see that approach to the problem for what it was—utterly unacceptable. Once again he'd forgotten his responsibilities. He'd become self-absorbed in a way he'd always sworn he wouldn't. He'd succumbed to emotions he hadn't permitted himself in years, and even more infuriatingly, while he was struggling to get a grip on them, it seemed that she had no such trouble compartmentalising. She'd evidently packed that night away, moved on and hadn't looked back.

He hated feeling as though he was at a disadvantage and out of control, and he hated even more that he had not managed to contain it. Yesterday afternoon spent in the country's second biggest city should have been a triumph. It should not have provided fodder for the country's small but noisy republican movement.

The situation had to be addressed, he thought grimly, as he glanced at his watch and set down his coffee cup. He was not having the monarchy brought down by a marriage designed to do the exact opposite simply because he'd somehow become too involved in it. Obviously he would have to follow Sofia's example and lock down the memories of bedding her once and for all. But first he had to confront the optics—which were important—and ignore any personal discomfort he might suffer as a consequence, which wasn't. And since they were due to arrive at their next destination in just under half an hour there was no time to waste.

'Sofia.'

'Yes?' she murmured impassively, without even looking up, damn her.

'We have a problem.'

Sitting at the other end of the long, narrow walnut dining table, which gleamed beneath the warm, dappled and shifting sunlight, Sofia stiffened and wondered if Ivo could somehow read her mind. Although, really, the problems plaguing her weren't so much theirs as hers alone.

Random snippets of the fifteen minutes they'd spent together in bed on Saturday night kept darting through her head, and whenever they did, her response was positively Pavlovian. Heat surged through her. Her head spun so fast she went dizzy. She wanted to seek him out, throw herself into his arms and kiss the life out of him, all of which was appalling because she was furious with him, with herself, with the entire bloody mess her emotions were in.

Once the marriage had been consummated, Ivo had not stuck around. In fact, he'd sprung off her as if she'd developed syphilis. Unable to get away fast enough, he'd muttered something about the early start and the busy day ahead and had then shot through the door before she'd been able to register what was going on.

Initially, once she'd got over the shock of his whiplash disappearance, she'd been relieved. She hadn't wanted him to linger. She'd needed the time to recover. The space to berate herself for yielding to temptation so pathetically easily, even if she had succeeded in getting him to lose control too.

But then, tossing and turning, unable to sleep, she'd asked herself what could have caused such a dramatic reaction. Had she revealed her feelings for him, as she'd feared she might? She didn't think so. No, she was *sure* she hadn't. So what else could have spooked him? She'd drawn a blank, which had resulted in a mad bout of second-guessing until she'd remembered that all he cared about was duty and everything had become clear.

Over the last couple of days she'd tried to ignore the hurt and rejection and get over the feeling of having been ever so slightly used. She knew that for him that night had been about fulfilling their contractual obligation and nothing else. She'd tried to convince herself that it wasn't personal and that there was plenty of time to produce the children he'd promised her.

Yet frustratingly, despite her extensive efforts to rise above the upset she felt, she couldn't, which was all the more annoying when, after nineteen years of her parents constantly prioritising their emotions over hers, she'd assumed she'd learned how to deal with such futile sentiments. But apparently she hadn't and as a result she'd done what she'd sworn not to do and allowed herself to be swayed by passion. She'd allowed her heart to dominate her head.

To prevent the collapse of her entire belief system and the potential detonation of their relationship, therefore, she'd had to put a stop to it. She'd vowed to toughen up. She was way too soft. If she wasn't careful, this marriage would eat her alive. She had to reinforce her defences. Add another course of bricks or two to the wall around her heart. Because it wasn't as if she could demand he clarify his thought process that night. She didn't do confrontation, which was another thing she could blame her parents for. And even if she *had* been the combative type, she'd have let sleeping dogs lie. What if she'd ended up sounding needy? What if he'd said something that had broken her heart? What if he'd pointed out exactly what it was about her that made her worthy only of second place, that turned people away or made them flee from her bed? How would she bear it? No. The best solution was to bury what had happened and how she felt about it and move on.

Irritatingly, however, this had proved easier said than done. She'd frequently found herself forgetting about the hurt and confusion and instead entertaining the appalling idea of begging him for a repeat performance. How could she want him so badly when she knew that he didn't want her at all? Where was her pride? Her dignity? In the end, to protect her self-respect as much as her heart, she'd had no option but to adopt frosty detachment and minimise contact as much as possible until she was sure she was bullet-proof.

But by Ivo directly addressing her now with this problem of theirs, it seemed the respite—which, in all honesty, she was slightly surprised he'd let her get away with for so long—was over.

Bracing herself against the impact of locking eyes with

him for the first time since she'd come apart in his arms, Sofia looked up from her laptop and channelled her inner ice queen. 'Just the one?'

'Several, actually,' he said, his face dark with displeasure and perversely all the more attractive for it. 'A number of unfavourable articles are circulating about yesterday's visit to Livigno.'

'I know,' she said, ignoring the objectionable shiver of heat that snaked down her spine. 'I've been going through them. They're not ideal, are they?'

His eyebrows shot up. *'Not ideal?'* he echoed in disbelief. 'They're a disaster. We're supposed to be presenting a strong united front to our people and capitalising on the goodwill of the wedding. But in some parts that is evidently not happening. What's going on?'

So much.

'I have no idea what you mean,' she said evenly, the outward epitome of cool, calm professionalism. 'Nothing's going on.'

His jaw clenched. 'Of course there is. You avoid me. You can't look at me. You barely even speak to me. The Arctic is warmer than you have been these last couple of days. And in private, that's fine. But in public, it is very much not. I married you because you were the one meant to be able to pull this off.'

As if she needed a reminder...

'You agreed to play a part. That was the deal. You're reneging on it and I want to know why.'

'I'm not reneging on anything,' she countered, having zero intention of thrashing out her complicated feelings with someone who wasn't remotely interested in hearing them. 'I'm just tired. And rather overwhelmed. You're used to all this. I'm not. The constant security presence, the cameras, the attention, the people… It's exhausting.'

'That explains nothing,' he said bluntly. 'You've dealt with seventy-two-hour crises and I've never once seen you flag. You thrive on the adrenaline.'

'This is different. The spotlight is on me. But I'll get used to it. And anyway, what's your excuse?'

His brows snapped together. 'What do you mean?'

'Well, you haven't exactly been playing your part either, have you? If I've been quiet, you've been positively Trappist. If I'm the Arctic, you're the *Ant*arctic. These headlines aren't all on me.'

Ivo's frown deepened, as if he were unsettled by her observations. 'I've been under a lot of pressure,' he muttered eventually, the admission that he'd been firing on less than all cylinders obviously an unpleasant and frustrating one. 'Which I grant hasn't helped the situation. But it must not continue. I simply can't allow it. So from now on, we need to focus on the bigger picture. We should up the eye contact. Smile at each other more. The occasional display of affection wouldn't go amiss either. I assume you're in agreement with this, yes?'

Well, no, she wasn't in agreement with that at all, as a matter of fact. Not only was she at sixes and sevens emotionally, her defences weren't up to smiles and touching. Despite how annoyed she was with him, she could hardly glance in his direction without swooning. What if they collapsed entirely and she had another altar moment? How mortifying would that be? How would she ever regain control then? 'There has to be some other way.'

'I'm open to suggestions,' he said, his irritation at being

challenged yet again evidenced by the muscle pounding in his cheek. 'You're the expert, after all.'

That was true. She was. And there was no situation she couldn't spin. With relish. However, she wasn't feeling very expert right now. She was having trouble focusing, and it had nothing to do with the sway of the train as the forest gave way to the beginnings of a town. She was in danger of losing herself in the mesmerising depths of his eyes. But that wouldn't do, so she blinked to break the connection and instead decided to turn her attention to the heart of the matter, which with any luck might be something she *could* understand. 'Is the 1 percent really that much of a concern?'

'What?' he said, the word slicing through the air like a lash. 'Of course it is. I'm surprised you even have to ask.'

'Why?'

'Because, unchecked, 1 percent can rapidly become 2, then 4, then 8. Especially in an age of instant news and social media. When my grandfather married my grandmother, he took her off to a secluded estate in the southeast and they weren't seen for six months. The attempted coup didn't come out of nowhere. There was a power vacuum. Disparate factions saw an opportunity to unite and grabbed it.' He leaned forward, the sudden intensity of his gaze fairly pinning her to her seat. 'I can't risk that happening again. I've worked too hard and there's still so much I hope to accomplish. We have to be seen to be believed, Sofia, and we have to be convincing. Loyalty requires a life of almost unlimited publicity to sustain it. My father spent decades bringing the country back together. I won't allow *anything* to jeopardise a legacy that he paid for with his life.'

A shadow darted across his features and, despite her resolve to remain aloof and unmoved, her heart twanged.

She'd been taught about the attempted coup that had taken place sixty years ago, of course, but she'd never thought of the emotional impact it might have had on those who came after. Yet it had obviously been significant. Whether or not he was aware of it, there was a trace of bitterness to Ivo's words that suggested he blamed his grandfather for his father's fatal heart attack at the age of fifty-eight.

'So *that's* where your sense of duty comes from,' she said, unable to prevent the ache that sprouted in her chest. 'You feel you owe it to your father.'

'Yes,' he confirmed with a short nod. 'But not just that. My responsibilities have been ingrained into me since birth. I eat, sleep and breathe them. There's no room for selfishness—for what *I* want—so it's fortunate I don't want anything. The country, the people and the monarchy always come first. *Always*. And now you're part of that. So you need to step up.'

This was the second time he'd denied or minimised wanting something, and Sofia had the feeling he protested just a little too much. But however intriguing she might find that, however much she might fancy comparing notes on playing second fiddle to something or someone else, there was no point asking him to elaborate. His intractability on the subject radiated from every pore.

And perhaps, she thought with a twinge of guilt and the ebb of her umbrage, she ought to take a leaf out of his book and stop thinking only about herself and her needs. The pressure he was under was immense and he was right, she *had* made a commitment to support him. She loved him, and people did anything for those they loved, didn't they? Besides, it wasn't as if she didn't know how to put on an act. She'd been doing it for at least the last year, and she'd learned from the masters, her parents, who, despite loathing one another in private, had been perfectly civil to each other in public.

So she had to get over herself and stop overthinking this. Ivo wasn't, was he? He wasn't struggling with feelings he had to suppress. Unlike her, he clearly had no misgivings about anything. His objectives were the same as they had been when he'd proposed. She just had to focus on those.

'I understand,' she said, nevertheless desperately hoping she wasn't going to be burned to a crisp by the experience. 'Whenever we're in public, I'll do what's required. You have my word.'

He gave a nod. His jaw relaxed. 'Good,' he said, glancing out of the window as the train pulled into the station. 'We're here. It's time to get the show on the road. Ready?'

No, not really. She had the horrible feeling that if she didn't exercise extreme caution, her emotions might get the better of her and snowball into the chaos she feared. That he could all too easily do her heart serious damage if she let herself care too much. But as long as she remembered that this was a performance, a role she'd been contracted to play and nothing more, she could handle the odd touch here and there. On the off-chance she did get carried away, she could claim it was part of the pretence. And in private, she would continue to guard her fragile heart with everything she had.

'Of course,' she said, plastering a smoothly professional smile to her face as she pulled her shoulders back, straightened her spine and lifted her chin. 'I've never been readier for anything. One happy couple? Coming right up.'

CHAPTER SEVEN

A WEEK INTO their agreement, Sofia thought that she'd never worked so hard in her life. Criss-crossing the southern peninsula, they'd visited ten towns in seven days. Quite apart from the relentless deployment of her professional skills, she'd shaken countless hands, her facial muscles ached from smiling and her brain hurt from the effort of remembering everything it was supposed to be doing.

Did she regret agreeing to Ivo's strategy and giving him her word that she'd stick to it?

Well, no, not in the round because she would do anything to defend the man she loved and protect the way of life they now shared.

But on occasion, she did, very much. Mainly whenever he looked at her with warmth and her heart melted and she nearly forgot that none of this was for real. Or when he took her arm or her hand and she had to fight the urge to lean in and rub up against him like a cat. Luckily, however, with the help of a sharp mental slap and an ultra-stern talking-to, she managed to pull herself back from the brink of madness every time.

The fact that he'd thrown himself into the role of devoted husband with the single-mindedness with which he did everything else didn't make remembering that it was only an act any easier. In fact, it made it harder, because all the smiles and touches were an unhelpful reminder of what she could have if only he returned her feelings.

But their physical interactions weren't the only source of her torment. In Pompetto she'd found out what it felt like to have someone in her corner for the first time in her life.

'Who are your people?' the outrageously snobbish bishop had enquired as they sat in the pews of his church awaiting an evening of choral delights.

'My people are the King's people,' she'd replied with a smile. 'But if you're referring to my family, I come from a long line of professionals—teachers, lawyers and doctors among them. My mother was in HR and my father was an accountant. I'm solid middle-class stock.'

'Ah,' the bishop had murmured with a trace of disapproval that had not gone unnoticed.

'I believe the phrase you're looking for is "what a breath of fresh air",' Ivo had said icily, his voice low and as dangerous as she'd ever heard it. 'The Queen is an asset this country is extremely fortunate to have. We would all do well to remember that.'

The colour had instantly leached from the bishop's face. 'Of course,' he'd stuttered, perspiration beading at his brow. 'I meant no offence.'

'Didn't you?'

The question had landed like a slap. The bishop had blanched even more and shrunk further into the pew. 'You have my sincerest apologies, Your Majesties. As well as my full support and my undying loyalty for as long as you desire them.'

Sofia had murmured her acceptance of the apologies and his backing but her thoughts had veered elsewhere.

The reminder of how powerful Ivo was and how coolly ruthless he could be had sent a thrill down her spine. She hadn't needed him to rush to her defence, but independence could be exhausting and it had warmed her soul nonetheless.

Then, in Roncanica, a village situated at the westernmost tip of the country, they'd been interviewed by a roomful of children about their plans for the future. Somehow they'd ended up batting ideas back and forth as if they'd discussed the topic beforehand when they hadn't, and she'd briefly wondered if they'd ever become the sort of couple who could mentally finish each other's sentences.

Even though she was well aware that they were simply presenting a united front to the world, Sofia had caught a glimpse of how a proper relationship might work and the togetherness that it might involve. Of course, she had no proof of anything. Her parents had not been good role models in that respect. In fact, they could not have been worse. Presumably they'd been in love at some stage, but by the time she was old enough to be aware of her environment, their marriage had turned into one of vicious animosity, with her more or less invisible. All she'd learned from them—apart from a strong sense of self-reliance and a keen understanding of façade—was a loathing of conflict and an ability to shut her emotions down in the face of it.

But now she'd had the taste of an alternative version. A shiny glittering version that called to her longing for love and the security of a close emotional connection. And she had to be *so* careful not to fall for it. She'd done an excellent job so far of switching off the public persona in private but it was getting harder by the day. Increasingly, she wanted to talk to Ivo over dinner about what they'd done and who they'd met. To share with him everything there was to know about her.

Yet such danger lay in following that path. It was lined with grenades of pain that would detonate every time he looked at her as if wondering why she was bothering him with unwanted conversation. She might find herself tempted to reveal her feelings for him and that was not a conversation she wanted to have, because she knew what the outcome of that would be and she knew that it would be crucifying.

She must never forget that all she was to him was a means by which he could execute his duty. That she filled a vacancy, nothing else. She must never read something into this display of solidarity that simply wasn't there. He'd never expressed anything more than a passing interest in her life, and even then only when it impacted on her work. She would be the biggest fool in the world to allow herself even a glimmer of hope that he might one day return her love. If she didn't want him to inflict irrevocable harm on her, she had to continue to keep everything she felt for him in check.

Never more so than tonight.

The ball at which they were guests of honour was being held at the kingdom's finest hotel. Built on a rocky outcrop, it was Art Deco in design and had terraces that descended to the sea. It boasted one hundred rooms decorated with exquisite luxury, employed the world's greatest chefs and staff and deserved every one of its seven stars. A thousand guests from the charity sector would be in attendance, the women in ball gowns, the men in white tie. There'd be a six-course banquet, champagne and dancing, followed by a night in the sumptuous Royal Suite.

How easy it would be to slip into the role of Cinderella and lose oneself in the fantasy, Sofia thought, resisting the urge to worry at her lower lip as the train pulled into the station and a flurry of activity ensued. To believe that she'd found her very own Prince Charming.

But she had to stay strong and resist the perilous temptation to think that all her dreams were being fulfilled. They weren't. They likely never would be. So she would smile in all the right places and waltz with him when required. But she would not get carried away. She would not lower her guard and care. Her heart *would* remain safe.

At six o'clock that evening Ivo paced restlessly around the teak-panelled lobby of the Royal Suite, his scowl so deep he feared it might well become permanent. He'd never felt so on edge. Or so at sea.

Over the past week, he'd given so many speeches they'd blurred into one, and been handed so many bouquets that any sort of floral scent now made his stomach turn. He and Sofia had attended three concerts, two football matches and one play, and met countless dignitaries and officials, not to mention great swathes of the population who'd come out in droves to see them.

However, the hectic schedule wasn't the problem. Nor was his queen. He couldn't fault her performance as they'd travelled around the southern peninsula. She'd kept her word and had proved herself to be exactly the asset he'd envisaged. The embodiment of grace and elegance, she'd met hundreds of people without complaint. Her smile hadn't faltered once, not even when the now unemployed Bishop of Pompetto had insulted her so monstrously. She waxed lyrical about how happy she was to be in whatever location they found themselves. She did her homework and had the knack of making everyone she spoke to feel special. And she could not have provided him with more support.

'Down with the monarchy!' someone had called in the middle of a walkabout in Cerbano.

Almost instantly a pair of personal protection officers had swooped in to remove the individual from the crowd, but Sofia had stalled them. To everyone's astonishment she'd walked right up to the woman and had asked, with genuine interest, 'Why would you want that?'

'No one elected the King,' the woman—Giulia, apparently—had protested. 'Or you. Inherited power is an outdated abomination. We want a say in the government. We want democracy.'

'But would it result in a better governing of the country?' Sofia had posited with a thoughtful frown. 'Isn't Montemare very well-run already? Name a state that has a higher GDP per capita than ours. You can't, can you? Because there isn't one. Investment is at a record level. Taxes are low. Every minute of every day the King works impossibly hard for each of you. I've seen it with my own eyes. He's tireless in his pursuit of fairness, justice and progress. Would an elected government riddled with ego and vested interests elsewhere be prepared to sacrifice personal desires for the greater good like he does? I don't think so.'

A reluctantly mollified Giulia had left with an invitation to visit the palace sometime, while Ivo had gone away thinking that he couldn't have made a better case for the monarchy himself, although Sofia had been wrong about the sacrifices she'd alleged he'd made. He hadn't, because he had no personal desires. Strong successful kings didn't.

Now that she was one hundred percent engaged, she was so damn good at her job that almost overnight the negative headlines had been wiped out. The press couldn't get enough of the royal couple who, to all intents and purposes, were besotted with each other. Everyone was fooled. The tour was progressing apace and in precisely the direction he and the palace had intended, all of which proved beyond doubt that in selecting her to be his queen he'd one hundred percent picked the right woman.

The cause of all his tension and stress, therefore, was Ivo himself. He was the one who'd suggested warmer, closer interaction, yet now he wished he'd come up with a different, less traumatic strategy. Eye contact with Sofia singed him like a laser. Her smiles struck him square in the chest and stole his breath so comprehensively that his head spun. The light touches on his back, his arm, his hand electrified every nerve ending he possessed and played havoc with his focus.

Two days ago, they'd met with the Mayor of Stallaglie, and she'd laughed at something the man had said. Ivo didn't think he'd ever heard her laugh quite like that before, and it had frozen him to the spot. Suddenly gripped by the need to elicit such a joyous sound from her himself, he'd instantly lost track of the conversation and would have looked an utter imbecile had she not stepped in to rescue the situation.

He was driving himself insane. He couldn't concentrate and couldn't sleep. He was in a permanent state of semi-arousal, which only added to his stress. He could feel his control unravelling faster with every passing minute, but the more he tried to hold on to it the more it seemed to slither out of reach.

Ivo was well aware that his desire for his wife was intensified by the allure of forbidden fruit, but that didn't alleviate the monumental sexual frustration he endured. His temper was frayed. He'd lost count of the number of times he'd had to bite back a snappish retort, and his mood was made worse by the knowledge that it wasn't just the press who couldn't get enough of the seemingly more affectionate royal couple. Deep down, in a part of him that lay buried under the crushing weight of his role—and which he did not dare acknowledge—neither could he, even though he *knew* that her performance was purely for the benefit of the public.

When had he experienced such unwavering support? the devil in him taunted when he recalled, far too frequently, how she'd sung his praises in Cerbano. When was the last time someone had defended him personally? *Never* was the answer to that. In fact, the last time he'd been in a relationship, he'd been attacked. The experience had convinced him that he was better off alone, and he'd always been absolutely fine with that. Love was for fools like his grandfather. Trust in anything on a personal basis was for the naive.

How he still saw the value in a team was something of a miracle, but he did. What he had not expected, however, was to *like* being part of a team. Or to feel so put out when, in private, Sofia took it all away and treated him once again to ice-cold indifference. After all, he was used to existing in both physical and emotional isolation. In fact, he *embraced* it. It meant he could do his job to preserve and strengthen his father's legacy to the best of his abilities. It meant his heart would never be diced into bits again. And it wasn't as if he *wanted* to know more about her parents. Or her life before the palace. Or anything else about her, in fact. He hadn't been *remiss*. He'd focused solely on what *was* important, not what wasn't.

Ivo neither recognised nor understood this version of himself. The flare of his temper. The questioning of the judgement that he'd never doubted before. The unspeakable desire for the act they were putting on to be real. None of it was him. For the first time in a decade he felt on unstable, treacherous ground, and he loathed it. But he had no clue how to climb out of the seething pit of confusion and uncertainty, and that only added to his teeth-grinding irritation.

'I'm ready when you are.'

At the sound of her siren's voice, which now reached into him and wrapped itself round his organs every time she opened her mouth, Ivo turned. His jaw nearly hit the floor. His head emptied of all coherent thought, which should have been a blessing when coherent thought was so troublesome, but it wasn't. Because all that remained was hot, sharp, crucifying need.

Her hair was up in an elaborate arrangement to accommodate his great-great-grandmother's diamond and emerald tiara. More emeralds sparkled in her earlobes and around her throat, complementing the green embroidery that wove around the shimmering ivory strapless ball gown she wore. She was so stunning his breath jammed in his lungs. For a moment, he couldn't speak. He couldn't even think.

It was she who eventually broke the ear-shattering silence. 'You look nice,' she said, snapping him out of his trance and crashing him back down to earth, because…*nice*? Was that *it*? She looked like a goddess and he looked *nice*?

'So do you,' he replied with staggering understatement as he stamped out the pique to his vanity, which was wholly unworthy of a king.

'Thank you.'

With yet another of the aggravatingly meaningless smiles she gave him when they didn't have an audience, she lifted her chin and sailed regally across the lobby towards him. Getting a grip and fighting back the appalling urge to propel her back into her room and keep her there until she smiled at him in a wholly more pleasurable way, Ivo held out his arm. 'Shall we?'

'By all means,' she said, inclining her head and accepting it.

'Let's go.'

At 9:00 p.m., Sofia was taking a much-needed break on the terrace when she felt the balmy air around her shift and her skin prickle.

Three hours into the evening, she was hot and all talked out. The effort of not swooning whenever she looked at the man she still couldn't quite believe was her husband had completely sapped her of strength. His black tail-coat hugged his broad shoulders as if he'd been stitched into it, and the crisp snowy white shirt highlighted the darkness of his hair and the stunning masculinity of his face.

Every time her gaze landed on him, longing clawed at her chest and made a mockery of her good intentions. She'd lost count of the number of times she'd been told what a beautiful couple they made. Worse, on each occasion, she'd had to fight back the alarming urge to snap that none of it was real, it was all just for show.

Her nerves were shredded. She felt as if she was fast

unravelling at the seams, and she just couldn't work out why she was finding it so hard to contain her feelings when she'd managed to do so perfectly well before. It was deeply alarming. The inkling of empathy that she was beginning to feel for her parents as a result was even more so. She'd dedicated years to behaving as unlike them as she possibly could. She hated feeling that tonight, swept up and lost in emotion as she was, she might be failing.

For the sake of the charade, her composure and her belief system, therefore, she'd wanted five, ten, maybe fifteen minutes to herself. To figure out what was wrong and fix it. But apparently she wasn't even allowed that.

'What are you doing out here?'

Eyebrows arched, Ivo leaned back against the stone balustrade over which she was gazing at the torch-lit gardens and folded his arms across his frustratingly distracting chest.

'Just getting a breath of fresh air.'

'I need you back inside.'

Emotion simmered away inside her, a seething cauldron of fatigue, resentment and impatience for this evening to be over, and she pressed down on all of it hard. She didn't know where it had suddenly sprung from, but she really had to get a grip. 'Now?'

He nodded shortly. 'The dancing is about to start and we're expected to lead it.'

'I know.'

'Good.'

'But can't people wait?'

'What?' He frowned, as if such a thing had never occurred to him before, and a muscle ticked in his cheek. 'No. Why should they?'

'Well, why shouldn't they?'

'Because we serve them, not the other way round. I thought you understood that. I've mentioned it often enough.'

It was the hint of censure she could hear in his voice that did for her control. It snapped like a badly frayed rope. The cauldron bubbled over and everything she was feeling poured through her like boiling lava before she could even think to stop it.

'I've done nothing *but* serve the people these past two weeks,' she said hotly, while trying to keep her voice down and resisting the urge to jab him in the shoulder with her finger. 'Do you know how many patronage requests I've received this evening? Twenty-eight. And I'll take all of them on if that's what's required. I'll play the part of the adoring consort and continue to defend you to the hilt. I'll dance with you and shake a million hands and do and be whatever you need. But every now and then, just for the teensiest-tiniest moment, what *I* need is a break.'

The warm air crackled with electricity, as if a storm had abruptly struck. Their gazes locked and held. She didn't know what hers was doing—firing daggers at him most likely—but his was dark, glittering, inscrutable.

Her throat was tight. Her heart thumped hard and fast as the seconds thundered by. She seemed to have rendered him speechless. What could he be thinking? Was he as horrified by her dramatic outburst as she suddenly was? Now it was out of her system, she felt ice-cold and shaky. Forget the faint flicker of affinity she'd had for her parents a moment ago. The shocking realisation that by allowing her emotions to overspill so violently she'd behaved exactly like them was battering her on all sides. Her head was spinning so fast she feared she was about to throw up.

But she couldn't lose it again. Not out here, in public, when one phone with a camera had the potential to destroy everything they were trying to achieve. Or anywhere. Even once was one time too many. She would not go down the road that led to chaos and heartbreak for all involved. So she took a deep breath and swallowed down the lump of mortification and dismay that was lodged in her throat.

'I'm sorry,' she muttered, because an eruption of such hideous passion was not what either of them expected of her. 'That was totally uncalled for.'

'The pressure is intense, isn't it?'

Her head shot up. *What?* Where was the remonstration she deserved? The unequivocal displeasure at her loss of composure?

Forgetting for a moment the horror of completely losing control like that, of revealing her true feelings for once, Sofia searched Ivo's face and saw that he no longer looked annoyed and disapproving. In fact, an unexpected glimmer of sympathy flared in his eyes, and it knocked the breath from her lungs. He'd never allowed her to glimpse the man behind the crown before. He'd never revealed even a hint of vulnerability. And she'd never *ever* imagined that she might not be in this alone.

'It is,' she said, the fireball of tension leaving her body in such an enormous rush that she went dizzy. What a relief he understood. What a relief he'd identified why she'd been so wound up in the first place.

'I forget I've had nearly thirty-five years to get used to it.'

'Whereas I've had little more than a month.'

'Quite.' He ran a hand along the strong line of his jaw, back and forth across the faint hint of stubble, slowly, mesmerising her, and then he nodded, as if he'd come to a decision. 'I don't think a short delay would make too much of a difference.'

'Really?'

'Yes.'

'Thank you.'

'You're welcome.'

'So I'll see you inside in say, fifteen minutes?'

'Oh, I'm going nowhere,' he said, seeming to press himself further into the balustrade. 'I'm staying right here.'

Sofia's heart lurched and then began to race. No. That couldn't happen. How would she be able to pull herself together with him by her side playing havoc with her senses? She required space, dammit. Solitude. Dealing with the fallout of having behaved like her parents was going to take time. As was trying to figure out what their shared moment of understanding, that brief emotional connection, might mean for their relationship. 'There's no need for that.'

'I think there is.'

'Why?'

'I can't risk you going nuclear again. What if you take off and disappear into the night?'

She stifled a shudder at the thought of it. 'I won't,' she assured him—and herself—with every drop of conviction she possessed. 'That urge has passed. Truly. I'll be fine on my own.'

'You won't be fine on your own,' he countered in a

tone that brooked no argument, the one she perversely found so attractive. 'You won't have any peace at all. As you observed, everyone wants a piece of you. You'll be approached and disturbed. My presence by your side will prevent that. We'll be left alone. It will be assumed we're having a romantic moment.'

A romantic moment? Imagine that. Imagine being glad of each other's company and taking comfort in it. Imagine knowing that someone was looking out for you and protecting you for real and you weren't alone any more.

'Besides, if I walked away now, when you're clearly agitated, what would people think?'

At Ivo's timely reminder about the optics of this little tableau, the heady dream Sofia had conjured up shattered, and she landed back in reality with a bump.

'Tell me something,' she said, not remotely irritated that he'd ruined her fantasy, but actually *grateful* he had, because if he hadn't she might have been in serious danger of getting carried away by it.

'What?'

'Do you ever do *anything* for yourself?'

His eyebrows arched as if he were taken aback by her question and then fell. 'No,' he said. 'You know I don't. And why.'

'Do you sometimes wish things were different?'

'Of course not. This has always been my life. It's my destiny to defend and protect my country from anything that threatens its peaceful existence. Including the frailties and whims of weak, self-centred rulers like my grandfather. There's absolutely no point bemoaning that fact. Or hypothesising about a life not led. Why do you ask?'

Sofia didn't know. What was she trying to prove? What

did she want him to say? Something that would alleviate her increasingly rampant frustration with him? The
dull ache that felt like…resentment? Where had that even
come from?

One thing she *did* know was that her feelings for him
were turning out to be not nearly as straightforward as
she'd assumed. They were intense, unpredictable, and
God, what if she wasn't equipped to deal with them?
What if she really had inherited her parents' inability to
contain volatile emotion and fiery passion? What if she'd
somehow created a situation in which she might suffer
untold damage, either by his hand or hers? None of that
bore thinking about.

She must never forget that every move he made was
with the monarchy in mind. She must never let her heart
dominate her head. His concern was not for *her*. It was for
his country—as he kept reminding her. And romance had
nothing to do with anything, so she must not read something into moments that were highly unlikely to mean
what she feared deep down she hoped they might mean.

'No reason,' she said, thinking that if she didn't want
to completely self-implode, she'd better reconstruct her
façade and her defences right this minute. 'Are you really not going to go away?'

'No.' He glanced at his watch. 'Time starts now, Sofia.'

'Fine,' she muttered, as she wrenched her gaze from
his with annoying difficulty and trained it once again on
the scenery, as if that would provide the strength she was
looking for. 'Do what you feel is right. Just please don't
spoil things by talking.'

CHAPTER EIGHT

BY MIDNIGHT, after six hours of pure unadulterated torture, Ivo's patience was at its absolute limit. In fact, he thought darkly, as he and Sofia rode the lift to their suite in thick, sizzling silence, he suspected that any minute now it was going to snap.

In light of his response to her touch and the smiles she saved for the public, he'd expected the ball to be tough. But he had not expected it to be such a downright nightmare. Yet the minute they'd entered the room he'd been overwhelmed by the feeling that he'd somehow stepped into a fairy tale. God only knew why. She was no Cinderella and he was certainly no Prince Charming. Furthermore, he had zero appreciation for such sentimental rot. Nevertheless, there'd been something about the space that had thrown him off balance. The billions of seductively flickering candles, perhaps. Or maybe the vibrant colours and the loud, happy chatter that had given him a headache.

Whatever it was, he hadn't been able to take his eyes off his wife as she circulated around the guests, leaving droplets of magic wherever she went. The stab of alarm he'd felt when he'd realised she was nowhere to be seen had been matched by the wave of relief he'd experienced when he'd found her on the terrace.

It was then that the night had taken even more of a turn for the worse. She'd looked pale and drawn, yes, and he'd found that he hadn't liked it one little bit, but what he thought he'd been doing by granting her wish for some space and then joining her, he had no idea. Not only had he broken his cardinal rule of putting his people first at all times but also those fifteen minutes she'd asked for had been some of the oddest of his life.

He'd tried to convince himself that he'd simply seen how close she was to breaking point and had felt the need to keep an eye on her. But he had the terrifying suspicion that, selfishly, appallingly, he'd also taken them for himself. Why else hadn't he left her there alone? He'd lied when he'd insisted she'd be plagued by other people. With one quick call he could have surrounded her with an invisible ring of steel. But he hadn't.

He'd felt as if they'd stood there for an hour. He'd been aware of nothing but her, the heat of her body and the heavy thud of his pulse. He'd promised her silence but suddenly his head had filled with clamouring questions about her life, her hopes and her fears and the absence of bridesmaids or friends on their wedding day. These he'd given free rein to because at least they'd put a stop to other more troubling ones, such as, why hadn't he been more appalled by her passionate outburst? Why, instead of lamenting her lack of composure, had he wanted more of the fire that obviously lay beneath her surface? Was that *something* he'd felt stab through him when she'd blown up relief at the thought that in her he'd found someone who understood the emotional burden of rule?

And why, when she'd asked him if he ever wished his life were different had he wanted to tell her that yes, he did, sometimes, in the dead of night when his responsibilities felt overwhelming and he ached with loneliness, or when he stood on a terrace with his wife and wondered about an alternative reality in which he wasn't royal and bound by duty? As he'd informed her in no uncertain terms, hypothesising was a waste of time. He was who he was. Had his father ever succumbed to such ridiculous whimsy? He didn't think so, and nor should he.

Naturally, he'd pulled himself together and switched his focus to the job, then taken her in his arms and waltzed her around the dance floor to the melodic strains of the thirty-piece orchestra. But the sensation that something wasn't quite right had nevertheless sat in his chest like a weight.

Ivo had no clue what he'd ever done to deserve such torment. Perhaps it was merely the intensity of being with one person 24-7 after a decade alone. Or the novelty of having someone whose job it was to back him when he'd only been backed by himself.

But luckily, after much mental wrangling, he'd come up with a solution. He and Sofia would be tied to each other for ever, and for the sake of his country he could not afford to permanently lose the plot like this, so the unbearable tension that arced between them had to be addressed asap. The hankering for something he could never have had to stop, along with the worryingly expanding feelings he had for her that kept breaking their bonds to mess with his head. He had to get the distracting desire out of his system because only then would everything else settle down, he was sure.

This he intended to do by indulging it. By removing the element of mystique that he was certain was blowing how he felt about her all out of proportion. Such a course of action would likely mean a complete loss of control in her bed, but if he was prepared for it, if it was temporary and contained in one locale, then he could live with that. What he could *not* live with any longer was the crippling and potentially destructive weakness he exhibited whenever he was in her vicinity.

'That was an enjoyable evening,' she said, putting down her bag on the table in the lobby and bestowing yet another of her irritatingly cool smiles on him. 'But an exhausting one. So I'll bid you goodnight. See you in the morning.'

No, Ivo thought, his jaw clenched so hard it was in danger of splintering. That wasn't happening. Not until he'd wrestled his desire for her back under control, at least. 'Wait,' he said, his voice cracking through the air like a whip. 'Not so fast.'

Halfway across the space, Sofia stilled, turned and stared at him, her eyebrows shooting up. 'Excuse me?'

'This isn't working.'

A flicker of confusion darted across her beautiful face. 'What on earth are you talking about?' she asked in bewilderment. 'It's working fantastically. Have you seen the terrible headlines recently? No. Because there aren't any. I've done everything in my power to ensure it. Apart from the minor blip on my part earlier, tonight was a triumph.'

'I didn't mean that,' he said, thinking that for him personally tonight had been unsettling as hell. 'The tour could not be going better. As I expected, you are brilliant.'

'Thank you,' she said, her flicker of a smile warming to two degrees above freezing, which did strange things to his chest and disrupted his train of thought—until he pulled himself together and refocused.

'What I meant was, you going to your bed every night and me going to mine is no longer acceptable. I'm all out of patience. Enough is enough. From tonight on, you and I will be sleeping together.'

For a moment, she just stared at him in frozen shock. The only sound to be heard was the faint crash of the sea a hundred metres below. Then twin spots of colour hit her cheeks and the pulse at the base of her neck began to flutter wildly. 'Are you serious?'

'Deadly.'

'This is rather out of the blue.'

'Not for me,' he practically growled. 'For me, this has been building for days. One room, Sofia. Yours or mine. You choose. I don't mind.'

'No.'

Ivo's brows snapped together, rejection stinging through him, the confusion now all his. *'No?'*

'That's right. No.'

'Explain.'

'I've already shared your bed once, and why would I agree to do it again when you so obviously don't want me?'

In response to that, Ivo reeled. Not want her? He wanted her so badly he was mad with it. So mad with it that he couldn't hear the voice in his head that was warning him to keep this about the deal, to remind her of her constitutional obligations, to not cross the line into the personal. The voice that was awash with longings he could never afford to indulge, for the sake of his country and his heart. 'What makes you think I don't want you?' he demanded, too far gone for caution.

'Well, our wedding night was a bit of a giveaway,' she said with a cool composure he wished to God he had. 'The clock struck twelve and you leapt from my bed as if it had caught fire. I understand we'd done our duty—and believe me, I am well aware that that's all this is about for you. I completely understand that you needed the boost of alcohol to get you through it. But quite honestly I'd expected a *little* bit more than a wham, bam, thank you, ma'am. Not that there even was a thank you, come to think of it.'

She paused, took a breath, then, before he could even think to formulate a reaction, continued with her devastating revelations. 'I get that to you I'm just a brood mare who has some handy professional skills on the side. Really I do. As you so astutely observed before, I signed up to this and I knew exactly what it entailed. You've been honest about that from the start, and it was therefore ridiculous to feel hurt, used and rejected. Nevertheless, I did, and quite frankly, it's all taking some adjustment. I'll dare say I'll get over your lack of interest in me personally, enough to be able to do my duty soon, but right now, if you don't mind, I'd prefer to stick to the current arrangements.'

Evidently finished, Sofia lifted her eyebrows, as if inviting him to respond, but, reeling with shock, Ivo could do no more than stand there and stare at her. Her words had rendered him incapable of thought. He was struggling for breath. He felt as though she'd punched him in the gut.

What the ever-loving hell?

That was what she thought?

She was wrong. She was far more to him than a competent PR and the future mother of his heirs. Yes, much of this last week had been for the cameras, and yes, it had caused him an abominable amount of grief, but it had also proved that they were a team. In sync. A partnership that could be dynamite.

As for her view of the wedding night, well, that cut him straight to the bone. He'd hurt her? He'd made her feel used and rejected? How on earth had he allowed that to happen? More importantly, what was he going to do to rectify it?

Ivo wasn't used to explaining himself. Not only was it the unofficial policy of the royal family never to do so, but also he'd never been questioned about anything ever before, until he'd decided to find a wife. Furthermore, life in the public eye had made him an intensely private man, and he took immense care to keep the majority of his thoughts and opinions to himself.

However, communication went both ways, and if ever there was an occasion to break the habit, this was it. He couldn't have Sofia continuing to believe he was merely using her when he wasn't. Where was the integrity and decency in that? Besides, if he stood any chance of finishing this tour with his reputation intact, he still needed to get her into his bed, and right now, that looked as though it was insanely far from happening.

He shoved his hands through his hair and cleared his throat to release the words he was nevertheless going to have to push out. 'I had no idea you felt that way,' he said, choosing to ignore the inconvenient fact that that was probably because he'd never asked. 'But let me clear up a few misunderstandings under which you seem to be labouring.

'Firstly, it was never my intention to hurt you on our wedding night. I was spooked by the strength of my response to you. What happened was totally unexpected. I lost control, which has never happened to me before. It wasn't part of the plan and it threw me for six. But I didn't handle it well and for that I apologise. Which leads me onto my next point. Namely that my interest in you is *not* purely practical. In fact, it is anything *but* practical and has been for days. I want you, Sofia. Like I've never wanted anyone before. You've been driving me wild ever since we kissed at the altar. It rocked me to my very foundations, which was why I needed time and a drink to pull myself together before coming to your room. But that was a pointless endeavour as it turned out because it didn't work. Nothing has. This last week I've never felt *less* pulled together. It's been complete and utter torture.'

Ivo thrust his hands into the pockets of his trouser and began to pace around the lobby, as if movement would ease the heated restlessness of his body and brain. 'I've tried my damnedest to ignore my desire for you,' he said, his voice low and tight as he sought to undo the impression he'd deliberately given her. 'It's crippling and I can't afford the distraction. I have work to do that needs my full attention, and you know what happened the last time a king allowed himself to be bamboozled by desire. An attempted coup and the near collapse of the kingdom. You mess with my head. You make me forget who I am. I'm not thinking straight. Yesterday, I fired a bishop. This evening, for the first time in years, I tossed aside protocol to *take the air* on a bloody terrace. It has to stop. I need it to stop.

'But getting you out of my system so I can focus on the job isn't the only reason I want you in my bed,' he said, on a terrifying roll he could not seem to stop. 'You asked me earlier if I ever do anything for myself. I said no, and that's been true for years. Until now. I'm doing *this* for myself, Sofia. I want you for *me*. Like I wanted those fifteen minutes earlier *for me*. Which is all kinds of wrong. I know that, in the marrow of my bones. But at this precise moment in time I don't care. All I can think about is making the most of tomorrow's twenty-four-hour break in our schedule and revisiting my original ideas for the wedding night. I want to take things nice and slow and explore every inch of you with my hands and mouth until neither of us can take any more.

'But I now realise that these desires of mine are entirely self-centred. I haven't considered yours at all, which is hardly a mark of the respect I promised you, and that's another apology I owe you. So while sticking to the current arrangements is obviously the very last thing I want, if you do, that's fine. It's *fine*. Really. Truly. I won't bother you again. You have my word.'

With nothing left to say, Ivo closed his mouth and came to a halt. He was sweating. Breathing harder than he ever had before. He'd never delivered such a long speech without prior preparation. He'd never had such an out-of-body experience. Felt so crazed. So horrified. Or been so desperate for a reaction.

Now was her chance to say something, he thought feverishly, his eyes boring into hers, the tension gripping his muscles so immense it hurt. Anything. But she just stood there, staring at him wide-eyed, as rigid as a statue in the deafening silence that stretched and stretched, and the wrecking ball of disappointment and frustration that slammed into him nearly took out his knees.

'Right,' he said gruffly, fighting back the urge to drop to his knees and beg, all out of heat and adrenaline, and needing to get the hell out of here while he still had a shred of dignity and self-possession left. 'Well. I'm glad to have got cleared that up. Now, if you'll excuse me, there's a cold shower with my name on it. Goodnight.'

* * *

Sofia watched in a state of utter stupefaction as Ivo clicked his heels together, nodded curtly, then strode across the lobby in the direction of his suite. Surely she'd stepped into a parallel universe these past five minutes. Had that conversation really happened? No. It couldn't have. She had to be dreaming. But if she was, why was her pulse thundering like a freight train? Why was her head spinning so fast she was in danger of passing out?

Assuming that that conversation *had* taken place, he'd just blown her preconceptions out of the water—the main one being that he didn't want her. He *did*. He *wanted* her. In a way that clearly had nothing to do with duty. He wanted her as much as she wanted him, if not more.

She would never have guessed, she thought dazedly as she tried to process everything else he'd confessed. His façade was as effective as hers, and she'd been so busy protecting herself that she hadn't given any thought at all to what might lie beneath it. She'd been utterly self-absorbed and as guilty as he was of taking things at face value.

But now she was beginning to realise that still waters ran deep, very deep indeed. All this time, he too had been tormented by excoriating desire. So much so that he'd had to take preventative action to keep it from devouring him, just as she had. So much so that this evening, he'd jettisoned the principles of a lifetime. He'd put himself and what he wanted first for once, which, unbelievably, was her.

She'd always believed him to be pragmatic and level-headed, a paragon of steadfastness and equanimity. But clearly, that was not all he was. She'd never heard him speak so heatedly. She'd never seen him look so deranged. He'd certainly never paced like that in all the time she'd known him. In fact, she distinctly recalled him once telling her that such behaviour represented a loss of control and was therefore totally unacceptable. Clearly, then, the depth of his feelings for her had taken him by as much surprise as hers for him had taken her.

But if he *was* more complicated than the saintly ideal she'd placed on an impossibly high pedestal, what did that mean for her love? That it was superficial and shallow? That it only valued the simple and the good and couldn't withstand the infinitely more layered and possibly even flawed reality of him?

No.

She refused to believe that.

Her love was true. It wasn't starry-eyed—at least, not any more. This last week had proved that it was messy, laced with frustration and disappointment, and it hadn't collapsed. It had survived.

She hadn't wanted to acknowledge the shift in her feelings because she'd been in search of a relationship as far from her parents' as it was possible to get. But now she could see that she may have been a little too harsh on them. Tonight, she'd felt for herself and witnessed in Ivo how swiftly passion could overheat and spill out as anger and frustration.

The difference was that between *them* things hadn't escalated. Things hadn't descended into acrimony and hate. Her outburst on the terrace had come and gone in a flash. Ivo had walked away from his just now without losing his temper. Neither of them had delighted in the feelings that had overtaken them. Both of them had managed to get a grip. And look at how cool she'd been when she'd had to explain how she felt about his behaviour the night of their wedding.

Ever since the crushing aftermath of that experience, Sofia had been doing her best to resist the attraction to protect her heart. She'd been fighting to keep her admiration for his strong sense of duty from turning into bitterness and resentment. Relentlessly reminding herself to heed the advice of her mother-in-law, she'd tried to rise above the maddening desire that challenged her sense of self-preservation.

Yet she'd been fighting a losing battle. The fifteen minutes he'd allowed her on the terrace had proven that. She'd tried to figure out what was going on with herself but had come up with nothing, which had been as worrying as it had been perplexing because she always had a plan. The fact that she hadn't been able to find a way through was why she'd had to cloak herself in extra ice to get her though the rest of the evening.

Now she could admit that it wasn't just the pressure of the job that had got to her earlier. It was the pressure of recklessly dreaming of things she knew she couldn't have, of struggling to keep her feelings under control when they were growing and changing and deepening in a way she'd never anticipated.

But some of those feelings weren't unrequited at all. The scorching attraction was mutual. What exactly had he planned to do to her, first on their wedding day, then tonight, and after that, tomorrow? How had he planned to drive her wild? She badly wanted to find out.

And, now she was thinking, *Why shouldn't she?*

This relationship wasn't as one-sided as she'd assumed.

If one removed love from the equation, it was actually pretty balanced, especially now he'd laid all his cards on the table.

And perhaps passion wasn't to be feared, after all. She'd worried about the damage it could do if indulged, but she'd discovered this evening that that didn't have to be the case. She could express her emotions, however volatile, and chaos would not necessarily ensue. If they kept it confined to the bedroom, they could find the physical release they both craved. The pressure elsewhere would ease. Ivo was right about the unfeasibility of the current state of affairs. They had to dissipate the unbearable tension somehow.

So why was she dithering? Why did she feel as though she could be playing with fire? Their connection would be a physical one, nothing more. She didn't have to confess her love for him. She wouldn't be risking her heart. She could still keep it safe from harm. She'd just have to double down on her efforts to keep it locked up. She knew perfectly well that the vision of a proper relationship, which she glimpsed when they were out and about, wasn't what he was offering for real.

But what he *was* offering was a safe, contained way to embrace the chemistry that was so real it burned. A chance to combine love and passion without it descending into chaos and destruction. So was she really going to stand here all night when she had a husband who wanted her as much as she wanted him? When the promise of spending the whole of tomorrow testing their attraction to each other hovered in the ether? When in this at least she was his number one priority?

No, she was not.

CHAPTER NINE

STANDING BESIDE THE four-poster bed that mocked him with its pristine vastness, Ivo kicked off his shoes and tore off his tail-coat. What on *earth* had happened back there? he railed at himself as he yanked free his bow-tie and threw it on the floor. All he'd meant to do was set Sofia straight. Instead, he'd ended up practically emptying out his soul.

Had he deployed logic? Thoughtful consideration? Restraint? Like hell he had. By the time he'd finished—and God, he'd gone on for *days*—he'd sounded desperate. Weak. Pathetic and powerless and utterly out of control. He'd even paced! For the first time in years he'd completely humiliated himself. And for what? For nothing. Because in response to his mortifying confession, Sofia had barely even *blinked*.

How could he *ever* have succumbed to such atrocious sentiment? he wondered grimly as he wrestled with the buttons of his shirt before simply pulling it apart so that they popped and spun off in a dozen different directions. Or allowed himself to want something for himself? How could he have crossed that line when he'd spent the last ten years avoiding it like the plague? Was there any coming back from what he'd done?

This was supposed to be a trouble-free marriage of convenience, not one riddled with conflict and tempestuousness. He needed to keep his emotions locked up to protect his heart and stay focused on the job for the stability of his country. After tonight's display of lunacy, his grandfather would be cheering from the heavens. His father would be turning in his grave.

Ivo had no idea how he was going to handle the storm raging inside him. He wanted to shake his fist at the sky and then slam it through the wall. But he'd spent two years in the army. He was no stranger to self-discipline. He'd get it under control somehow. The minute he'd undone these bloody cuff-links, he'd cancel their day off tomorrow. God only knew what had been going through his head when he'd instructed it to be scheduled into the itinerary. A break? How self-centred was that? And then to have contemplated abandoning the plans he'd made for an all-day sex marathon instead... He must have been even more out of his tiny little mind than he'd thought.

He'd soon come to see that it was a good thing she'd turned him down, he assured himself as he finally freed the discs of gold. The last thing their physical relationship needed was emotion. He'd sworn a decade ago that he would never get sucked under again. How had Sofia described her outburst on the terrace? A blip? Well, that was what the last half hour had been for him. He'd forget it ever happened. As ever, denial was his friend.

The cuff-links that he'd inherited from his father he set on the bedside table. The shirt he ripped from his back and hurled at the chair. He was just about to tackle his trousers when the door flung open.

Ivo jerked round.

At the sight of Sofia standing in the space, he froze. His pulse spiked. His blood shot to his feet so fast that his head spun.

What the hell was she doing here? Hadn't he borne enough this evening? 'What do you want?' he snapped, sounding as though he'd swallowed a bucket of gravel.

'You,' she said hoarsely. 'I want you.'

The words flew across the room like darts and lodged in his chest. Every cell of his body began to cheer but he gave his head a sharp shake and ignored them. 'No. You don't.'

'Yes, I do. I know what I said earlier, but the truth is, I've never been as attracted to anyone as I am to you. I've been trying to deny it and doing my best to hide it—just like you have—but this week has been impossible for me too. All those touches. Wishing they were for real while despising myself for wanting someone who I believed didn't want me. God, if you knew the torment I've endured, the battles I've been fighting… I am desperate to know what you had planned for me on our wedding night. I can't think of a better way to spend our day off tomorrow than making up for lost time. Take me to bed, Ivo. Please.'

Yes, screamed his body. *No*, cautioned his head, which was advising him to tell her to get out of his sight. She was simply too disruptive, too damn dangerous. He had the dreadful sense that she had the power to undo him completely, and he couldn't exist in her orbit until he'd worked out how to stop behaving in ways that terrified him.

Yet she looked so sexy standing there and confessing that, despite appearances to the contrary, they were on the same page, that his agonies were also hers. So achingly beautiful in the soft shimmering golden light cast by the chandelier that now only one body part remained capable of thought, and it wasn't his brain.

He didn't want cold showers and distance. He wanted heat and proximity. There'd be time for a reckoning in the morning. Right now, nothing mattered more than slaking this maddening need he had for her, and he couldn't wait a second longer.

'There'd be no going back,' he growled, and it was as much a promise as a warning. 'Not until I can look at you without wanting you, without *needing* you.'

Her eyes sparked. Her chest heaved. 'I've never wanted anything more.'

'Are you sure?'

'I'm sure.'

'Then get over here.'

She was across the floor and in his space in a matter of moments. She threw her arms around his neck, pressed the entire length of her body right up against him and crushed her mouth to his.

Relief and desire poured though him with such force that his legs shook. He wrapped her in a tight embrace and took command of the kiss until it turned ferocious, a clash of teeth and tongues and heat so scorching it could melt the sun.

Every instinct he possessed urged him to back her up against a poster, delve beneath her skirts and take her fast and hard. To then toss her onto the bed and do it all over again until she couldn't move, let alone think straight. But he'd told her he'd take his time. There'd been mention of slow devastating exploration, and he was a man of his word, so that was what she'd get.

Grappling for control, Ivo eased the pressure of his mouth on hers and dug his fingers in her hair to angle her head. He embarked on a kiss that was deep and languorous, and within moments she was moaning at the back of her throat and softening against him.

When he finally broke away to drag in a much-needed breath, his heart pounded heavily. Every fibre of his being was tight with anticipation. But he ignored the drumming insistence of his body, and her faint whimper of protest, and turned her round. As he worked to undo the delicate buttons that fastened her dress, her head fell forward, presenting him with an expanse of smooth soft skin and an opportunity he simply couldn't resist.

He pressed his lips to her upper arm and she shivered. As he trailed his mouth across her shoulder and then up her neck, his fingers began to fumble, which frustratingly slowed his progress. But then, thank God, he found a zip. Breathing harshly, he slid it down inch by inch, savouring the gradual reveal of her back, the curve of her spine and the sliver of lace at the top of her bottom.

Rock-hard and aching, he turned her back to face him. Her eyes shimmered with heat. She clutched the dress to her chest, and he wondered for one brief baffling moment whether she might be suffering from another attack of nerves, when she suddenly let it go. With a soft swoosh, the dress fell to the floor. She stepped out of the puddle of satin, kicked it aside and then stood before him in nothing but emeralds, a whisper of underwear and sky-high heels.

'I'm feeling a little underdressed,' she said, which drew his attention to her mouth, red and swollen from his kisses, and filled his head with images that made him ache even more.

Ivo ran his gaze over her and felt a rush of blood to the head. 'Then fix it,' he muttered, although he'd be quite happy to freeze this moment, to capture the vision in front of him and store it away so he could revisit it whenever he wanted.

Not needing to be told twice, Sofia reached out and undid the button of his trousers. When she brushed her fingers over his straining erection, his breath hissed through his teeth and his hands clenched into fists. She pressed her mouth to the throbbing pulse at the base of his neck and then worked her way across his chest. She moved her hands to his abdomen and the muscles there flinched.

She took her time trailing her fingers and her mouth over him while he stroked his hands over her back, and then she sank to her knees. She pushed his trousers and shorts down and when he was free of them, as if she'd read his mind, she held him first in her hand and then slid him between her lips.

Ivo let out a harsh groan as she took him deeper, and slowly, agonisingly began to move her head back and forth. Fire sped along his veins. His heart thudded so hard it was in danger of cracking a rib. He made the mistake of looking down. Light bounced off the emeralds in her hair, hanging from her ear lobes and circling her throat. The hand that wasn't holding him slid beneath the waistband of her underwear and when she moaned, he felt the vibrations so strongly that all of a sudden release rushed towards him like a rocket.

His knees shook and his breath stuck in his lungs. He

closed his eyes but that didn't help. This wasn't going to be slow. It was going to be over far too soon, which was very much not the plan, so with Herculean effort he put a hand to the back of her head and encouraged her up.

'What did you do that for?' she protested huskily, all tousled and pouty and gorgeous.

'Delayed gratification.'

'I've never seen the point.'

'You will.'

He lifted her into his arms and deposited her on the bed. Then he arranged himself above her so there was no escape. Her eyes glittered. Her cheeks were flushed. Supporting himself on his elbows, Ivo thrust his hands into her hair, lowered his head and kissed her until she was clutching at his back and writhing.

His heart thudding hard, he cupped a breast and then wrenched his mouth from hers to turn his attention to first one nipple and then the other. He felt her shiver and heard her sob and then he inched his way down her body until he settled between her thighs and set about driving her to the brink as she'd done to him.

He paid no attention to her protests, or her pleas that he put an end to her torment. He was relentless in his determination to make up for the hurt he caused her the last time they'd been in a bed together and to punish her for putting him through such hell this evening. It wasn't enough that she twisted the sheet in her hands and arched her back. He wanted to make her scream. Which she did. And while she was trembling and panting and gasping for breath, he repositioned himself and thrust fiercely into her.

She was so hot and tight and wet that his mind went.

She wrapped her arms around his neck and her legs around his hips and, driven purely by primal instincts he couldn't begin to comprehend, he started to move.

She matched him thrust for thrust and he tried to slow things down but within seconds she was biting into his shoulder and shaking all over again, and he was lost. The tingles that had started in his toes shot up his legs, collided with the contracting muscles of his stomach, his chest, his groin to trigger the hardest, most intense climax of his life. The tension gripping him shattered. And, as he buried himself in her as hard and deep as he could, he exploded into a spiralling fireball of blistering ecstasy that was unlike anything he'd ever known before.

CHAPTER TEN

SOFIA WOKE UP when the shaft of bright midmorning sunlight slowly moving over her face eventually reached her eyelids. For a moment, as she blinked away the sleepy fuzz clouding her vision, she couldn't work out where she was. Something was missing… The sway of the train… But then she heard a rustle to her right, felt the faint brush of a hard male leg against hers, and it all came flooding back in glorious technicolour detail.

What a night, she thought with a wide satisfied smile. It had been everything she'd dreamed of. Better, actually, because her imagination had not had the ability to conjure up some of the things Ivo had done to her. His dedication to the job wasn't limited to his position as King. His passion had collided with hers and detonated with the force of a nuclear explosion. More than making up for lost time, he'd repeatedly drenched her in pleasure and by the time they'd finally succumbed to exhaustion just before dawn she'd barely been able to string a sentence together.

She'd never been so in sync with anyone. He'd understood what she'd needed before she had. Again. He'd taken her to heights she'd never dreamed of and she was still in one piece. And because she had not imploded as a result of the experience, it occurred to her now, while she was feeling all warm and sated and mellow, that rather than being something to avoid, perhaps this intense connection they shared was something to build on instead. They were tied to each other for life. They had to forge some sort of a relationship outside the bedroom and work, and she couldn't deny that, after his ardent and unguarded confession last night, she was fascinated by the thought of what else might be going on beneath his very attractive surface.

How much of a risk to her heart would it be to find out a bit more about her husband, the man behind the crown? How dangerous could simple conversation be? Not a lot, surely. It needn't get heavy. And, OK, so the trouble she'd always had in making friends indicated that she wasn't exactly an expert in this field, but Ivo was going nowhere and she did enjoy a challenge. And maybe if her parents had talked more about how they felt instead of letting their grievances fester, they'd have argued less. So the voice in her head that was trying to remind her of both her intention to keep this strictly physical and all the reasons she should not be encouraging even the lightest of emotional entanglement could pipe down. She'd keep her guard up and her feelings contained. Everything would be fine.

Deciding that there was no time like the present to activate this plan, Sofia summoned up every drop of strength she possessed and glanced over to find Ivo lying on his side, propped up on his elbow. Their gazes met, his dark and smouldering, and longing shivered through her. She could scarcely believe she and the man she loved were actually in bed together. It didn't seem real. Beneath the sheets, she pinched herself. Hard. Too hard, in fact, which was why she winced and let out a gasp.

'Good morning,' he said gruffly, as she surreptitiously rubbed the stinging spot on her thigh and wondered how on earth she'd survive the day if he put his mind to surpassing the night.

'Good morning.'

'Are you all right?'

'I'm fine. Just a little achy.' It wasn't a lie. 'Muscles I wasn't aware I had are making themselves known. I've never had a workout like it. You definitely proved your point about delayed gratification. Plus, I seem to have stubble rash everywhere.'

He ran his gaze over her, hotly, languidly, as if cataloguing every spot he'd set his mouth to, which was why it took a while. 'Not everywhere.'

'No,' she agreed, as fire licked through her in the wake of his scrutiny. 'You avoided my face. That was clever of you. The press would have had a field day if I'd appeared in public with red patches on my cheeks and chin.'

'I know what I'm doing.'

'You certainly do.'

'Want me to prove it again?'

Her blood thickened and slowed and desire began to throb in the pit of her belly, but she ignored it. She was on a mission of a different kind. 'Later.'

'Why waste time?' Leaning over, he ran a hand from her jaw, down her neck, and would have slipped it beneath the sheet she was clutching to her chest had she not removed it and given it back to him.

'You're insatiable.'

'And you aren't? I distinctly recall you begging me for more on a number of different occasions.'

Sofia swallowed hard. He wasn't wrong, but this little trip down memory lane wasn't helping her focus one little bit. 'I need a break,' she said. 'And sustenance,' she added, flushing when her stomach chose that moment to rumble.

'I'll order breakfast. We can't have you fading away.'

He rolled back to reach for his phone and she fought the urge to reacquaint herself with the bumps and ridges of his abs. 'I know what we can do while we wait.'

He glanced up from the device and a gleam lit the dark depths of his eyes. 'That's an excellent idea,' he said, evidently thinking of something she hadn't. 'Showering together is good for the environment. And I would enjoy lathering you up.'

She'd enjoy that too. But not just yet. 'I meant, we could talk.'

He stilled and arched an eyebrow at that. 'Talk?'

'About last night. Before this—' she waved a hand between them '—happened.'

Ivo deposited his phone back on the bedside table and frowned. 'I'd rather not.'

'It was quite a speech.'

'Yes, well, as I said at the time, I'd reached the end of my tether.'

'I could see that. You paced.'

'I did,' he agreed with a grimace.

'You looked and sounded crazed.'

'As if I need reminding.'

'It was actually rather flattering,' she admitted, shifting so she lay a bit more upright. 'I've never had that effect on anyone.'

'No one's ever had that effect on me.'

'Now I'm even more flattered.'

'I've also never been married before or spent so much time with one woman in such intense circumstances,' he said. 'So don't overthink it.'

Right. Of course. Good of him to set her feet back on the ground, because getting swept away by fancy was not part of the plan. But was that all it was? Would any old wife have driven him to such distraction? 'So how long *have* you wanted me?' she asked, silently cursing her need to be told she was special despite her best efforts to kill it.

'For about a month,' he said, confirming what she'd known since the start—that she wasn't special at all—which tanked her spirits even though it shouldn't. 'As my Communications Secretary you were automatically off-limits. I didn't even go there until the moment I decided to take you as my wife. I'd summoned you into my office to instruct you to launch a marketing blitz that would broaden the country's appeal, and mine. Then it struck me how suited to the role of Queen you'd be, and suddenly your hair reminded me of the cornfields in the north. Your eyes made me think of the sea where it meets the beach. The poetic nature of my observations came as quite a shock.'

'I can imagine.'

'And all you admired was my integrity.'

'Don't forget your sense of duty and responsibility and your equanimity.'

'How could I?' he observed dryly. 'I never thought I suffered from vanity until you mentioned those.'

'They're valuable traits.'

'I know. But they're not all you admire about me, are they?'

No, they weren't. Because, as she'd come to realise, they weren't all he was, and her feelings were expanding to embrace every new glimpse into his character she got, despite the depressing fact that to him she merely remained convenient.

And then there was his body, to which no doubt he was referring. 'I think I've made that abundantly clear,' she said with a shiver as she thought of the many inventive ways she'd worshipped him with her hands and mouth. 'If you could have read my mind when I joined you in the lobby yesterday evening before we went down to the ball, you'd have been shocked to the core. Or maybe you wouldn't, given the past twelve hours.'

'You said I looked *nice*.'

Had her understatement stung? Surely not. For that to happen he'd have to care what she thought of him, and he didn't. He just desired her body. 'I lied,' she admitted, thinking back to the moment she'd laid eyes on him and almost forgotten her name. 'You looked magnificent. You always do.'

His eyebrows lifted. 'Always? How long have *you* wanted *me*?'

Damn. That was careless of her. The last thing she needed to do was admit the truth and invite questions it would be too risky to answer. So she'd better get that guard back up—and fast. 'I'll admit to having a crush on you when I was fifteen,' she said, choosing her words with care. 'But I can't have been the only teenager in the world to have an image of you pinned up on my wall. The crush faded soon enough. As did the poster. And naturally I've been aware of your looks since we've been working together. I'm not dead. But it was never a problem until you proposed.'

Which was true. Sort of. It *hadn't* been a problem, at least not on a professional level. 'The kiss at the altar threw me too. And you aren't the only one who unintentionally lost control on our wedding night. It's been a struggle getting it back.'

'I'd never have guessed.'

'That was the point. My self-respect was under attack. And anyway, you're hardly one to talk. You're just as good at concealment as I am.'

'A lifetime in the spotlight can do that to a man,' he said. 'So much of me is public property, my head is the only space I have sole access to. But we're not talking about me. We're talking about you. And I find I'm intrigued.'

'By what?' she asked with a frown, noting the way he was now regarding her, which sent a ripple of trepidation curling down her spine.

'By you. You're an interesting mix of hot and cold. One minute you're all buttoned up, the next you're erupting on the terrace of a ballroom. Last night in the lobby you stood there like a statue while I lost my head and then you burst into my room to whip up an inferno. All sorts of things are going on behind that ice-cool façade of yours, aren't they?'

Sofia went still. Her heart lurched and then began to pound. 'They really aren't,' she said, horrified at the thought of being so transparent.

'And you know what?' he continued, as if she hadn't even spoken. 'Suddenly I find myself wondering what else you might be hiding.'

What? No. She couldn't have him wondering *that*. He might be tempted to go one step further and probe, and what would he discover then? That she didn't just want him physically but loved him body and soul? Whatever character flaw it was that had prevented her parents from caring about her enough to put her first? Her innate tendency to push away people who tried to get close, even when she didn't want to? Absolutely not. A conversation like that would be anything but simple. It would expose far too much. Her heart would likely get involved, and she could not allow that to happen.

'I'm not hiding anything,' she said, nevertheless alarmed by the thought that if he chose to pursue this line of questioning she wasn't sure she'd be able to stop him wheedling out all her secrets. She knew how tenacious he could be. At countless international conferences she'd watched him persuade people to do whatever he required. How long would it be before he ground her down and she told him everything? And why was he interested anyway?

Clearly, it had been a bad idea to embark on a plan to get to know him. She should not have allowed the sweet lassitude of sexual satisfaction to mess with her head. She should have listened to the voice of reason and stuck to the original plan to keep this physical.

And maybe *that* was the way out of the tricky spot she found herself in.

'But you're right about one thing,' she said, deliberately lowering her voice and running her now-smouldering gaze over him so slowly and thoroughly he could not mistake her intentions. 'I *am* blowing hot.'

She placed a hand on his hair-roughened chest and

traced the hard muscles that she couldn't get enough of before sliding it down the delicious contours of his abdomen and under the sheet that bunched around his hips.

His muscles twitched as she went. His erection stirred. But he did not flip her onto her back and have his wicked way with her as she'd hoped. Instead, he gripped her wrist, stalling her progress before she could wrap her fingers around him, and gave it back to her. 'Don't try and deflect.'

'I'm *trying* to seduce you. I feel we need to test your theory about delayed gratification again.'

'Yet I'm sensing evasion.'

'I can't think why. Apart from keeping how much I wanted you under wraps, which I've explained, I'm an open book.'

'Honesty works both ways, Sofia,' he said, the glint in his eye deepening her alarm about his tenacity. 'And didn't you promise to obey?'

She had, dammit. And honesty did work both ways. Yet if ever there was a time to renege on her wedding vows and ignore a condition of this arrangement, this was it. She would do anything to keep her heart under lock and key. He didn't want it, and she couldn't let it loose to ache for things she could never have. She wasn't special to him. She never would be. She didn't know why she'd found that depressing when it had been ever thus.

But what if she couldn't hold him off? He was perceptive and determined and more or less holding her captive. What if he kept on and on, and she wound up telling him everything? What chaos would that unleash? What damage would that do to her? How—

There was knock at the door.

Sofia jumped. Her spiralling thoughts stopped in their tracks. She heard the muffled announcement of breakfast, and she could have wept with relief. 'Oh, good,' she said brightly, as she slid off the bed and into her robe with as much control as she could muster. 'Just in time. I'm famished.'

Polishing off his second espresso of the morning, Ivo watched Sofia tuck into a plate of pancakes with a focus that precluded a return to the conversation—no doubt deliberately—and thought that although he probably should be concerned about the complete override of his head by his body last night, he wasn't. He didn't regret a thing. The experience had been astonishing. A mind-blowing feast for the senses. He'd never encountered such compatibility. Or such stamina. And to think he'd been prepared to accept 'tolerable'. What a tragedy that would have been.

It had taken him far longer than her to fall asleep. In that time, dark and quiet, he'd revisited the events that had led to the most incredible sex of his life and come to realise that the mad mental ramblings that had plagued him as he'd undressed like a dervish had been nothing more than a consequence of severe sexual frustration. He'd completely overreacted. There was no need to cancel their day off. No line had been crossed really. And so what if he did want Sofia for himself? He could still honour his father's legacy while enjoying passion in the bedroom. He'd feared distraction, the selfishness of putting his own needs first, but the world hadn't ended when a waltz had started fifteen minutes late. He was no longer a bedazzled twenty-four-year-old about to drop a major ball. Knowing exactly what he had to do when and where was now second nature. He gave every waking moment to his country and he didn't begrudge that at all, but why couldn't the nights be his?

The strange conviction he'd had that she was finally where she was meant to be—in his bed, in his arms, in this marriage—was nothing to worry about, he'd assured himself as he'd listened to the oddly soothing sound of her breathing deeply beside him. It was a bonus to be so attracted to his wife. It boded well for the production of heirs. He saw no reason why their physical relationship should stray into deeper waters. He would certainly do nothing to encourage it. He had no intention of pushing that self-destruct button ever. He would put neither his country nor himself at risk. What they had here was more than enough.

Ivo had therefore been looking forward to spending today exploring Sofia and the chemistry that blazed like a wildfire further, before it settled into something considerably more manageable. But twenty minutes ago, those plans had changed. Now he wanted to find out what she was hiding. Not because he thought it might be something detrimental to the monarchy—his courtiers, who'd commissioned a report into her background upon their engagement, would have alerted him of anything like that. But his curiosity was piqued to such an extent that, left unaddressed, it might prove more a distraction than she was.

So it was back to the original itinerary and the trip to Rafifi Castle he'd already arranged. Only they wouldn't be doing their own thing as they recharged their batteries before returning to the tour tomorrow. They'd be spending the day together so he could get to the bottom of her caginess.

Sofia put down her knife and fork and dabbed her gorgeous mouth with a napkin. Ivo recalled all the clever things she'd done with that mouth and briefly contemplated a delay.

'Where are you off to in such a hurry?' he asked, as she pushed her chair back and got up from the table.

'The shower.'

'I'll join you.'

Her eyes widened with alarm and he thought, with some amusement, *Not so cool now, was she?*

'No, no,' she said, with a quick smile that was no doubt meant to mitigate the sharpness of her tone. 'Thank you but I'd prefer to shower alone.'

'Think of the environment.'

'I'm thinking of efficiency. And...work.'

Ivo raised his eyebrows. 'Bored with me already?'

'What? No. Of course not. I just feel we ought to get back to it. This day off is unnecessary,' she said, warming to the theme that had clearly just struck her. 'We're neglecting our duty, and I know how important that is to you. An impromptu visit or an event of that sort would be excellent PR. It would demonstrate our dedication to the people and the job. I'm sure something could be rustled up somewhere.'

She really was desperate to avoid being alone with him. Why? What did she not want him to know? Whatever it was, he hoped she'd continue to resist his efforts to dig beneath her surface. He rather enjoyed watching her sweat and squirm. Her on the back foot and him in the driving seat was a very satisfying dynamic. It returned the control to him, restored order and meant that he was back to being the man he recognised, thank God.

She would yield in the end, of course. She was no slouch when it came to the effective deployment of words, but he was an experienced orator who could tie her in knots if he chose to. He had skills that had been honed on the battlefield of diplomacy and could force the most intransigent of world leaders to bend to his will. Up against that, she wouldn't stand a chance.

'I appreciate your commitment,' he said, thinking he'd relish the challenge nonetheless. 'But we have other plans.'

'What other plans?'

'I've arranged a day out.'

She frowned. 'A day out?'

He nodded. 'That's right.'

'Are *you* bored with *me*?'

Hah. As if. He didn't think he'd ever be bored with her, further proof he'd made a wise decision by choosing her to be his bride. The rest of his life was hopefully going to be a very long time. It would be infinitely more bearable with someone who held his interest out of bed as well as in it. 'Not in the slightest,' he said. '*I* feel, however, that we could do with a change of scenery. Fresh air and space, away from the masses. Especially after yesterday evening's episode on the terrace. Such a build-up of pressure needs more than a few moments of gazing out at a darkened garden. There's a place about an hour from here. A crown estate. It's remote. We'll have privacy. We can relax. It'll be fun.'

She stared at him as if he'd suggested running through the streets naked, and he empathised. He was almost as surprised as she was by the thought of relaxing. Whether or not the experience would actually turn out to be fun, of course, was anyone's guess, Presumably that would depend on what she was keeping from him. But with no protocol to follow, no protection officers, journalists or camera crews milling about, it would certainly be novel.

'It's not a date, is it?' she asked, looking faintly alarmed by the thought.

'Of course it's not a date,' he said, ignoring the unfathomable tightening of his chest and responding instead to the suddenly pressing need to nip any notion of that in the bud. 'Why would you even think that? A marriage of convenience has no call for such a thing. So don't go getting the wrong idea, Sofia. We can't afford such sentimental nonsense. We are who we are and there's no point wishing otherwise. This isn't some romantic claptrap. It's merely some timeout to kick back and unwind. An opportunity for me to get to know what makes you tick. That's all.'

CHAPTER ELEVEN

THE LAST THING Sofia wanted to do was spend the day alone with Ivo when he was so determined to get to know her. She'd have to be constantly on her guard, and after last night she was exhausted enough already.

But what choice had she had?

She'd run out of options.

And as a result, she was now sitting in the passenger seat of a low-slung black convertible that wound through the hills inland to the north of the south coast, thinking that, despite his insistence this wasn't a date, it certainly felt like one. The wind whipped through her hair. The sun was warm on her face. The gorgeous man handling the powerful car like a pro was her lover, her husband, who'd arranged a day off, a day out, who'd loaded the boot with a picnic and wished he wasn't who he was.

Was he aware of the whisper of regret that had tinged those words? she wondered as she stole a glance at him, her breath catching at the sight of his handsome profile and strong sexy forearms. She couldn't imagine he was. He'd be appalled.

She, on the other hand, couldn't seem to let it go despite her attempts to do exactly that. What did it mean? For all his protestations to the contrary, did he actually *want* romance? Deep down, did he yearn for love, like she did? What would be the implications if he did? A relationship that didn't have to be the loveless match she'd signed up to? A chance that he might actually come to return her feelings?

Ivo slowed to turn off the main road and onto a narrow lane that led through a village and then up yet another hill. Sofia similarly applied an emergency brake to these dangerous and oddly seductive thoughts. He was bound by duty—and he accepted and embraced that—but he wouldn't be human if he didn't experience the occasional *what if* himself. She must not 'get the wrong idea' and fall into the trap of imagining things that didn't exist. She *had* to keep her feet on the ground and the convenience aspect of their relationship at the forefront of her mind and remember that this wasn't a date and she was glad about that.

As for finding out what made her tick and the questions he was no doubt lining up to fire at her the second he had a chance, she'd just have to get in there first. Go on the offensive and ask *him* some questions for a change. Wheedle out *his* secrets and expose *his* vulnerabilities to uncover the man that nobody else saw. He wasn't the only one with tenacity.

They pulled up at a set of huge wrought iron gates and the two pairs of outriders veered away and disappeared, leaving them alone. The gates swung open and he depressed the throttle to roar up the cypress-tree-lined drive, a five-second burst of recklessness that was as unexpected as the faded jeans and untucked polo shirt he wore.

After bringing the car to a sharp stop at the top of it,

kicking up gravel some distance from a huge gleaming white structure, Ivo levered himself out of the driver's seat and strode round the bonnet to the passenger side. With a yank on the handle, he opened her door and stood aside.

'Here we are,' he said, as she swung her legs round and rose from the seat in a move that would have been a lot more elegant had his gaze not fixed on the bare skin below her skirt and darkened, as if he was remembering those legs entwined with his.

He slammed the door shut, jolting Sofia out of similar hot and distracting memories. Getting a grip, she shaded her eyes and looked up and around. The plain, almost round monolith rose from the high ground into the bright blue sky, dominating the view for miles. In the distance, beyond the undulating landscape, she could even see the sea. 'And where, exactly, is that?'

'Rafifi Castle.'

'It doesn't look much like a castle,' she said, scanning the building and its environs. 'Where's the moat? Where's the drawbridge? Why doesn't it have any of those long thin openings for archers?'

'Who knows?' He reached into the car for the floppy wide-brimmed sun hat that she'd placed on the back seat for the ride. 'It was built in the thirteenth century but there are no relevant documents as to its purpose. It was obviously never designed to be a military building. It has no stables or dungeons and up until a hundred years ago didn't even have any bedrooms, let alone a kitchen. What it *is* is a perfect octagon. One theory is that it was built as a sundial. Something to do with the mysterious laws of the stars, I believe.'

'How fascinating.'

'It sounds completely far-fetched, if you ask me. It was probably built as a folly.'

Sofia took the hat from him and positioned it on her head while he strode round to the boot and opened it. A distant memory from her history lessons flitted into her head. 'Isn't the estate where your grandfather honeymooned with your grandmother and almost collapsed the monarchy nearby?'

'It is.'

'Worth a visit?'

'Absolutely not.'

'If it's anything like this place, I can see why they didn't emerge for six months. Peace, privacy, views to die for. What's not to like? It must have been idyllic.'

'I'm sure it was, for *them*,' he said, as he extracted the picnic basket and set it on the ground before delving back inside for the blanket. 'For everyone else, scrabbling around to see off the army and restore order, it must have been horrendous.'

'They were in love.'

'They were selfish.'

'Surely you can empathise.'

He straightened so sharply he nearly cracked his head on the lid of the boot. 'What on earth are you talking about?'

'Not what. Who. Carolina, Countess of Vila Real. According to the tabloids at the time, you were mad about her.'

Ivo's jaw clenched. He seemed to turn to stone right before her eyes. 'The tabloids were wrong.'

'She was very beautiful,' she said, recalling the extensive press coverage, the envy their relationship had aroused and the shameful relief she'd felt when they'd split up.

'Only on the outside.' He gave the boot lid a good shove down and picked up lunch. 'She cheated on me and afterwards tried to sell the story of our relationship to the press. If the palace hadn't killed it, I'd have been crucified. No one would ever have taken me seriously, either then or now. It was not a pleasant experience in any shape or form.'

No, Sofia thought with a pang of sympathy as they set off for the giant oak door. She could imagine. He'd have been mortified and appalled to have been shamed so publicly, even if only the breakup had hit the news. Who wouldn't? And she could understand his abhorrence of drama because of it. But to be betrayed like that… Whether or not love had been involved, it had to have hurt, and her heartstrings twanged at the thought of him in pain. 'No wonder you're once bitten, twice shy.'

'I will never put myself in that situation again.'

'That's understandable,' she said, wishing she could get her hands on his faithless, treacherous ex.

'It's also one of the many reasons I picked you for the role of Queen.'

Oh? 'What do you mean?'

'You're as interested in love as I am. Not at all, in other words. I couldn't have married someone who hoped for more than I'm prepared to give in that regard. It's a tough enough gig as it is, without throwing unreasonable expectations into the mix.'

Sofia nearly tripped on a stone. Forget the unreasonableness of expectations. He thought they were on the same page about love? When had she ever given him *that* impression? 'What makes you think I'm uninterested in love?'

'No evidence of a boyfriend in all the years you've worked at the palace,' he said with disconcerting conviction. 'Plus, you're as devoted to your job as I am. It's so all-consuming there's little time for anything else. An external relationship would never survive the neglect.'

'I see,' she said faintly. 'You seem to have it all worked out.'

'I know,' he said. 'I do.' He opened the door and stood aside to let her pass out of the hot bright sunlight into the cool dark of the cavernous hall. 'Come on in. I'll show you around.'

Unable to work out why the proximity of his grandparents' honeymoon hideaway was suddenly playing on his mind, Ivo concentrated on giving Sofia a potted history of the castle, complete with dates, figures and any other facts he could recall. She, however, didn't seem to be appreciating his vast wealth of knowledge on the subject.

'And then eighteen months ago,' he said, as they stood in the space at the centre of the structure. 'I guillotined the Lord Mayor in this very courtyard.'

She nodded vaguely. 'Right.'

'Are you paying attention to *anything* I'm saying?'

Her gaze jerked to his. 'Huh? Sorry. I'm a little distracted.'

Yes, he could see that. 'By what?'

'By what you said at the car. About your ex-girlfriend and the effect she had on you.'

He stilled. Frowned. Why the hell would she be thinking about *that*? 'What does that have to do with anything?'

'Love doesn't *have* to be dramatic and destructive, you know.'

His frown deepened into a scowl. Now what was she doing? Why was she talking about love when neither of them had any interest in it? And what was that emotion that laced her voice? It was the same thing he'd caught when she'd mentioned how his grandparents had felt about each other. Was it...*wistfulness*? It had better not be. That would suggest a hankering for something that this marriage was not—and never could be—about. 'It has the potential to bring down a monarchy,' he said, determined to banish such an unfathomable sentiment, if that was what it was. 'To humiliate and weaken those foolish enough to indulge it. And let's not forget, it drove your parents over a cliff.'

'Well, yes, but that was passion of the most toxic kind. And by the end of their marriage they hated each other.'

'It's still selfish.'

'But it can be quiet, supportive and enduring.'

His eyes narrowed. Despite the heat of the day, he was suddenly feeling a little chilly. 'You sound as though you speak from experience.'

She shook her head and averted her gaze but not before he caught a glimpse of something that intensified that chill. 'You only have to look at your mother to see it.'

'My mother?' he asked, more baffled than ever. 'What are you talking about?'

'She loved your father.'

His pulse leapt but he ignored it. 'Don't be ridiculous.'

'That's what she told me.'

'Theirs was a marriage of convenience.'

'Not for her.'

'You must be mistaken.' She had to be. Because if she wasn't, then that meant his father had lied every time he'd hammered home the importance of the head ruling the heart, and that simply wasn't possible.

'Perhaps you should ask her.'

Now why would he do that when she'd only just begun to get over his father's death? He loved his mother. He didn't want to set her back. He had briefly questioned the depth of her grief, of course, but they'd been married for thirty-five years. Naturally she was going to miss him. However, familiarity was all that was. A successful royal marriage didn't involve love, and theirs had been the epitome of success.

'Absolutely not,' he said, refusing to give Sofia's preposterous theory any credence whatsoever, because if he did, everything he believed to be true would crumble to dust and where would that leave him? Floundering around, confused and helpless and dropping so many balls that his country would suffer the consequences? Not on his watch. 'We don't discuss that sort of thing. Besides, I'm not wrong about this.'

'If you say so.'

'I do say so,' he said with a grind of his teeth. He was right about everything. Always had been, always had to be, always would be. Sofia knew the score. She was just messing with his head, for some perverted reason.

Nevertheless, all this talk of love was curdling his stomach so violently he felt as though he were about to throw up. He didn't want to think about his ex. Or his parents' marriage. He was the one supposed to be digging beneath her surface, not the other way round. Although, that now didn't seem a wise course of action at all. In fact, it seemed deeply unwise, because for some unfathomable reason he didn't want to know what she was hiding any longer.

What he *did* want was to get the hell out of here and surround himself with other, infinitely less confusing people. But that would invite more questions to which he wouldn't have the answers, so instead he banked everything but the attraction that still burned like fire. He raked his gaze over her and welcomed with open arms the resulting surge of heat. It was preferable to continuing the ludicrous conversation they'd been having.

'A swim in the river before lunch?'

'I didn't bring a costume.'

'That doesn't matter,' he said, taking her elbow and guiding her back inside to collect the picnic things en route. 'You won't need one.'

Ivo did not like talking about love, Sofia thought, trying to keep up as he took her on a route march to the river. That much was clear. And before today she'd never have brought it up, because what would be the point in a marriage of pure convenience? Why would she deliberately set herself up for pain by acknowledging she cared?

But something had changed since breakfast. Something that made her not bury her curiosity but embrace it. Something that made her wonder if she couldn't use that curiosity to try and change his mind about love without it hurting at all.

It had occurred to her, as he'd shown her around the castle, whether there might be more behind his determination to continually deny romance than a lack of time and an abhorrence of drama. After all, a decade had passed since his ex-girlfriend's betrayal. Surely he'd have got over it by now, if that was all it was. Its lingering effects made more sense, then, if the wound he'd suffered was an emotional one. One which had cut deep and lacerated his heart as well as his pride. Under those circumstances, she could absolutely understand why he might want to protect himself at all costs.

And now the questions that ricocheted around her brain were: *Was there any getting past it? Should she even try?*

This morning she would have said definitely not. She shouldn't even *want* to. She knew what this arrangement was about. He reminded her of it often enough, and she had no intention of risking her heart for nothing. But now she couldn't help wondering whether there wasn't nothing, but *something*. Whether, if she *did* have any expectations, they might actually not be unreasonable.

She kept thinking about the moment on the terrace when he'd revealed the pressure he was under. The regret in his voice when he'd told her they were who they were and there was no point wishing otherwise. Deep down, did he know it wasn't a binary choice but that he was simply afraid of being hurt again? And if that was the case, what if she could show him that he had nothing to fear from her? That he could have both work and her without it resulting in drama and distraction? What if she could show him that they could serve the monarchy and the people *and* have love and romance too? That it didn't have to be a zero sum game.

Sofia knew these were unwise thoughts. They loosened

the ropes that kept her safe and opened her up to heart-break and pain. However, her feelings, which swelled and deepened with every new facet of himself he revealed, were increasingly hard to contain. They were beginning to overwhelm her.

But if the risk of chaos and devastation wasn't as great as she'd always believed, maybe she had nothing to fear from setting them free. And if there was even the tiniest flicker of hope that he might one day be able to return her love, maybe, instead of fighting to keep it to herself, she ought to reveal it.

Not in words, of course. It was far too soon for that and, given the assumptions he'd made about her and his attitude towards his ex, he might consider it a lie by omission. He might feel deceived, possibly even betrayed. But perhaps she could unwrap her feelings subtly. Through her actions. She could start by opening up a little in the hope that he might reciprocate, step by tiny step, until after a while, with any luck, he started to see her in a different light.

She wouldn't expect immediate results, of course. She wasn't a *complete* fantasist. This would likely take a long time. It was certainly a strategy with an uncertain out-come and if she'd got this all wrong, she'd suffer rejec-tion more painful than any she'd endured at the hands of her parents.

However, she didn't think she was wrong. She thought that deep down he wanted all the things that she did. She thought that, if he could get over his fears and allow himself to love her as much as she loved him, they could have happiness beyond their wildest dreams. She could have everything she'd ever wanted. And so, if she was right, could he.

But first, she thought dizzily, as he stripped off and a wave of lust consumed her, she was going to do whatever it took to make sure that he didn't get bored.

By the time they finished their late and long lunch beneath the draping, waving branches of a willow tree, Ivo was at his wits' end. With the exception of a couple of interludes in the river, which had involved no swimming at all, 'fun' was not how he'd describe the afternoon.

Unnerved by their earlier discussions about love, he'd decided that he would control what they talked about over cold chicken and an array of salad. He would not allow another foray into a topic that roiled his stomach. Instead, he'd turned his attention to getting the answers to the questions about Sofia that had plagued him the evening before at the ball. A deeper understanding of who she was and why would add to their partnership and strengthen the foundations of the monarchy, he was certain.

'Tell me about your parents,' he'd begun, deciding to start with a continuance of the conversation they'd begun in her room on their wedding night, which had been aborted by constitutional obligations and the clock.

In the process of uncapping a pot of fat green olives, Sofia had shot him a startled glance. 'I'd rather not,' she'd said with a grimace. 'It's far too beautiful a day for such a gloomy topic. Let's talk about something else instead. Like… I don't know… Any unreasonable expectations *you* may have. Or who you'd be and what you'd do if you weren't who you are.'

God no, Ivo had thought with a shudder. What was there to say anyway? All his expectations were entirely reasonable and, as he'd told her several times now, hypotheses were pointless. He could not afford to indulge in such ridiculous fantasies. Fifteen minutes of doing so on the terrace outside a ballroom was quite bad enough.

'I've talked about myself ad nauseam over the past few weeks,' he said, recalling the endless history lessons and myriad explanations he'd given her for his decisions and conduct. 'Now it's your turn. You wanted communication. So communicate.'

'Fair enough,' she agreed with a nod. 'My parents were a nightmare. As I told you, they argued a lot, pretty much all the time for as long as I can remember. It was horrendous. I used to dread coming home from school. The unpredictability of their personalities and their relationship meant that I never knew what I'd find. The simplest of conversations would descend into a row. They were so loud the neighbours must have been able to hear every word. Things were frequently thrown.'

'How did you cope?' he asked, unable to imagine how awful such conflict must have been for her.

'I had to block it out.'

'By listening to music with your headphones on and dancing the negative energy away?'

Her eyebrows rose. 'You remember that?'

'Of course. I have an excellent memory.'

'That was one way,' she said. 'Another was by daydreaming about life at the palace.'

Now *his* eyebrows were the ones to rise. '*My* palace?'

She nodded. 'Yes. I frequently transported myself from my house to yours, where it felt like nothing would ever go wrong. I envisaged beautiful royal people doing beautiful royal things, in perfect peaceful harmony, with never a cross word. Of course I realise how unrealistic that was, and I probably did then, but at the time I didn't care much for reality. I just needed an escape. Which was another reason I married you. Regardless of what was actually going on behind the palace walls, the monarchy got me through some tough times. I feel a strong sense of loyalty towards it, so strong that I even pursued a career doing what I could to support it. I didn't want to see the crown fall into the hands of someone who didn't care. I couldn't allow everything you and I had worked for to go to waste.'

'You're not a dreamer these days,' he said, trying to equate his uber-professional communications secretary with the troubled adolescent she must have been, and failing. 'So what happened?'

'I toughened up,' she replied with a shrug. 'Despite the music and the fantasies, my childhood was a pretty lonely time. There wasn't a whole lot of love going round and I could hardly bring friends back, even if I'd had any. On the upside, though, I learned to be resilient and self-reliant. My parents were both so awful I couldn't side with either one so I chose to side with me, instead. I didn't like the rage I felt at their dysfunction. The volatility of my emotions felt too much like theirs, so I did my level best to control it. I still do. I also try to avoid confrontation and prioritise communication over letting things stew, which was another point in your favour. You have a solid grip on your emotions. You offered a relationship free from drama and chaos, which I wanted, and I value honesty and steadfastness, which you have in abundance.'

The conversation had then moved on to his childhood, which had been considerably less traumatic, and then they'd stopped talking to lose their minds in each other's arms again.

But now, but with the sun sinking towards the horizon, Ivo wasn't feeling very steadfast. The grip he had on his emotions didn't seem solid at all. His stomach was churning and his chest was tight. He had no clue as to why he could hear the rapid thud of his heart in his ears, but it felt dramatic. He felt…*chaotic*. He was being hammered by the more troublesome aspects of her upbringing, such as loneliness, neglect and a stark lack of both affection and friends. Battered by the need to dig deeper to tease out her hopes and fears and find out whether she did in fact have any dreams and, if she did, what they might be. For all she had said, he could feel there was much more she was holding back.

He couldn't shake the unsettling sense that his foundations weren't built on impregnable rock but shifting sands instead. His feelings for her were supposed to simple. Basic. Centred on respect and liking and nothing more. But they were turning out to be anything but simple. Mixed up among them was lust, madness and other dark swirling things he couldn't identify, and suddenly, it seemed imperative to remember why *he'd* married *her*. To focus on the admirable character traits *she* possessed.

Her resilience was an asset to the crown, he told himself, recalling the pragmatic nature of their relationship that, for a moment, had got lost. As was her deep unwavering loyalty, which was evidently not to him but to the institution, exactly as it should be. Her self-reliance meant that he would be able to attend to business without having to worry about her. Her focus on peaceful resolution and transparency matched his, which augured good things for their marriage and the country. Once again, he congratulated himself on having identified an excellent queen in Sofia. Once again he congratulated himself on restoring order.

The job was what mattered, he reminded himself as he glanced at his watch and snuffed out a rogue pang of resentment when he saw the time. His duty. His responsibilities. Continuing the charade for the good of the crown. Nothing else.

'We should go,' he said, pushing off the tree trunk against which they were watching the sun set in companionable silence. 'The train will be waiting to take us to our next royal engagement.'

'Do we have to?'

He bit back the 'no' that was on the tip of his tongue and got to his feet. 'Yes,' he said, as he extended his hand to help her up. 'We do.'

CHAPTER TWELVE

ON THEIR RETURN to the train, Ivo had Sofia's things brought to his carriage on the basis that his en suite had a double shower, of which, over the next week, they made ample use.

Every time she thought about the dreamy afternoon they'd spent at the castle, a bloom of warmth spread across her chest. He hadn't run a mile from everything she'd told him. On the contrary, he'd reciprocated, just as she'd hoped. He'd seemed as reluctant to leave as she had been. He'd taken her hand as they'd headed back to the car at sunset, when there had been no journalists around and no members of the public to convince. He hadn't had to do that. She'd have followed him regardless. She'd follow him anywhere.

Drawing encouragement from how that afternoon had gone, Sofia doubled down on her efforts to subtly show him how she felt. When they weren't on show, discussing the tour or driving each other to the heady heights of pleasure, she shared with him more of her life before their engagement. She told him about the jobs she'd had prior to working at the palace, where she lived and how she spent the little time off she had. Some things required deflection, of course, such as why she had no friends to speak of, not even a bridesmaid. The last thing she wanted to hash out with him was the fundamental flaw she had that pushed people away. But the more mundane things, like her favourite food and what books she enjoyed reading, she was perfectly happy to reveal. So too, it seemed, was he, and it was these little things, the things that no one else knew about him, that fanned the flame of hope that flickered in her heart.

She'd recently worked out that the disappointment she'd begun to feel at the thought of the convenience aspect of their arrangement had indicated a deep, burning desire for a proper marriage to a husband who loved her the way she loved him. She'd always believed that that was an impossible dream, and she'd done her very best to accept it. She'd tried so hard not to care. So hard not to wish. Not to resent him for his honesty. But it had been so very tough. And now she felt as though she could both care and wish, because she had the sense that she was beginning to matter to him and not just because of the practical skills she could offer or for the sake of the monarchy. He paid attention. Sometimes she caught him looking at her with such warmth that her bones melted. They were developing the connection she craved so much.

What was happening filled her heart with growing joy. She felt as though he was beginning to see her in a new light, which was quietly, wonderfully thrilling. The bright shiny future she'd dreamed of felt within closer reach than it ever had before, and she so badly wanted it she felt giddy.

And she wasn't the only one to have noticed the shift in their relationship, if the article in *Ciao!*, the country's leading celebrity magazine, was anything to go by.

Today is the last day of the Royal Tour...

She read the words for approximately the hundredth time as she sat in the back of the car that was winding through the streets of Oviense.

And, oh, how we'll miss it. This past week and a half would have melted the most cynical of hearts.

Who could have remained unmoved at the sight of the King catching the Queen in his manly arms when she stumbled at the ruins of the Temple of Zeus at Neapolis?

How cute was it when, at the launch of the Navy's newest battleship, they finished each other's sentences?

The long, lingering glances they shared over the magnum of biodynamically produced Pinot Noir, bottled in honour of their nuptials, made this fan want to yell, 'Get a room!' Their chemistry is off the charts.

Despite the rumours that once abounded, and its inauspicious start, there is clearly nothing convenient about this marriage. If the way their hands are practically welded together is anything to go by, they're mad about each other!

How long will it be before The Palace of Montemare hears the pitter-patter of tiny feet?

We say, watch this space in nine months' time...

Sofia switched off her phone but the words she'd committed to memory danced through her head. The accompanying photos were burned onto her retinas. She could recall each of those occasions.

When she'd tripped at the ruins and Ivo had caught her, she'd gazed into his eyes and the world had ground to a halt. The concern on his face had brought her heart to her throat and stuck it there. He hadn't seemed to want to let go and neither had she.

At the launch of HMS *Indomito* he'd had to address the Navy. For fun, she'd challenged him to incorporate the word cornucopia into his speech. She hadn't expected him to comply but he had, twice.

At the vineyard, over a glass of the most delicious wine she'd ever tasted, he'd suggested some of the things he might like to do with it if they took it back to bed with them, and she'd nearly dragged him off right then and there.

And then yesterday, in front of the crowds that had gathered to greet the Royal Train when it pulled into the station, he'd responded to calls for a kiss by sweeping her into his arms and giving them exactly what they wanted. Thoroughly and at length.

Had she shown him that he could both work hard and play? That love was nothing to be feared? Could she dare to believe that he was beginning to return her feelings?

The little voice in her head warned not to get carried away, to remember how fragile her heart was and the harm it could come to if she didn't take care. After all, Ivo hadn't said anything to indicate that his feelings for her had changed, and he'd never been anything but up-front with her. But her misgivings were drowned out by the conviction that actions spoke louder than words, as she herself had demonstrated every minute of every hour of the last ten days.

What to do when they returned to the palace and the

real work began now occupied her every waking thought. Should she tell him how she felt? Ask him how *he* felt? Or was it too soon? Would it give him the nudge he needed or send him back to square one? She was in a constant state of flux. Her emotions were whipping about all over the place. But she had to keep it together this one last time.

The car drew up at the square in the centre of which a statue of Ivo's father—a tribute to his long and stable rule—was due to be unveiled. They got out and, with a wave to the crowds, he took her hand. He must have done so a hundred times over these past ten days but the contact still sent a sizzle of electricity up her arm. Only now she felt protected, special and wanted too.

They walked up the approach to the fabric-draped statue, smiling and talking and engaging with the people that lined it. They stepped onto the stage and with effort Sofia pushed aside the complicated tangle of thoughts and emotions that pulled her in so many different directions. She had to concentrate. This particular event meant a lot to him. The fact that he'd trusted her enough to request she take a look over what he wanted to say meant a lot to *her*.

'Today,' he began, his deep, authoritative voice carrying across the crowd, 'we gather here not just in the presence of stone and metal, but in the shadow of a legacy—a legacy that shaped this kingdom and whose influence will echo for generations yet to come. It is my privilege and my honour to stand before you as we unveil this statue of my father, who acceded to the throne at a time of great unrest and whose reign defined an era of prosperity, unity and strength.

'When I was young, he often spoke of duty and the

weight that rests on the shoulders of the sovereign. He never sought glory for himself. He led with wisdom and humility, and under his rule, our kingdom flourished.

'Let us remember the ideals that he embodied—courage in the face of adversity, an unwavering dedication to peace and a work ethic that put some of his ancestors to shame. Let us remember that our actions in life echo beyond our time, and that the true measure of a ruler is not in how long they rule, but in how well they serve.'

On cue, the shroud slithered to the ground to reveal a life-size bronze standing on a square marble plinth. Sunlight bounced off it, imbuing it with warmth, and the marble sparkled. Like him, his father had been an imposing man, thought Sofia, who stood so close to the statue she was almost blinded by its shiny newness. Like him, he wore ceremonial dress well. Could she hope that this and a devotion to the country was where the similarities ended? That the ability to love might be where they differed?

'I vowed to continue the legacy that my father passed down,' Ivo said, recapturing her attention once the applause had died down, 'and will endeavour to do so for as long as I am able. And so the Queen and I would like to take this opportunity to thank each of you for your support and loyalty these past three weeks. It has meant a great deal to us to see so many of you on our travels throughout the land and we will treasure every single moment.'

'We won't!'

The angry shout came from the edge of the crowd at the front. Accompanying it was an arc of bright crimson that sailed through the air. The splodge of paint hit the statue with a wet slap. Because she was standing so close, some of it spattered her face and the bodice of her dress.

For a moment, there was utter silence.

Next came a collective gasp.

And then suddenly, amidst the shouts, the panic and the chaos, with the wind knocked from her lungs as she fell backwards, flailing, Sofia hit the deck.

'Are you all right?'

It was the third time in an hour that Sofia had asked Ivo that, and now, as on both previous occasions, he nodded shortly and replied with a curt 'Fine'.

However, sitting in the back of the armour-plated car for the journey to the palace, having been advised to forgo the less protected Royal Train, he knew he wasn't. He wasn't fine at all.

The tour had ended in disaster.

His father's memorial had been desecrated.

But blowing that and everything else out of the water was the devastating memory of jerking round in response to the heckler, seeing the splashes of red all over Sofia's chest and face, and believing she'd been hurt.

He'd never experienced terror like it. His response had been so visceral it had wiped all trace of reason from his head. Acting on pure instinct, he'd flung himself at her, taking them both down, and had covered her body with his to shield her from further attack.

No matter that it was only paint.

No matter that within seconds the perpetrator had been apprehended and removed.

His only thought had been keeping her safe. And not

because she was the Queen but because she was his wife. Because she was his and he would protect her with his life.

Before logic returned to assure him she wasn't—and never had been—in any danger, a vision of his future without her in it had slammed into his head, in shocking, stark detail. It had been bleak and colourless and so agonising he'd felt as though his chest had been ripped apart and his heart torn out. He'd still been shaking when they'd been helped up, rushed back to the car and bundled into it. He'd feared it would never stop. He'd wondered if he'd ever get over the gut-wrenching fear of losing her. He hadn't been able to think. He'd barely been able to breathe.

But now the adrenaline and panic were ebbing and he was regaining control. Cold hard reason was returning and with it, horror of a different kind, because it was becoming blindingly clear that he had a problem. Of epic proportions.

His violent overreaction to what had really been a minor threat to Sofia's safety suggested that at some point over the last month he'd completely lost the plot. And now that he was trying to figure out what the hell he thought he'd been up to recently, he found he wasn't short of examples.

From the moment he'd decided to make her his wife, he'd embarked on a downward spiral to insanity. He'd told himself that he'd known what he was doing, but he clearly hadn't had a clue or he would have paid more attention to the warnings he'd acknowledged and then, like an utter idiot, ignored. Such as the feeling that she might be dangerous. The rings that flashed at him non-bloodystop. The kiss at the altar.

Ever since then, his behaviour had been unfathomable. He'd nearly lamped his second cousin at the wedding reception. That night, he'd dithered, ducked and dived. On tour, he'd fired a bishop and delayed a waltz. He'd driven to Rafifi Castle like someone who didn't care if he crashed, and then stripped off his clothes and swum naked in a river. He'd altered speeches for fun. He'd tried to make her laugh. He'd grabbed her hand at every available opportunity and he'd kissed her in public. Not for the optics. Not even for the crowd that had bayed for it. But for himself. He'd prioritised his needs and concerns over duty because he'd wanted to.

These weren't the actions of a serious ruler with a destiny to fulfil. This was the sort of reckless, self-absorbed behaviour his grandfather had indulged in and Tommaso favoured, and it had to stop before he forgot for good what he was supposed to be doing.

He had to crush the growing confusion he felt about his parents' relationship and the unnerving suspicion that it wasn't just the crown that was lucky to have Sofia championing its cause, but him too. He could not keep hunting down articles that came with photos of the two of them gazing at each other and imagining what might be if he wasn't the King and she wasn't the Queen. He'd never even read *Ciao!* before this morning, when he'd come across one fan's take on this latter stage of the tour. Mad about each other? No. He was just mad, full stop.

Why had he held her hand that afternoon as they'd left the river for the car, when there'd been no one around to witness it? Why, when she'd expressed a longing to stay there for ever, had he thought for a moment, *Me too*? And since when did he feel empathy for his grandfather and regret that they hadn't been able to take a proper honeymoon? When they'd got in the car to meet the train, for one mind-boggling moment he'd thought about scheduling another day off to visit his grandparents' hideaway and to hell with what would have to be cancelled.

These past ten days he'd enjoyed hearing about her life, her thoughts and her opinions so much that he hadn't put a stop to it, even though he should have. Instead, without a care for the consequences, he'd reciprocated like a man who couldn't get enough. He'd let her into his head, the space he guarded like Cerberus. He'd even contemplated addressing his work life balance.

This wasn't the pragmatic approach he'd decided on when he'd set out on this endeavour. This had become a battle between his head and his heart, one he hadn't even been aware was waging and one that, if he wasn't very careful indeed, the wrong organ would win.

Ivo might like to think he was always right, but he'd been profoundly wrong to think that she was the dangerous one in this relationship. *He* was. He'd lost focus. He'd let his emotions get the better of him. And once again it was his own damned fault.

He felt sick at the thought of identifying even for a nanosecond with his grandfather. Or Tommaso. He hated that on occasion he'd come across as needy. He hated even more that he'd started to doubt his father's insistence that personal sacrifices had to be made for the sake of the crown. And how could he have forgotten the abject humiliation and crucifying pain when it all went wrong?

He could not afford to continue down this perilous path. He and Sofia weren't a couple in any sense other than the contractual. He couldn't believe that even subconsciously he'd actually begun to feel they might be. When had that started? What had he been *thinking*? Anarchy didn't just happen on the streets. Chaos and the breakdown of order was happening in his head, and he had to get a grip before everything he was trying to achieve imploded, leaving nothing but a gaping hole in his chest.

Despite the disruption that today's incident at the unveiling had caused, Ivo was glad he'd been forced to come to his senses. He was glad that what was important had been brought back into sharp relief. Now the tour was over, he would put it behind him and concentrate on the only things that mattered—shutting down emotion, turning his back on self-centred recklessness and ruling the country as well as he could.

The silence was heavy in the car as it purred through the streets of the capital and out the other side. He was blisteringly aware of Sofia's gaze on him but he couldn't bring himself to so much as glance at her. He didn't want her concern. Or the curiosity he could feel burning him like a laser. He simply couldn't risk weakening again and heading ever closer towards destruction. Which was why, when they arrived at the palace, he vaulted from the car, headed straight for his study and didn't look back.

CHAPTER THIRTEEN

SOFIA DIDN'T THINK she'd ever seen anyone look as pale and terrified as Ivo had when he'd launched himself at her that day by the statue. She had no idea how long she'd stayed trapped beneath him on the hard floor of the stage. Time had slowed right down. All she'd been aware of was his arm tight around her waist, his hand clamped to the back of her head and the frantic banging of their hearts—until, unable to breathe, she'd pushed at his shoulders, once, twice, and eventually, as if electrocuted, up he'd leapt.

During the long, thundering seconds he'd lain on top of her, however, she'd had the strange impression that he'd been transported to another place, and in the car back to the palace the feeling had grown stronger. Seemingly lost in thought, he'd completely disengaged. The frown on his face had been etched so deep it had looked in danger of becoming permanent. He certainly hadn't appeared to be 'fine'. In fact, his inability to make eye contact with her and his abrupt disappearance upon arrival suggested that he'd been the very opposite.

Prior to the last week and a half, Sofia would have been worried by this. She'd have wondered what could be wrong. Now, however, she knew that there was nothing wrong at all. Everything was very right indeed. In fact, everything was completely and utterly brilliant because the miracle she'd never expected, never even thought possible, had happened.

He loved her.

He had to.

Why else would he have leapt to her rescue like that instead of leaving it to the professionals? Why else would he have kissed her with such desperation when she'd opened her eyes? The way he'd held her to him as if she were the most precious thing in the world... And the look on his face as they'd got to their feet... The stark, naked terror... The shaking and withdrawal indicative of feelings that ran soul deep...

In that moment, he hadn't cared about the monarchy. He'd cared about *her*. She'd been his only priority. Because he loved her. She knew he did. She'd felt it in every touch, every smile, every conversation they'd had. When was the last time he'd reminded her that theirs was a marriage of convenience or warned her not to get the wrong idea? She couldn't remember.

As a result of these realisations, her senses were heightened. Colours seemed brighter, smells more intense. Her heart was so big in her chest it felt as though it would burst. She was giddy with relief and happiness. All those doubts and fears she'd had, all those struggles...gone.

Desperate to see what the future held, she wanted to proclaim her love from the rooftops. Issue a communiqué or schedule another interview with the nation's favourite chat show host. But something held her back. She sensed he needed space to get over the shock of what had happened and work it all out for himself. Redefining the principles he'd held for years would take some adjustment and it wasn't something that could be rushed. But that was fine. She could handle a strong powerful man in a state, she assured herself, light-headed at the thought of Ivo, the husband she adored, in bits over her. Like Penelope, she could wait for him to have the epiphany she longed for.

Sofia hadn't given any thought to a time frame for this lightning bolt of discovery. A day or two, maybe three? She had not envisaged still being given the cold shoulder a week later.

Yet that was precisely what happened.

They slept apart. They dined apart. On the rare occasion they did occupy the same space—generally on some work-related matter—her attempts at conversation continued to be met with gruff monosyllabic answers.

He was increasingly withdrawn and uncommunicative, opaque and cold. The more she tried to engage, the further he backed off, and she just didn't understand what was going on. Why was the door that connected their suites locked? Why did he take his meals where she wasn't? Surely he couldn't still be traumatised by what had happened? She'd got over it in the blink of an eye. She understood that he had a lot of work to catch up on. So did she, in the aftermath of #statuesplat, but they'd both been ridiculously busy before and had still had time for civility. So had she done something wrong? Did he somehow blame her for the incident?

Riddled with confusion and disappointment, Sofia didn't know what to do about any of it. She felt rejected. Hurt. She missed him. Because it had been considered prudent to give the public a break from their ubiquity, they didn't even have any functions to attend. There was no audience to hold hands and touch for, and the one attempt she made to initiate a kiss had resulted in such a brutal rebuttal that she hadn't tried again. This wasn't just a hitherto undiscovered steeliness. This felt callous, cruel and directed only at her, and it slashed at her chest like a knife.

Professional experience had taught her that any problem had to be nipped in the bud before it mushroomed into the sort of issue that eventually became insurmountable, but the thought of confronting him and trying to persuade him to talk to her made her want to jump into bed and bury herself under the covers. She was terrified of discovering for real that *she* was the reason for his baffling conduct. That he'd discovered the fatal flaw she must have that drove people away. Her emotions raged ever more wildly, and she didn't want to end up having the sort of row that resulted in the hurling of both insults and objects.

However, this morning something had happened to change her mind about a face-off. Her usually regular as clockwork period had failed to arrive and she was now a day late.

In the bathroom that adjoined her room, Sofia stared at the positive pregnancy test, which shouldn't have come as a shock, given how much unprotected sex they'd been having, but did. Within moments, however, the shock receded and in swept a whole host of other highly charged emotions. Sheer joy at becoming a mother to the child of the man she still loved despite the way he was acting. Deep satisfaction that she'd fulfilled another of her royal obligations. Dread over the fact that because she'd had such terrible role models she might mess it up. Determination that no child of hers would *ever* suffer from the self-centred whims of its parents, like she had.

It was because of this resolve, which point blank refused to allow history to repeat itself, that Sofia put down the test, jumped to her feet and went in search of him. She'd had enough of the silent treatment. She'd made it clear right from the start that it wasn't what she'd signed up to. She had to find out what was going on because this state of affairs could not continue, certainly not now there was a baby involved. She'd let it go on long enough already. The conversation would not become heated, she vowed, channelling every skill she possessed as she scouted out the palace. It would not descend into acrimony.

Eventually, despite the lateness of the hour, she found Ivo in his study. He sat behind his desk, scowling at whatever he was reading on his computer screen, but the minute he clocked her presence his face cleared of all expression.

'I gave instructions not to be disturbed.'

The icy flatness of his voice struck her like a snowball to the face and she inwardly winced. Instinctively, she wanted to turn tail and run. But she wouldn't. And she refused to be deterred. This wasn't about just the two of them any more. 'I know you did,' she said coolly, advancing into the room and mentally batting away the bewildering daggers he was shooting at her. 'Yet here I am.'

'Please go.'

She came to a stop in front of his desk and shook her head. 'No.'

'I'm busy.'

'I can see that.'

'All right,' he muttered, shuffling some papers and then getting to his feet. 'If you won't leave me in peace, I'll find it elsewhere.'

'Sit down.'

In response to the instruction that sliced through the space between them like a whip, he recoiled as though she'd slapped him and his eyebrows shot up. 'I *beg* your pardon?'

'I said, sit down.'

He didn't. Instead, he straightened his spine and pulled his shoulders back, his expression becoming stonier than she'd ever seen before. 'I am not accustomed to being ordered about like this.'

'Yes, well, there's a first time for everything,' she said, with the set of her jaw and a lift of her chin, because two could play the intimidation game. 'You and I need to have a chat.'

'For someone who claims to avoid confrontation at all costs you're giving off very belligerent vibes.'

'Is that what you were hoping for?' she asked, keeping her eyes locked on his and off the distracting pulse that was hammering at the base of his neck. 'You being all moody and withdrawn this past week and me just accepting it?'

A dull flush hit his cheekbones. 'Don't be absurd.'

'Don't be dismissive.'

'You're being ridiculous.'

Ridiculous? *Ridiculous?* With effort, Sofia kept a lid on the emotions that were beginning to roil and took a deep breath to steady her suddenly racing pulse. 'You've been avoiding me all week, Ivo,' she said, wishing she could shake him out of his mule-headed obstinacy but suspecting that he wouldn't budge an inch, either literally or figuratively. 'Every time I come within six feet of you, you disappear, or at least try to. Just now being a case in point. We don't touch. We don't speak. You barely even look at me. Where's the fun we had? Where's the closeness? What happened?'

'What happened is the job,' he shot back, radiating tension as he flicked a glance at the door in obvious desperation to escape. 'While we were on tour, matters of state were put on hold. We were allowed some leeway. Now it's over, the real work starts. There's no time for fun, Sofia. Or for self-indulgence. This is it. For the entirety of our lives. You'd better get used to it.'

No. She refused to believe it was just that. There had to be something else afoot. The personality change was simply too huge. He'd never reacted like this to anything, not even when Tommaso had caused a potentially catastrophic diplomatic spat with Hungary last year. 'I miss you,' she said, doggedly trying to reach him, regardless of what she discovered as a result. 'I miss us.'

His jaw clenched and she could practically see the shutters slamming down around him. 'Royal personages don't have the luxury of such sentiment.'

It sounded as though he was citing from a handbook. He looked like an automaton and, in growing despair, she grappled around for something, anything, that might jolt him out of it. 'I'm pregnant,' she said, and held her breath.

Something flared in the depths of his eyes, but it was there and gone in a flash, barely making a dent in his rigidity. 'That is excellent news.'

She waited for more, but none came. 'Is that all you have to say?'

'What else is there?'

Was he *serious*? 'There is so much,' she said, the stirrings of anger sweeping away the confusion and dismay. 'You could ask how I feel about it, which, by the way, is a bizarre combination of excitement and terror. You could tell me how *you* feel about it. You could express at least a *modicum* of interest in your heir.' She scoured his face for a sign of what might be going on beneath the surface, but his façade was more effective than hers. 'I don't understand your indifference,' she said, hating the way her voice cracked but still determined to avoid theatrics as she sought to get to the bottom of the problem. 'I don't understand you. I thought we'd moved on from this. I thought we'd agreed to communicate. You promised me honesty and respect. The opposite of that is what's going on here. It makes me wonder if I've done something wrong. It feels as though you're punishing me for something I don't know anything about. You said my life would be better for marrying you, but right now it doesn't feel that way. And I am well aware that thanks to my parents' neglect my self-esteem isn't the most robust, but I also know that I'm not imagining the distance you're creating between us. I refuse to let whatever it is fester. This isn't what I want for our child. Do you? Do you want our child to go through what I went through, feeling invisible and unloved, parents at odds, only with ice instead of fire?'

For several long moments, he just looked at her. Then came what sounded like a grind of his teeth, and he eventually muttered, 'No. I don't.'

'So talk to me.'

His gaze drilled into hers. She sensed that he was waging some kind of war with himself. All she could hear was the heavy ticking of the grandfather clock and the pounding of her heart in her ears. Was he about to walk out? Would there be any coming back from it if he did?

But then he gave a nod and she felt a dizzying rush of relief. 'All right,' he said, his jaw so tight it looked as though it was about to shatter, although his expression remained ruthlessly impassive. 'I'll tell you exactly what happened. Oviense happened. I thought you'd been shot. There was a shout, and I looked over and you were covered in what I thought was blood. It scared the living daylights out of me. I think, for a second, my heart actually stopped. I've never been so petrified. My life without you in it flashed before my eyes and it was dreadful. In more ways than one. I cannot afford to feel like that. I do not want to be behave the way that I do around you. Loitering on terraces, driving too fast and messing around with speeches is not who I am. I don't even understand it. But what I *can* do, what I *must* do for the sake of the monarchy, is put a stop to it before I take my eye off the ball once too often and destroy everything I've worked for.'

By the time Ivo finished speaking Sofia was reeling so hard it was a surprise she was still standing in the same spot. He might not understand what was happening to him—and why would he when, thanks to his treacherous witch of an ex, he'd spent a decade suppressing his feelings?—but she did. She understood perfectly. And as the emotions she'd been trying to keep under control burst free, she thought helplessly, dazedly, joyously, that all he needed was a helping hand. Which she'd give him, because she no longer had any reason to hide her feelings. The days of agonising uncertainty and second-guessing were over. The risk of heartbreak was virtually non-existent. Every single thing she'd ever wanted was hers for the taking. All she had to do was reach out and grab it.

'It *is* who you are,' she said, her heart pounding so hard it was in danger of cracking a rib. 'You can be both excellent ruler and loving husband. You can be all that and more. Together, we can be everything. There's nothing to fear about any of it. You're so strong and determined I can't imagine you ever allowing anything to damage the monarchy whatever the circumstances and however much you catastrophise. So you don't have to put a stop to anything. You don't have to fight. And don't think you're alone in the way you feel. You're not. Because I'm in love with you too.'

Ivo flinched and went white. Right before her eyes he seemed to age a hundred years. *'What?'*

'I'm in love with you too,' she repeated breathlessly, light-headed with the relief of finally getting it off her chest. 'I have been for months. Possibly even years. That's why I've never been interested in anyone else. I've only ever been interested in you, Ivo. It's always been you. That's the main reason I married you. I didn't just want to save the monarchy. I don't just admire your integrity and decency. I love everything about you. You have no idea how hard it's been, living with that. How painful it was to see you interviewing all those women before you settled on me. I've never experienced jealousy like it.' She blew out a breath, her head still spinning madly. 'God, it feels good to tell you.'

He stared at her dumbstruck, the muscle hammering in his cheek the only sign of movement.

'Say something,' she said, when she couldn't stand the excruciating silence any more.

'Is this true?'

'Every single word.'

'So you lied to me.'

At the chill in his voice, the giddiness evaporated and she went cold. Nausea rolled up her throat and for one terrible moment she thought she was going to pass out. Was that his takeaway from her declaration of her feelings? After she'd poured her heart out? 'Not really,' she said, an icy sweat beginning to break out all over her skin, her pulse thudding so hard her temples throbbed.

'By omission.'

'Does it matter?'

'Of course it matters. Love was never part of the arrangement. How many times have I told you this is a marriage of convenience and nothing more?'

'Dozens.'

'Which bit of that do you not get? I thought we were on the same page.'

Battered by his unyielding attack, Sofia felt every word like a lash. Her eyes stung and her vision blurred. What she'd feared had come to pass. He didn't appreciate her confession at all. But why not? Why was he so determined to deny what they both felt? 'Are you saying you *don't* love me?' she asked, doing her best to keep the neediness she hated from her voice, desperate to hold herself together.

'I'm saying you shouldn't believe everything you read in the press. I'm saying it doesn't matter one way or another. Feelings are irrelevant. Duty will always come first. If you think I've changed my mind about that, that's your mistake. I've made my position abundantly clear on numerous occasions. I can't comprehend why you'd suddenly believe otherwise.'

Well, she'd believed it because…

Because…

Because she'd dared to dream that his feelings for her would trump all else. Because she'd actually hoped that if he loved her, he'd see that his fears about destroying the monarchy were unfounded, that together they could be brilliant, and choose to put her first.

But why would he? she thought numbly as the scales fell from her eyes and all she was left with was blinding, heartbreaking clarity. No one else had ever made her their number one priority, so what had made her think he'd be different? What had made her think *she'd* be different? She'd tried so hard to secure her parents' devotion by being the best she could be, but she'd failed then and she'd failed now.

Did he even love her anyway? He hadn't denied it, but nor had he admitted it. Would it be worse to know that he did and denied it or didn't in the first place? Either way, the truth was that she wasn't enough. She was never ever enough. And *this* was why she hadn't wanted to confront him. Because she'd feared it might hurt, and it did. It was pain unlike anything she'd felt before. Pain that sliced her chest in two and ripped out her heart.

But he would never know, she vowed, blinking back the sting in her eyes as she swallowed down the hot tight lump in her throat. He would never, ever know. Because her self-respect was all she had left.

'You know what?' she said, needing to get away before her strength and composure deserted her completely and she made even more of a fool of herself than she already had. 'Forget it. Forget I said anything. In fact, forget I was even here. I see no reason why our paths should cross in the future unless absolutely necessary. Our offices are perfectly capable of liaising with each other on our behalf. I'll let you know when the pregnancy is confirmed but apart from that I won't bother you again. Oh, and one other thing…' With hands that were trembling, she tugged the rings that weren't even hers off her finger and set them down on the desk. 'Please see that these are put back in the vault until required. Goodnight.'

CHAPTER FOURTEEN

As instructed, Ivo did everything he could to forget that awful night in his study. He couldn't think of it without shuddering. The drama. The passion. Sofia's complete wrongness about everything.

Where the hell had his cool, level-headed Communications Secretary gone? he wondered in bafflement whenever the image of her standing in front of him, clearly overcome by emotion, slammed into his head, which was far too often for his comfort. When precisely had the asset turned into a liability? How had he never noticed? And as for all that guff about love… About her feelings and his… What had she been *thinking*? As if either of them could afford to indulge in such self-centred nonsense. Was *this* what she'd been trying to hide at breakfast the morning after the ball? God.

She stayed out of his way, as promised. He'd accepted her emailed request to stand down from her role as Communications Secretary. He agreed with her assessment that her position had become untenable upon their marriage and she had other responsibilities now. One of which, presumably, was the child she was carrying. *His* child. His heir. Which he couldn't let himself think about because it put too much pressure on his chest. When she'd told him the news, his first instinct had been to leap over his desk, gather her into his arms and kiss her into oblivion. He'd buried the urge, of course, but it kept trying to surface, and he simply couldn't handle the unacceptable possibility that one day soon he might not be able to resist.

Only once had they been forced into each other's company for any length of time. The reception to welcome the new Spanish ambassador to the country had required a united front. Just before they'd entered the Long Gallery, he'd handed her the rings that for some reason he hadn't got round to placing in the vault, and she'd wordlessly put them on. She'd pulled her shoulders back and lifted her chin, looking so stunningly magnificent that he'd filled with the sudden, clamouring urge to take her back upstairs and beg her for forgiveness. He hadn't, naturally, and had buried that urge too. Instead, he'd offered her his arm and together they'd performed a masterclass in royal protocol and duty. No one but him had noticed the strain of her smile or the tension that had gripped her. No one at all had noticed the strain of *his* smile or the tension that gripped *him*.

Ivo had every reason to rejoice in the fact that Sofia finally understood that the monarchy was and always would be his number one focus. And he did, initially. He was relieved to discover that his judgement was sound, after all. He was absolutely certain that in time she'd get over whatever feelings she thought she had for him, he'd recover from the madness that had temporarily engulfed him and things would be back on an even keel.

Gradually, however, he began to feel as though something was off. Everything seemed to be conspiring against him. He lost track in meetings and forgot names. Carrying out the simplest of tasks was like wading through treacle. He was nearly dropping balls left, right and centre. The daily comms briefings with her replacement just weren't the same. The damn rings kept winking at him from the bowl on the desk in which he'd put them, telling himself he'd deal with them later.

Because he'd had years of experience in the field of international diplomacy, he held it together so effectively that no one had any inkling what churned beneath the surface. Or in how many directions he was being torn. But unfortunately his mother knew him too well to be fooled.

'What is going on?' Elenor asked, having finally secured the audience that he'd repeatedly put off until he'd run out of excuses.

Shifting uncomfortably on the sofa in his private sitting room, Ivo wondered darkly why the women in his life kept asking him this. 'I don't know what you're talking about.'

'Don't be dense,' she said with the bluntness he'd inherited. 'I'm talking about Sofia. Or more precisely, you and Sofia.'

Suddenly, the cushions felt like knives. His shirt was as tight as a vice. He jumped to his feet, strode to the window and resisted the urge to pace. 'Other than the roles we perform as King and Queen, there *is* no me and Sofia,' he said, ruthlessly ignoring the denial that surged through him.

'That's the trouble,' said his mother. 'She's having your heir. She needs you. Meanwhile, you're doing your best to avoid her, which is not what I would expect of you when such behaviour is the opposite of honourable. And then there's the job. You're operating at 50 percent. You're making mistakes. You're getting away with it at the moment, but for how much longer?'

'It's a temporary affliction,' he muttered, not needing to be reminded of how badly he was in danger of failing at everything.

'Is it?'

'Absolutely.'

'Did you know she's in love with you?'

The memory of her admitting how she felt slammed into his head and for a moment his lungs seized. He forced out a breath and cleared his throat. 'She did mention it, yes.'

'I warned her about the pitfalls of hopeless expectations, but she clearly paid no attention.'

Right. Enough. He was fed up with his. He couldn't handle being slammed with any more home truths and he didn't have time for any more crypticity. Needing to clear up yet another thing that had been driving him nuts, he whipped round to face his mother and shoved his hands in his pockets. 'Talking of hopeless expectations,' he said, locking his eyes on hers so as not to miss a thing. 'I understand you had a few back in the day...'

His mother considered him for a moment before saying, 'Yes, I was in love with your father, more fool me.'

As Sofia had maintained. The floor beneath his feet seemed to shake and crack. He set his jaw. 'Why?'

'What do you mean, why?'

Was steam coming out of his ears? It certainly felt as though it was. 'That's not what we do.'

Elenor looked at him with disconcerting shrewdness.

'You could if you wanted to,' she said. 'As could he. But he was frustratingly stubborn. He refused to acknowledge how I felt. He refused to give us a chance.' She sighed and a flicker of grief and regret darted across her face. 'But I wish he had, because we could have shared the huge demands he faced. He might not have had that stress-induced heart attack. Because of the actions of *his* father, he saw emotion of any kind as a weakness instead of the strength it can be, and I know he taught you to believe that a marriage of convenience was the only option open to you. But it's not too late. You're in love with Sofia. There's no point denying it,' she said, holding up a staying hand when he opened his mouth to issue an objection. 'I watched the footage of you on tour. I read the articles and saw the photos. With love like that you could take on the world. Do not make the same mistake your father did, darling. I really couldn't bear it.'

His mother rose from her chair, gave his arm a squeeze and left Ivo standing there, his head spinning with all the unnerving observations she'd made, which he turned upside down and inside out, until he all he was left with was the blinding realisation that of *course* he was in love with Sofia. He probably had been for months, ever since the day she'd started working for him. He'd come to depend on her more than he'd realised. He'd looked forward to their daily meetings. He'd enjoyed her no-nonsense approach and the fact that she'd never been intimidated by him. Pretty much every rash, out of character thing he'd done since deciding to make her his queen, his wife, *his*, proved he was crazy about her.

But that wasn't the point.

The point was that he didn't *want* to feel any of those

things. He feared the sort of distraction and disruption that could bring down the institution he'd devoted his life to. He dreaded handing over his heart only for it to be decimated. Once was quite enough, and with the benefit of hindsight he could see that he hadn't even been in love with Carolina. Sofia, though... She'd be able to do irreparable damage.

But then, why *would* she decimate his heart? She loved him enough to marry him even though he'd told her he'd never return her feelings. She loved him enough to sacrifice life as she'd known it for the crown. For him. The last ten days of the tour, she'd shown him in a thousand different ways how she felt about him, and he'd welcomed every single one of them without thought. By demanding answers from him the night she'd cornered him in his study, she'd risen above her abhorrence of confrontation to fight for what she wanted. She had more courage in her little finger than he did in his entire body.

Meanwhile, what was *he* doing?

Wallowing in hang-ups a decade old.

Using the excuse of the monarchy to protect the heart that was softer that he'd ever wanted to acknowledge.

But no more.

Heavy was the head that wore the crown, and he was done with putting himself last, with sacrificing the desires that weren't unreasonable and suppressing his feelings. He wanted Sofia's love. He wanted her loyalty and support, not for the sake of the monarchy, but for himself. He wanted every wild emotion she had to give him and to return them in spades. If he had anything to do with it, she'd never feel lonely again. She wouldn't spend the next fifty, sixty, seventy years yearning for something out of reach, as his mother had.

He could not contemplate heading for an early grave through stubbornness. He had to accept that, although his father had been an icon whose legacy he—Ivo—had worked so tirelessly to defend and grow, he had also had flaws. He wasn't a saint. Nor was his grandfather a sinner. He'd been a man in love.

And then there was his heir, which he was *thrilled* about, not just because the line of succession would be assured, but because they were creating a family. His mother had been right yet again. He shouldn't be avoiding her. He should be looking after her. Could babies hear in the womb? He'd read somewhere they did. His stood to inherit a kingdom. There was a lot to pass on and he ought to be doing precisely that, even at this early stage.

Filled with purpose, vowing not to stop until he'd fixed the mess he'd made of things and fervently hoping it wasn't too late, Ivo strode into his study. He scooped up the rings that had sat there so accusingly, a blistering reminder of what he cast aside through stupidity and fear, and then stormed into her office.

'Where is the Queen?' he demanded, glaring at each of the four stunned functionaries in turn.

'I—I believe she's gone, sir,' stammered her usually unflappable private secretary.

What the hell?

'Gone?' he echoed, feeling as though his head was about to explode. 'Gone where?'

'Rafifi Castle.'

Right. Well. That wasn't a problem. 'Get me the helicopter. Now.'

* * *

Sofia sat beneath the weeping willow by the river at the castle, the bright sunshine of the day dappling the ground and making a mockery of her misery.

She shouldn't have come here. The memories of happier times were too hard to bear. But she hadn't known where else to go. Her diary was empty for two whole days that stretched out before her, and she hadn't been able to stay at the palace where there were constant reminders of what a fool she'd been. At least here she was in no danger of accidentally bumping into Ivo. And her wretchedness would ease soon, she was sure, even though it was still so fresh, still so intense that she couldn't imagine when.

She hadn't cried in over twenty years, ever since she'd realised that no one would ever ask her what was wrong, so she'd be better off bottling up how she felt and doing her best to move on. She was making up for it now, though. In the twenty-four hours she'd been here she'd hardly stopped. She was wrung out. Her entire body ached. Her heart was shredded. She'd loved and she'd lost and she'd never felt pain like it.

Yet she had no one to blame but herself.

She should have never allowed herself to care, she told herself for the thousandth time as she stared desolately at the river that glistened and sparkled in the sunshine, and shuddered out a sob. She should have been stronger. Been satisfied with what they had. She should not have reached for the moon.

So desperate had she been to fill the well of loneliness inside her that she'd allowed a crush on the King to get way out of hand. She projected all her hopes and dreams onto him. She'd expected him to provide the close loving family she'd lacked, and save her.

Now the truth was revealing itself to her in all its devastating detail, she could see that she hadn't been at all fair. It wasn't Ivo's job to fix her. To prove that she wasn't unlovable. Of course he wouldn't put her first. It wasn't personal. He wouldn't put anyone first. He wouldn't be the strong successful ruler he was if gave his country anything less than his full, undivided attention.

All her hopes and dreams had been built on sand. The house of cards she'd built had collapsed into nothing. She should never have tried to manipulate his feelings into more than they were. She should never have ignored the voice in her head that had warned her over and over how much damage he could inflict. Ignorance had been bliss. Reality was devastating.

But at least she knew now exactly where she stood. No more would she imagine heightened senses and bask in attention that wasn't really there. No more would she read something into nothing. That bubble had well and truly burst. Her feet were now firmly on the ground. So firmly on the ground, in fact, it occurred to her that perhaps she'd set her sights on him *because* he was unavailable. Her dreams had been safe. Pain and rejection had not been a possibility—until he'd turned her life upside down, her heart had conquered her head and then they'd stared her squarely in the face.

And perhaps she *had* no fatal flaw and *wasn't* unlovable. Perhaps she simply pushed people away before they did the same to her. A self-defence mechanism she'd developed to protect herself from the sort of pain that her parents had caused her. An act of self-preservation. How would she have made friends anyway? She had no idea about the give and take of relationships. Her expectations had always been distorted, so really, this marriage hadn't stood a chance.

What she *was* was resilient. So she'd get through this. Despite the arrows of agony that still stabbed at her heart no matter how hard she tried to deflect them, she'd eventually find a way to navigate her relationship with Ivo and the rest of her life. She'd have a child, his heir. She'd have patronages. She could make a difference. Performing with him for the public would get easier with time, she was sure. They'd settle into the marriage of convenience this was always meant to be, and she'd come to find that she was…content.

The faint *whop-whop* of a helicopter had her looking up through the gently swaying branches of the weeping willow and shading her eyes. The small dot grew larger and noisier as it approached and then landed out of sight.

With a sigh that seemed to involve her entire body, Sofia pulled herself together and got to her feet. She brushed off her dress, took a series of deep steadying breaths, then headed in the direction of the helipad to find out what was up.

She was halfway across a meadow strewn with daisies, poppies and cornflowers when she saw Ivo striding towards her, looking like some dark avenging angel as he made a beeline for her. She halted in her tracks. He carried on mowing a path through the wild flowers and grasses, his gaze fixed on hers with such intent that her heart began to crash wildly against her ribs. Nerves twisted her stomach into so many knots she feared she might be about to throw up.

Had she forgotten an appointment?

Surely the office would have called.

So why was he here? Had something happened? What could she have done now?

She must not speculate, she reminded herself frantically, swallowing hard as, without even stopping, he took her arm and propelled her back to what she must not think of as 'their' tree, fairly blowing her away with his impact. She'd fallen into that trap one time too many. It was so hard to forget the fantasy she'd created to fulfil her craving for love and connection. She'd clung to it for such a long time and he looked so very good. But she had to remember how the conversation in his study had crucified her. How weak she'd come across and how vulnerable she'd been. She must not crumble. She had to stay strong.

He pushed aside the draping branches, then let her go and jammed his hands in the pockets of his trousers. She rubbed the spot on her arm where he'd held her, which burned. 'What are you doing here?'

He opened his mouth, then closed it. He peered at her more closely and his brow furrowed. 'Have you been crying?'

'Pregnancy hormones,' she lied, nevertheless having to work for her composure like she'd never had to work before. 'And I asked you a question. What are you doing here?'

'It's my castle.'

'That's not an answer.'

'No?' he said, radiating an energy that snapped and sizzled around him. 'Well, how's this for one?'

Her breath caught. Her heart hammered like a pneumatic drill. The entire world seemed to grind to a halt. Even the river stopped in its tracks.

'I'm here to apologise.'

The world started up again. The river flowed once more. Her lungs released their grip on her breath, and Sofia wanted to wail in despair because hadn't she learned *anything*? Was she *still* so deluded she'd expected a declaration of love? 'For what?'

'My complete and utter stupidity.'

'You're not the stupid one,' she told him, vowing to get through whatever this was with her pride intact, even if it killed her. 'I am.' *In so many ways.* 'And if anyone deserves an apology, it's you. I got it all wrong. I was totally misguided to think I was in love with you, and you me. I see now that I created this idiotic fantasy with you at the heart of it. I was trying to create the family I never had. I was trying to fix something in me that I believed was broken.'

'Broken?' he echoed in disbelief. 'There's nothing broken about you.'

'I know that now,' she agreed. 'And a lot more besides. I'm appalled that I let my emotions get the better of me, not once, not twice, but on a number of occasions, when that was never part of the deal. I realise I haven't been the wife you need lately and I'm aware we can't divorce, but I promise I'll work on my self-control. I'll stick to the page you're on like glue. I'm totally over whatever madness took hold of me. I'll keep what this relationship is at the forefront of my mind at all times. It'll be nothing but duty, duty, duty from here on in.'

'Well, that's inconvenient.'

She frowned. 'Why?'

'Because I'm not just here to issue you an apology. I'm also here to tell you that I love you.'

She blinked. Her pulse spiked. Her breath stuck in her lungs all over again. 'What?' she managed as her head began to spin.

'I love you.'

'No,' she said, clinging to her defences with everything she had. 'You don't. You made that exceptionally clear the other night.'

'I didn't mean a word of it.'

'You sounded as though you did.'

With a flinch he yanked his hands out of his pockets to shove them through his hair and then scrubbed them over his face. 'I thought I did at the time,' he said, beginning to pace around the spot where they'd picnicked. 'But I was wrong. I'm so in love with you I can't think straight. I can't eat. I can't sleep. I'm just about holding it together, but it won't be long before I bring down the monarchy single-handedly.'

'I see. You need my help.'

He stopped abruptly gave his head a sharp, decisive shake. 'No. That's not it at all. Hear me out. Please. Even though I know I don't deserve it.' His gaze burned into hers, and she couldn't avert hers, no matter how much she wanted to because it hurt so damn much to look at him. 'I need *you*, Sofia. And not because of the kingdom or the constitution or anything else related to my position. But for me. Just me. That's what I've been struggling with. You turned me inside out. You had me wishing for impossible things and abandoning principles I've lived my whole life by. I was brought up to believe that a royal marriage is not supposed to be that way. That a dedication to duty necessarily precludes love. On a personal level I've always been convinced that love was for the weak, that it would render me vulnerable and open to exploitation. My heart isn't hard. It's as soft as a marshmallow. I had to protect it. Telling myself I neither needed nor wanted love became a habit. But I think, deep down, I've yearned for it for years. You're not the only one who's been lonely. I suspect that's why I put off finding a wife for so long. It wasn't a question of busyness. I was waiting for you. Realising that was terrifying and, once again, I didn't handle it well. You were right to call me out on it. You were right about everything. Not least my mother's feelings for my father. That's another piece of history I will not allow to be repeated.'

'You asked her?'

'Yes. She confirmed what you'd said and then she pointed out all the other things I haven't wanted to acknowledge. For nearly thirty-five years I've had a one-track mind. I've been obsessed with the idea that success in the job necessitates selflessness and the sacrificial suppression of feelings. But not any longer. I love you. I want to share everything with you. With us both at the helm the country will thrive. I know it will.' He drew in a deep, shuddering breath, his Adam's apple bobbing as he clearly swallowed hard. 'Without you, though, I won't. I might not even survive. I'm sorry it took so long for me to come to my senses. I'm more sorry than I can say for the cruelty I showed you the other night. You will never know how much I regret that. I will spend the rest of my life trying to earn your forgiveness if you'll let me. I honestly don't know what I will do if I've blown it for good. Have I?'

He stopped. Sofia reeled, beginning to shake with the force of the emotions she so badly wanted to let loose, yet couldn't. She was desperate to believe he meant what he was saying, but something held her back, and she was done with ignoring caution. 'I don't know,' she said, her throat tight with the swirling emotions she was trying so hard to contain. 'I emptied my soul to you and you crushed it. You broke my heart. What if it happens again?'

'It won't.'

'I wish I could take that risk.'

'You can,' he said, buffeting her with conviction that she wished she could embrace. 'I promise. Take it. Take it with me.'

'But you'll never put me first,' she said wretchedly. 'And I know I shouldn't expect you to. I understand that the country has to be your number one priority. But no one ever has ever put me first, and if I let myself care and you aren't able to do that, it might well destroy me.'

He stilled. He looked her steadily, thoughtfully, for several long thundering seconds, then took a step towards her. She tried to take one back so she could breathe air that wasn't filled with his scent but somehow the tree was behind her. 'Do you know where I'm supposed to be right now?'

What? Given her access to his schedule, she probably ought to. But her brain didn't seem to be working. Nothing seemed to be working. 'No.'

'Munich. At a conference on renewable energy, which, as you know, is something I feel really quite strongly about. I'm the keynote speaker. Or at least I was. The minute I realised how I felt about you I had to come and tell you, so I sent my mother to deliver my speech instead. You're more important to me than anything, Sofia. Even duty. Which is something I'm still trying to get my head around. But what I do know is that I'll *always* put you first. I can no longer imagine doing anything else. It simply won't be possible.'

Sofia's head swam and her heart banged against her ribs. 'Is that true?' she said, her voice little more than a hoarse, strangled whisper.

'Have I ever lied to you?'

He hadn't. Not once. Not even when decimating her heart in his study. 'No.'

'And I don't intend to start now. Or ever.'

Which meant what? That she could believe him? That she was as important to him as he was to her? God, how she wanted that to be the case.

'So what do you think?' he asked intensely, as if her answer was the only thing in the world he wanted to hear. 'Are you really over me? Am I really just a fantasy? Have I killed your feelings for me permanently? Or will you take pity on me and give me a second chance?'

It was his uncertainty and the crack in his voice that blew to bits the last vestiges of her resistance and released the ropes holding her heart. Here he was, this strong proud man, spilling out his soul, adjusting the principles he'd held for a lifetime for her, prioritising her because he loved her, because she was enough for him, and it was everything she'd ever wanted. All she had to do was believe him. Trust him. And in the end, with the proof of how he felt radiating from every pore and in the hoarse sincerity of the words he spoke, it wasn't even difficult.

'Of course I'm not really over you,' she said, her heart

overflowing with so much joy that she trembled with the force of it. 'You're everything I've ever wanted. You always have been. I thought I wasn't enough for you, like I wasn't enough for my parents. I've been so miserable, Ivo. I tried to tell myself that I was tough and I'd get over it, but it would have been so hard. It would have been impossible.'

'You'll never be miserable again,' he said as if it were a vow, pulling her into his arms and kissing her so fiercely she thought she might faint, as much from an overdose of happiness as a lack of air. 'You are more than enough. You are everything. I'm sorry for letting you think otherwise. I'm so very sorry for making you cry.' He leaned back a little, searched her face and frowned. 'And for that terrible speech. I'm sure I've missed something… Like our child. God. You have no idea how happy I am about that. I can't wait to meet them. And add to our family.'

'Your speech was perfect.'

'It could have been better organised. But I didn't have you to tidy it up for me.'

'I've missed you.'

'I've missed you too. I love you, Sofia. Let me show you how much.'

He kissed her again and they fell to the ground, where they tugged off each other's clothing until there was nothing between them but heat and desire and love, until it was impossible to know where she ended and he began. They moved as one, perfectly in sync, and when they hit the dizzying heights of ecstasy together, it was so intense, so beautiful, she could have wept all over again.

'I nearly forgot,' Ivo said, glancing at their joined hands as their racing hearts quietened and the sweat cooled on their entwined bodies. 'You left something behind.' He shifted off her and reached out to rummage in the pocket of his jacket that lay in a heap by their feet, then took her hand and slid the rings on to her finger. 'Don't ever take them off again.'

Sofia looked at the symbols of their unity, their commitment to each other and the crown, watched the diamonds winking in the sun, as if to say *Dreams can come true*, then kissed him with all the love she felt, the love that she would never have to hide again, and murmured, 'I won't.'

EPILOGUE

The sun shone down on this morning's corona-
tion, fifty years to the day since the last. But what
a difference five decades make. Then, only King
Ivo and the dowager Queen Elenor appeared on
the palace balcony. This afternoon, he and Queen
Sofia were joined by their five children, four sons-
and daughters-in-law and twelve grandchildren to
celebrate the accession to the throne of the former
Crown Princess, Marina.

The King's decision to abdicate was one we feel
it's safe to say that no Montemaran truly wanted.
His has been a reign of unrivalled peace, prosperity
and longevity. It's seen the smooth transition from
an absolute to a constitutional monarchy and tire-
lessly supported thirty years of flourishing democ-
racy. Its success will be hard to beat.

But the new Queen Marina has learned from
the best. The crown is in very capable hands. And
how can anyone begrudge our beloved octogenar-
ians the desire to enjoy their twilight years together
at Rafifi Castle? They've devoted their lives to the
country. Now they have time to devote to them-
selves.

Apparently, the King is most looking forward to a daily swim. When the Queen Mother revealed she'd join him if the river wasn't so cold he said he knew exactly how to warm her up and mentioned a certain weeping willow beneath which to do it—a rare insight into their private lives that raised more than one blush in these offices!

It's clear that they're as mad about each other today as they were on their first Royal Tour all those years ago. They might be older but they still make a beautiful couple. They still look at each other as though there's no one else in the world and melt our hearts with every single smile. All of us here at Ciao! *wish them well and a long and happy retirement.*

* * * * *

Were you blown away by
King's Emergency Wife?
Then make sure to check out these other sparkling stories from Lucy King!

Virgin's Night with the Greek
A Christmas Consequence for the Greek
The Flaw in His Rio Revenge
Boss with Benefits
Expecting the Greek's Heir

Available now!

DRAGOS'S
BROKEN VOWS

MILLIE ADAMS

MILLS & BOON

For Voltron, the instigators behind many shenanigans and the receivers of many outraged texts.

If not for you, this one wouldn't exist.

CHAPTER ONE

Cassandra

I'M THE MAD *wife in the attic.*

The realization hits me like a closed fist, and my knees buckle with the force of it. I lean against the wall, hand pressed to my heart.

I stare around the room at the paintings I've done over the last six months. Each one a testament to my degrading mental health, growing darker and darker, the last one a black hole with only a spot of brightness at the center. The light at the end of the tunnel? Or a fall into nothingness? I can't tell anymore.

The trouble with dreaming of finding your own Mr. Rochester is that it's tempting to believe you'll be Jane Eyre.

That's the hubris of youth and inexperience. The belief you'll be different somehow than all those other girls. The belief that you can save him when no one else could.

I admit defeat, then and there.

I can't save Dragos Apostolis. Not from his inner demons, or himself. I can't save *us*.

When I'm alone in this house—and I am far too often,

wandering the halls like the ghost of a girl who used to believe in love—I forget how I ended up here.

I can forget the way my world stopped the first time I saw the man I now call my husband.

Six foot five, broad shoulders, short black hair. His eyes a surreal crystalline blue, a scar on his cheek keeping him from looking too close to pretty. His knuckles were tattooed in severe black ink, one letter on each finger, the words in Romanian.

I found out what it meant later. He spelled it out for me, counting on those fingers as he thrust them into me.

Even now that memory makes me shiver.

That's my madness, though, and I know it.

I knew he was dangerous from the first, even though he was dressed in a bespoke suit, a guest at the exclusive fundraiser I was waiting tables at to make ends meet while I studied abroad in London, away from my small town, away from my loving family.

But I wondered, how dangerous could he be?

I had been a very naive girl. Though not naive enough not to realize the definition of a bad-boy fantasy, and at twenty I'd held onto my virginity for far too long and I'd been overcome by the desire to beg him to take it.

I hadn't had to beg. Though he likes me to do it.

But I'm not pathetic enough to do it, not anymore.

That first night is still burned into my memory. He approached me with the smooth grace of a shark cutting through the water, and I was stunned that the man who had caught my attention and held it had sought me out.

As I stand there, in my perch in the attic, looking down at our manicured garden—*his* manicured garden—I see that night play out in my mind.

* * *

I'm holding a tray of drinks when the man comes over
and lifts it up off my hand and sets it on a nearby table.

"It's my job to carry that."

His eyes are so dark they're nearly black. They catch
mine, then they rake over my body so intently it feels like
a touch. "Your hands are far too lovely for such a menial
task. I can perhaps think of a better use for them."

His accent is gorgeous, though I can't place it. I know I
shouldn't be thinking about his accent. I should be angry
that he's made such an indecent comment. I'm not.

"As far as I'm aware I take answers from my boss.
And not from you." I'm not sure what instinct spurs me
to come back at him like that. To engage in what might've
been banter if this were a meet-cute.

I'm quite certain, based on the shiver of fear that skates
down my spine, and the shimmer of attraction in my
stomach, that this is not a meet-cute of any kind.

"I can also thing of better things for you to do with
your mouth."

There is no way of mistaking the meaning in his
words. He looks at me directly. Those eyes are so fath-
omless in the dark. He has the beautiful face of a fallen
angel, and I'm stunned. I'm like a little goldfish swimming toward a lure.

I know it.

But I can't stop myself. I take one step toward him,
and he reaches out and grips my arm, pulling me up
against his body.

"I want you." His voice is low, rough; it echoes inside of me.

"I…" I should tell him that he needs to take me out.

I should tell him no. I shouldn't be thrilled by his attention. I shouldn't respond to his possessiveness. And yet I do. I have never felt so attracted to a man in all my life. I have never wanted a man like this before.

"I really have to finish my shift," I manage to say.

"You don't," he says.

I look around, certain we've drawn the eye of the people in attendance—or worse, my manager, Lisa, who I hate with the fire of a thousand suns. "I do… I'll lose my job."

"You *won't*," he says.

"Do you own the company?"

A slow smile spreads over his face. "I own this place." He indicates the sparkling venue that we're standing in and I can't figure out if he's a liar or not. He's certainly not the old white guy I'd associate with ownership of a building like this. "Do you not know who I am?"

I shake my head. "No."

"How interesting." He looks at me like I'm an artifact. Something to be studied. "You're beautiful."

He says both things with a tone of wonder. My heart is beating so hard I think I might pass out. I can't remember if I've ever been this close to a man before. I have. I know that I have. I've kissed men before. And yet, it didn't feel this close. This intimate. Sharing the air with a man like him is something else entirely. He's a predator. I feel that in my bones.

A shark.

And yet, I am the little fish that keeps on swimming. Maybe the snare is a hook. Still I swim.

I tell myself that having a modicum of self-awareness in this makes me less pathetic. And yet, I know the truth.

I'm not the first woman to fall from grace over a sinfully handsome mouth. I won't be the last.

"Come with me."

Do I want this? Do I want my first time to be with a total stranger who's never going to call me? Because he won't. He's clearly a wealthy, powerful man who can have anyone he wants. He walked up to me and grabbed me like I was an item that he could purchase. I suppose I should be grateful that he didn't offer to cover my evening's wages.

But I want him. I have never felt the need like this before. It's insistent, driving. And I have the deepest, most profound sensation that if I don't go with him I will regret it for the rest of my life.

Live.

That's what my mom said before I left home. When I left our sweet little house on the street that I grew up on, in Idaho, heading to Europe for my grand adventure. She said: *Live, Cassandra.*

I'm sure she didn't mean this. But maybe she did.

Maybe she meant that I should make mistakes sometimes.

God knows I've never made a mistake before.

I had to get the best grades. I had to be at the top of my class, so I could get the scholarship that I wanted, so I could go to the schools that I wanted to go to. My family loves me. My dad works so hard for me, for my siblings, but paying for four children to go to college has never been in the cards.

I knew that if I wanted to get into a good art program it was going to have to be based on my achievements.

I did all that. But what I haven't done is live.

And right then I wonder, what the point of being an artist is if you don't have messy experiences.

I can feel that I'm justifying. I want to do this. I want to do him.

Before I can rethink it, we're leaving. I'm in the back of his shiny town car, and he drags his finger along the line of my jaw, down to the center of my chin. *"Dragostea mea."*

I don't know what that means, but I don't want to ask. I don't want to break the spell.

Then he kisses me. His lips are hot and hard on mine. I've been kissed before. I can't remember those times. Because this is something entirely different. The way his mouth was over mine. The way he claims me. His lips, his teeth, his tongue.

I am trembling. I want him so badly I'm ready to tear his clothes off in the back of this car. Ready to tear my own clothes off. I realize then that I didn't even look to see if there was a barrier between ourselves and the driver. I'm having a hard time caring.

We separate, and I look up at him, my heart pounding so hard it's all I can hear in my ears. "I don't understand what's happening."

"What is there to understand?" He pushes his hands through my hair, and I shiver. "This is the most honest thing there is. The most real thing. When two people want one another."

So I give in. I throw myself at him. I kiss him. The town car stops, and we're ushered into a beautiful building, whisked to the top floor.

Once we get inside, he closes the door. We're alone.

It's spare. There are no artifacts that point to who he

is, but I wonder if that's information all on its own. Everything is black. Polished.

There is a large couch in the living area, a massive window that offers a view of the city below.

He moves toward me, and kisses me. I realize I don't know his name. He doesn't know mine. Does it matter? Do I want to do anything to break the fantasy, or do I want to live in it? Live in this.

I don't want to stop and talk; that much I know.

He'll be gone by the morning. Or rather, the truth is, he'll throw me right out into the night, I'm sure.

Why exchange names? He kisses me down my neck, down the edge of my rather respectable neckline. Then he takes hold of the front of my dress with both hands and tears it. Well, he isn't going to throw me out on the street in this same dress, that's for sure.

He peels it away from my body, and I'm in nothing but the black bra and underwear that I put on this morning. I'm breathing hard, trembling.

He kisses me, smooths his thumb over my bottom lip, then dips it into my mouth. I bite him. And he growls. I don't know where that instinct came from, only that it was strong and powerful. That with him, all I can do is follow my instinct, because it's all I have.

He kisses down my body, holding me firm, holding me steady as he trails a line of hot open-mouthed kisses over my skin.

He bites my hip, pulls my panties down. I'm only wearing a bra and my black high heeled shoes.

Then he pushes me against the wall, and begins to lick me there at the center of my thighs. I'm shocked. Motionless. And yet, I'm also prisoner to the pleasure that he creates inside of me.

He's relentless, merciless. And I like it.

Then he pushes two fingers through my slick folds, thrusting them deep into me, and I gasp at the unfamiliar invasion.

He continues to move his tongue over the sensitive bundle of nerves there, and I shudder. Then I wish I knew his name because I would call it out like a prayer. Instead, I just cling to his shoulders, digging my nails into his skin.

Then he rises back up, rips my bra away and kisses me hungrily. He's still fully clothed.

My legs are shaking. He takes me to the couch, lowers me down onto it and then sits beside me, running his fingertips along my thigh, lifting my foot up into his lap, where he slowly begins to unbuckle the ankle strap on one of my high heels.

Then he turns his attention to the other one. The movement is so civilized, so careful, and in contrast with everything else, so delicate it makes my heart ache.

The intent expression on his face does something to me.

I am in another world. I'm outside my body, and yet somehow more fully inhabiting it than I ever have.

I move my hands up because I want to take his tie off; I want to take his clothes off. He reaches up and grips my wrist, pulls it away, his hold iron. "No," he says, pushing his forefinger up against my mouth. "You are not in charge."

The dominance in his voice makes my internal muscles clench. Yet another thing I feel I should be angry about, but I'm just aroused.

Then I find myself being pushed back on the couch, and he looms over me, his hand coming up to my throat, where he squeezes tight, and my breath exits my body. For one moment, I wonder if I've made a grave mistake. But then he lowers his head slowly and starts to kiss me. And there's something about the way he's holding me combined with the sweetness of the kiss that brings me right back to the edge of erotic dysfunction. I can hardly think.

While he's kissing me, he releases his hold on me, and I am conscious of him making movements, but barely aware. I realize that he's gotten a condom, freed himself from his suit, and before I can tell him that I haven't done this before, he thrusts inside of me.

I gasp at the unfamiliar invasion. He's so big I can barely breathe. I find myself beginning to panic, my breath coming too fast, making me dizzy.

He begins to shush me, like I'm a panicking animal, but he stays inside of me as he holds my face steady and looks at me. "Are you a virgin?"

"Not anymore," I say, trying to keep the edge of panic out of my voice.

I don't want him to stop.

He makes a pained sound, somewhere between pleasure and torture, and then he begins to move inside of me.

With each movement I find my pleasure building. The pain becomes a distant memory, and I am lost in the rhythm.

And when I finally do come, I arch my back up off the couch, and scream. He covers his mouth with mine, and freezes above me. I feel him large and pulsing inside of me as he surrenders to his own climax.

I am certain that I will never see him again.

* * *

I laugh then. In the emptiness of the room. If only I hadn't seen him again. But I was a silly girl. I wanted to be in love. I wanted my ill-advised one-night stand to be forever. So much that when he asked me to stay the night I stayed. And then I stayed every day after. I tried to keep doing my studies for a while, but there was a point when being with him became overwhelming.

We exchanged names, obviously.

He showered me with gifts. He made me feel special. And he married me quickly. The most lavish event you can possibly imagine. An old church in Romania with roses climbing all over the old stone structure. Lights wound around every pillar and trellis. Thousands of people came. I couldn't say that I knew any of them, apart from my family and a couple of my friends. All of whom wanted to be supportive, but were clearly overwhelmed.

Who can blame them? It was like I'd had a personality transplant. Dragos was my whole world. When before my whole world had been my art. My achievements.

And then once he had me...

I look around the empty space. My decision is made.

Yes. My decision is made.

I can be Dragos Apostolis's mad wife in the attic. Or I can go back to being Cassandra.

I miss her.

And so, I know I need to leave.

CHAPTER TWO

I'M SURPRISED WHEN Dragos comes home that night. It's deeply out of character for him as of late. There was a strange in-between space in our marriage, when he had isolated me from everything and everyone, and he was always with me. It was always us. In this house. And it was heaven and hell all at the same time. My whole world was him.

But the problem with the two of us is that we don't talk. It isn't love. That's what it's taken me nearly four years to understand. He is obsessed with me. And I'm obsessed with him. Or rather, he *was* obsessed with me. Now he's obsessed with... Something else.

It's distressing to me how little I know about my husband. He's from Romania. He never speaks about his family. I get the sense that he's deeply enmeshed in a business that is connected to his family. Another thing I know spare little about. He keeps me separate. From everything.

He's paranoid. He says that he's afraid for my safety because he is a powerful man. And yet it all feels like being on a leash to me.

The dominance that's so exciting in the bedroom is much less exciting when enacted in our actual lives.

One thing I do have is money. He's given me my own account so that I can shop whenever I like. I know it has never once occurred to him that I might leave him. If I act quickly enough I should be able to use that money to get a place to stay.

I don't know what he'll do if I leave.

The truth is, there's so much I don't know about my husband, and it's because I haven't wanted the answers.

What I wanted was a fantasy, with no reality intruding, but now that I've begun to question the fantasy it's dissolving.

The plan is coming together. But tonight, he's in the house.

I need to figure out exactly…

I close my eyes; they're welling with tears. The problem is I still love him. The problem is the idea of leaving him seems as absurd as cutting my own arm off.

I'm dependent on him. He has become part of me. And I hate it. I hate it because it doesn't feel nice.

Because it feels rough. Because it feels…

Overwhelming. All-consuming.

And I have to ask myself, as I make my way down the stairs and head toward his study, if there is a sinister reason that for me, the straw that broke the camel's back is his absence, not his overwhelming presence. Because God knows I should've left him the first time he refused to let me go out when I wanted to. The first time he denied me a trip home when he couldn't supervise me.

The first time he told me I could no longer invite people to our house.

Yes. I should've left then.

He's not cruel to me. But I am a thing. One of the many that he owns.

That's all I am to him.

I move down the stairs like a ghost. I do everything like a ghost.

I'm shocked when I see him in the kitchen—all black like everything in Dragos's life—cooking like he's a domestic of some kind. He's barely been home for months and now he's in the kitchen. Cooking.

I watch as he grabs a large knife, and quickly chops an onion. His movements are efficient and ruthless. I can imagine him taking that knife and stabbing it through my heart with the same efficiency.

He wouldn't, of course.

I'd bleed on the rug.

It would be an inconvenience, and Dragos abhors an inconvenience.

"You are lurking," he says without looking up from his task.

I slip into the light. "I wasn't lurking, but I was surprised to find you here."

"Why is that, *dragostea mea*?"

My love. I know what it means now, and yet I preferred it when I didn't know the meaning, honestly. It's just a mockery of everything I once believed in now.

One thing I do know about Dragos is that his sex drive is insatiable, and he hasn't been exhausting it with me.

It's way too easy for me to think of him, out at some function where he sees a waitress. Twenty, pretty, innocent.

I would never have suspected he'd want anyone but

me at first. I interpreted our physical connection as love for him, just as it was for me.

I saw it as the beautiful tapestry, woven before our time on earth. Magical and fated. We were meant to meet that day; it was written in the stars. Why would I question it?

That's what I told myself.

But there was a loose thread, and I could see it, even then. I didn't pull it. I didn't even want to get near it.

But now, as he's grown distant and I've grown more unhappy, I've begun to pull at the thread, and now it's unraveled everything. I can't see the beautiful picture of us that I once did. I'm suspicious of everything he does, of all of his motives.

As quickly as I fell for him, as quickly as I leaped into that fantasy of us, I've destroyed it by asking the questions I refused to ask before.

Now I let myself wonder about his life before me. Maybe I'm not his first wife? He's never really said. I never really asked. I thought that meant I was the first for certain, but the longer I live with him the less I know him. The less certain I am.

Maybe this is something he does every few years. Find some young, dumb creature, seduce her, shower her with jewels and clothes, then trade her in for a new one.

If that's true, then what I can't understand is why he married me.

I thought he loved me. That's the very sad thing. I thought that because I loved him, he loved me, and it never occurred to me that it might not be true, even though he didn't say the words.

I thought he was showing me every time he touched

me. I thought the diamond ring he slipped on my finger when we were naked, in his infinity pool on the roof of his penthouse in Singapore, was the evidence. I thought it was love, the way he looked at me that first night. I convinced myself I was different. Why would he keep me with him all day every day from that moment on if it weren't?

But he's never said he loves me; I just decided he did.

So much of this relationship has been in my head, in my heart. I can see myself now for the fool I was. I saw a dangerous man with tattoos, and wanted to believe he would have a heart of gold. I saw a man who was aloof, mysterious and decided I could decode him, never allowing myself to believe there was nothing before behind that hardness.

I saw a field of red flags and decided they were roses. Because it was what I wanted, what I craved. I wanted to mold this man into the fantasy I desired, but you cannot reshape a mountain.

Only in the last six months did I start to question it, and to my shame it was because he wasn't paying attention to me. I could accept all of it—the mystery surrounding his work, his past and his feelings. That sex was a replacement for discussions of emotion or romance. Gifts instead of words of love.

I could accept it all, as long as I was sure he belonged to me.

As long as his obsessive attention insulated me, I could accept the fantasy. Believe it wholeheartedly.

I was happy until I realized he didn't feel the same way I did. Until I realized I couldn't simply rest on my belief that when I said *I love you*, and he responded with sex, it didn't mean for certain he loved me.

It was the distance that made me tug the thread.

The dissolution of the fantasy didn't mean I no longer loved him; it was only that I could suddenly see he didn't really love me.

Once I accepted that I started to realize…

It wouldn't last.

I'm scared of what that means. I'm scared to ask too many questions.

Part of me would rather wonder forever if he did love me, than know for certain he didn't.

And so I drive myself mad. Day after day.

"I'm surprised because in the last six months you've been home a handful of days and you certainly haven't cooked."

"I missed you." My heart hits my sternum, and lurches up into my throat. "I wanted to have dinner with you."

Why am I still so susceptible to him? Why did that make me hope?

I guess I should be relieved that even after all this time the pull to him is so powerful. If it wasn't I might hate the girl who left the charity event with him that night, a little more than I do now. That girl with her eyes full of stars, about to embark on her very first night of wildness.

But I still feel like her when I look at him sometimes. Especially when I look at his hands and remember all the wicked ways he's ever touched me.

Great sex isn't a marriage, alas.

If it were, we'd be the happiest people on the block.

I want to take what he's just said at face value, but the small, mean part of me that finds everything he does suspicious and painful simply can't.

It wasn't always like this. No, when we were first to-

gether it was fire and stars and beauty that obsessed me
in ways I could never explain. It made my art feel insuf-
ficient for the first time in my life. I'd never loved anything but art until him.

He told me I was beautiful; he told me my art was
special. That I was special. My parents are such lovely,
sweet people but have always been worried about me getting a big head or dreaming too much. Dragos made it
his mission to make me feel powerful, talented and particularly singular.

After a lifetime of taking in the importance of work
ethic and practicality, a man who showered me with
praise, gifts and affection like none of them were in short
supply, or anything I had to learn was thrilling.

But over the years it's changed. Slowly, over time, he's
gotten distant.

It feels like he's trying to make up for something. Apol-
ogizing to me by cooking for me.

Another woman.

I keep obsessing about that, I've been thinking it constantly. It sneaks into my dreams at night and I wake up
howling—more points for my theory that I'm going mad.
I ask myself why I even care.

If he's betrayed me then I should rejoice, honestly,
because it gives credibility to this deep dissatisfaction
I feel, to my resentment. If he's sleeping with someone
else I can leave him easily.

I let myself imagine it, those hands on someone else's
body.

It fills me with fury, and absurdly, makes me want to
grab him. Kiss him. Remind him.

We're the best. He and I. When we're together we

break furniture and sound barriers. He leaves bruises on me, I leave bite marks on him. We aren't like anyone else.

I don't have to have a long list of lovers to know that.

He loved that I was a virgin. He told me. He loved that he claimed me. That he was the only man to ever see my body, to ever touch it. He recited poetry about it while he thrust deep inside me. The idea that it hadn't actually meant anything, or that my inexperience might have actually bored him made me want to die now.

Or maybe kill him.

I might be more likely to stab him than he is to stab me, if I'm honest. I'm almost certain I'm being figurative.

"Did you?" I ask. "Miss me?"

"Yes, though if you're going to be unpleasant I might revise my opinion." He says all this in the same smooth voice he's said everything else in.

"Have you been working on a big project or something?" I ask.

Apostolis Enterprises is a Death Star–level conglomerate. It's not a moon; it's a giant megacorporation coming to kill you.

It keeps him busy and that's understandable. Maybe it's something to do with that.

"No," he says. "Nothing new."

I feel certain he's goading me with that. I move into the room and walk behind him, sliding my fingertips over the black marble. "I think I'd like to go visit my parents."

"I don't have time to take you to America right now."

I stop. "I didn't ask you to come with me."

"You aren't going alone."

"Don't be unhinged, Dragos." I frown. "I managed to travel the world without you when I was much younger."

"Now you're my wife, Cassandra Apostolis, and that puts you at risk." There was a dark flame in his eyes that rose up suddenly and it set me on my back foot. "It's not safe for you to travel without me."

"I'm not your prisoner!"

"When do you want to go, perhaps I can arrange a security team for you."

"I don't want to bring a massive security team with me to Idaho. This is silly. They live in a small town, nothing is going to happen."

"You're naive," he snarls, and then turns back to his cooking. "Go upstairs. I've left a dress for you for dinner, and some other gifts."

My stomach feels sour with suspicion and anger now and in spite of all that, my heart beats faster when he says that because it reminds me of the earliest days of our marriage. It reminds me of how things were when I thought these kinds of gestures were love.

That he showered me with designer dresses and jewelry and flowers because it was how he showed me the depth of his feeling.

But the trouble with a man whose wallet has no bottom is that spending money means nothing to him. That took me a long time to figure out. I'm firmly middle-class. Money means something to me, and it always has. Every dollar comes from someone's labor. I used to calculate how many hours of work it would take for my dad to pay for something Dragos gave to me.

I stopped because the answer was too depressing.

Over the years the meaning of money has shifted to me too, and I don't like that. It's like I've forgotten something else about myself. That girl who believed in hard work, in sacrifice. My parents were always so supportive. I wanted to be an artist, and even though they're practical people to their souls they supported me in that as long as I was serious in the career path.

As long as I went to school.

So I worked for that. And then I dropped it like it was nothing so I could hold onto him.

Still I find myself doing his bidding now, out of curiosity more than anything else. I go back up the stairs, but to my room this time, not the attic.

We have separate rooms. In the early days of our marriage that really didn't mean anything. My room was a glorified closet. I kept my belongings there, but I kept my body in bed with Dragos.

The room is just so pretty; I've always thought so. I have a view of a meadow and trees, and I used to find it soothing. Now I think about escaping.

I walk to the four-poster bed and touch the dress he left there. Gorgeous and very brief. He likes me to wear as little as possible. I like to wear as little as possible for him. Driving him mad with my body is my power in the relationship. Of course, he drives me equally mad with his.

When it comes to sex, we're aligned. It's what brought us together after all.

It's a green velvet that will hug my curves, and there are very high heels to go with it. Along with several jewelry boxes, and elaborate, see-through undergarments. I put it on, because this might be the last night I do something like this for him.

I put it on because no matter what, I'm still his wife. *Right now* I'm his wife.

My hands tremble as I dress, adrenaline building inside of me. I put on makeup. I style my hair. I want him to react to me. I want to feel like I used to. I want him to feel like he used to.

When I go downstairs he's finished with dinner, and is nowhere to be seen, but I know where I'll find him. I walk through the kitchen, the dining area, to the terrace at the back of the estate house, where I find Dragos, sitting at an elaborately set table, candles all around.

For a moment I question everything. For a moment the flicker of a candle flame is more like a gaslight.

Am I being dramatic?

Am I making up issues because I'm lonely?

Am I spoiled and entitled now?

Do I just have regrets because of my own choices?

Dragos didn't ask me to leave university; I chose to do that. I was swept up in our passion and I couldn't imagine caring about anything as much as I did him.

I threw myself into the fire.

But over the years it has begun to feel more like a trap. He's become more restrictive with travel, included me less. But I put the handcuffs on.

The realization makes me want to try. Why am I planning to leave him without trying to reach him first?

The dinner he made is lovely, the dress I'm wearing is beautiful. He's never said he doesn't love me, I'm the one that decided because he doesn't communicate his feelings that I've been wrong about them.

The truth is, he did marry me.

It has to mean something.

I move to the chair across from him and I sit down, my hands in my lap, clutched together tightly. "Thank you, I'm sorry I was in a bad mood earlier."

"It's nothing," he says, waving his hand.

It wasn't nothing, but I wasn't going to press that issue. "So you aren't working on anything new, but has work been chaotic?" I ask.

"No more than usual, you can't run an empire the size of mine and not run into chaos."

I nod. "Of course not. Property management or manufacturing or…"

"All of it," he says, nearly dismissive. "It's very dull, Cassandra. Have you been painting?"

I think of the grim paintings upstairs. "Yes. But I don't like them."

"You're too hard on yourself. If you wish to have an exposition I could arrange it."

He could rent out a room and let me hang my paintings there. It's not a real gallery. Not something I earned with talent. Those lines get oh-so-blurry when you marry a billionaire.

What is this life I'm in? I can hardly fathom it. Sometimes it feels like a dream. Not in a fun way, just in a surreal way. Like I can't connect the dots between where I started and how I got here, even though I remember every single thing that's happened along the way full well.

"I'll think about it," I say, because I really will. I'm not ungrateful for the offer. He asked about my painting. It almost feels like him caring. "I'm not sure my work is ready."

He looks utterly confounded by this. "You can have it if you like."

"That's not how things work," I say. "You need to earn them. What if no one wants to see my paintings? What if they're terrible? And how will I know if you rent out a room for me?"

He looks even more confused. "I don't understand what it would matter. You can have an exhibition and people will come. Not everyone will like it, but some will, so it goes."

He is so practical in his way, even when he's being extravagant and it's one of the things I've always liked about him, actually. I worry about so many little things, and he just cuts right to the heart of the matter.

He isn't wrong in some ways.

"I just would feel silly. Having a vanity gallery I only got because my husband paid for it."

"I don't understand this, but if that's how you feel."

If he's shocked he doesn't show it. But we don't talk. We take meals together. He tells me that I'm beautiful. We make love. Except, it's not even making love. It's ferocious and fearsome, and the passion between us hasn't dimmed.

Except it has. Lately. He hasn't been home. I am accustomed to walking around our home in clothing that barely covers my body because Dragos likes it. And yet, he hasn't even been around to appreciate it recently. I look at him and my heart starts to beat faster. So fast that it's painful. So fast that I think it might burst altogether through my chest.

"Just let me think about it," I say. I take a sip of the wine he poured for me and then stare down into it, pondering. "So, my parents."

"I will have to make an arrangement with the security team."

"I don't want a team."

"I will not allow you to go if you don't take them."

I look at him and I feel a challenge rise up inside of me. "Will you lock me in my room?"

"I won't give you use of my jet."

"Oh, noooo, will I have to fly commercial? Economy? I wasn't born with a silver spoon in my mouth."

He looks up at me and something flashes in his eyes that chills me to my bones. "Neither was I, *dragostea mea*. It was a silver dagger."

Silence settles between us and I twirl my glass. "Was it? Does that mean you're actually ready to tell me something about your childhood?"

He lifts a brow. "You say that as if there was a time I didn't tell you about it. You know many things about my childhood."

"I suppose, though it seems superficial." I never push him, but now I feel I have nothing to lose. So I am.

"My parents are dead, what is there to say?"

"Some people would maybe have something to say *about* their parents."

"I am not some people."

That was an understatement. "I understand that, it's just that I don't know anything about your life and that's weird."

"It has never bothered you."

I look down, then back up at him. "It has, actually, I just never said anything. You've been to my parents' house. You've met my siblings. You know all about the schools I went to and how I got teased for being a nerd, and how I had a hard time making friends because I'd tell them they were unserious for not having goals for their future. You know about the time I planned a big sixteenth birthday party at the bowling alley and only two people came, and my mom put on bowling shoes and paid them to play my favorite band over the loudspeaker and embarrassed the hell out of me, bowling and dancing, and also saved the whole entire day. You know me. You're like a locked box."

"Has it ever occurred to you that I give you nothing more or less than what is good for you to know?"

I have no idea how to interpret what he's just said. "Dragos…"

"The night you met me you went home with a stranger. You were happy to let that man have you in every way he wanted. You have been happy with that for four years, we do not need to change it. We live this life, here, and that is sufficient. The past does not matter."

"I'm not even involved in your present. We used to travel, at least. We haven't gone anywhere for eighteen months. I've been stuck in this house other than the odd event and then…and then six months ago you stopped coming home. You do all these things without me now and you're acting like nothing has changed."

"And somehow you think my childhood is the key to all this?" He laughed, a booming crack of a sound that was divorced from humor. "Yes, *drogostea mea*, my father did not hug me and my mother was a drunk and so now I have trouble with emotional intimacy."

I can't tell if he's joking or not. "Well, is that true?"

"My father was a hard man, that's true. He made me into a hard man, that is also true, but I have no sadness about it. No regret. It is what had to be in order to make me the man who could carry on the family legacy, and so I have done it. My mother…she does not matter. She did not raise me."

I huff a laugh. "Some would argue that suggests she matters all the more, or at the very least it indicates that you might have some issues around that."

"You once told me you were too middle-class for some event I took you to. I suspect you are too middle-class here as well. Issues. Those are middle-class."

I nearly snort. "Hardly. Everyone in the middle class is too busy working to go to therapy. But we do talk about things with our friends."

"Friends may yet be another bastion of the middle class, I fear."

This conversation is frustrating, but I feel like I've actually learned some things about him, though I sense him getting irritated. Normally, when I sense his irritation I pull back. It's one reason I never get this far.

"How was your father hard?"

"He was Romanian."

"That doesn't mean anything to me, I'm American. You're the only Romanian I know."

"You have met many since marrying me."

"You know what I mean."

"Perhaps I don't."

"If you can't even tell me about your father I'm going to assume you have some deep trauma associated with him and you're too scared to tell me about it."

My heart is racing and I fear I've gone too far, and when he looks at me with flat, ice-blue eyes, I know that I have.

"You think I'm afraid of trauma? What is it you think might happen? Do you think I will weep, Cassandra, is that it? Do you think I fear emotion?"

"S-sometimes."

"Let me put your mind at ease. I do not speak of my life before you because of your own delicate sensibilities. But if you are truly curious, I am happy to tell you about the last time I saw my father." He leaned back in his chair and laced his fingers together behind his head. "The last time I saw him he was standing in front of the family estate, and then suddenly he fell, and a large pool of blood spread out beneath his head. He was killed right before my eyes by an assassin's bullet. And you question why I have security."

I sit in stunned silence. I don't know what to say to him. I don't understand what he's just told me.

"I…"

"Do you wish to give me condolences?"

"Yes. I'm sorry. I… Of course I didn't know that happened to you. How old were you?"

"Sixteen." He stands up and pushes his chair in. "It was not the first death I ever witnessed, though, so I was not terribly upset by it. When I was eight I found my mother's body in the kitchen, though I think my father was responsible for that."

"Dragos…"

"Do you feel better for knowing that, Cassandra? Does it make you feel as if we have the intimacy you so crave?"

"I…"

"If you expect that it will make me emotional to relive this, I am sorry to disappoint you. People live, and they die. It is a brutal thing but there is no reason to remain tortured by what is."

"Your mother…"

"My father wasn't a good man." A smile curves his lips. "I cannot lie to you. When I saw him there, his eyes lifeless, I said a prayer to St. Isaac for justice to be done. For my father that will mean burning in hell, and I take joy in that." He pauses for a moment. "This does not disturb me, though I can see it does you. I will leave you to finish your night in peace."

Then he turns and leaves me alone.

Again.

The sadness mingles with fury inside me and I know one thing for sure.

I can't try anymore.

CHAPTER THREE

I SPEND THREE hours crying in my room, and I hate myself for it. Sitting on the bed in the dress he bought me weeping like an infant because…

Because he saw his father die.

Because his father killed his mother, and Dragos had once been a boy who had found her.

Because he used it to hurt me, rather than using it to tell me something real about himself.

Because I don't know him.

I don't.

All this pain, all these scars, and he acts like they don't touch him. Like they mean nothing. I can't figure out if he's being honest, or if this is all how he protects himself, but I don't know if I can possibly bear the weight of that unknown anymore.

I wanted to unlock him. I wanted to find my way to him but he doesn't want to let me and I find that so unbearable to face.

Maybe I should fight harder but everything feels hopeless tonight. Like I'm wandering through a maze and whenever I think I just might have found the way out, I hit another wall.

I'm beginning to think he isn't a maze after all. Just a trap.

I stand up, and I walk to the mirror. I wipe the mascara trails off my cheeks, because *Good God, Cassandra, get it together.* I lift my dark hair up off my neck. I'm sweaty and upset and the air feels cool on my skin. I look at myself. I really, really look at myself. At the stranger I've become.

I think I wouldn't mind her so much if she wasn't so lonely.

But I feel like there's a surging channel between myself and Dragos and I can't swim across it.

I'm angry then, so angry, all mixed together with my hurt because we were really something.

We were.

That first moment we met was magical. Like a miracle I hadn't even known to pray for, and instead of taking that magic and making more with it, he'd wrapped his fist around it and trapped us both, stagnant and locked in this tower where we can never, ever get closer to each other.

I can't leave this alone tonight.

I can't let it go.

I leave my room and I make my way down the hall.

I don't knock on his study door, because if this house is the only place I'm allowed, then I refuse to act like part of it might not be available to me when I want it. I refuse to act like *he* might not be available to me. Even though I know he feels differently.

Dragos is in charge. We both know that.

Made even more difficult by the fact that we like power games in bed. We play lots of games, but in some of them he's my master and I surrender everything to him. Sometimes, he puts a collar on me and it makes me feel good, because it makes me feel like I'm his.

But there are times that it bleeds into our lives, and it picks at my own insecurities. When we met I was nothing more than a waitress. He took my arm, he led me out of there and he made me his. But he is the one with money.

He is the one with power.

I feel that every single day. The wedding ring has become a manacle.

He is sitting behind a wide black desk. Polished, gleaming. Just like him.

Like we didn't just have an earth-shattering conversation. Like he didn't just tell me about childhood trauma I could never have guessed at.

Perhaps I should have.

Perhaps my mistake has been thinking he's a man with a rough surface, who must have humanity beneath.

Maybe he's rough all the way down.

His tattooed hands are pressed down on the surface of the desk, and he is focused on something in front of him. He looks up when I walk in.

"Yes?"

"I need to talk to you."

I love him. That's the thing that enrages me then. I want him. That's the thing that hurts.

If I could only despise him. Then I would've left him. I would've left him six months into the marriage if I would've known what was going to be, as long as I didn't love him. But the problem is I do love him. With every fiber of my being, with every part of my soul. And I try to tell myself that it can't be love because it isn't like we behave the way that a normal couple does.

But I wouldn't know normal. I know Dragos. And that's it. He is my only experience of men. He is my only experience of love. I want to leap over his desk and… Maybe strangle him. Maybe make love to him. I'm not entirely sure.

The feeling is too powerful to keep contained inside of me, though. I am finding it nearly impossible to breathe past it.

"I thought you might need your rest tonight after the conversation we had on the terrace." He says this with his head tilted to the side, and someone who doesn't know him observing the scene might mistake it for concern. Compassion.

I know him, however. Which means I know it's neither of those things.

He does such a fantastic impersonation of a human man. And yet, in his deepest heart, he is more machine than anything else.

The way he took me to bed that first night and held me. The way he looked at me whenever he bought me a new dress. The way he proposed, with rough desperation in his voice, as if he didn't understand what was happening between us either. Like I wasn't the only one who was inexperienced.

If only that could change the way that I feel about him. It hasn't yet. It probably never will.

"I'd like to know why you said that and then walked away. Why you didn't even give me a chance to respond."

"I didn't need your response," he said.

"Why?" I ask, my tone filled with desperation and I'm not even in the mood to hide it.

"Why would I need it?"

"When people marry they share things. When they care for each other they talk. I want to be there for you and you won't let me."

"I do not require you to be there for me in that way. I don't need anyone to do that for me. If I had needed it, I would have told you so."

Is he getting what he needs from other places? Other women? I'm undone by all of this, and I can't even pick which thing wounds me the most. That he might have betrayed me. That he doesn't care about me. That he doesn't share with anyone, or that he shares with someone who isn't me. That I might want to stay, that I definitely need to leave.

I just don't know.

"But I'm your wife," I say.

"Yes. You are my wife. And you are a very good one. Very beautiful."

I reach my breaking point then. All of my hurt, all of my regret, my pain, my everything wells up inside of me and explodes. "Is that all I am to you?" I'm yelling. In the sacred space of his office, I am *yelling* at this man. Who is fearsome and frightening, who just spoke to me of smiling over his father's dead body and yet I don't care.

Because I need to say this. I need to say what I've been holding back. I need him to hear me. I need him to see me.

"That is all a wife needs to be," he says.

"No. I'm not *a wife*. I'm Cassandra. And I'm an artist. And I had dreams once, Dragos, and they were not to simply rattle around your house waiting for you to come to my bed."

All the lies I let myself believe crash through me. Back

in the beginning with him it seemed like I wouldn't need art school when every moment with him was a canvas of inspiration.

Now all I have are canvases filled with black and gray.

"I told you I'd buy you a gallery."

"*I* told *you* it isn't the same! You hear the words that I'm saying, but they don't mean anything to you. You don't know me, you don't understand me. I've given you my whole life story and you still don't know. The information is just sitting inside of you like facts written on note cards but you haven't…learned what that means to me. How it makes me who I am."

"You are hysterical. You know full well that we often do not make it to bed."

"But that can't be all there is."

Maybe I'm the one who isn't being fair. Maybe I'm the one who's changing the rules, but I don't think so. I'm sure that even the sex used to be different. I'm sure of it.

"What is it you expect?" His voice has gone hard.

The word is on the tip of my tongue, but I'm almost afraid to say it. Still, I know this is it. This is the end. There's no point holding anything back. Not now.

"Love. I would like love. For you to say it as well as show it, and it can't just be…it can't just be gifts and orgasms, because that's not the sum total of a relationship. Of a marriage. If you wanted a mistress then you shouldn't have married me."

"Cassandra. That is not what marriage is to me. And I thought that we agreed on this. That what we have is all that is needed."

"I'm telling you that it isn't."

"Are you?"

I lose my temper then, and I do move. And I find myself reaching across his desk. I grab hold of his black tie—why is he wearing a tie at home?—and I pull him toward me.

Our faces are nearly pressed together. "I'm unhappy."

"Why?" he growls. "Look at this place that you have. You're ungrateful."

"Yes. The prison is very nice."

"This is not prison," he says. "You know nothing of prison. You're having a temper tantrum, and I find it unseemly."

"I don't care what you find seemly. I am not an object. I'm not a mistress. You *married* me."

"So I did."

"Are you having an affair?"

He looks furious. Offended, even, and I can't say I've ever seen Dragos *offended*. "You ask me this?"

"You've barely been home for months."

"First you object to the fact that there is sex in our relationship, and now you are acting as if you would be wounded if I gave that sex to someone else. Which is it?"

He was scratching at the inconsistencies I was already enraged at in myself.

"It can be all of those things, actually. Because most people are complicated. But you… You are desperately simple, do you know that? I feel that you fancy yourself very important because you have a lot of money and you are constantly working, and everybody seeks out your opinion on things, but you don't do anything except work and…"

"I know full well how I spend my time. And because you have given such a well-stated opinion on me, allow me to remind you of who you are. A waitress. You say you're an artist, where's your gallery? The hallway of your husband's home does not signify. You were serving champagne to people with more money than you would have ever seen, and I elevated you."

"You elevated me to the obscurity of the top floor of your house," I say, his cruelty nearly taking my breath away, but I refuse to let him see it. I refuse.

"You hate me so much now," he says, his eyes filled with a strange sort of wonder, and I think for a moment maybe regret.

A moment passes between us, and his eyes glint. "You still want me, though," he says, and I want to kill him.

"I don't know that I do. You haven't touched me for two weeks."

He grips the back of my head and holds me steady. And then he's kissing me. And it reminds me far too much of that first night. Because I am lost in it. It's not natural. We've been married for four years. We've had each other countless times, and I'm on the verge of leaving, so there's no way this should capture me the way that it does.

Dragos has always been my form of addiction. His kiss is my drug. And I can't turn away from him. Not now.

His kiss turns carnal, and he pulls me on top of his desk, sweeping everything else aside.

He strips his clothes off. It's so rare that he does this, so rare that I get to see his body. He is fond of taking me while I'm naked and he's nearly fully clothed. I know that it has something to do with power. Control. Because he is nothing if not a man who values his dominance.

But this time he gets naked. This time, I can see every line on his body. All of his scars. All of his tattoos.

Stories that he has never told me about his life, but that I can trace with my fingertips.

I don't know him. That makes me want to cry. Because I never will. This is the last time, I realize, as he pushes my dress up past my hips—the dress I know he bought to take off of me—and claims me in one smooth stroke. As he takes me to new heights, each stroke of him within me a revelation.

It's the last time. I know that it is. Because I am going to leave. He doesn't care. He can look at my pain and return that pain with cruelty. He doesn't love me.

And I have to go.

Some of what he said is true, and it's my own fault. I've surrendered to him, utterly and completely. But this ends now. It has to end.

I arch up against him, and cry out my pleasure, and at the same time I want to weep. He shudders, spilling himself inside of me. I look around the room, and I see the destruction left behind by our passion.

My life is destruction. I am in the debris that surrounds us now.

I move away from him. "Good night."

"Have you nothing else to say?"

"No," I say. "I have nothing else to say. This is all we are. It's all we will ever be."

"You say that as if it's a bad thing."

"It is. It is, Dragos. How do you not know that?" I want to scream at him, but I know I could do that until I'm hoarse and it wouldn't change a thing. He sees the world in this one, intractable way and he won't let me reach him.

"What is love? What is it you think should pass between married people? I cannot understand you. This is passion. We have had it from the first moment we met, and it is unlike anything I've ever experienced in my life."

He has never said anything like that to me. There's something desperate in his voice, and I find that...

No. I can't let him appeal to me. I can't let it affect me.

"I only know that it isn't this."

I leave my clothes. I leave him. I go to my bedroom, and I wonder if he's going to follow me. He doesn't, of course.

Of course he doesn't.

I let myself sleep, and then in the morning, when I wake up I search around the house, and I discover that he's gone.

I pack one bag. I don't want his clothes. I don't want all of the things that marked me as Dragos's wife. I leave my wedding rings on the dresser. I find some clothes that I brought with me into the relationship. A pair of black leggings and a sweatshirt. A baseball cap. I leave my computer, my phone. They could track me. I know that. But for all that Dragos is controlling, I can't imagine that he's going to pick me up and bodily carry me back to this house. The truth is, the lock and key have been in my possession this entire time. I'm the one the let myself become a prisoner. I did it to make him happy.

I did it to preserve the relationship. But now... I'm done.

I regret that I'm going to have to take the car that he bought me. The car that I never drive. I never drive it because he never lets me go anywhere. I don't want to take anything extravagant.

I stand there and have a momentary fantasy about going to France. Living in a garret, waiting tables and painting in my spare time. I won't need any men. I'll stay by myself. I'll focus on my art. I'll make myself happy. I'll be poor, but I'll be… Myself.

That's what I haven't been for a very long time. Myself.

I open up the door, and for a moment I'm shocked that it isn't locked. But of course it isn't.

All of the barriers were in my mind all along.

He has security outside the house, but there's always a shift change. I wait until then.

I close the door behind me. The silence out in our driveway is deafening. It's a gated house. We have security. Perhaps I won't be able to get out of the gate. That's possible.

I open the garage and get into my little blue sports car. It's a beautiful car. Maybe I'll sell it. Maybe it will fund the beginning of my new life in France. Maybe it will fund my croissant habit. Maybe I'll buy canvases and oil paint with the money.

A parting gift seems fair. But I really don't want anything else from him.

I hold my breath when I pull the car up to the gate, but it opens for me. And as I drive away I take my first full breath in four years.

CHAPTER FOUR

I WON'T LIE, I'm somewhat surprised when he doesn't come after me. And yet, it also feels like confirmation. Maybe this was what I was afraid of all this time. Not that he had me locked in, a prisoner serving a life sentence. Not that he would hunt me down in the streets.

That he wouldn't come for me at all.

Maybe he's moved a new woman into our home. It's shocking how easily I can imagine that. His hands, his mouth, on someone else.

Someone who's willing to play his games and live by his rules.

If it's regret I feel knotting my stomach, I do my best not to acknowledge it.

I stay at a hotel in London. I work on selling my car for some cash. I find a little attic apartment in France and laugh because *I'm* putting myself in the attic now.

After three days, while I'm preparing to board a train to Paris, I call my mother.

"Cassie," she says. "I've been worried about you. I haven't heard from you."

I smile at the wall, because I want to sound like I'm fine. "I... I separated from Dragos."

There is deafening silence on the other end.

"That's probably for the best," my mother says after a good while, and her certainty about that hurts.

"Do you think so?"

"He's very…cold." My mother is quiet for a moment. "Your father and I never wanted to interfere, and really, we couldn't. You were so in love with him. But it wasn't like you. I imagined you with…a nice guy who might want to bring you back here."

Of course my mother didn't imagine me with a man like Dragos. I'd never even imagined a man like Dragos existed.

I see flashes of the two of us together. Of our passion. He isn't cold physically. But in so many other ways he is.

I try to imagine what it was like watching me fling myself into my relationship with him, like nothing else on earth existed, but I just end up missing that feeling and I hate myself for it.

"It just wasn't working," I say.

I've been back to visit my family since the wedding. Three times. And Dragos went with me every time. I was never allowed to travel home without at least his security detail, but him preferably.

I know that it bothers my family, that they never were able to see me alone.

I know my father has been worried. And who can blame him? I brought home a rich man who rarely smiles, has tattoos all over his body and never lets me out of his sight. I'm actually aware of how it looked, I just wanted so badly for it to be okay that I pushed all of that down, and I never invited any conversations with either of my parents about it.

"He's never hurt me," I say.

"That is a very low bar, Cassie," my mother says softly.

I want to shout at her that *I love him*. Can't they understand that? It was so big I couldn't do anything but rearrange my whole life around it. It was love. It was love and it was real and it changed me.

But what's the point of defending something that I'm killing? I can't figure it out. Why I still feel the need to defend the choices that I made.

Why I need to hold onto how real it was.

I suppose because if it was never real there's no point in me being scarred and bloody inside over it.

"I've decided to move to Paris," I say.

"You're not coming back home?" I can tell she's disappointed and that makes guilt twist in my chest.

But I can't do that. It's for small, petty reasons. But I can't go back. Because I was this overachiever. I was going to *make it*.

I didn't date. I didn't go out. I threw everything into my art and a perfect GPA so that I could get the scholarships I needed, so that I could leave Idaho and travel the world and not be so stuck.

I thought that I was better than the other girls in my hometown who were going to stay there and marry their high school sweethearts. I'd had goals and aspirations that reached beyond the main street of that little place.

I can't face going back with my tail between my legs.

My own ego makes me want to laugh bitterly now.

I would've been better off marrying a Kyle or a Josh. That's the honest truth.

I flew too close to the sun and I got my wings burned off for my sins. I understand all too well now why some people never want to leave their homes. Why they don't want to reach high.

The fall is a bitch.

I'm still falling by the time I arrived in Paris, and take up residence in the small apartment with a window that faces the Seine. It is small, but the sort of place I dreamed about as a child. The building is ornate, with glorious scrollwork, and the walls inside are robin's-egg blue and gold.

I eat bread and cheese and drink the most glorious wine. It is a fantasy I had often when I was in high school. A small nook in Paris to live the romantic life of an art-ist, comfortable and cozy, glamorous in its simplicity.

And yet for me, it is not the Paris I came to that first time.

It doesn't feel as bright or beautiful or glorious, no matter how many opulent galleries I visit. No matter how many architecture tours I take, or how many designer shops I go into.

It is like a different city altogether.

I spend a week or so pondering that. Was it really more beautiful the first time I came here, or was I just with Dragos? Was I still seeing the world through rose-colored glasses that are shattered now?

I remember it all too well.

I'm giddy. Because not only do I have a boyfriend who touches me in ways that intoxicate me, he's… Obsessed with me.

It feels naughty, and I feel a small amount of guilt over the pleasure I take it. He's in his thirties, and if the girls that I hang out with at university knew, they would retch and gag about *age gaps* and how *problematic* it is. They would shout at me about *power dynamics*.

I love the power dynamics.

He makes me feel like he holds the whole world in the palm of his tattooed hand, like he could take care of anything I needed. Like I didn't have to try so hard. He didn't know me, he just saw me and wanted me. Not for what I could do, and he wasn't drawn to me because I'd worked so hard to get where I was. He just was. Like it was magic.

Every boy my age around me in class now looks so insipid by comparison. They wouldn't know how to do the things Dragos does to me in bed.

But it isn't just the sex, though it's incredible.

It's everything. He loves to take me shopping. He takes me to gorgeous restaurants. He shows me off. Like he's proud of me. He's a very important man. The owner of a major conglomerate that has its hands in nearly every industry on earth.

Another thing my friends would be horrified by. There are no such things as ethical billionaires, after all.

But there's something about even that which makes it all feel that much more amazing. The truth is, he can have any woman he wants just because of his money. He can have any woman he wants because of his raw physical appeal. He can have any woman he wants and he wants me.

What am I supposed to do with that? How am I supposed to fight that? And why would I want to?

Secretly, deep down, I've always wanted to be special. I've accepted that I have to work hard to get what I want, but part of me has always wished someone would look at

me and see me. See the hard work, the talent, and just…
recognize me and lift me up.

He has.

No, it's not my art, but he seems to see me. I've been
so focused on this, all my life. I ignored men, I ignored
any desire for romance and now I feel like I could drown
myself in this feeling and be happy forever.

When he asked me if I want to go to Paris for the week-
end, I imagine a long train ride, and instead, we take his
private jet. We stay in the most gorgeous penthouse that
I never could've even imagined. It overlooks the Eiffel
Tower, we have private dining on the rooftop and the
first night he draws me a bath with rose-scented water.

I sink into it, and he sits behind the tub, lathering up
my hair and washing it for me. I look up at him, and he
smiles, and I'm certain that no one has ever been this
happy.

I imagine explaining this to my mother.

I haven't told my mom and dad about Dragos.

What is there to say? *Hi, Mom and Dad, I was waiting tables at an event and I met a man who told me I was
pretty so I fell into bed with him without asking his name
and let him take my virginity, and now I'm in the world's
most delicious whirlwind courtship?*

Now I'm rethinking everything I ever thought I knew
about myself and planning a future that can't actually
happen because there's no way a man like him will ever
marry me.

But I don't care. I let him take me to Paris and I'm letting him give me a bath.

Letting him wash my hair.

"I was not looking for this," he says, a note of wonder in his voice.

"Well, I wasn't either."

"No?"

I laugh. "No. I was a virgin, Dragos. Men were not on my mind. They still aren't. It's just you."

I wonder if I've said too much, but he doesn't look upset. In fact, he looks pleased.

"What are you going to do after university?"

"I don't know. I've spent so long working so hard. To get the scholarship, to keep my place in this really competitive program. I haven't had time to think about what I want to do after."

"You're an artist."

"Yes. Well, I want to be."

"That's not how being an artist works, my Cassandra. You don't need school to make you an artist. That's something you find in your soul, I am told. Having no soul of my own, it's very difficult to say if that's true." He lifts me out of the tub, carries me to the chaise lounge where he sits behind me and combs his fingers through my hair, braiding it with deft skill. I want to tell him I know he has a soul. It has to be a beautiful one. Because it captured me from the first.

Surely, surely, I never could have fallen for a man who didn't.

I *am* falling for him. I have to admit that to myself as he holds me, his hands gentle in my hair.

He delights in showing me around Paris, especially when he finds out that I've never been there. He has the Louvre closed down so that we can tour it just the two of us, and I know that I should feel guilty for such extravagance, but it's magical. We eat croissants, and he brushes crumbs off my face like I'm cute and it's not embarrassing. Then he takes me back to the penthouse, and makes love to me until neither of us can breathe.

I brush his dark hair out of his eyes, and stare at him. "I think I might love you," I say.

I wait for the ceiling to fall down on me. The whole world. He doesn't run. Instead, he smiles at me. "Do you really?"

"Yes."

"That is a gift, my Cassandra."

He doesn't say he loves me, but he doesn't leave me.

I let that memory fade away. He didn't love me. I wanted it to be love. I feel silly with how much I wanted it to be.

I'm angry that Paris feels gray.

"He's a stupid man," I shout into the emptiness of the apartment.

I buy canvases, so many canvases. I put minimal furniture in the room. Because I decide that it's going to be a place devoted to my art.

Unfortunately, I only have one muse. I spend all day every day painting my husband.

The honed sinew of his bicep, a close-up, detailed rendition of his hands, on my throat. The tattoos, the strength.

His hands digging into my hips. The hard cut of his jaw, all that black stubble, his chin, his mouth. Close-up pieces, and no one would be able to identify the muse.

But I know.

After weeks of this, I accept it. He's all I can paint, and I think I have to paint him if I want to even begin to wash out the memory of him.

I do an interpretation of him as *The Thinker*, his head in his hands, his scarred, tattooed body in living color rather than white marble.

It's precision work, and yet I find I have no difficulty painting him from memory.

It's not an ode to love. It's an exorcism. Dragos Apostolis is my demon. My personal monster. But I don't only need to paint him to remove him from me. If I paint him, then maybe I'll understand him. If I paint him, maybe I'll have power over *him*.

I have so many memories of him, of us.

I wish that I could look at those memories objectively, but I just feel so sad for myself. For how badly I wanted to believe in him. For how badly I wanted to believe in us.

A kiss in front of the Eiffel Tower, engagement in Singapore, the wedding in Romania. The honeymoon in the Swiss Alps. I can see his face in those moments, all the times I thought he was giving me a look of love.

What *was* it?

That's why I have to paint him.

If I can look at that expression rendered in front of me, then maybe I'll be able to understand it.

But I'm still working on my tortured thinker. I've been trying to get the muscles on his thighs just right, and the black dragon he has tattooed there.

I know it intimately. I've traced it with my tongue.

I paint and paint, and when I leave I smell like turpentine and have blotches of color on my fingers and arms. I eat in one of two cafés just beneath the apartment, every single day. Every single day, I see the same man in line. He wears a tan trench coat, and a nice suit. His hair is light brown, his eyes the same color. He is none of the extremes of Dragos. With jet-black hair, cold ice-blue eyes and he looks at me in that very particular way.

He looks like the nice man my mom thinks I should have ended up with.

I feel nothing. I don't want to. I'm still married to Dragos, after all. He's ruined me for men.

There's a woman who sits at the window every day, and she smiles at me in a particular way, and I'm not interested in her either. Logically, I entertain the thought that if he's ruined me for men perhaps I should go on a date with a woman. But I can't even muster up interest for that based on novelty.

The realization I have in that moment is that he's going to have to become my ex-husband at some point, officially.

He is going to have to find me. He's going to have to send papers.

I don't want any of his money.

I smile politely at the woman, and at the man. I sit down with my pastry and my coffee. The man is the one who approaches me, and this doesn't surprise me, because men.

"Hi."

I'm surprised that he speaks English, and even more surprised to discover he's American.

"Hi," I say.

"I'm Luke. I've noticed you here every day. And I've heard you talking to the cashier so I knew that you were American."

"Yes. I am. Is my French that bad?"

He laughed. "Better than mine."

"Where you from?"

"California."

"Idaho. So… West Coast also, kind of."

He nods. I don't invite him to sit down.

"I'll probably see you here tomorrow."

"Yes," I say. "You will."

It wasn't bad talking to him. I get up and I bus my own table, then I walk out onto the street. A dark shape catches my eye, and I am immobilized. I look over quickly, but I don't see anything. I don't see anyone.

I swallow hard. It's not Dragos. He would never come for me himself. He would send one of his people anyway. It would never be him.

I walk quickly back into the apartment. I spend the rest of the day painting.

When I sleep, it's fitful. And filled with flashes of memory. Filled with Dragos.

I can see him clearly in my mind standing on a street corner in Paris. I wake up in a cold sweat, and I paint until the sun comes up. Then I go downstairs for my breakfast. Luke is there.

"Can I join you?" he asks.

"Yes," I say definitively. He sits down, and I push my mug back and forth. "I have to warn you," I say. "I'm married. I mean, I fully intend on divorcing him, but I just left."

He nods. "That's okay. I don't really know anyone here. So… If I could just know you, that would be nice."

It's the nicest thing someone could've said to me. I find out that he's twenty-five and has taken an internship here, and feels homesick. I tell him that I'm an artist, and he isn't dismissive at all. We laugh about the fact that I'm a cliché. An American in Paris working on my paintings.

He doesn't ask me about Dragos. I'm grateful for that, because it means that I can pretend. I can think about other things.

"Would you like to go out tonight? Just… For company. I don't expect anything."

He is so nice. "I would. Thank you. I'm… Going a little bit crazy cooped up in my apartment all day."

"Same. Anything I can do to help out a fellow American."

"Cue eagle screech," I say.

"I'm not going to do it. Everyone in here already hates us."

"True," I say.

I want to tell him that my soon-to-be ex-husband is Romanian, and do an impersonation of Dragos's grim voice as he monologues about large American chain stores and consumerism. Because it's something I always found funny, because he's a billionaire, so…whatever with the consumerism rant and also he married an American.

But I stop myself, because I don't actually want to think about Dragos. And I don't want to talk about him. I'm angry that I had a good memory of him. A thing that I used to find amusing.

"Are you all right, Cassie?" he asks.

I told him to call me Cassie. That's what everyone calls me back home. It's really only Dragos that insists on Cassandra. "Yes. Everything's fine. I'll… I'll see you tonight. I just live upstairs? But we can meet down here in front of the café."

"Great. Seven o'clock?"

"Perfect."

He leaves to go to work, and I stay seated for a minute. I feel just a little bit lighter. Just a little bit happier. I feel like maybe everything isn't ruined.

I'm not attracted to him. But I've met someone. Someone nice. Someone I can have a conversation with. After feeling like I was descending into madness for so long, it's a relief. Of course, spending the rest of the day working on my painting of Dragos pulls me back into a strange place. And by the time I'm on the street waiting for Luke I'm feeling edgy.

The streets are busy, but still, there is movement that catches my eye, and I look quickly. I'm sure that I see a man with black hair, wearing a black coat slip around the corner.

My nerves rattle.

Dragos.

No. It can't be. It can't be Dragos. I tell myself that repeatedly. But I become more and more anxious until Luke arrives with a small bunch of roses. "I know," he says. "But, I wanted to get them for you."

"That's very nice," I say.

Of course then I have to carry them for the whole evening, because I'm not about to invite him up to my apartment before we even eat. I'm not about to invite him up at all, not under any circumstances.

I couldn't even imagine.

Please come in, ignore all of the paintings of my naked ex-husband.

Yes, I am extremely horny, but not for you, for his jawline.

I wince. Thankfully, Luke doesn't notice.

The restaurant he chooses for dinner is lovely, modern. We are seated by the window. I'm a glass of wine deep in the conversation when the hair on my arm prickles. I look out the window, and I see him. Standing there across the street, his hands in his pockets. Looking right at me.

My jaw drops, my heart begins to race. A bus drives by, obscuring my view. And after it passes, he's gone.

"What is it?"

"I… I don't…"

"You look scared," he says.

"I'm not. I… I…" I shake my head. "I thought I saw someone I know. But they can't be here. They aren't in the country. It was just one of those uncanny things." I try to smile. "I'll slow down on the wine."

I try to calm myself down, and soon I find myself relaxing. Dinner is lovely. I learned more about Luke over the course of that dinner than I ever did about Dragos in the four years we were married. And I still don't want to see him naked. It's too soon. That's the thing.

Someday maybe I'll want to.

I think of all my paintings. I guess you can take the mad wife out of the attic but you can't take the madness out of the wife.

I've locked myself back in the attic so to speak. But I am trying.

When Luke and I leave the restaurant, I'm still carrying the roses, and I carry them in the hand closest to his so that there is no attempted hand-holding. If he notices this, he doesn't let on. He talks while we walk, and I'm overcome by that same sensation of being watched again.

I look over my shoulder, and I don't see anything. My heart starts to beat faster, and the one thing that begins to frighten me is I don't know that I've ever had a great instinct for whether or not I'm being watched. But what

I have always been in tune with is Dragos. The way that he looks at me, the way that it feels when he's near me.

No. I refuse to believe that I maintain any sort of mystical connection to that man. I refuse to believe that I'm having intuition. I'm being paranoid.

We arrive at the front of my apartment. "Thank you again. For the roses. For dinner."

"Can we do this again?"

"Yes. But I really don't want to disappoint you. I... I really just got my heart broken. And when I tell you it was an extremely dysfunctional relationship..."

"Is he who you're afraid of?"

It's a logical question, and in some ways the answer is yes. But... The truth of it is I'm more afraid of myself.

"It was very intense," I say. "And he is very controlling."

Luke looks angry. "No man has any right to control a woman."

"I appreciate that. But I'm just trying to give context for...me."

"I like you, Cassie. But I'm okay going slow. I won't lie to you and say that I don't feel something. But it's okay if it only ends up being friendship. We're two Americans in Paris. We might as well see, right?"

"Yeah."

Though I don't need to see. I know.

"Good night," he says, and I'm grateful that he doesn't make a move toward me, or wait for me to walk away. I stand there for a moment, until that strange sensation creeps up on me again. After that I go back inside quickly. Very quickly.

I make my way up the stairs and lock myself in the

apartment, then put a chair in front of the door for good measure.

And here I am, left alone, surrounded by paintings of Dragos.

I sigh heavily, and pour myself another glass of wine, and I sit in front of my nearly finished painting. I take out my sketchbook, and I start to draw. I don't intend for the drawing to be pornographic, but it is. Dragos, over me, his hand gripping my chin as he enters me from behind.

I won't paint that.

I'm startled out of my guilty artistic fantasies by the sound of tires squealing on the street below, a strange thick whisking sound and a shout.

I run to the window and look out at the street below. There, bathed in the light of the streetlamps, I see a man dressed all in black lying on the sidewalk, with a pool of blood spreading around him.

And I freeze. Because all I can think of is the story Dragos told me about his father.

Dragos.

I run to get my phone, but I can't remember where I put my purse. My hands are shaking. It's not Dragos. But someone is hurt. Maybe they've been hit by a car? I have no idea what just happened.

But they need help. I need to call the emergency line. But I can't find my stupid purse. I can't find my stupid phone. The apartment is too small for it to be this difficult.

Finally, I find it, and I run back to the window with it in hand. But the man is gone. If it wasn't for the red smudge on the sidewalk I would believe that I made the entire thing up.

And then I hear a large thump against my door.

My adrenaline spurs me, and I'm not thinking about anything but the fact that there's an injured man who needs help.

I move the chair, and open the door. And my whole world falls apart.

CHAPTER FIVE

Dragos

I KNOW HER FACE.

It's the *only* thing I know.

There are great black holes in my mind, spaces where I'm sure knowledge once was. Or maybe not. It's blank. I have nothing but instinct, driving and intense. There's danger; I'm certain of that. I'm injured and it was no accident. I'm certain of that too.

And her.

I'm certain of her.

In the tangle of gut response and blind, feral emotion, there is one image. One memory.

I remember the first time I ever saw her.

She is dressed in yellow, and she's laughing. She's like the sun.

Something in me changed that day that I saw her. I know that. The before and the after, though it is an impression inside me and not a series of images. I remember her, but I don't remember my name.

I remember her, but I remember nothing else.

Her name is a vapor, escaping me, eluding me, just like my own.

My head is pounding. I feel blood dripping down my face.

I do know that this is not the first time I've been injured this gravely. I can't recall how. Only that I'm sure I have been before. Guns and violence and near-death experiences fit me like the clothes I'm wearing.

"Dragos."

She says that word. I don't understand it. Her eyes are wide, and she's fluttering around frantically. She's not helping me, but she seems to know me.

"What are you doing here?" she asks.

"I don't know," I say.

The room tilts, and I do my best not to tilt with it. One thing I know I'm not used to is struggling. I am used to a fight, but I am used to winning that fight with ease.

"I need to sit down," I say.

She gestures to a chair that's in an odd spot in the room.

"That is a strange place for a chair," I say.

I know this, even though I don't know how I know it. There are truths that exist inside of me, even if I'm not certain where I come by them.

"I'm sorry you don't approve," she says. "What happened?"

"I don't know."

"You don't… You don't know?"

"I don't know. I woke up bleeding. I… I felt like I needed to go upstairs."

She looks at me, those clear blue eyes grounding me, holding me to the earth. She is the only thing that is. "Dragos, do you know who you are?"

"No. I don't." I close my eyes. "I'm Dragos?"

"Yes."

I open my eyes again. "That is a stupid name."

She only stares at me. "I… Why do you think it's stupid?"

"I don't know. I only know that it is."

I feel frustrated, because she's asking me questions that are ridiculous. My head is bleeding.

"Should get something to stop my bleeding," I say.

"I need to call the emergency line."

Something in me knows that's the wrong thing to do. "No. No. We cannot do that. Because if I end up in the hospital then…" I have an instinct. *Danger.* "If I go to the hospital they'll try again."

"Who?" she asks.

"I don't know," I say. "I don't know who has tried to do this. But somebody did. I was…" I close my eyes. "I was shot at." I turn toward her and touch my shoulder. There is a burn mark on my coat, a scorched line that cuts straight to the fabric. "It was a bullet. I fell and hit my head on the curb. They probably think they got me. Because of the blood."

"Except if they come back to check your body will be gone."

"True."

I'm trying to put thoughts together, but my brain is an abyss. My thoughts don't make sense, the order they come in, the way that things occur to me.

"This was not an accident. I cannot tell you who has done it, but I can tell you it was intentional, and it means that we are both in danger. Because you know me."

She does know me. I know her. I remember her.

Not her name. But I know she's mine.

I stand up, because I need to close the distance between us. I grab her arms, and only then do I realize my hands are bloodied. She gasps, like she's scared of me, and then I look around the room. The room is filled with paintings. Paintings of naked men.

No. A naked man. The same one. Broken into parts and pieces, a close-up examination of him in different parts.

I look at one canvas of a man's hand curled around a woman's throat. I stare at the tattooed fingers, and then look down at my own.

This is me.

Every painting in this room is of me.

"What is this?"

She looks around, her eyes wide. "Nothing. I…"

"I don't know what's going on," I say, letting go of her, looking down at my bloodied hands. "Someone tried to kill me. And I knew that I had to go to you, but I don't know how I knew you were here. Do we live together?"

"No," she says.

I knew the answer to that, honestly, because she looked so surprised when I came in, and I had the overwhelming sensation that I had been looking for her and finally found her.

But then, I am her muse.

And we…have been very intimate. That much is clear.

That much seems right.

"Dragos, sit down," she says.

"I will not sit down. We need to leave. We need to leave this place. If they saw me coming here then you are in danger too."

"Do you remember anything?"

"You," I say. "I remember you. Remember the first

time I saw you. I… You were wearing yellow and you were talking with your friends."

"No," she says. "I was wearing black. And I was working. I was not talking to friends. You're hallucinating."

"I'm not hallucinating," I say.

"You don't know your name. We need to find a doctor. If you won't go to the hospital, then you need to…" I can see a realization dawning in her eyes. "You don't know yourself. So you don't know where your houses are," she says.

"No," I say. "I don't."

"How to contact your physician."

"No."

"And someone tried to kill you."

"I believe so."

She looks defeated. "I know," she says. "I know those things."

"How?"

"Because, Dragos Apostolis, I'm your wife."

CHAPTER SIX

Cassandra

I'M AFRAID THAT he's lying to me. Except he's bleeding profusely, and I know that I need to help him. He was following me. He has been for days. I'm sure of it. Every time I thought I saw someone. It was him. I'm not in any doubt of that now.

I am shocked, furious. I have no idea what I'm supposed to do with this or him.

But I love him. And I hate that I love him. I love him, and I can't let anyone… Hurt him.

"You've always been paranoid," I say.

Though his paranoia might be rooted in reality, I have to now admit.

"I have?"

"Yes," I say. "You would never let me go anywhere without security."

"That's very controlling."

I laugh. I can't help myself. Of course the amnesiac version of my husband, a man who has never been afraid to call out bullshit of all kinds, is quick to call out his own as long as he can't remember that it's his.

But I know that we need to get out of here and quickly.

Because suddenly I think… Perhaps he wasn't only controlling for the sake of it. What I know is that he's a very rich man, and I know that people hate him. I still wish that I knew more about why somebody might actually try to kill him, but unfortunately since the man never let me into a single thing in his life, I wouldn't know.

"Okay. Do you have your phone?"

"Yes," he says. "I think."

"I'll find it," I say, leaning in and fishing my hand into his left pocket, where I know he keeps his phone, because he's left-handed. I'm so close to him, and suddenly, I start shaking. Because he's here, after two months of me not seeing him, and he was very nearly killed. We might not even be safe. My heart squeezes so hard I think I might die.

He might've been killed. Right there in front of me.

I can't handle that. And so I open his phone up and I call his head of security. "Where are you?" I ask.

"In London, where Mr. Apostolis has asked me to be. Why are you on his phone, Mrs. Apostolis?"

"Someone tried to kill him. And he has no idea who he is."

"We'll send an emergency vehicle to the location."

It goes dead. I have a fair idea of exactly where we'll go, because I've been there before, and I recall him saying it's a property that is listed in his name, and it even has a panic room.

He said this to me offhandedly, and I laughed, and now I think it was not a joke.

"We need to get down the stairs," I say.

Thank God he can move on his own two feet, because

there's no way I could carry a man his size down those stairs.

We wait behind the door until the phone lights up, and everything after is a blur. He is rushed to a private medical facility and I'm on edge the whole time. They scan his brain to make sure he isn't dying. A concussion, but nothing more. I'm given instructions on how to safeguard him, but I want to ask for…for help, for something else. Something more. But I am his wife.

And then his security team says the larger imperative is to get him somewhere safe and private, they trust no one, not even these doctors enough to have them come with us, to have them know the location of where we might go.

We're instructed to go to the roof of the facility and await a helicopter, which touches down the moment we reach the roof, the rotors causing windstorm that throws my already chaotic heart into disarray.

As we climb up inside, and are whisked off into the Parisian sky, I feel like I'm leaving behind everything again for him. And I don't know how I keep doing this. Maybe he is lying to me. Maybe this was all an elaborate ruse to get me to come with him.

Maybe I've walked into a trap again.

All I know is that in spite of my best efforts, I'm back with Dragos.

I want to weep. For all of the reasons that a person can shed tears. I don't. Maybe because I'd have to be connected to my body to manage that. Right now, I feel like I'm not just flying above Paris, but above myself.

Were the last few weeks a dream?

Or maybe the last four years were some dire fantasy and I'll wake up at home in my bed.

The flight itself lasts two hours, and I'm thankful he doesn't try to touch me. When we land in the snow at his mountaintop home above Geneva, I'm not surprised. This was where I thought we would go.

We spent our honeymoon here, and he told me then it was a secure property that only very few people knew about, and a helicopter is required for access.

It's a beautiful home, set into the side of the mountain, nearly concealed by the craggy rock around it, the angles of glass designed to allow the house to fade into nature.

It's beautiful. But that's not my prevailing thought right now.

I usher him into the house, and the crew flies away. Which means that I'm alone on a mountaintop with Dragos. Who doesn't know who he is. Probably.

I press a security lock on the wall behind us, like he showed me to do the first time we were here.

He's looking around, pacing like a caged panther as he regards the parameters of this place. It's dark outside, but the snow still glows a fearsome white. It's eerily quiet. So different than the apartment in Paris I was in only a couple of hours before.

I feel like I can't catch my breath. I'm not sure if I've been able to catch my breath for weeks.

I wait. To see if he's going to pounce on me. To see if he's going to collapse. I still haven't decided whether or not I think all of this is a ruse. Or whether it's really happening.

"Sit down," I say. In spite of myself. "We need to call a doctor. We need to figure out how to get him up here."

"Not necessary. I simply won't sleep."

"Oh. I suppose I'm going to stay up with you, then?"

"You are my wife."

It's on the tip of my tongue to tell him I'm trying to *not* be his wife. I don't know what to do with an amnesiac, though. If you're supposed to tell them, or if telling them the truth is like waking up a sleepwalker.

"How do you know you're not supposed to sleep?" He's so confident and certain in some things and I have no idea how or why.

I want to laugh, though, because the truth is he's no less confusing with amnesia. I've never understood what was happening inside of him. He's a wall and I've never known how to climb him.

"I don't know," he says. "There are certain things that I know, and many that I don't. Some of this is simply feelings. A gut instinct."

"You knew me," I say.

He nods slowly. "Yes. I told you. I remember meeting you."

"Okay," I say.

He *doesn't* remember that. He thinks he does. He probably would have felt this way about any woman he happened upon after this accident. Though, he clearly did go up my stairs to my door for a reason. Which means he knew where I was living. He has been watching me this whole time.

Impossibly, foolishly, my heart begins to beat faster. Because he *came* for *me*.

I thought he wasn't going to. I thought he didn't care or that he had another woman in our bed already but he did come for me.

The joy that gives me is momentary and then I want to fling myself out a window. Because how is it that I can be joyous that my husband chased me down? When I was afraid of it. When I knew that it was necessary for us to be apart.

Truly, I am tired of myself. Of my obsession with him.

I'm in shock, I realize. I want to rage at him, at the world, at everything. I realize that the problem with myself and Dragos is that there was never a pattern for us from the start. There is no guidebook for this.

One thing I never imagined, though, is that it could get more absurd. So kudos to the universe. Hilarious stuff.

"I don't think you know me," I say. "Not in some magical way. I think I was maybe the last thought in your head because you were in front of my apartment, and clearly you knew that."

I'm desperate to prove to both of us that me still existing in his washed-out memory doesn't mean anything.

"I *do* know you," he says, his tone fierce, his blue eyes wild. "And you know me. You painted me."

I am *wretched* that he saw that. It was humiliating enough to let myself exist in that cycle where all I could think about was him, but I never imagined him seeing it. I never imagined him witnessing my obsession.

The trouble is, I think he's unhealthy. Unwell.

The trouble is, so am I.

"*Everyone* has to have a model for painting," I say, gritting my teeth. "You've been mine."

"The paintings are *erotic*."

Heat races over my skin and my face gets hot. "How nice that you understand the concept of the erotic there among your scattered memories."

He regards me, his perusal slow. I feel that gaze like hands on my skin and it's far too easy to remember what it's like. We have a very low success rate with not touching each other when we're alone together.

We don't even do that well with it when we aren't alone together.

I can recall a business event he took me to where he put his hand in my lap beneath the table and…

No. I'm not going to remember that.

"For my wife, you seem to not like me very much," he says.

Well, not-waking-the-sleepwalker approach be damned, because I'm going to tell him.

"I'm trying to become your ex-wife," I say.

Silence settles between us. "What?"

"I left you." I'm shaking as I say this, my whole body threatening to vibrate apart.

"Why did you leave me?" He looks desperate then, upset. How strange, because he doesn't remember anything, so why should that upset him?

I wrap my arms around my midsection. Maybe that will keep me together. "Our marriage wasn't going well."

"Then why was I in Paris?"

I clutch my head. I'm sure I look like my painting of Dragos right now.

Then slowly I release my grip on my own head, and curl my hands into fists, trying to get ahold of myself, trying to stem the rise of emotion inside me. "I actually can't answer that question. I don't know why you were there. I don't know why someone would try to hurt you. You're a rich and powerful man, but for all that we were married, I don't know you. You could ask me to give you the details of your life and you would have just as much luck with an internet search."

He's silent for a long moment. "Is that why you left me?"

"One of the many reasons," I say, my throat tight with emotion now.

"You don't love me?"

I swallow hard and try to banish that tightness. "You don't love *me*, actually. And you made that very clear in our last interaction."

"Do I live in Paris?"

Even without a memory he's infuriating. He's not asking the questions I wish he would. He's asking stupid questions.

"No. You live in London. Usually. But you have houses all over. Like here, in Geneva." I pause for a second. "Or rather, a mountaintop above Geneva."

"So I followed you to Paris."

"That would be my guess. I thought I saw you, over the last few days, but I convinced myself that I was hallucinating, because you haven't made any contact with me since I left."

He sits back and rubs his chin, the stubble making a rough sound beneath his fingertips. "That seems out of character. I must've had a plan."

"You don't know your name, how do you know your character?"

"I told you. I have feelings about things. Instincts. Not specific memories. But you… You are very important to me." He pauses. "What is your name?"

It's such a simple question, and it shouldn't nearly send me to my knees. It took him three days to ask my name after the first time we had sex, and it was only because

I asked him his. This version of himself without memories cared about my identity much faster than the man I met initially.

I'm tempted to tell him it's Cassie. But something—not something, I know exactly what, that small, needy part of myself—wants him to know what my name is. Wants to hear him say it in that way of his. "Cassandra."

He closes his eyes. "Cassandra." He says it like he's purring. Like it gives him deep satisfaction. I stand there feeling outside of myself. He has blood on his face, and it's a face that I hoped I would never see again. And now that he's in front of me, I'm just… Glad.

I swallow hard. And I walk past him, through the palatial, all-black living area and into the kitchen.

"Black on black on black," I mutter as I open up a drawer and find a rag. Well, rag is kind of an understatement. It is a lovely very expensive square of fabric that I would never want to get dirty in normal circumstances. Or, rather I wouldn't have in my former life when I was much more connected to the value of things and hadn't been married to a billionaire for four years.

They dressed the wound at the hospital, but didn't take the time to clean his face properly.

I run water on the cloth, and I walk over to him slowly, like I'm approaching a lion and not a man I know intimately.

"Don't you ever get tired of black?" I ask, leaning in and wiping at the dried blood on his face. Our eyes meet, and he is so close to me, it makes my stomach clench.

"I don't know," he says, his lips so close to mine.

"All of your houses have this same motif. At least every one I've been to. It's very boring."

"I don't let you decorate."

"You don't let me do anything."

His eyes never leave mine, and my heart flutters like I'm a schoolgirl with a crush and not a married woman standing two inches from the man who broke her.

This is ridiculous. I can't be lusting after my near ex-husband, who I hate, who was stalking me, who now has amnesia.

I've made a lot of questionable choices with him, but this would be a bridge too far even for me. Even for us.

Still, I notice that my breathing gets shallower and my heart begins to beat faster. Then he reaches up and touches my face, his rough fingertips dragging down my cheek.

I move away from him. "Don't."

"If you insist."

"I don't know what you're telling yourself. I don't know why your brain is trying to protect you from the truth of how you actually feel about me, but the truth is, you don't love me. I'm one of your possessions. That's why you came after me. You were pursuing me just like you would a stolen car. In fact, I did take one of your cars, maybe that's really what you were looking for. I sold it."

He's looking at me blankly. "I didn't come for a car. I came for you. That much I know."

"You don't know that. You can't know that."

"I can," he says. And then he gets up out of the chair, his movements surprisingly fast and fluid. He grips my arms, his expression ferocious, and I try to move away from him but he holds me fast. "The only thing I knew in that moment after the bullet grazed, when I hit my head on the ground, and I came to, the only thing that I knew was that I had to get to you. I could see you in my mind before I went upstairs. I knew where I was going."

"But don't you understand that you only do that because you were stalking me? Because you're imbalanced and unhinged."

"And what about you? With those pictures you painted of me all over the room."

"Call it an exorcism," I spit back at him. "Because I did love you. But I was dying living in that house. I was dying."

"Did you tell me?"

"Yes," I say, the word a choked, pained whisper. "And here's the thing, Dragos, you don't remember how we met. You reminded me of how we met before I left you. When I told you that our marriage was suffocating me you reminded me that I was only a waitress. That's how you met me. I was waiting tables. I was young and vulnerable. Ripe for you to pick me, and you did. And I thought it was exciting, sleeping with a stranger. But it is far less exciting when four years on the man you're sleeping with is your husband but still a stranger."

He releases his hold on me, and begins to pace in front of me. "You are the only thing I know," he says, looking at me. "You are the only thing I know for sure."

I should leave him. Honestly. I should have left him in Paris.

Left him to die? The very thought makes me feel like I'm the one dying.

"You don't mean this," I say. "You think you do right now, but you don't. If you came for me, it's only because you're obsessed. We both are. But you weren't even that obsessed with me in the end. You were avoiding me. I think you're having an affair."

I wait to see what he'll say to this. Because his guard is down, and even though he is in some ways maddeningly the same as ever, he also feels different. I'm wondering if he'll tell me more than he did before.

"Were you?" I ask.

"No," he says.

"How do you know that?"

"I just do. I cannot remember another woman. Not a single one. I cannot remember another woman's touch, another woman's kiss. And no, I cannot see the times that we were together, but I feel them. They exist inside my bones. They are more real than I am to myself right now. You are more real. I don't even know what I look like except for the paintings that you did of me. But I knew what you looked like. And I know what I look like through your eyes."

I don't know what to say that. It is a stunning realization. I have somehow become this man's north star, and after years of him being mine it feels…

It should feel triumphant. But I wanted to escape this, not become more deeply enmeshed in it.

I shake my head, and I turn away from him.

"It's true," he says. "You are the only thing that's real to me."

"I really sort of hate you," I say. "What you think of that? What you think of knowing that the one person you can remember can't stand you?"

"Then why didn't you leave me to die, *dragostea mea*?"

I despise him for that. "I'm not your love. I never have been. Don't torment me." I lose my temper then, I cross the space and grab the shiny vase sitting on a stand in the corner, I wrap my hand around it and I throw it right into the side of the wall, watching as all the black glass splinters and shatters onto the floor.

"Are you even being real right now? This isn't just another way that you're looking to manipulate me? Because you love to manipulate me. I think that's the only thing you ever really liked about me. That I was a young virgin who wasn't armed against all of your machinations."

It's my turn to start pacing. "You took me to Paris, and I thought it was beautiful. I thought it was romantic. You said that you wanted to marry me, and I thought that it was because you loved me. What I've learned in the time since is that you never actually loved me."

"You left me," he says, his voice grim. "I must have done something terrible I…" His gaze goes distant, blank. "What is it I do?"

"What?"

"For work. What is it I do?"

"You own Apostolis Enterprises, and it is basically every industry you could ever imagine."

"I… Am I a good man, Cassandra?"

I stop and stare at him. The question is absolutely sincere, entirely genuine. He looks different than I've ever seen him, the expression on his face totally unguarded.

"I… Why are you asking me that?"

"Because I have the feeling that I'm not. I was in danger, you left me. Those things together make me wonder…"

"You told me you're certain you weren't having an affair." I despise myself for how much I want that to be the truth.

"I am. I am certain of that. I know that you're the only woman I want." I can't ignore the sincerity in his gaze, but I also know it might not be true. He thinks it is, but that doesn't mean I can trust a man with a head injury. "But I wasn't good to you."

I feel bad that he thinks… Well, I'm not sure what he thinks. "You didn't hurt me, if that's what you're thinking it's… I felt like I was isolated and alone. I can't actually tell you what you do for work on a daily basis. You've never explained it to me. I can't tell you about your childhood. I can't tell you if you had any pets, or where you went to school. I can't tell you what your hopes and dreams are, if you ever wanted to do anything beyond running your father's company. I don't know the answer to that because it's something you wouldn't share with me."

"Then I am afraid I'm right and I'm not a good man. It is entirely possible I deserved what happened to me today."

I can only stare at him. He's a stranger to himself now, and it's terrifying to think that of the two of us, I know him best, because I don't know him. Not really.

Except…

"You were never cruel to me, not… You were mean. You were mean to me when I told you I was unhappy, that is true. You said I was only a waitress. You tried to push me away and it very definitely worked. But you never harmed me. You never made me feel like I was in danger. The truth is, Dragos, I kept myself locked in your house. You didn't lock me in."

I swallow hard and I turn away from him. "I was afraid of you not wanting me anymore. I was afraid of that from the beginning, so I did everything you asked me to do and I didn't rock the boat because I didn't want to lose you. But in the end I lost myself." I take a deep breath and try to ease the knot in my chest. "That actually isn't your fault. That's my fault. Some of this… I felt too much for you. So much that it eclipsed all of my other dreams. I think that's who I am. I was that way with my art for my whole life and I thought it meant I loved art and it wouldn't change. But I met you, and you filled me up all the way and I couldn't love anything else. That's my fault. Plenty of people have relationships and they stick to their own convictions about their life and they don't give up their dreams. I did."

I turn away from him now because I can't look at him while I'm feeling this much.

It's hard to own my part in the mess.

But I have to.

His lack of love might have been toxic, but so is my love.

CHAPTER SEVEN

Dragos

SHE'S CRYING. SHE'S TRYING not to let me see, but my Cassandra is crying, her back to me, the shattered pieces of that black vase around her feet. It's late and my head hurts, but I know I can't sleep. I wouldn't want to even if I could, not when faced with her pain like this.

What manner of bastard am I?

That's the question I'm most obsessed with answering.

My wife left me. She ran from me.

She's here with me, weeping, yelling. I can see how much I hurt her, and I have no idea what I did.

I'm certain I didn't have an affair. I cannot imagine ever wanting to touch another woman. She makes me ache. Even in my present state, my desire for her is intense. Nearly all-consuming.

Even without memories, with an injury, my need for her feels like the most essential thing.

"I am sorry," I say. "I'm not a good husband, clearly."

"No, you aren't," she says, her voice watery.

"Why did you marry me?"

Her shoulders sag and she turns to face me. "I didn't know better. I thought that our attraction was everything.

I thought it was enough. I thought it was what made us…
us. And my family couldn't tell me I was being silly, even
though I think my mom wanted to."

"Tell me," I say. "Tell me how we…met."

"I was working at an event."

She has mentioned that before, but it doesn't feel right
to me. She tells me again, though. She was wearing black,
waiting tables. I approached her and took the tray from her.

No. I didn't approach her.

I close my eyes. She's sitting in Trafalgar Square, on
the edge of the fountain and she's wearing a bright yellow dress. Her long legs are stretched out in front of her,
as one of her friends tells her a joke. Then a man—a boy
really—sitting to her left leans in toward her and I fan-
tasize about killing him.

I remember the fantasy. Vividly.

It makes me think I've seen someone struck in that
manner before, it's so vivid, and I know at the time I felt
no remorse for wishing death on him. I'm not sure I feel
any remorse now.

But she's moved on in the story, to me taking her home.

"I thought that you'd send me away that night but you
didn't. Then I thought you were being nice because I was
a virgin." She blushes just slightly when she says that. I
feel a deep sense of possessiveness, knowing I was her
first, and I don't think that was the point of the story.

She clears her throat. "You let me stay, and then you
took me shopping. You took me to Trafalgar Square."

It's so odd that she says that considering my memory
and I wonder if somehow my mind has put two different events together.

"And then?" I ask, desperate for more.

"You took me back to your place again. I had to text my roommate and tell her. I mean, if I'm honest I texted her and bragged because she was also a virgin and we'd both sort of started despairing of ever seeing a naked penis."

She laughs ruefully, but I'm only filled with curiosity. "Why hadn't you?"

"What?"

"Why had you not been with a man? It isn't because you aren't appealing."

"I was too busy."

"You were busy the night you met me, according to you, and yet you made time for sex. So why not before?"

She looks away from me. "It was love at first sight for me, I fear." She blinks. "Not really. You can't love someone on sight, that's all chemicals and pheromones and all of that, but it felt like it at the time. It felt like something bigger than myself and I… I wanted that." She pauses for a moment. "You've never asked me about this before."

"I haven't?"

"No. I've told you some of this, I'm sure, but you never really asked. When we first got together I chattered at you constantly, and I think you found it amusing but… you weren't really asking for my life story. When you met my parents—"

"When was that?"

"After we got engaged. When you met them, I think you were completely bemused to find yourself in such a domestic situation."

"Why?" I ask the question with a burning sense of frustration inside me.

"You didn't have a good childhood."

"You said you didn't know anything about me."

She looks the other way. "Right before I left you, you told me that you saw your father die. And you also told me... You said that you found your mother's body in the kitchen when you were a child. And that you're certain your father had killed her. When I took you to meet my parents I didn't know any of that. In hindsight I can understand why my life confounded you."

I sit with that information and I try to assemble it into something I recognize. But I can't picture myself as a boy, much less imagine my parents. What sort of house did we live in? Was it in Romania? In the country or the city? Did I love my mother?

Did I love my father?

I can't see anything but Cassandra. She is every memory, and suddenly more than just the one. I see her in the yellow dress, I see her in the black and I feel a great sense of achievement and satisfaction as I cross the room and take a tray of champagne out of her hands.

I see her on the couch, I wrap my hand around her throat and my body responds to this image. I remember her painting then.

"We liked it rough, didn't we?"

She nearly chokes on a laugh. "We did. It's the one place we always agreed and everyone was happy."

Why did I fail her so profoundly emotionally then? Why was I such a bad husband to her?

"What?" she asks, sounding irritated.

"I'm thinking," I say.

I can't be in the dark about who I am. It's an issue of safety, first and foremost for Cassandra. But I also feel compelled to look at the records of who I was as a man, so that I can fashion myself into a different one. One who can be with her. One who can have her.

Love her.

"I love you," I say, because it is the only truth I know and right then it's brighter than any image in my head. Right then, it is the only thing I know for sure.

She goes white, the color draining from her cheeks, her whole body going rigid. "You don't."

"I do. I woke up knowing nothing but your face. It's the only memory I have now. I see it, the night we met at the gala. I went straight to you. I knew I wanted you and no one else. I knew I had to have you." I don't remember the words I was thinking, or what my plan was. What I'm experiencing is the echo of the feeling.

The certainty that I needed her more than anything or anyone. That I would give up my life for her if it was required.

But you didn't. If you had done that she wouldn't have left you.

True. It was true. And yet, I'd had my life stripped from me. My memory of who I was. She is all that remains and I will not make the same mistake again.

I won't lose her to hold onto something that I can live without. I've been given a gift, I think. Everything unnecessary was taken from me. Cassandra is what remains.

I was clearly a foolish man who thought that other things mattered more than my wife, but I cannot argue with this thing fate has given both of us.

"Let's walk through the reality of the situation," she says, her voice caustic. "I told you I loved you and that I needed more from you and you wouldn't give it. No, I don't think you believed I'd leave you but that's because

I was such a sucker for you and you were so egotistical it never occurred to you that someone would defy you in that way."

"I can't know that, so what you're doing is writing a one-sided narrative that I have no ability to rebut."

"Well, Dragos, you didn't do anything to fight that narrative when you knew the truth either. You let me sit with my own presuppositions and you did nothing to tell me about you, who you were, what you felt. And then you followed me to Paris."

"Because I needed you."

"Or because you lost, and you hate to lose."

I reject that. Wholly. "Or because I couldn't live without you."

"Do you know what I think? I think you're desperate for this to be true because for some reason I'm the only thing you have to hold onto. And maybe, for some reason, this version of yourself wants to believe you contain some sort of basic human decency or a modicum of emotion, but let me tell you something, Dragos, when you remember everything, you don't care about that. You don't care about being a good man. A good husband."

She shakes her head. "I can't do this. I can't." Then she leaves me standing there in the room with nothing but the shattered vase.

I don't know the layout of my own house. I don't know where to go or what to do but I find myself walking through the house as if some GPS coordinates were entered into my body without me knowing it. I arrive at a door and I expect to open it and find a bedroom, but when I push it open that's not what I find.

Don't you ever get tired of black?

I recall that as I step inside and look at another severe room, totally absent any color.

I walk to the desk, a large, horseshoe shape with columns of drawers, and I sit in the plush leather chair positioned there.

The computer sees my face and wakes up. I sit there, staring at the screen, and then my left hand goes to the third drawer from the top just beside me. I open it, and inside there's a key.

I sit there staring at it. I know something then, even though I'm not sure how. It's muscle memory that guided me to the key, and that sees my hand picking it up now.

I don't keep anything important on computers. Anything can be hacked. I know that with a certainty that defies logic.

There is a door at the back of the room and it has a keyhole in the doorknob. I stick the key in and it fits. But the key doesn't unlock the door; rather it ignites a light up at the top that shines into my eye, and only then does the door give.

I open the door, and behind it is a keypad. I don't think. I simply enter numbers that mean nothing to me but that follow a pattern my hands seem to know, and then another door gives.

And behind that door is a room filled with files.

I feel a deep sense of foreboding as I walk inside. And I'm not certain why. Something Cassandra said echoes inside me. I didn't care then if I was a good man.

Why do I care now?

I have been dropped into a life, some thirty years into living it, with no knowledge of good or evil. She is my compass. And the arrow pointing to her is demanding that I be someone worthy of her, and I know…

Deep down I fear I'm not.

And that the proof of that may lie here.

The file cabinets pertain to business, I'm certain of that. But there is a box in the corner that isn't the same. Not a neat file cabinet, but a box that looks like it came from a moving truck.

I make my way to it, and I pick it up. It's heavy.

I need to go through all of these things. I need to try and piece myself together. But I decide that I need to do it with Cassandra.

Because I knew what sort of man I was when I first met her, and I saw a reason to hide it.

My instinct now is to continue to hide except…

I already know how that film ends. I don't like that ending. It ends with her leaving. It ends with me chasing her to Paris and her doing mad paintings in her garret, missing me and hating me all at once.

Even without the bullet and the head wound, this isn't the ending I want.

Insanity is doing the same thing over and over again and expecting a different result.

I think she said that to me once. I hear it in her voice.

I might be insane, that's the trouble. I don't know. But I am capable of making a choice right now, and with that agency I'm determined to not simply walk in these same footsteps I walked in before.

I carry the box out of the office and I try and trust my feet to carry me to where I think she might be, but this time I do find a bedroom and she isn't in it. It's clearly mine, but there is a door inside, and when I open it, it takes me to another bedroom.

"Cassandra?"

She comes out of the bathroom wearing a white robe, looking like the fulfilment of every fantasy I can't remember.

"I told you, I can't do this with you. I'm exhausted. I know you don't remember what happened, I know you remember me, but believe me when I tell you that you don't want me."

"I do."

"You don't. You have always had a fantasy in your head. The woman you think I am, the woman you want me to be, and I didn't do anything to disrupt that for a long time. I just…let myself love you like a fool, but I was foolish because I never knew you and you can't love someone you don't know. What we had was lust, insane chemistry. I was young enough and naive enough to think that was all I needed. And yes, the amazing trips, the money, the gifts, all of that made the fantasy that much more compelling, but it wasn't the real you and it wasn't the real me. When we had to actually live life together it became abundantly clear."

I can't argue with her because she remembers, and I don't.

"Then let's get to know each other now. I do not know you and I do not know me. We can find out who I am together. I think I've found my secrets," I say as I set the box down on her bed. "And there are more. I am willing to do all of this with you. With no protection. I will not filter it, and I will have no lies I can tell you because I will be seeing all of it for the first time. Get to know me, Cassandra, as I do. And then decide if you can love me or not." I make my way to her and I put my hand on her face. "For my part, I know already that I love you. All this will do is make me more certain."

She looks away from me, but not before I see tears in her eyes.

"If this is what we need to do to put the whole thing to rest then yes, I'll do this with you." She takes in a deep, shuddering breath. "I tried to just hate you. I tried to leave. I tried to paint you out of my dreams and it didn't work. So yes, I'll do this with you. But it's a postmortem for me, Dragos. I need you to understand that. I already know that what we were…is dead and gone, and there's nothing we can do to bring it back."

CHAPTER EIGHT

Cassandra

I'M EXHAUSTED AND I need to sleep. This whole day has been an extended nightmare. But he is standing there implacable and immovable and I know he probably shouldn't sleep anyway because of the head injury.

But I feel wretched.

Of course, even now with no memories, my feelings mean nothing to him.

Except…

Suddenly he looks at me and his expression changes.

"Cassandra, you are so tired."

I laugh. "Of course, I am. I got stalked by my ex-husband when I was on a date and then he got shot at and now I'm in Switzerland with his amnesiac ass. That's exhausting."

"You were on a date?" he asks, and the moment of him actually caring about my feelings is clearly past.

"Yes."

"Are you sleeping with him?"

"If I was?"

His eyes go black and I can see him grappling with a rage that terrifies me. I'm immobilized. I've never seen him look like this before. There is a violence in his stance that is unlike anything I've seen in him before.

Yet, I realize I've always known he was capable of this.

"I think… I think I would kill him," he says, and there is a note of honesty and self-discovery in that statement that seems to jar him as much as it does me.

I know he isn't speaking in hyperbole. He would kill that poor nice man.

It's not the first time that I've looked at him and had the realization that he isn't a bad-boy fantasy. He might actually be a dangerous man.

But I've told myself, always, that I can handle it. That I can handle him.

"I'm sorry," he says, looking up at me with genuine regret in his eyes. "I cannot bear the thought of another man touching you."

"He didn't." I don't know why I feel compelled to give him peace of mind. He doesn't necessarily deserve it. Maybe it's for my own comfort. Because I don't need to share space with him when he's…like that.

"Good. Now I…" He puts his hand on his forehead. "I'm sorry. I'm not…myself."

"I think you're perfectly yourself."

There's a haunted look about him when he makes eye contact with me. "I am sorry, then. Sorry that this is who I am."

"I chose you," I say.

This is the fundamentally difficult part about all of this. "I'm really angry at you. I have been. But the further I drill down into all of it, the more I realize I'm angry at myself too. I married you without knowing you. I realized that what we had wasn't enough for me, but it was exactly what you gave me when we were first together. I'm the one who changed the rules."

I feel disloyal to myself admitting this. Because it is true, but I also feel like my anger at him is justified. I also feel that I'm owed my outrage. My hurt. My heartbreak. I do feel sorry for the twenty-year-old who met him and thought she had won some kind of lottery. Who thought that love was going to be that easy. That desire was simply a magical thing she could get carried away on.

"What were the rules?" he asks me.

"Don't you want to open the box first?"

He considers this, and then he sits down on the bed next to the box. "First, tell me the rules."

"It was nothing quite that structured." I look at him and I feel the first squeeze of pity that I felt the entire time. He genuinely doesn't know who he is. He's genuinely lost. He doesn't know what happened between us. He doesn't remember any of the unkind things that he said to me. He doesn't know who tried to kill him tonight.

He isn't the architect of our disaster. Or maybe he is. Answering that question requires me to grapple with questions I really don't know the answers to. Are we our memories? Is he even Dragos without them?

Is he someone innocent now?

Is he the man I love?

I remember that moment of violence on his face, and I know for certain that he is. In a way that terrifies me.

Because the violence in him does not repulse me as it should. I didn't fall for him in spite of the edge of danger. No. I rather fear that I fell for him partly *because* of it. That part of me wanted a love that would hurt. That would skim too close to my bones.

It made me feel alive in a way nothing else did. When school and art and the rest of my life was perfection and hard work and contorting myself to be the very best.

Not with him.

He said we liked it rough, and he's right. It always has an edge. It always has. I marvel at that, and wonder for the first time about my own part in that, and why I wanted it so very badly.

But none of that is an answer to his question.

"It became clear to me very early that you didn't want to answer too many questions about yourself. That there were certain things that were off-limits to me. Aspects of your business. I'm not stupid, you're a very rich man, and I definitely wondered if some of it was… Not aboveboard. But everything was good between us, so I didn't see the point of questioning it. Not too deeply. That was one of the rules. If I ask a question, and you don't answer it, that means don't ask again. It means you weren't going to answer. You also never liked to share details about your childhood. About your parents."

He nods slowly. "I don't remember them. Do you know where I grew up in Romania?"

"Yes. We went there. You don't live in your family home, but you do still own it. We had our wedding in a church nearby."

"What was it like?"

"It was a large estate. Very old. You said that it had been in your family for years. You said that one day our children…"

He frowns. "I said we would have children?"

I look away from him and stare at the wall as a crushing sensation in my chest makes it hard for me to believe. "Sometimes I wonder if both of us were living in a fantasy. Sometimes I wonder if you thought you wanted something that later you couldn't actually take hold of."

Those words settle between us. Hard and sharp.

He touches the box, and opens it. The first thing he takes out is a photograph. It's of him as a boy. I know, because it looks so much like him. The man beside him must be his father. He's tall and imposing, handsome and stern. He looks so much like Dragos it's startling. The woman on the other side of him must be his mother. He looks nothing like her. She is beautiful and tall, far too thin. There is a deep unhappiness embedded in the smile she is giving to the camera. And I feel instantly like I understand her better than I would like to.

His face is frozen, a mask of shock.

"These are my parents," he says.

"I think so," I say, my voice thin, choked.

"And me. I was unhappy. The house was very unhappy. It was…"

He closes his eyes. "I don't like to remember this."

"You don't like to, or you can't?"

"When I have my memories, I don't like to have these." He is insistent, his voice firm. And it takes me a moment, but then I understand. He doesn't think about this time of his life. Not ever.

There is a strange, haunted expression in his eyes, and I hate to see it. So much more than I would've thought. I don't want him to be hurt. That truth rings through me sharp and clear as a bell. No matter how complicated my feelings are for him, I don't want him to be hurt.

It's such a terrible thing. Because I love him, but I don't know him. Because I love him, but it might be the death of me. I never thought in the literal sense, but now I'm beginning to wonder.

"Do you remember anything now, looking at it?"

He pushes the photo away. "My father's a bad man. He hurts my mother." He turns to me, and he puts his hand on my face. "Did I ever hurt you, my Cassandra?"

My Cassandra. Like he always calls me.

"No. You never put your hands on me like that, Dragos. I never feared that you would. You're a brick wall, but you're not a wrecking ball. Those are two very different things. You have never raised a hand to me. And I…"

"But you were afraid of me. When I found you in Paris, you were afraid."

"Yes. Because you did come after me. You did come to find me, and as much as I never thought that you would hurt me, I didn't know what you would do. And I did have to accept that there was very little that I knew about you."

"You think I have the potential to be dangerous."

"You said yourself, that if I were sleeping with the man that I went out with in Paris you would kill him. I don't think that you would ever hurt me, but that doesn't mean you wouldn't hurt someone else."

"I see."

I'm trying to be as honest as possible, but I feel guilty. Which is ridiculous. I'm only telling him the truth about himself. What I know to be in his character.

"What am I?"

"I don't know. I spent a lot of years not wanting to know."

"Then maybe I don't want to know any of this." He grips my chin. "Can we start over? Can I just have you? Can I just love you?"

This is absurd. It's also the thing that I want more than anything else. I want him to love me. I, in many ways, have been given the most absurd fantasy that I could've ever asked for. This man, completely different in some ways, sitting there asking if he can love me. Wanting to forget all of it. All of the negative things that we went through. All of the toxic things between us.

I'm weak. Because I miss his body. I miss his touch. *This isn't him...*

I stand up from the bed, my hand pressed to my chest. My heart is beating so fast I can hardly breathe. "I can't. Dragos, we can't have sex. That's what we do. It's what we do instead of talking, it's what we do instead of getting to know each other."

"But you don't know me. And I don't know me. We cannot know each other. Except through our bodies. I want you, my Cassandra."

"I want you too. But I always want you. I told you... The day that I left we had sex. On your desk. That's who we are. If you can understand one thing, then I need you to understand that. You sitting on this bed and giving me soft promises of love is not us. It never has been. I feel things for you. I want you, I always have. From the moment that we first met. But we don't make sense. Whatever this is will end because you'll remember and you'll go back to being you. A life cannot be built on this kind of sharp dangerous desire. It's a fling, it isn't a relationship."

"But perhaps it can be."

"Based on what? Do we just stay here forever? Me a woman who paints, and a man with two memories?"

"What is life? I don't know anything outside of you, Cassandra. And I'm not certain that I want to. All that is waiting for me is more of this," he says, pointing to the picture. "More bad things. Everything is bad. You were the only thing… The only thing that my brain saw fit to hold onto. Perhaps you were the only good thing in my life."

"Then what is the good thing in mine?"

I feel racked with guilt as I say that, as I walk out of the room and leave him there. I feel like I might as well have shot him myself.

I go downstairs, back into the living room. That broken vase is still there. I wish I could forget something. I wish I could forget one moment of our time together. I wish that I could forget how I feel alive when I'm with him, and how terrible and dry and pointless everything feels when I'm not.

I wish I could go back to being the good, overachieving girl who wants nothing more than to succeed at her art.

I sit down on the couch, and I put my face in my hands.

Why do I want him so much?

Why do I want the darkness?

I think about my painting. About the paintings that I've done of him, and how different they are to everything else I've ever done. The paintings that I did while I was in the attic.

The truth is, the work that I've done with him, in the depths of my misery without him, those paintings are better than anything I did before, which were more about wanting to be good, and not about wanting to express a feeling. But I hate the idea that perhaps I simply need a broken muse to make art.

Any therapist would say that's a terrible thought. An

artist doesn't need to be tormented in order to produce good work.

They certainly don't need to be in an unhealthy relationship in order to do it.

And yet, he calls to a part of myself that I never acknowledged before I met him. Sexual. Imperfect. Dramatic. Wild.

Joyful.

Because the truth is, while I've had a perfectly happy life, I don't know that I've ever felt anything big, all-consuming. Nothing other than the need to succeed, the need to be perfect. The need to make my parents proud. And none of that was ever really about me.

It was about the way that other people saw me.

In his arms, for the very first time, I simply felt my feelings.

Understanding the gifts that I've gotten from him don't make me feel better. They make me feel worse, in fact. Because it makes me feel like he was giving more than I realized.

I made it sound like he never gave me a thing. Like he never did anything other than hurt me, and that isn't true.

I hear footsteps behind me, and I turn. There he is, looking wounded, which was nothing I ever thought I possessed the ability to do to the great Dragos.

"I hurt you very badly," he says.

He did, it's true.

"Remember you asked me if I slept with him?" I ask.

"Yes, I remember that, it happened only a few minutes ago. I'm not forgetting what we're experiencing now, and I think you know that."

"I don't know how your amnesia works." I sigh. "It made you want to kill somebody."

"Yes. Though, not somebody. Him."

"I understand that." I sit there for a long moment. "I convinced myself that you were sleeping with another woman. Perhaps more than one other woman. But you were distant from me before I left. And I would love to say that I left because our communication was dysfunctional, but some of it was that a lack of trust invaded me. Once I started thinking that you weren't having sex with me as often because you were with someone else I couldn't let it go." I stare at the wall, because I can't look at him right now. "I wanted to kill her. Whoever she was. I don't like that part of myself. I don't like the intensity, I don't like…" I close my eyes. "But it's always been there. I just pushed it into my drive to succeed. You actually make me *feel* it. In real time. Not just this deferred daydream of things that I hope I do with so much fervency that I forget to live in the moment. With you, I'm always in the moment."

"We sound exhausting."

I laugh and laugh and laugh. It's not funny, but it's true. So very, painfully true. "We are. We are terribly exhausting."

"I'm sorry."

I want to melt into his arms. And what if I do? He's my husband. What if I melt into his arms and let him hold me? What if I let him kiss me? I'm stuck with them either way. We are stuck here. Except… I need to keep my distance from him. I need to prove that I have some sort of strength.

Just to myself.

I stand up, and I began to walk toward the kitchen, but he reaches out and grabs my arm. "Stay here. Are you hungry? I will get you something to eat."

"You don't have to…"

"Sit," he says. "I am the one that has to stay awake so that I don't die. Let me move. You take a rest."

So I do. I just sit there. I sit there and for a full minute I don't think about anything. When he returns with a tray full of fruit, cheese and cold cuts, I don't even know what to say. He's like a dream pulled from my deepest fantasies. He's like a Greek myth. A god offering a woman fabulous, irresistible temptation.

"That looks amazing."

"I hope you like it," he says.

"What's not to like?"

"Would you like some wine? I thought that I probably had better not. With the head injury."

"Yes," I say. A moment later he returns with a large glass of red wine, and I wonder if I just should've grabbed him and instigated sex instead, because it might have made me feel a little bit more in control. Dragos being controlled by a softer aspect of his soul is disconcerting to say the least.

"Do you want to know what made me feel drawn to you?"

I look at him. "Do you know what made you drawn to me?"

"Yes. I feel it so clearly. It was like I could see the sun for the very first time. When I saw you… And you were smiling. Though then you smiled at another man."

"I don't know what you're talking about."

"In Trafalgar Square. You were dressed in yellow."

"You keep talking about that. But you didn't meet me there."

"I did," he says, insistent. "I didn't *meet* you, no. I saw you. You were sitting with your friends. You were sitting with him."

I shake my head. "I don't even know what him you're talking about. You did take me to Trafalgar Square. After we met, though. We met at an event that was hosted at a venue your…company owns. It was a charity thing, I think. And the catering company that I worked for was hosting it. I was attracted to you instantly. And as we've discussed, I was a very good girl, so I didn't even consider, not for a moment that I would… I just thought that I would look at you, and I would go home and nothing would change. But then you approached me and we started talking, though it very quickly turned into a proposition and I… I wanted to say yes. I thought it would be a one-night stand."

"I didn't," he says. "Not for one moment. I knew that you would come home with me, and that you would never leave me. I knew that I had to keep you. Because you were so beautiful. But more than that. It was more than that. I can't explain it. I just know that I feel it. Like it was dark, and then it wasn't."

It's so strange to see him like this. Trying to communicate with me when before he would have rather cut his throat out than speak to me about anything of substance. Now he can't find the words, and he wants them desperately. I feel sorry for him. Almost.

"Dragos, this version of you is so dramatic." I pause for a moment. "I kind of like him. I mean, I especially like the cheese platter."

He moves nearer to me. "I can make you one every day. I don't care if I never remember."

"That's not true. You do care."

"Well. Yes, I do care, because I could never stand not knowing everything. Everything I might need to know to keep you safe."

"You actually have a life that doesn't revolve around me. The trouble is, I'm the only memory that you have. So you think that I'm the only thing that matters, but that isn't true. You care about your work so much. You spend most of your time on that. And you don't even share it with me. Which is how I know I am not a huge priority in your life, whatever you might think."

He frowns. "I don't like this interpretation of me."

"I would welcome your perspective. But the truth is, you never gave it. Not even when you could."

"I'm trying to give you some of it now. About you."

"I understand that. But I'm telling you that as much as you might feel this way now, you didn't really show it when you could have."

He shakes his head. "I was afraid. Afraid. Of something." He puts his hand on his forehead. "It's got something to do with my father. Because I do think he was a very bad man."

I feel bad, because I'm taxing him, and I can see that. I should probably be more concerned about that than I am.

But I've lived *so many* taxing lives with this man. Too many.

Yet here I am.

He reaches out to me, and I can't help myself. I let him take my hands in his. I smooth my thumb over the ink on his.

"I worry that I am a bad man," he says.

This isn't the first time he's expressed this concern.

"I know that you're a rough man. A hard one. The ink on your hands is a warning that you're not afraid to use force if necessary to get what you want."

"I told you all of that?" he asks.

"No. You didn't. I… Have guessed that. Based on knowing you. I told you, I don't know all that much about you. But that doesn't mean I don't have some sense for who you are."

"And you're different."

"Yes."

"From a nice family."

"A very nice family."

"They probably told you to stay away from me." He grins, showing all his teeth. Every inch the predator.

I laugh. "No. They knew that they couldn't tell me that. Because the moment that I met you I was… I was lost."

He frowns. "This is why I think we could start over. If we can feel all of these powerful things without truly knowing one another…"

"The trouble is, I also know where that leads. To where we were. To all that unhappiness."

"I don't want you to be unhappy."

His words wash over me like a healing wave. He doesn't want me to be unhappy. This form of him, this version of him, whatever I want to call it, he doesn't want me to be unhappy.

"That is really, very nice, Dragos." My words are strangled.

"It seems like the bare minimum that one should want for their wife."

We're still holding hands. And I can't stop myself from tracing the letters on his knuckles. "I didn't know. I just felt mounting sadness every day, and I didn't know if you wanted anything for me at all. Or if you just kept me out of habit. Out of a sense of pride. And I can't ask you now."

"I'm sorry. I am useless in so many ways, it turns out. And in many that I did not foresee."

"I don't think anyone can really foresee amnesia."

"I don't suppose. You need to go to bed," he says.

"But you can't go to bed."

"I will sit," he says. "And I will keep watch."

"Over what? We are out in the middle of nowhere. No one's going to find us."

"I will keep watch," he says firmly.

Then he pulls me up from the couch. He sweeps me up into his arms, like it's our wedding day all over again. And he begins to carry me up the stairs.

I cling to him, looking up into his face, carved with hard lines like granite, at his hard obsidian eyes. The trouble is I can see the man that I fell in love with. I can see the man that I want him to be. I can see a whole future that I wish was a possibility, but that I know isn't. It would be insanity of a kind to continue to cling to the idea that it could be.

I'm beginning to think the definition of insanity is not simply doing the same thing over and over again.

The definition of insanity is love.

And that is a terrifying realization.

He lays me down on the soft mattress and I cling to him for a moment. Because I don't know what it is to be put to bed by him without sex following. We know the steps to this dance. His body does, even if his mind doesn't. I'm confident in that. I see it, in the barely banked black flame in his eyes. Every other time he would've kissed me. Touched me. Held me down, restrained my hands, thrust into me and made me cry out his name.

He doesn't do that. Instead he smooths my hair back from my forehead and gazes at me as if I am a sight that he has longed to see for millennia.

Time ceases to exist.

There is nothing beyond the two of us. The affection in his touch. Something that I've never felt from him before.

"Like the sun coming out from behind the clouds," he says softly. "Like finding a missing piece to my soul. Like finding a lifetime of missing peace." He lets out a hard breath. "I don't remember everything, in fact, I barely remember a single thing. But that feeling inside of me is so large, so all-consuming. I think nothing could banish it. That's why I remember you."

He's talking about me like we might be soulmates. That's how I felt. From the first moment I saw him I thought…

No. I tried so hard to stop romanticizing that moment. To sit and recognize it for what it was. Lust overtaking sense. I'm not immune to that. Who is?

"It was sexual attraction," I say. "Us and all of humanity. It isn't that unique. We start wars and religions to try and contain sex. We paint our feelings and turn them into song lyrics, poetry and films. It's a playground game. Kiss, marry, kill. There's a reason those three go together. We kiss and marry and kill the one we love." I touch his face. "I don't want you to go thinking that we had some beautiful life and I'm denying us. Our feelings were real, but I'm not sure that I believe in love anymore."

As I say that, I feel my heart begin to crumble. I feel like I'm doing to him what he did to me. I looked at him, hoping, praying that he would give me something. That he would tell me that he cared for me.

That he loved me.

Now he's looking at me like he wants the same reassurance and I'm refusing to give it. And I can't figure out if I'm being punitive, or if I'm just trying to save us both.

He moves away from me, but stays sitting at the foot of the bed.

"Sleep," he says.

"You don't have to babysit me."

"I don't want you out of my sight. You're the only thing I know. Without you I'm… I don't exist."

My eyes begin to drift closed. I think I've been awake for twenty-four hours. I don't want to sleep, actually, I want to answer him. But I feel myself being dragged under into unconsciousness. And when I wake, none of this is a dream.

I am still living in Dragos's nightmare.

CHAPTER NINE

Dragos

I WATCH HER sleep all night. I know this isn't the first time I've done that. I know it the way that I know so many things about her. Things that she continues to dispute.

The hours pass quickly. She wakes on a gasp, and I immediately want to comfort her, but understand that I might also be the source of her fear.

"Good morning."

"Dragos," she says.

Yes. She's still surprised to find herself here with me.

"I will make you coffee," I say.

"Thank you," she says, sitting up slowly. I'm overcome by the urge to kiss her. I was last night, too, but I could sense her pulling away from that. I understand why she didn't want that. But I want it. I want *her*.

Still, I'm listening. She says that we default to the physical because talking is so difficult. But talking is especially difficult when you don't know anything about yourself. And the things I do know she rejects.

I make my way downstairs, and marvel at the way muscle memory carries me through the motions of making coffee. The way that I am able to perform basic functions without knowing anything about myself. I don't remember how I learned these things, and yet my body still knows them.

Like it still knows that I love Cassandra.

But what is love?

I have not asked myself that question even one time since my head injury. Instead, I've just been confident that the thing that I felt when I first saw her was love.

How could it be anything else?

Yes, I have felt confident in that. But what is it?

A flash and an image assault me. My mother. I know it's my mother. Lying on the kitchen floor, looking up at the ceiling sightless. She doesn't move. She doesn't breathe. There is blood.

My stomach turns violently.

What is love?

I see my father, staring, without tears, without emotion, as we watch her coffin being lowered into the earth.

What is love?

The coffee finishes brewing just as I feel like I might be violently ill. And right then she comes down the stairs.

I see her, but now it feels complicated. Cluttered by this memory of my father. I can almost feel the ice radiating from him in that memory.

The lack of feeling. For me, for the woman that's being lowered into the ground.

"Are you feeling all right?" she asks me.

"No," I say. I have no capacity to live. I don't know enough.

"You probably need to sleep. We should have brought someone with us…"

"We don't know who we can trust. I don't know what's caused this, because I don't know—"

I have another memory then.

I want out. Completely. I have to detach myself, my name from all of this.

Do you think it will clean the blood off of your hands?

No. The blood goes back generations. It will always be there. But it must stop.

I'm speaking to someone else in the memory. And that man is talking about blood on my hands. I look down like I might see it there.

"Dragos?"

"I have been remembering some things this morning."

"Oh."

"My father killed my mother. I told you that," I say.

That pulls me away from that more recent flash of memory, back to my childhood. Back to those two things that I saw. I know that what she said is true.

"You told me that recently," she says.

"I told you the truth. I can remember… Finding her. They say that you repress traumatic memories. Why is it that that's the first one to return to me?"

"I don't know," she says. Her voice is gentle, compassionate, and that makes me feel like the situation must be dire. Because she has seemed halfway angry to have to deal with me from the first moment I can remember, so her pitying me feels like a bellwether for tragedy.

"I didn't tell you in the beginning," I say, trying to put all of these things in order. Trying to make sense of them.

"No. You really didn't tell me anything about your past. I think… I didn't much think about that because I was so young. My past… It barely existed."

"I wouldn't have told you," he says. "Even if you had asked."

"When you told me, you did it to hurt me. Not to help us get closer. You thought that it would shock me."

"Did it?"

"Yes."

She walks over to me, and very slowly lifts her hand, and places it on my face. I feel instantly calm. And yet again I understand entirely what happened to me when I met her. But looking at her right now I cannot understand what drew her to me. I am nothing but a shell. A hollow man filled with memories of her and trauma. Why would a young woman with so much ahead of her tie herself to me?

I put my hand over the top of hers. Scarred and tattooed, and I find it so ugly. She is so soft. So untouched by this world. I am the pain that she has experienced.

"Why did you want me?"

"I told you," she says. But then tears fill her eyes and she turns away from me. "I'm sorry about what I said last night."

"Which thing?"

"That what we feel for each other is common. It's not. If it were common then I would've felt it before. If it were common then I wouldn't have filled canvases with paintings of you. I guess, maybe it is common, but it doesn't make it any less powerful. It is the thing that drives people. It's what makes us all do things that we regret. Things that hurt ourselves, things that hurt the other. Lust is a powerful force."

"And that's what's between us?"

"I don't think it's only that. I'd like it to be. There is a Bible verse about love. Do you know it?"

"I did not know my own name yesterday," I say.

"Well, I thought it was a long shot, but still. It talks about all the things that love is. Patient and kind. That isn't us. I struggled with that. Because I learned that verse when I was a child. And I knew we weren't that from the beginning. But I thought maybe we were something that burned brighter than people who lived normal lives could ever understand. I thought maybe we were special. And now I don't know."

"We can not know together."

I despise the fact that memory has introduced doubt. She is not wrong, though. I already know that nothing about the thing between us was patient or kind. It was greedy and insatiable.

It has been from the beginning.

She makes more coffee, and then makes a cup for me, putting cream and a very specific amount of sugar in it. I like it, and I marvel at the fact she knows this about me, and I don't.

"You're going to have to sleep eventually," she says.

"I don't need very much sleep."

I have practiced going days at a time without sleep. I trained to be able to do that. I know it then, as certain as I know anything else.

These memories, they don't come in a way that's rational. It's like I get the core first, and then the external layers begin to wrap themselves around it. A feeling, followed by an image and a reason.

We sit together at the island in the kitchen, the only

sound our cups occasionally making contact on the high-gloss black countertop.

I know we didn't have many moments like this in our marriage. Based on the things that she said. And based on feelings. Things that feel right and wrong about myself. As a husband and as a man.

We were a thunderstorm, and we never managed to reach the eye of that hurricane.

"I need to go through the things today. The room that I found, and the box. I need to remember. Because if I don't, we cannot leave here."

"I can," she says.

I shake my head. "You can't. They knew that I had come for you. They know that you can be used against me. That is the truth of it."

"I… I don't think that in your original state I could be used against you."

"You could be. Believe me. I did not come after you with the intent to let you stay away from me."

Her eyes narrow. "Did you remember something?"

"No. I feel it. I feel it burning inside of my chest. I would never have let you go. I would never have let you stay away from me." Suddenly, the fire in my blood is too hot to control. I reach out and wrap my hands around her wrists. I pull her toward me. "Do you have any idea what it felt like to return and have you be gone? You were nowhere. Nowhere in the whole house, I turned everything upside down. My security said you'd gone out shopping—something you never do—but they didn't know where you went. I told them what fools they were for not tracking you. And then… Then I began to find your trail.

You sold the car. I was able to trace your phone. And then I began to make a plan."

I wasn't conscious of remembering those things. But they're coming out of my mouth, and I have to pause and see if they're true. Are they memories?

Yes. I'm almost certain they are. I can see myself clearly in the house now, running barefoot up and down the halls, calling for her.

My first instinct was to be afraid. Afraid that something happened to her.

Yes. There has always been an aura of danger. A certainty that she would be taken from me.

I release my hold on her and I sit there, letting the feelings wash over me.

"What?"

"I thought they had done something to you."

"Who?"

"I don't... I don't know, Cassandra. I don't. I only know that I... I only know that I fear for your life. And then when I found out that you were safe I was angry. So angry. You left the safety of my care. I went to Paris and I was watching you. I had to keep you safe. But then you started talking to that boy."

"You were watching me?"

"Yes. You're my wife. You're mine. You decided to leave the marriage, I did not decide to let you."

This violence rising up inside of me...

This is what I lead with. This is the man that greets the world. This is the one that I know. The one that makes my decisions. The one who married Cassandra. This is the man that she knows. This man who is so dead set in his ways, and so certain of what he wants that there is no room for discussion.

And I know that he exists because without him he wouldn't be alive. And Cassandra certainly wouldn't be safe.

Whatever she thinks.

I let him take over me then. This man who knows things I don't. It's the only way I can think of him. It is not two personalities. But there is an instinct there I have not earned.

"You're my wife," I say. "Till death do us part, Cassandra. And not a moment before."

"You were killing me," she says.

She gets up, pulls away from me and storms out of the room, but I follow her. "Stop," I say.

"No. Is this…? This is who you are. Even without your memories, this is who you are."

"You don't understand. I'm remembering things. I remember… I remember that day, and I remember how I felt. I was so afraid for you."

"That's what you say. But the truth is that you just don't want me to leave you. You don't know how to lose, Dragos. I do expect that everyone is going to fall in line, especially me. Because you put a spell on me the first time we met."

I close the distance between us, and I grab her wrists and pull her up against me. "The spell was mutual. You wrecked my life the first time I saw you. I knew that I would do anything to have you. *Anything.* There has never been another woman…"

I stop, because I don't know what to say next. Because suddenly, everything I think I know ends. Like a cliff.

There's nothing. It's just her. Her, her, her. I don't have facts anymore. I only have my beating heart, the way that it hurts to breathe. I only see her.

So I do the only thing I know to do.

I kiss her.

I kiss her because I'm starving for her. Because I can't hold myself back from her anymore.

The kiss is full of violence. It has to be. *I* am full of violence. I don't know where it comes from, and I don't know where it's going. But I can't stop myself. I can't hold myself back. I expect her to turn away from me. I expect her to push me. To make it clear that she doesn't want this. That she doesn't want me. But instead she clings to me. And I feel all the desperation that passes between us each and every time.

I understand now why she stayed for four years in spite of claiming misery. I understand now why she married me in the first place even though she barely knew me.

Because this thing is bigger than we are. It's bigger than memories. It's bigger than what we know is good and what we know is bad. It's bigger than logic, bigger than reason.

I kiss her, and trace her lower lip with my tongue.

I cannot remember sex, and that fuels me. I know the steps, and yet there's a novelty to it all the same, and it… Excites me.

"I'm a virgin," I say.

She laughs against my lips. "Hardly."

"I might as well be. I cannot remember this. But I know it. The feel of it. The way of it."

"Well. It's only fair. You took my virginity. I suppose it's right that I should take yours."

She snarls, the sound feral, as she pushes me up against the wall and tears at my shirt, ripping it from my body.

Her nails rake across my chest, and a guttural sound escapes me.

I grip her chin and hold her steady as I deepen our kiss. Deepen our connection. I taste her deeply, and she gasps, leaving claw marks in my skin, her breath hot as it tangles with mine.

"I don't know what you look like naked," I say. "I can't remember any woman." I move my hands over her clothed body. Cup her breasts, trace the outline of her glorious figure, and I let myself relish in that feeling of the unknown.

Where that cliff was my enemy before, now it becomes my most cherished friend. I let the unknown stoke the fire of the delicious longing I feel. And then, I pull her dress up over her head. She is wearing nothing more than black lace. I growl against her mouth. "Were you going to let him see this?"

"No," she says.

There's a challenge in her eyes, and I know that she considered lying to me. Just to make me angry.

I know, because it's who we are.

"I told him that it wasn't going to be like that. I told him we were only going to be friends."

"He wanted you. That was why he went out with you. All he could think about was being inside you."

"Probably. And I probably went anyway for that reason. To defy you."

"Such a dangerous game, little girl."

"You're the most dangerous game a woman can play. And I keep doing it. God help me."

She bites my neck, kisses her way down my chest, and I wrap my arm around her shoulders, taking us both down onto the stairs, her knees planted on a step, positioned over me. She presses her palm flat to my chest, and my heart is raging. "I like this," she says. "Maybe I should take control for once."

Yes. I like it. My Cassandra, the warrior, poised to take me. I move my hands up her slim midsection, skim my thumbs over her nipples, still barely concealed by the lace cups of her bra. "Then take me. As I did you."

She's breathing hard, and she undoes the closure on my pants, freeing me before squeezing me tight in her soft hand. Then she licks her lips, and positions herself so that the blunt head of me scrapes against that black lace. I can feel that she's wet beneath the fabric. But she teases us both. I grit my teeth, tormented by the near penetration. Until she sweeps the fabric to the side and impales herself on me in one smooth stroke. The cry of triumph on her lips nearly sends me over the edge then and there.

I grip her hips but I let her set the pace.

I watch her face. I memorize it. There are no memories. There is nothing. Just this first time. Me, as I am, with her.

Yes, there is darkness threatening to close in on us. Yes, this began with anger, but it continues now because of what has always driven us.

This extreme desire for one another. This need that is never ending.

I reach up and grab the edges of those lace cups, pull them down so that I can see her bare breasts. I reach up and cup one, squeeze, and look at my dark, ink-covered hand on her soft pale skin.

She begins to breathe hard, fractured, as I can feel her get wetter, closer to climax.

"Yes," I growl, unable to help myself now. I thrust up inside of her, taking over. I begin to bring her down hard against me, setting the pace now where before I was content to let her have control. But we are both lost now. We need release. More than either of us need to breathe.

This is fucking as only we can. I don't need memories of other partners or other times to know that. That this is us, and it could never be anyone else.

I realize that this is always where I have known her. Where I have tried to let her know me.

I understand her body. It's like we're one person in this moment. As if her pleasure fuels mine. As if what she wants drives me.

I know it so beautifully and perfectly as I thrust up inside of her, as I bring my thumb to the center of her body, to that bundle of nerves right there, and begin to stroke her as we continue to race toward release.

And when she throws her head back and shouts my name, I thrust up one last time and empty myself inside of her.

Only then do I become aware of how uncomfortable the steps are as they dig into my back. Only then do I become aware that she has actually drawn blood on my chest with her fingernails.

I smile.

This is happiness.

It is the only version of it I know now, and the only version of it that I have ever known.

Something I realize then, as clear as I ever have, is

that I have never been happy a single moment in my life before Cassandra.

That thing that I felt the first time I saw her was happiness. It was like I felt her happiness inside of me as she laughed and smiled, wearing yellow, bathed in the sun.

I knew that I could never let that leave me.

Because I had tasted joy. I could feel it now.

She won't believe me. She doesn't believe me.

I already know that. But I also know that it's true. More than I know anything else.

I cup her face. I bring her down and kiss her. She stays on me, keeps me inside of her. And I simply hold her for the moment. Then I feel tears on her cheeks. She moves off of me, but not away, curled into a ball on the stairs. She lets out a watery laugh. "This is really uncomfortable. Why are you still laying here?"

"I don't care that it's uncomfortable."

"Of course not. You're probably used to it. You probably trained to be uncomfortable."

"I think I did," I say.

"Dragos…"

"No," I say. "Don't turn away from me. I'm sorry. I got angry, because I remember the feeling I had when you left me. It broke me, Cassandra. Whatever you think about me, losing you broke me."

"I don't understand why."

"Find out who I am with me. Because when we find out, then we'll know. I won't hide it from you. Not anything. And if the man that you uncover is still a man you want to leave, then leave. I won't come after you. I promise you that. I will let you have the life that you want."

I mean this. From the very bottom of my soul. My soul. Do I even have one?

I must. Because without memories, I want her to be happy. And with them, I know I didn't want her own happiness more than I wanted my own. I know that because of the blinding, red rage I felt when I realized she was no longer there.

"I will be honest with you," I say. "When I found out that you had left me, I was determined to bring you back to me even if you didn't want to come. I would have taken you prisoner. I was intent on doing so."

"Haven't you done that?"

"Yes. But because of… I want you to be safe. I promise you, when all of this is sorted out, if you don't want to be with me, you may go off and live your life. I will get you a security detail if that's what it takes, but you can be without me. I want you to be happy. You have given me… You've given me great joy, Cassandra, and I feel as if I have given you none. It cannot go on that way."

She looks shocked by those words, like she doesn't know what to say. She says nothing. Instead she stands up, and I can see that her legs are wobbly.

Mine are too, in truth. But I rise with her, and we begin to walk up the stairs.

I follow her to the bedroom, where she pushes the door open, and reveals the box of all of my things.

"Then let's start here."

CHAPTER TEN

Cassandra

I'M COMPLETELY SHAKEN by everything that just passed between us.

I don't know if I believe him or not. About any of it. That he was intent on actually kidnapping me. Keeping me captive, or that he won't do it now.

I'm disappointed in myself in some ways. Because I didn't just cave to his seduction. I attacked him. I drew blood. I was the one who was feral. Who was beyond myself. I proved to him that I'm half the problem.

I proved it to myself.

But I sit at the edge of the bed and I let him pick the box up and set it down. He's only wearing his pants, his muscular body on display, and I'm wearing my underwear. I look down at myself, and bring the cups of my bra back into place.

"You don't need to do that," he says.

"I'd rather not have my tits out while we go through your childhood trauma."

He laughs. And then he seems dumbfounded by the fact that he did.

"Is this what it's always like? A storm and…"

"There isn't actually very much laughter." I relent, and force myself to be fair. "There was. In the beginning. You really liked taking me places. Showing me new things."

"I suppose I did. Tonight you showed me something new."

That makes me blush. Which I hate. I shouldn't be able to blush. The things I've let this man do to me.

Everything. Every hard line I thought I might have with a partner got erased the minute I met him. He pushes me to places I never thought I would go, and makes it all sexy.

So it seems stupid that I'm blushing like the virgin I was the first time he found me.

"That's one of the few things we haven't actually done much of. Me on top. You like to be in control."

"Do I?"

"There's a reason I have a collar with your name on it."

He lets out a low, rumbling growl. And that's how I know he is still Dragos.

"Do you remember that?"

"No, but it sounds to me like you wear it willingly, so it says as much about you as it does me."

"I guess it does," I say.

He opens the box up, and instantly, my chest seizes up. Because all the niceness is about to go away. I can feel it.

"I'm not going to understand half of what I'm looking at," he says as he takes out a stack of photographs. I take the first one from his hand.

"This is the house," I say, pointing to a manor with a wall covered in climbing roses. "This is where you grew up."

"I see."

I study his face to see if he feels anything.

But this doesn't seem to bring out strong emotion. Not the way other things have.

He takes out another photo. It's of him. He's a small boy but I can see it in his eyes. He doesn't have that spark of mischief or joy you see in children's eyes. That grimness is there already. That hard, implacable nature.

I take the photo from him, and he moves on, but I can't. I stare at the small boy in the photograph, and I wonder how he became the man sitting beside me. The man whose body I know better than my own.

All of this has made me question what I know. About who we are, about who we can be.

I don't know everything that happened to him; neither does he. But it doesn't make him less real. And I wonder if that doesn't make my love for him less real. Just because I don't know every single thing about him.

I don't know every brick that went into building him, but I do know the wall. It's the wall that's the problem, because if he could open up and give me some of himself, then the details might not matter so much. But I have to be included in the life he's living now, complicated by the fact that he doesn't seem to know what that life is. He did, though, before all of this.

He takes another photo out of the box. "My father," he says, his jaw going rigid.

"You look like him," I say.

I sense a shudder go through his body. "I suppose I do."

"You didn't want to grow up to be like your father."

He shakes his head, very slowly. "I did want to be like him. I didn't think I had a choice."

"Are you remembering?"

"I…"

He closes his eyes, and then opens them again, staring resolutely at the photograph. "I loved my father. Very much. I… It is not normal for a parent to raise their hand to their child."

"No," I say softly.

"I think I know that now. I think I know that a man should not strike his wife or his children. But I didn't. I didn't, because I didn't go to school. I had tutors at home. I did everything at that house." He takes the photo of the house back from where he has said it. "Yes, I didn't leave there. Not for a very long time. So what my father said was love, it was love. What he said was for my own good was for my own good."

I'm sitting there with a growing sense of horror dawning inside of me. I feel a deep sense of pain. A deep sense of sadness emanating from him. Or perhaps that's just me. My grief. My resolute sadness over where this is going. Because I already know how it ends. His father killed his mother, so of course his admiration of his father couldn't have extended beyond that.

"Everything that my father touched turned to gold. He was a man of extraordinary control and a clear way of doing everything. Yes. I wanted to be like him. I very badly did. Because my father had everything. And he was the best father."

"How?"

"He was strong. He was strong and I idolized him for that. Because he told me that it was what I had to be. He told me it was what I had to want. So you see, it is very easy to manipulate someone. When they are all you know.

When you tell them that they are what you want to be. I didn't know any better."

"Surely after he killed your mother…"

He clutches his head like he has a headache. I touch him, and he pulls away.

He is quiet for a long moment, and I don't say anything. My heart is pounding so hard.

"She deserved it," he says. "She deserved it, he told me that she did. Anyone who defies him meets their end. He runs everything as he must to keep us safe. To keep so many people safe. The business is everything. If it collapses so do many lives. And she… She was going to ruin everything."

He looks up at me, his ice-colored eyes haunted. "My mother deserved to die."

I watch his face as the words leave his mouth. I watch the dawning realization that deep inside, he believed this.

I don't know for how long. I don't know why.

Does he still believe this?

I know it's because of his father. His father brainwashed him. Clearly from the earliest age, his father had been manipulating him, shaping his mind, shaping his view of the world.

His father controlled him.

"Dragos, you know that a woman doesn't deserve to be murdered, not for any reason."

The silence between us has a pulse of its own.

"Yes, I know," he says, his voice harsh, sharp like a dagger. "I know," he says.

"Your mother didn't deserve that. Your father is a monster."

"I know that too," he says, his words sharp. "I do know.

I didn't. I… I didn't for so long. He told me. He built my entire world. How could I ever look at it and say that it was false?"

And suddenly I realize something I never have before. Dragos doesn't live in the same world that I do, and it isn't because he's a billionaire. It isn't because he has money and privilege. It's because his world was shaped by something altogether broken. And whatever I've believed about him is wrong, because I made assumptions about the fact that we must have some shared morals. A shared idea of what love is. Of what marriage looks like. But he grew up in a home with a maniac who convinced his son that his mother deserved to die.

"You've never harmed me. You've never made me feel unsafe physically."

"That isn't true," he says, his voice rough. "You were afraid of me when I came for you in Paris. What if I did intend to hurt you? How would either of us know?"

"I don't believe that you did. I don't believe for one moment that you intended to harm me when you came after me. I think you were angry, and I think you wanted me back in your possession. But hurting me wouldn't get you what you wanted."

"How could I have ever thought my father was justified?"

"I'm trying to figure out how to say what I want to say. Without sounding… Without sounding like I believe you're beyond hope, because I don't think you are. But there's an old song about a wise man who built his house upon the rock, and a foolish man who built his house upon the sand. Your house was built upon something else altogether. Something broken. Something destined to make a person… Fall to pieces eventually. Or…"

"Become a psychopath?"

"Maybe. I had thought that our foundations were the same. I knew that you didn't seem to have a relationship with either of your parents, I think I assumed they had passed away. But it never occurred to me that you had grown up in a house like that. So broken. So damaged. I just never even thought for one moment… It's making me reevaluate."

"Reevaluate what?"

I look down at my hands. I miss my wedding ring for the first time. Not just because I wish I had something to play with to distract myself, but because it was part of what bonded us together.

I've done a good job of reducing us to sex. But it has always been more than that. We're husband and wife. And yes, our attraction was a key part of that. It always has been. That instant attraction we felt at first meeting, the way we couldn't stay apart after.

It's why I married a relative stranger. But he did too.

He was caught up in that same sweep of inevitable fate I had been caught up in.

He still has his ring on his finger. I reach over and I put my hand over his, the metal of his wedding band warm under my palm.

I'm the one who decided it meant nothing to him, because he wasn't showing me affection the way I expected to see it.

I'm the one who decided he might have violated his vows, when there was no evidence beyond his emotional distance.

Now, looking at reasons why, at the origins of who he is, I feel like I'm the one who failed.

"I expected you to behave like a man who grew up with two functional parents," I say, slowly. "I expected you to see marriage the same way that I did based on how I grew up. With my two functional good parents. But that's a completely unrealistic expectation for someone who grew up under threat of violence. For someone who grew up believing that abuse was normal."

"I know better now," he says.

"I know that. You never hurt me."

"I never *wanted* to."

He says this with a great degree of authority. He says this in such a way that makes me believe him.

"You are right," he says. "I accepted a great deal of wrong. I accepted it because it was what I grew up with, but I never wanted to lay a hand on you like that. I only wanted to make you feel good. That's all I ever..." He drifts off again, like he's lost in a memory. "But for a very long time I wanted to be his soldier. I hated that my mother was gone. She was..." He winces. "I remember her slapping me across the face. But I was a difficult child. She was unhappy. She... My father was very bad to her. It wasn't her fault that she couldn't be patient with me."

I'm horrified by this. There is not one happy place for him in his childhood. There's not one good thing to grab onto. He has no idea how a parent should look at their child, how they should treat them.

"My parents were so good to me," I say. "I remember how much effort they put into the holidays, even though we never had a lot of money. It was never about the presents, it was about being together. About going up to the snow to get Christmas trees, and telling stories by a campfire outside even though it was freezing cold."

My memories, all that happiness, rush through me now. It's my foundation. It's the truth of who I am, of how I was made. It never occurred to me that he had been forged in a very different fire. How could we ever see things the same?

"They came to all of my school events," I continue. "They told me that I could be whatever I wanted. I never quite felt good enough. But that was me. They were so proud of me, and I just wanted to live up to their faith in me. They're practical people. My dad works a difficult, physical job. But they supported the idea I had of being an artist, as long as I could get myself there. As long as I was taking the practical steps and making plans instead of just daydreaming. And so I did. Sometimes that felt difficult. Sometimes it felt like I was rolling a giant boulder uphill, but I always had support when I needed it. Help when I needed it. You didn't have anything. And that…" I shake my head. "You didn't tell me. In fact, you actively refused to tell me anything about yourself so I couldn't have known. Except, I wish I had guessed. Really. Because I held you to a standard that wasn't fair."

"How does my terrible childhood change what you deserve? It doesn't. You deserve to be treated the best, regardless."

It's such a clear, concise statement, and one that cuts through to the heart of everything. He isn't wrong. His words are a revelation in some ways, and yet I'm still lost in my previous realizations. I treated him like the knowledge of how to be a good husband was innate to him. Why would it be? No one ever showed him how.

"Marriage is a partnership," I say. "I deserve to be loved like you've never been hurt. But you deserved to be cared for in a way that considered you had. I should've been more patient with you."

"I don't know about that. I don't know that I deserve patience of any kind."

"The things that you're describing are so horrendously abnormal. Truly. They are not just or fair. They're not anything that anyone should have to go through. And I... I expected you to know things that you couldn't know. You were born speaking Romanian. I was born speaking English. I would never be able to speak Romanian the way that you do, just as you have an accent, even though your English is excellent." I add that last part because I know comments on his accent irritate him. "It isn't your native language. Just the same as this sort of life, this sort of connection, it's not your native language. I treated you like it was. Like it should be. Like there was something wrong with you because you didn't understand what I wanted. But it's... Conjugating verbs you don't even know."

"No, I think you might be going a little far to absolve me."

"What made you decide that you didn't want to be like your father?"

He looks up. "I didn't decide that. I am my father." He looks at me, and his eyes are so blank and cold they terrify me into my soul. "I am, my Cassandra. I grew up to be him."

CHAPTER ELEVEN

Dragos

I'M DRIVEN IN that moment to go and search the closet. That room filled with so many files. Because it holds a key, though I'm not certain what it's a key to. If it's a key back to a life I even want. All of my childhood has come back to me. It feels like knives have lodged themselves in my gut, and every breath drives the blades in deep.

I'm having a difficult time even explaining everything to Cassandra. And it's funny that she mentioned English and Romanian. Because my memories are in Romanian, and there is a disconnect, a difficulty in taking that native language and simplifying it into English. Trying to explain these meanings. Or maybe that's just trying to explain the crooked foundation of my life.

Because that is certainly part of it.

She's not wrong.

I was raised believing that up was down, and black was white. As simplistic of an example as that is.

I was raised to believe that ruthlessness was the only true virtue. That a heavy hand was the only hand that could ever be respected.

As I said to her, my father made the rules, made the mold, and told me that fitting it was the only option. I did.

I don't know what that means, not in its entirety. But I feel a darkness in me, and heaviness. And I'm not sure if I'm racing to that darkness or away from it as I stand up from the bed and head back to my office.

Cassandra follows me, and I almost want to tell her to go back. But I promised her this. I promised her the opportunity for us to do this together. For us to learn who I am at the same time.

Of course, that was before.

Before the starkness was little more than a creeping suspicion.

But the visceral rage I feel in my memory for my dead mother has told me something about myself that I wish I didn't know.

It never occurred to me what a blessing the loss of memory might be.

To never know that at one time I felt a sort of acrid hatred for a helpless woman.

He made you feel that way.

I know this. I know that it was my father who poisoned my mind, poisoned my soul, but I wish I had no memory of it. For just over twenty-four hours I've lived free. Unencumbered by anything except my love for Cassandra.

A gift I never knew I wanted.

A gift I need more than air, I realize now.

I cling to that as we walk into the office, and I go into the file room.

I'm looking for something. Something specific. I feel driven. My heart is pounding heavily. And then, I know exactly where I'm going. But it's not to one of the files.

I walk toward the back of the space and open up the cupboard. Inside is a large canvas. A new self-portrait, painted by Cassandra.

I know exactly what it is. And I have a memory of procuring it. It is sharp, and it is clear. It is also linked with that first time I ever saw her.

The memory returns to me in a rush, and I am more confident in the truth of this memory than I've ever been.

The deal I've just inked with a group of guerilla arms dealers is going to make me very rich. I don't mind funding a revolution. The authoritarian government has it coming. I wouldn't consider myself benevolent, not in any capacity, but I also like to believe I am somewhat principled in the lucrative world of crime. I would never traffic people, and when it comes to weapons…

There are plenty of men who have sealed their own fates with violent deeds.

If one will live by the sword, they will die by it.

My father exemplified that. I am, in many ways, certain I will too.

I feel no guilt.

I never have.

Not once in my entire life. Because my father told me that as long as I'm winning I can't possibly be doing anything wrong.

At least, that's the sort of thing he said when he was alive.

I pity for him that he could not win our game.

He was darkness. An all-encompassing cloud over everything he touched.

Now, I am that darkness.

My steps are decisive, and I head to my next destination. To the next deal. Whatever it might be, I don't concern myself with it. It is nothing. Nothing makes me feel a thing. I am hollow.

I look over toward the fountain and suddenly everything stops. My footsteps, the world around me, my heart. Everything.

Then I stop. And so does the whole world.

It's like the sun has come out from behind the clouds for the first time. I knew I was darkness before, and it never bothered me. But now it's like the light burns, but losing it will destroy me.

I am overcome by the sudden realization that if I have to go back to the man I was a heartbeat earlier I may die.

Because of her.

There she is.

A goddess. A vision. The most glorious creature I have ever seen.

She's smiling. Sitting on the edge of that fountain, her dress bright yellow, the sun a halo around her head. She's laughing. The hem of her skirt rides up, and I see the glory of her thigh. But I've seen any number of female thighs, and more. This moment is not only about sex.

There's something different. Something hungry. Something so intense I cannot move past it.

I don't want to.

I didn't know I was falling. I didn't know I was drowning. And suddenly, there's a lifeline. Right in front of me. Suddenly, there's something for me to grab hold of.

Now it's all I want.

I know in that moment I will remake myself and everything around me to have her.

I take my phone out. I snap a picture of her. I send it to my head of security. I demand that he find her. I need to know her.

I melt into the crowd, and by the time I get home that night, I have a dossier on her. Cassandra Martin. Twenty years old, from Twin Falls, Idaho. Majoring in art. I know the names of everyone she was sitting with at the fountain as well, but I don't care.

I also find out that she works for a catering company. I arrange an event to hire them at a speed that would be impossible for anyone with less money. A charity event. Which I've never concerned myself with before. But this isn't about charity. It's about making sure I have access to Cassandra.

I got to the university and linger at the edges of the art studio. I see the back of her as she walks out the door. A black bag slung over her shoulder, her dark hair in a neat, low bun. The art professor is a man, the sort that resembles a ferret, and I instantly dislike him, because I peg him as the sort of man who uses his influence over the women in the classroom to talk them into compromising positions.

Nothing about the interaction I have with him following dissuades me of that. I ask him which art belongs to Cassandra.

And not only does he show me, but he agrees to sell me the stunning nude, which I buy because I cannot stand to have it hanging there for all the world to see. For this ferret of a man to see.

I buy it. For an exorbitant sum.

And then… Then finally it's time for the event. We meet and she thinks it's spontaneous. She thinks it's romantic.

I know that she'll be leaving with me because I know that there's no way I can let her out of my sight.

I don't need to kidnap her, but I'm prepared to.

I was prepared to.

But I didn't have to. She came with me.

I hid the painting, so she wouldn't know I'd orchestrated it all. So that when I took her to my room and made love to her there for the first time she wouldn't know I'd been looking at her body, rendered beautifully on canvas long before she ever knew I existed.

I flash back to the moment, and Cassandra is standing behind me staring.

"I painted this at school. It was still… Well, I never knew what happened to it, I didn't get it returned to me when I left."

"No. Because I bought it."

"When?"

"In March. Of the year we met."

"But we didn't meet until April."

"I am very well aware when we met, Cassandra. But I wasn't lying to you. And I wasn't remembering wrong. I saw you for the first time in Trafalgar Square. You were with your friends. You were talking to them and laughing." I stop because suddenly that resonates more. Harder. It's like a bullet has gone through me. "I saw you. I felt something."

"Slow down," she says. "You… What?"

"That's all I remember. I don't remember any more about that. Except I… I saw you. I saw you sitting at the fountain, and I knew that I had to have you. Because… It was like my life was dark. Always dark. From the moment I was born. You're right. I was born into something entirely different than most anyone. And I... I didn't know how to meet you. I had my head of security track you down."

"Instead of coming over and saying hi to me?" she asks, her eyes going round.

"Yes. I didn't... I could not risk losing you. I had to know who you were. I went to the university, and I saw you there. I bought that painting."

"You bought a painting of me. One that I did of my own naked body."

"It was hanging publicly. And your professor... He is... I didn't like him seeing it."

"My professor was very nice," she says, looking at me like the monster we both know I am. "And not at all creepy."

"He sold me the painting," I point out. "And pocketed an exorbitant amount of money. Do you still believe that he isn't creepy? Because he willingly sold that artifact of your body."

"And you bought it."

"I'm your husband."

"But you weren't. You weren't... How did we meet, Dragos?"

"I hired your catering company to work at a charity event. An event which I planned for the sole purpose of hiring your company. I insisted that they send you that night."

"You insisted that they... And they agreed to that?"

"If you pay enough money you can have anything you want."

"No. You can't. That just isn't... It isn't true, not in

any regard. You cannot buy people. You cannot buy their affections."

"You can buy their loyalty. And you can buy favors, and those were the only things I wanted or needed. I got you. I got you into my proximity. I got what I needed. And then we met. At the perfect moment."

"You pretended that you were simply… Attending."

"I didn't," I say. "I told you that I owned the venue."

"You didn't say that *you* arranged the entire thing."

"No, I didn't, because that would've been counter to my goal. But had you not left with me…" I feel a lashing of shame. Which I know is an unfamiliar sensation for me. "I would've taken you."

She looks at me like I'm a stranger. I suppose I am.

This is a truth I was avoiding telling her. This is a part of myself I wanted to keep hidden. Because I knew she would look at me this way; I knew it would change things.

She thinks she hasn't been patient enough with me, that my broken upbringing set me up for dysfunctional relationships. But I know when I'm doing something most people would think is wrong, it's an easy enough thing to recognize. If you feel the need to hide your actions, there is a reason.

My reason is, and has been, that I knew she would find me to be what I am.

A manipulative bastard who puts his own needs before the needs of others.

But I don't want to lose her. I can't lose her.

"I thought… I thought I had a spontaneous meeting with the only man that I had ever felt chemistry with."

"But it doesn't matter," I say, because I need to believe

it. "You felt it too. When you saw me for the first time you felt the same thing that I did when I first saw you."

She shakes her head, and she takes a step away from me. "No. I didn't feel the same thing that you did. I didn't feel like the sun was shining on me. I didn't feel like I was suddenly no longer in darkness. I felt like you were dangerous. To everything that I was. And I was right. But I dismissed it, I told myself that it was just a little bad-boy fantasy. But a bad boy's different than a bad man, Dragos, and every time I think I can connect with you, every time I think…"

"I had to have you," I say, moving to her and taking hold of her, my thumb and forefinger gripping her chin. "And I didn't know any other way. I have never felt that way about anyone before. I can have any woman I want. And I have had any woman I wanted. But then there was you, my Cassandra, and I needed you. In a way that went beyond sex, though I needed the sex. Badly. But I needed you. I needed you with me. Always. You must understand that I never even envisioned getting married. And once I met you there was no question. I knew that you would be my wife. Because I knew that you had to be mine."

She pulls away from me and holds herself, wrapping her arms around her midsection. "You don't understand, do you? You took this thing that I thought was a beautiful, spontaneous, fated thing and now I know it's… It's more of your machinations. It's more of your manipulation."

"Please," I say, feeling desperate. I move toward her again, and I palm the back of her head, holding her still. Keeping her from running away. "It was fated for *me*." I'm breathing hard; I can scarcely think. "It changed me. If you cannot… If you can no longer feel as if it was fate for you because I made sure we met again, surely you can see that it was still fate. I did not have to stop that day. I might never have seen you. But I did. And it changed everything. Absolutely everything."

I have no practice at making others understand me. I've never had to.

"Dragos… I can't…" She clutches her head like I did only a little while before. "Every time I think I am starting to know who you are I realize I don't."

"I feel that way about my own self," I say. "Because it's true. I don't know the whole story of who I am, but what I have known from the beginning of all of this is that you were an extremely important part of it. That you are integral to the man that I am."

"Dragos…" She puts her hands up against her eyes now. "Why are you making this so difficult? Why is every new revelation like an assault?"

"I don't want to hurt you. And yet I understand that I have. Continually. I was…the day I met you I was doing an arms deal."

There was a pause.

"Is that what you do?" she asks, her voice thin, shocked.

I sit down on the floor, rest my forearm over my knee. I feel dizzy. Disoriented. Perhaps it's a lack of sleep. Perhaps it's something more. And then suddenly all these pieces come back to me in fragments.

Layer upon layer of truth. So many truths that I didn't want to again.

The truth about me. About where I come from and who I am. About how I idolize my father. About…

"I killed my father," I say. Even now as I'm horrified by the images washing through me, I feel no pity. No remorse. He was a terrible man. He was a terrible man who was about to harm or potentially kill a child and he needed to be stopped, but I'm not certain that's why I killed him.

Revenge.

He killed my mother.

Yes. All of this is true. All of it. But still, I was not fueled by a sense of justice, not then. I was fueled by the thing my father taught me to obey. The drive to win. The drive to succeed. To be the baddest, the cruelest, the most powerful possible monster.

It was what he trained me to be, and in the end, I dispatched him when he proved to be a liability. His actions caused great and terrible destruction…

He was threatening the son of one of the men in our village. Our home.

And I stopped him from harming that boy.

My father did bad things in our village, but I never did. I thought it should be our duty to care for those people, not terrorize them.

It's the closest thing to the Mafia a place like ours would've seen. It supports most of the town. Everyone worked for my father. But he also enforced that. His was a reign of terror, and I began to believe that it wasn't the most efficient way to run a business, or anything else.

He went too far, trying to kill a child in the village. There was no more putting up with it. There could be no more looking the other way.

It had to be stopped. He had to be stopped.

And then, following, they worked for me.

I don't realize that I've said all this out loud until I look and see her face. Leached of color, completely horrified.

"Dragos. You said an assassin killed him…"

"I was the assassin. I had to be. There is nothing good about my family. Nothing good about my father. Nothing good about us, about the way we did business. Nothing. And there is nothing good about the way I do it either. I have taken over the helm of a doomed ship. It is rotten to its core, as is its captain."

"Dragos… Please. That can't be true."

"Of course it's true. Why you think you know nothing about me? Why do you think that we were married and I kept everything from you? Because I thought… Dammit, Cassandra, I thought that if you could just see me, if I was all you knew, then you would not leave me. I thought that you would remain untouched by it. I thought that…"

"You brought me into this world, and you didn't even ask me if I wanted it."

"I know."

"You… No wonder you were so afraid for my safety. You live in a world of monsters."

"I know. And I knew that if you knew this truth you would not want me. So I could never let you know. I have never cared for my life or my death but when I saw you for the first time I suddenly had a reason to live, and a very clear understanding that I would die without you. It was the most painful paradox one can experience. Life in my estimation is short and brutal, and I never wanted to extend it until that moment."

"You're trying to tell me that you fell in love with me at first sight, and because of that you had to manipulate me. You had to bring me into the space where I could be killed."

"Yes."

"And you knew you had to lie to me, because I wouldn't go with you if I knew this."

I step forward, and I put my hand on her face. "Is that true?"

CHAPTER TWELVE

Cassandra

I'M FILLED WITH HORROR. With a sick sense of betrayal.
Shame. Embarrassment. Because I believed…

I believed in our beautiful fate.

All the while it had been a manipulation. He had
shaped our fate with his tattooed hands. Hands that have
blood on them.

I should be afraid, but I can't bring myself to be afraid
of him. I don't understand why. He should be scarier to
me now than he ever has been. He's confessed that he
killed his own father, even if he did deserve it. Even if
he did it to protect a defenseless boy. A desperate act
in a moment of desperation. But I genuinely believe he
doesn't think he did it because he cared.

I think he did.

But he can't see it.

He's… He's not a *good* man.

Not in the way society measures such things. Not in
the way I should measure them.

And if I had known that the day that we met then…

I look at him, and I want to tell him I would never
have gone with him. I *want* to tell him that all of this is

insane. That what he's told me is so far beyond Greek myth we'll never be able to get past it.

Hades and Persephone look functional by comparison. And yet…

I'm breathing hard; I'm on the verge of tears.

"We'll never know if it's true," I say, because that is the truth. It's a truth that I wish I could overcome.

I wish I knew. But he didn't give me a chance.

He's given you one now.

"You said that I could leave you. That if I found the truth about who you are, what you did, and I couldn't bear it that I could leave you and you would allow it. Now that you remember who you are, Dragos, do you still stand by that?"

"Yes," he says, the words broken, "I do. I promise you, that if you cannot abide by this, then you can leave me. I will see that you're protected. I will… I will protect you from anyone who wishes to harm you."

"Who will protect me from you?"

"You can hire someone. I will finance it."

My heart is pounding. "What if you would've told me? All of this."

"Oh, yes, that is fantastic. In your mind I could have gone up to you having your happy friend time in the sun, and said come with me to the underworld, and you would've gone?"

A shiver of fear races down my spine. "I just might have. Because I ignored every warning sign that flashed in front of me that first night. I knew that you were… Something I wasn't going to be able to handle. And I still… I still wanted to go with you. If you would've given me a chance, maybe I would've gone."

"Well. This is the truth. Of me. And so now what decision do we make?"

"Why don't we start with giving me more than five minutes to decide. You're not who I thought you were. We're not what I thought we were."

Panic is rising up inside of me, and I decide that I have to leave. I just have to get away from him. I have to think. It reminds me of when I ran in London. When I could no longer bear the weight of the two of us and I had to go be by myself. So that I could untangle it alone.

I push myself away from him, and I run out of the office, down the hallway and back to my bedroom. I close the door, and I lock it. I know Dragos well enough to know that a lock won't stop him if he decides that it can't.

I'm shaking. I sit down on the bed.

All of this is a lie. All of it. He manufactured us meeting.

It wasn't fate; he's a stalker.

I tell myself that, over and over again because I know it's what I should think. Because I know that I need to be looking at this for what it is. Any therapist would tell me that it was dangerous. That he's dangerous. He's a criminal. As much as I was able to understand about his… His family business… He's the Romanian Mafia.

And our entire marriage is a contrivance that he created.

I tell myself that, and I wait for it to… To matter.

I wait for him to be something other than Dragos to me.

We have never had it sweet; we never had it romantic.

But against my will I remember Paris, and him washing my hair. I'm lying to myself. We have had it romantic.

There has been sweetness.

It's been forgotten these last couple of years, but it was there.

But he was… Lying.

I take a deep breath; at least I tried.

I don't know what to do. I can leave him. I realize that. He's given me… Not permission, but his word that he'll allow it if it's what I need. But is it what I want?

I don't know where this leaves us. I don't know what marriage vows mean when you discover that everything about your relationship is a lie.

But I can't hide from him. This is the business of us, and we have to work through it. I tried before. He didn't allow it. But he's different now. He's told me that he loves me, and in all the years of our marriage he never did that. Now he has his memories. His memories and this time that we shared here.

Maybe I can try to talk to him again. Maybe it will be different.

He hid things from me, but I'm not blindsided by that. I knew he was.

I overlooked everything I didn't want to see. I went willingly. People might look at him and see a monster, someone controlling. I told myself he was, but didn't I walk into his house? Didn't I stay out of my own free will? I wanted him, and I looked at him and saw a man could never be called normal and I went anyway.

I did what I knew he wanted because I wanted to please him, not because he forced me.

He never once forced me to do anything. He didn't manipulate me. He never harmed me, never threatened me.

I built my own cell, brick by brick, out of my fear. My

fear that if I knew everything about him I'd feel obligated to leave. My fear that if I asked how he felt about me he'd say he didn't love me, and I'd have no more excuses.

I gave everything up for him, because I chose to. Then when I missed those pieces of myself, I left him because I have never figured out how to be…balanced. How to love art and have a life, how to love him and maintain friendships and do my art. How to leave him and…live. I was still in the attic, even then. Painting and painting because I'm not any more balanced than he is.

I don't have the excuse of a tortured childhood. Just my own mind. My own passions that own me, control me.

In him, I've found a match in so many ways. A man who gets off on my passion. A man who can meet me there, but I have to learn to master myself. It's not enough to just ask him to master me, and I know that.

I wait until I'm done shaking. Until I have a little bit more control over my breathing. I stand up and I open the door. There he is, sitting on the floor, leaning against the wall with one knee drawn up, and one leg out straight. He looks despondent.

Like I've never seen him.

"We need to talk. Not just about things you *want* to talk about. But the things I feel like I need to know."

"If that's what you wish," he says.

"It is. It's what I need. I need to know how you saw our marriage. Did you feel like you were tricking me? Did you feel like I was your…thing? That's how I used to think of myself. A piece of your collection."

He shakes his head. "No. That has never been how I saw you. I was never laughing at you. I was never enjoying keeping secrets from you. I wanted to keep you safe. What I found with you was something separate to the life that I'd been raised to live." He lets his head fall back against the wall.

I reach my hand out. "Come inside," I say.

He reaches out slowly and he takes my hand. I lift him up, drawing him to his feet. And we look at each other for a long moment. I think of all the times that he picked me up to take me to bed. But we aren't going to bed. Not right now. Now we're going to sit, and we're going to talk. And say the things that we should have said all these years.

"Let's go back into the office. I want to be able to look at everything. To understand everything."

I shake my head. "I don't need you to lay out the proof. I don't really care about it. I… What I need to know is your heart. Not the things that you've done. Though I think I need to know those too. But whatever you tell me, I'm going to believe you. Whatever you tell me."

He nods slowly, and leads me into the bedroom. We sit down on the edge of my bed, holding hands, and it reminds me of how we held hands at our wedding. He looks up at me. "I was never making fun of you. What I built for the two of us was an escape for myself. A sanctuary. You believe better of me than I've ever believed of myself. Than anyone ever has. You made me feel like there was something in me that was worth caring for. I told you, the minute that I saw you for the first time I suddenly cared about my life in a way that I never had. I was never laughing at you. I wanted to spare you. I thought that perhaps I could keep that life away from you. That I could keep that part of myself away from you. Because I had to from you in the beginning so I thought that maybe I could do it forever."

"Oh… Dragos. I don't think that works when you're sharing a whole life with someone."

"I wanted it to," he says fiercely. "I wanted for the two of us to have something, to have more than I'd ever had. I wanted to cling to what I felt the first time we met, and I wanted to hang onto your feelings for me. You said that you loved me so quickly. So easily."

"I thought that it would chase you away."

He growled. "Never. No woman had ever told me that she loved me."

"And what were your other relationships like?"

All these questions, some of which I avoided asking because of jealousy. Some questions that he simply refused to answer. All things I know I need to ask now.

"I didn't. I had physical encounters. Consensual, always. I have never delighted in hurting people, whether you believe that or not. Yes, the business that my father established is…"

"It's criminal," I say.

"Yes. It is. Though he has never bought or sold human beings, and neither have I. He has never contributed to the global oppression of people. But there's no way that it can be victimless. Can any corporation be considered victimless? No matter how you look at it, if someone is making profits on the level that my family always has, that many of these aboveboard corporations are making, someone is being exploited at one level or another."

"Yes. But that is deflection. From the reality of the situation."

He is silent for a moment. "Yes. It is. It's such a funny thing, because I care now. It's like my world got put back together in a different order and suddenly I can see the truth of it all."

"I think that's another thing I need to understand. When you were a boy you bought into your father's view of things completely."

"Yes."

"When did that change?"

"I think… When he hurt that boy."

"Can you explain that to me?"

"The entire village that my family home sits in is employed by my father's business. The family business. It is a generational thing. It's always been this way. My family has been running their operation, weapons and the like, for hundreds of years. They own the land in the village, they collect rent and they also provide the money for the villagers to pay it."

"That doesn't really sound like a charity so much as exploitation."

He nods. "I would agree. Now. But at the time it was presented to me that the village depended on our family. It was up to us to provide. We had to continue to earn profits. The lives of everyone in the village. Everyone."

"How did your father explain…breaking laws?"

"Our government was unjust. Authoritarian. It stifled the rights of the citizens, and it especially left poor villages like ours unable to defend themselves, care for themselves. So… We took it on."

"Out of the goodness of your hearts?"

"That is… Not exactly how he positioned it. There was never any goodness. It was all uncompromising, hard and ruthless. If I'm honest, his focus was about being a firm leader. He talked about responsibility, but never about benevolence. There was no pretense about benevolence."

"Well, I guess at least there's that."

"I suppose. Except I was never taught to care about goodness. There was responsibility, and a need to be seen as strong. To be an uncompromising leader, because you had to be. Because any crack in the armor could lead to anarchy."

"Well, no dictator can have that."

"Of course not. And that was my father. A dictator in the confines of his own village. But of course, the operation was actually much larger than that. It was global."

"But then… Someone displeased him and…"

"He was going to hurt a child. And I have never cared for right or wrong, except there is fairness, and to my mind there was nothing fair about that. I was never an innocent child. So I cannot even say that I looked at the boy as an innocent bystander. I had no childhood."

I knew that. Because I had seen it in his eyes in those pictures.

"But you stopped him."

"Yes. For good, though it was not my intent, it is how it happened. I hit him until he didn't get back up. But it was finished. And then that made me the leader."

"Were you different than your father?"

"Yes. I'm not a man given to violence, though you may not believe that. I get no pleasure from it. I do not find it to be overly motivating to the people around me. It is not something that I foster."

"When did you realize it was wrong that he killed your mother."

"Today."

"That can't be right," I say.

"It is. Because I didn't think about it. It happened. It was one of the many terrible things that happened that I witnessed in my childhood. And I didn't revisit it. I don't revisit those things. This is forcing me to do it. But of course it was wrong. Of course it was... I hate him. I'm glad that he's dead. But it isn't enough. Because I'm him. I've carried on his legacy, because I didn't pause and take the time to change everything about myself. There are things I do differently, I don't exult in holding my authority over people's heads, but didn't I manipulate you? I will do it when it does serve me. I just get my kicks differently than my father did. But it doesn't make me any different."

I have to sit there and think about that. I have to think about whether or not it's true. Because I don't know. I've never had to think about things like this. My life is so easy in comparison to his. I know that I should be looking at him and seeing someone frightening. Someone who might even be considered a monster. I know that I should. But I can't. Because he is still mine. And he just wanted to cook food with the two of us. I want to believe that. That he wanted the fantasy as much as I did. That he wanted us to be sacred, the same way that I did. The same way that I do.

Except we can't afford to stay in a bubble. We have to find a way to make it real. We have to. Or we won't survive.

"I don't think you are a bad man for doing what you did to your father. And I don't hold the past against you. I don't. I won't. But the future... You can't keep living this way. I don't mind going back to Idaho and living in a small house. I'll do that. I don't need you to have money. I can forgive you for everything that you've ever done. None of it's important. You were raised by a psychopath. He twisted your view of things. He twisted your whole life. You deserve to live differently if that's what you want. And if you want that, then I'll help you." I take a breath. "I'll be brave enough to ask for what I want, even if it's hard. I'll ask how you feel, even if it might hurt."

A sob rises inside me, and I try to push it down, but I can't. It wrenches its way through me, and comes out on a painful gasp. "If you want to learn how to do this, how to be a different man, then I want to be there for you." A tear falls down my cheek. "It's not even as simple as you being a different man. If I wanted a different man, I would go find him. I'm sorry that I said it that way. I don't want you to be different. I want you to…be the man that you are, but have a chance to be one that walks in the light instead of the darkness. You want that. Whether you realized it or not, you must have always wanted it, because when you saw the sun, you wanted to stay in it. Didn't you?"

I can see a well of emotion in his eyes. I also understand that he doesn't know how to express it. I keep holding onto him. I keep that connection.

"I think I was trying," he says. He's quiet for a moment, and I don't want to say anything, because I don't want to break the spell. I don't want to stop him from remembering whatever is about to come forward. "I was. That's why… That's why they came for me."

"Who?"

"The men who tried to kill me. I know who they are.

I know who they are, so we don't need to hide anymore. We can leave here."

I don't know what to say to that. I'm stunned. "Go backward. What do you mean?"

"I was dismantling the organization. For the last six months. That's why I was distant. It's why I was gone all the time. I was preparing to take it down from the inside out. And I had done. I'd been liaising with Interpol, and the CIA. Making sure that every branch of the organization was undone."

"You were in charge of it."

He shakes his head. "Only this branch. Organized crime is vast. And I have no interest in continuing on. I... I was afraid for you. I knew that the longer I stayed in, the more impossible it would be for me to ever have a life with you. I would always have to keep you locked away, as I had been doing. I received a threat. Against you."

"And that's why you wouldn't let me leave the house."

"Yes. I was afraid for your safety. But I also knew that I had to end it, and I had to do it decisively."

"You're really... Ending it all. For me?"

"Yes."

"Were you going to go to prison?"

He shakes his head. "No. And it's probably unfair that I won't."

"You did your time. You had your father."

"That is possibly true enough. Either way, I'm finishing it. It ends with me," he says.

"Then... Then I'll stay. Then we can try to... To be married. To give this a chance."

"Only a chance?"

The way he says that makes my heart feel broken.

"Dragos, I was married to you for four years. You couldn't give me what I wanted, and I was dying a slow painful death. I know you want to fix it now. But who knows if we can do this. As… Functional human beings. And I want more for us. Neither thing that I did with you was right. When I didn't get exactly what I wanted I left. I ran from you. And before that I just let myself get swept along in the current. I don't want either of those things now. I want for the two of us to be able to talk. And I'm just getting to know you."

"You want me to date you?"

"Yes."

It seems an absurd thing. To ask my husband, the criminal, if you would like to date me. To try and start all of this over again. To try and find a way forward.

"We can't just do the same things. We can't just go right back to doing the same dance, because we know it doesn't end well."

"All right," he says. "I will give you whatever you need. And I'm going to call my contact at Interpol tonight, and as soon as there isn't any danger, we can go back home."

I don't know what home is going to look like for us. There are so many truths laid bare, and everything feels different, and yet somehow the same. I feel like I'm floating in a surreal environment. I feel like I actually know what has just happened to me. To him. To us.

And I feel like until we have time, none of it will make any sense. We have so much to comb through. But the one thing that I'm certain of is my feelings for him. I know that they're real. The question is are they compatible with life?

That's the one thing I think neither of us really know at this point.

"I have some work to do," he says, standing up. But this time it doesn't feel like abandonment. This time I know exactly why he's leaving.

He's doing this for us. He has been acting for us all this time. And that revelation is something that's also going to take me a long time to fully understand.

I sleep for a while, and when I wake up it's to Dragos's hand on my back. "Cassandra, my love, we can go now."

CHAPTER THIRTEEN

Dragos

I WALK INTO my own house feeling like a stranger to myself. Because while I am the same man who left this house in a rage, a fury of fear and anger, looking for his wife who ran away to Paris, I am also something entirely different. Something is changed in me fundamentally. Because even when I was on the verge of dismantling my father's crime empire, I wasn't doing it for the greater good. Or for good at all.

This is something I finally speak out loud to Cassandra as we take dinner on the same terrace where we had dinner the night she left me.

I've cooked for her again, in hopes that I can redeem that last time together, when I fundamentally destroyed everything.

"I wasn't aiming for a redemption arc when I decided to turn everything and everyone over to the authorities, not with the broader world. I wanted *you*. I wanted to be someone you could…talk to. I wanted to be someone you were safe with. And it was becoming clear to me that it was going to be difficult for me to keep you if I was having to oppose my father's enemies at the same time."

"His enemies? I thought they were all part of the same organization."

"It's a difficult balance. There is a constant threat of betrayal, backstabbing. Everyone is on guard always. How can you trust the person you're forming an alliance with when they're all murderers and thieves?"

"Isn't there a pirate code, or something?"

"Only in the movies."

"It sounds like ungentlemanly warfare."

"It is. But I have never claimed to be a gentleman."

She's silent for a long moment. "If you were really doing all this for me, then why did you say those things to me that night before I left?"

I have to sit there and try to remember. I have to dig through all the detritus in my mind, trying to make sense of what exactly did happen. Why I said those things. Because she's not wrong. If keeping her was the most important thing to me, why would I say that? Why, when she bore her soul to me, did I say that she was nothing? A mere waitress. Beneath me. When I was in the process of moving heaven and earth for her?

"Love," I say finally.

"You did not say all of that because you love me."

"I said it because I was afraid that I loved you. I… Love is not something I was ever taught to esteem. Love is not something I was ever taught to want. My mother and father never even said that they loved me, let alone each other. It was something that my life was completely void of. And then I met you. I could never figure out quite what you were. I could never sort out what we were. And when you came to me, demanding certain things, I found it confronting. I didn't want to face it."

"Well, you very nearly destroyed us both."

"I don't know how to do any of this." For the first time, maybe in my entire life, I feel close to being defeated. There is so much work to do. So much unpacking of the baggage inside of me, and I'm not certain that I want to. I was willing to dismantle this empire on her behalf. More than willing. Money means nothing. Power means nothing. Not if I can't have her. But all of this? Digging down to the very bottom of all that I am? Digging down into what makes me feel, what makes me act, that I do not enjoy.

I'm not even certain it's possible.

"How do people do this? How do they go to dinner and share their lives and… What? They decide they want to be together based on all this?"

"I do believe that historically they generally also want to sleep together."

"Well, I did that without having to take you to dinner."

"Yes. But look where that got us."

"Married."

"Dysfunctionally," she points out.

"I've never had a friend," he says. "I don't know how to do this."

Cassandra looks at me as though I just told her the most heartbreaking thing she's ever heard. "Dragos. You've never even had a friend?"

"What good would a friend do me?"

"I don't know. But that's not really what it's about. It's about human connection."

She sounds far away when she says this, and I wonder if perhaps it's too late for me. If maybe I'll never truly learn how to have all this. I feel like I love her. When everything was erased inside of me, that felt like the one truth that remained.

But here and now it feels like a mountain I can't quite climb and I'm not certain what I meant to do with it.

"They've done studies about that," I say. "Babies who are neglected, and miss out on fundamental attachment phases, then they can't ever bond to another human."

"You can't seem to let me go," she says.

And that is perhaps the most encouraging thing anyone could have ever said to me. Because maybe I can care about another person then. Though I know my version of it is sharp, I suspect that love is supposed to be soft.

But then, how would I know?

"I am not going to be bankrupt, you know," I say.

"Well, that's nice to know."

"I had begun streamlining my business. Sectioning off the parts that were legitimate. And I'm going to make sure that I devote some of my profits to charity. That's a good thing." I feel very much like I'm lost in paint-by-numbers morality. Hoarding too much wealth is bad. I've seen that in many articles. Giving it away is good, and I'm trying to be good. I have to make sure that I do all of this by causing the least amount of harm. But really what I want to do is build palaces for Cassandra, and wrap her in silks and jewels. Really, she is the only thing that I care about.

I find everything else quite boring.

But I want to change. Because she has asked me to do that.

Because she needs me to do that.

And what she wants matters to me. It matters so damned much.

"That's… That's great. And if you want help with any of that…"

"Actually, what I would really like is to have a gallery. An auction. Anyone you can think of from your school who you thought was quite talented. And perhaps your art. If you will allow me to arrange it. I know that you didn't want me to give you a gallery…"

"An art auction? For what?"

"A charity."

"What charity?"

"It doesn't matter. Does it?" I ask, feeling frustrated.

She looks at me for a long moment. "Think of something that you care about. Your charity is allowed to be one that you choose. It's allowed to be an issue that matters to you. What matters to you?"

Something inside of me feels shaken. I don't know how to respond to this. And yet, there is one looming issue that comes to my mind. As I remember watching my father strike my mother. As I remember both my parents lifting their hands to me. Slapping me into silence. My father hitting my face with a closed fist.

"Domestic violence," I say finally.

What a mundane thing. I was a victim of child abuse. My mother a victim of domestic violence, as well as a perpetrator of it.

These are things that every person deals with. My father made it seem like we were special. Kings of the sort. People who mattered. Above the law, above all manner of petty things, and we were just a home full of violence.

One of the most common ills in all the world.

"That's wonderful," she says. "And I would love to contribute work to that. And I'd love to contact my…my old friends."

"You haven't had them in your life much since you met me."

"No. I haven't. Things have been too different."

"Then contact them. We will… We will have the charity event at the place where… The place where you met me. And I suppose it is still where I met you. Even if I had seen you before."

She takes a deep breath. "I'm not angry at you about that anymore. It's another thing that you didn't understand. You didn't know how to go about meeting somebody that you wanted to meet. But you could've just come over and said hello to me. The effect would've been the same. I was drawn to you from the first moment that I met you. You made me act out of character. You made me do things that I never wanted to do before. It would've been the same then. But actually realizing that… Realizing that made me think that being mad at you about that is silly. You can't go back and know what you didn't know. And I would've gone with you either way. That is the actual truth. Likely, if you would've told me that you were a crime lord, I probably still would've let you take my virginity."

"We sound unhinged."

"I think we are."

But I know some measure of peace after that conversation. And then I throw myself into the charity event. Not just to make myself good. But because I find I actually want to do something to change some of the ugly things in the world.

And I wonder, for the first time, if I might actually be changing myself.

CHAPTER FOURTEEN

Cassandra

WE'RE BACK FOR a month before I contact my friends about the art auction. The contact is tepid and awkward at first—I basically ghosted them after all. But eventually things thaw.

It culminates with the four of us going out for coffee. The three that Dragos saw me with at Trafalgar Square that first day. We've barely been in contact since Dragos and I got married, though they did come to the wedding. I think Stephanie, Michael and Cheyenne were always a little bit upset that I left school.

Understandable.

"My husband wants to have an auction, and he told me that he wanted me to talk to my friends I thought were the most talented. Naturally I thought of you."

"Oh," Cheyenne says, looking down. "That's… That's really surprisingly thoughtful. I didn't think that he cared about that sort of thing."

"What makes you think that?"

"But you dropped out of school after you married him. And we've barely heard from you since then," says Michael.

"That was me," I say. "I let myself get very consumed by the relationship. And we had a little... Rough patch. Recently. But we're trying."

"Trying?" Stephanie asks.

"That makes it sound precarious. Or like maybe I don't want to be with him. That's not true. What we're trying to do is learn a different way of communicating. And that's difficult when you spent four years not doing it."

"Love's not supposed to hurt," Michael says, sounding sage.

I'm not sure that I agree with him.

I think anything that consumes you with the desperate enormity that Dragos consumes me with is bound to hurt sometimes.

But I think of art, and my relationship with it. How badly I've always wanted to express myself that way.

It hurts too.

Everything I've ever wanted has been painful.

That's just who I am. I'm passionate, and I tend to wrap it up in the mask of overachieving. Dragos was the first thing I ever flung myself into that I was willing to fail at. He's given me access to the messier parts of myself. The parts that don't have to be perfect.

There's a lot of good in the difficult.

And since we came back from Switzerland, we've been better. So much better. He talks to me now. And yes, some of it is moral triage. But I have to give him credit where it's due.

"He had a very hard childhood," I find myself saying. "And I didn't really appreciate how much that affected him until recently."

"He's very controlling, it seems to me," Cheyenne says.

I bristle. "He's actually not. He was…" I want to call him paranoid, but that's not really fair. There were real threats. He was involved in bad things. But I don't exactly want to expose him either. "He has a lot of trauma in his past," I say, because I know they can understand therapy speak. "And he's working to unpack that. But it didn't actually come from a place of wanting to control me. He wanted to protect me. He's learning to accept that that needs to take a different form. He's also trying to get involved in acts of charity. And I think it was really… It was really a lovely thing that he wanted to include me. And all of you."

Whether they can understand it or not, I can.

I feel protective of him. Which is silly. My big bruiser of a Romanian husband hardly needs me to defend his honor. Such as it is. But I find that I want to.

I realize right then that I don't have to please them. They don't have to understand.

I understand.

I feel free of a burden I didn't even realize I was carrying.

This need for people to understand what I'm doing and why.

Because honestly, who cares?

I've been burdened by that for a very long time.

I'm just not now.

It takes a while, but eventually my friends are satisfied that I'm not a prisoner of some kind. After that, I get to work on my paintings. Not the dark, gritty series of paintings I was doing of Dragos's body, though someday, I would like to do something with those paintings, which have since been rescued from the flat in Paris.

Instead, I decide to paint concepts of home. I'm halfway through the series when I decide to call my mother, and invite my parents out to the auction. I also take it as an opportunity to tell her what I've been meaning to tell her for a while now.

"Dragos and I are back together."

Her indrawn breath lets me know she doesn't approve. And that butts up against all that perfectionist people-pleasing inside of me.

"He's a good husband," I say. "Maybe our marriage doesn't look exactly like yours and Dad's, but…"

"I don't understand it," my mom says.

It doesn't come from a place of wanting to be mean. I can see that she doesn't understand it. But I've always wanted a life she didn't understand. It's just that Dragos is a bridge too far.

"You really can't understand?" I ask. "Have you *seen* him?"

"You've been married to him for four years, I would imagine if it was only sex that it would have faded," my mother says, obviously deciding to go ahead and be bold.

To call my bluff, since I thought I was being the shocking one.

"It hasn't," I say, pushing right back. "And that might've been what brought us together, I'm not going to lie. But I love him. He is an extraordinary man. He's been through so much and he…" I'm suddenly infused with conviction about this. Suddenly completely understanding of why I love this man. "No one ever taught him what was right, and he's finding it anyway. No one ever taught him that love was something human beings needed, and he found it anyway. It's a miracle, actually.

And I want… I want to see this journey through with him. Yes, it's a journey. And it isn't perfect, it isn't necessarily always easy. But I could've married some normal boy from the same kind of street that I grew up on, and maybe we could've fallen into a rhythm, and it would've felt like easy, but I don't think it would've felt like this. Like…finding the most beautiful, rare art piece. One of a kind. It takes my breath away every day."

"To me, love is something steady. Something that keeps you safe. Security." She sounds so weary, wary too. And I get that. I've never been what my parents expected, and I can understand why this looks…

I can understand why she's worried. But I want what I want.

"But I never wanted the same life as you. Not because I don't love and appreciate the life that you gave me. I do. It's that life that gave me this one. But I always knew that there was something different out there. Something I'd never seen before. And Dragos is that. I could paint pictures about that man to the end. But I can also paint home. Loving one doesn't mean I don't love the other. And it doesn't mean that I don't think… That what you're saying is important. I do."

"Oh, Cassie. I… I just want you to be happy."

"Me too. But I'm looking for something more than that. I'm looking for joy. The kind that fills you. The kind that makes you into something totally new. I know it's with him."

She pauses for a moment. "You're going to stay with him and have kids with him?"

I want that. His forever. His child.

"I think so," I say slowly. "But you know what, if I

need to leave, I'm strong enough to do that. Because you taught me to go after what I need. So don't worry about me. And please come to the auction."

"Of course we will."

She doesn't understand. And I'm okay with that. I understand. I'm the only one that needs to.

And that's a revelation I didn't expect to have. It was one I wasn't even looking for. The focus has been on fixing Dragos. But this new firmness I'm finding in myself is something I needed.

Because suddenly all my actions make more sense. I've felt this whole time like I got caught up in his current. But the current was mine too. It always has been. We are mutually undeniable. That means I am too.

What we have is something that not everybody understands, and I don't need them to. I cannot please everybody. Which means I'm going to please myself. Because I want the kind of wild passion and joy that I can find with him.

I don't want staid and steady.

And yet, I find that more and more we seem to have both. And that seems like something altogether magical.

CHAPTER FIFTEEN

Dragos

IT'S LIKE I'M living an entirely different life in the same body that experienced all of the disastrous things that it did. But Cassandra was there with me. My Cassandra. And she makes everything feel endurable. My sunshine.

She keeps me from descending into the darkness.

This charity event is the first thing I've ever done for the broader good. I've done good things that served me, but never for the sake of it. I feel like my skin is too tight for my body. I've been meeting with women who are survivors of domestic violence, representatives who are going to speak tonight, and encourage donors to open their wallets.

Their stories feel so close to my own experience of growing up in a house where violence was normal.

I never thought that I would have something in common with a housewife from Essex. I do, though. The problem with all of this is that I'm becoming human. Where before I think I existed somewhere outside humanity.

But this is doing nothing but driving home the truth that my father was a man like far too many men.

And he turned me into something a bit too close to him.

The one thing that makes me feel even a little bit proud

is that I never raised my hand to a woman. At least I can look at these women knowing that he didn't manage to make me into the kind of person who relished harming those weaker than himself.

Cassandra looks beautiful. Dressed in bright pink, her dress hugging her glorious curves.

The artwork she's done is truly stunning. Idyllic images of home. But there is something dark underneath the surface. For those that have experienced home in a manner that didn't mean safety, these paintings of houses on manicured streets, family dinners, create a sense of disquiet.

It is exceptional, I think. The emotion that she has packed into these pieces.

The pieces by her friends are good. But they are nothing in comparison to what she's done.

Perhaps I'm biased. But I don't think so.

I take her hand, and when the band starts playing I pull her in for a dance. We've never done things like this. She looks up at me, delighted. I twirl her, and she comes back to me. I hold her against my body, and I feel my heartbeat quicken.

We can't stay away from each other. In an ideal world, perhaps we might've abstained while we worked on our relationship. But for us, this physical connection is so much a part of who we are, that even when we try to keep our distance, we can't.

But there are moments like this, which feel different. This romance. I experienced it for the first time with her. I remember when we went to France, and I got to watch her experience Paris for the first time. She loved it. She fell in love with it while she fell in love with me, and I hoarded all of those good feelings to myself.

But I didn't want to give them back.

Because that felt frightening. As I hold her close against me, nothing feels frightening.

She looks up at me. "What are you thinking?"

She would think that my thoughts were absurd. "I was thinking about how my feelings for you frighten me."

There. I said it. I'm honest. For perhaps the first time. In my life, the life that I experienced with my father, there was never any room for fear. It wasn't an acknowledged emotion.

Such a strange thing, to live beneath the iron fist of an awful man, and to never be given a vocabulary for the wrenching terror that you felt.

Because a man was never afraid, and I was never a child. I was only ever supposed to be a man.

Telling her now that I'm afraid of anything... It's like peeling off a layer of skin.

"Me?"

"Yes. Because I don't know how to hope for anything good. I don't know how to hope for anything softer, lovely. I don't know how to hope for us. I was never given a framework for that. I was never given... A path toward hope at all. I wonder now if I had known what it would be like to try and hang onto this sunshine if I would've done it."

"Is it too difficult for you?" She asks this with a soft, husky voice. I can tell that right now she's afraid too.

"It might be. But I want it."

So she clings to me, and we don't talk anymore. It's time for everyone to be seated for the auction. But ahead of the auction, three brave women stand up to tell their stories.

They are ugly stories. And I am bruised by each and

every one of them. More than that, they remind me of things I've left in dark spaces inside me.

Memories I wish hadn't returned.

I am left with my own brokenness. I despise it.

As each woman talks, I remember cowering as my father kicked me. Hit me. I remember saying the wrong thing, and not understanding why my mother's face went from something placid to something filled with rage. Slapping me. Yelling at me. Telling me that I'm worthless.

Both my mother and my father hurt me, but in different ways. My father told me that I had to be ruthless. That I have no emotions. That I feel no pain. He told me that I was strong.

My mother told me that I was the worst thing that ever happened to her. That I was small and pointless.

Somewhere in there, is me. I am neither of the things my parents wished for me to be, or accused me of being. I'm just a black hole of pain. The place where my mother poured her helpless rage at being stuck in a relationship with a man who would ultimately take her life. The place my father sought to make an image of himself.

And none of it was ever about who I was. None of it was ever about what I wanted, or what I could become.

I am shaped by violence. And I don't know if I can ever be made into a different form.

The auction begins, and they start with art by Cassandra's friends, and I take that moment to leave the room.

I walk outside into the night, and stand beneath the stars, barely able to breathe.

"Dragos?"

Her soft voice surprises me.

"You can go back inside to the auction."

"What's wrong?"

I don't want to tell her. I don't want to tell anybody. Because those two things inside of me are fighting with each other. The desire to be bulletproof, like my father told me I had to be, and the desire to protect the boy who felt very small when his mother looked at him like something she hated.

I don't want to tell her. And I wouldn't have. Not in the past.

I would've shut her down; I would've lashed out at her. Like I did that night she left me. I would have pushed her away.

But I have to do something different now. Because that's why we are in this marriage again. Because she's decided to give me a chance to change. Which means I actually have to do it. Now. When it is so difficult. When I can barely breathe around the pain inside of me.

"I don't know how to talk about these things," I say. "I never have before. I've told you about what happened. I told you about my childhood. But it's... Seeing this pain and other people. Realizing that it's real pain. That the fear I felt was not small. And that it's... It's shaped me into what I am. No one ever loved me. Not ever. And I feel so much... Sorrow. For that boy. Whose parents only saw him as something to vent their rage on, something to mold and shape and manipulate." I wince. "And then I manipulated you. What if this is the only way that I ever know how to relate to other people? What if I am actually doomed to repeat the same things?"

This is the deepest fear I have. That no matter how badly I want to change, no matter who I want to become, it's too late for me.

I had a window into what I could be like as a new man, with a clean slate.

What if it was only ever a glimpse into a life I can never have?

"You aren't," she says softly, putting her hand on my shoulder. "Dragos, you're not your father. I know you're not, because you just dismantled everything he spent a lifetime building. Because you have actually decided that there is something more important than winning. You've decided there is something more important than amassing wealth. Control. He never did. He died hurting a child. He lived by the sword and he died by it. But you've decided to put it down. That is different."

"But you… You want children. You want children, and I… My mother hated me. She saw me as something that got her stuck with my father, and she wasn't wrong. She was killed because she was trapped with him. And how can I even hate her, even though she hurt me? She was stuck in a terrible life. With an awful man. One who was literally the death of her. Yet she made my life hell, and I never found that I could mourn her. I had no safe space in my home. My father acted like he was proud of me, but that didn't come with anything better. It didn't come with anything less… Painful. What if I don't know any better?"

"We just have to keep trying," she says.

I realize that it's time for her art to go up for auction. Her parents are in there. We have to go back inside.

"Let's go. We can talk about this more at home."

"Can we? You won't shut me down?"

I shake my head. "No. I don't know if I'm going to like the answer to any of this. But I know the answer isn't in hiding."

She takes my hand, and we go back inside. The auction begins, and I feel badly that I have taken her away from this moment. Because her work goes for an astronomical sum. I consider bidding on it, but I don't have to. And I know she would be happier if it isn't bought by her husband.

Her triumph is happening right when I am falling to pieces.

It feels like a disservice to her. She married a strong, ruthless man who didn't know how to give love in any capacity. But she has ended up with a man who wants to give her things he's not sure he knows how to find. A man who is fraying at the edges.

Perhaps we are altogether too combustible to exist in any sort of peaceful capacity.

When the auction is finished, the event is a triumph. And there are several gallery coordinators in attendance who can't wait to speak to Cassandra about her doing an installation. It has nothing to do with me. I've manipulated nothing. It's just about her work. I step away and let her talk to them. I don't loom, to the best of my ability. Because I'm trying to exhibit the differences in our marriage that I know she needs. I want her to have freedom. A life of her own, separate from me.

Well, I can't say that I want that. But she does. And so, I need to give her space.

What I don't expect, is for my mother-in-law to approach me.

"This is a spectacular event, Dragos," she says.

She's a small woman with a weathered look around her eyes. Her hair is gray and short. She's wearing a practical black dress, and sensible flat shoes. I've never seen her in a dress before, and I can't imagine she would wear one for anything other than her daughter.

"It is really all Cassandra's work. All of the artists are her friends. And they produced amazing pieces for tonight. And of course the women, who have told their stories. They are powerful."

"But you arranged it."

"Yes," I say.

She regards me for a long moment. "I've had trouble figuring out what Cassandra sees in you."

I nearly laugh. Because very few people would ever say such a thing to me. And I'm a billionaire. I'm also not vain, but not blind to the fact that I have physical charms.

I do know that Cassandra's mother has never been overly impressed with me.

"All I ever wanted for myself was a normal life," she says. "Stability. That's the key to happiness, at least for me. But she's a dreamer. And you seem to be her dream. But then, so is all this. When she gave it up to be with you, that was what upset me. But seeing her here with you tonight, and seeing her living her dream with you by her side, for the first time I say I feel good about the two of you together."

"My hope is that I'm on the right path," I say.

"You don't know?" She fixes me with hard, gray eyes. "I'm *trying*."

This is a painful, alarming admission.

I've never tried in my life. I've only wanted and succeeded.

It is only in this vast forest of emotion that I feel like I might fail.

"Life is much more difficult when you have to consider the feelings of others," I say.

She laughs at me. As if this revelation I've only had recently is something obvious. "Well, yes. That is what makes life difficult. You live in a society, and you have to consider others. I guess maybe when you're as rich as you are, you don't often have to consider that."

"No," I say.

"I know she left you for a while. It must be very interesting for you. To find something that you can't buy."

She's not wrong. There's never been anything I couldn't buy. There's never been anything I couldn't manipulate my way into. I thought Cassandra would be the same. In fact, she started that way.

But that couldn't last.

Which is why I have to give her honesty now. Real and unvarnished. And I find that to be a truly difficult thing. Because I'm not even that honest with myself.

"It has been. And you're right. I can't buy her. Least of all her love."

"My advice would be that you just love her back. Because she loves you more than anything. I know she does, because Cassandra has always wanted to please us. But anytime I've ever told her I think she might be making a mistake with you, she hasn't listened. She knows her own mind. She knows her own heart. And I think that's you."

It's not exactly a warm and fuzzy conversation. Not exactly one filled with reassurance. And yet.

When we get in the car to go home, Cassandra moves into the vehicle beside me. "What did my mother say to you?"

"She told me not to mess this up. Because you love me very much."

"Did she?" she asks, sounding shocked.

"Yes. That was the gist of it."

"And are you? Going to mess it up?"

"No," I say. "I won't." I pause for a moment. "I love you."

I say nothing after that, and she says nothing. We just let it sit there between us. On the short car ride back to our house. And when we get inside, I say it again.

"I love you."

I feel it begin to cover all the other things that have ever stood between us. All the terrible things that have ever happened to me.

"That's why I pushed you away. Because I loved you, and I didn't want to. It terrified me. I don't know how to love another person. God, it's awful. It is the worst thing that I have ever felt. This desperation. This knowledge that another person is now inextricably linked to my happiness. If I don't have you, I might as well not be here. I also want to live because of you. That was the feeling that I had right from the first. I went from never knowing love at all to feeling all of it in a single moment when I saw you there."

I am on the verge of laughing hysterically. Because of course that's what it was. All this time. It wasn't sex. It never was. It was always love.

"From the very beginning," I say to her. "It was love. I didn't know how to express it properly. I didn't know how to show you. Because I didn't even know what to call it inside of myself. I didn't even know how to feel it. I turned it into manipulation because that was what I understood. I've never loved anyone. And no one has ever loved me. But you said that you did. That night in Paris, and I have never wanted more of something as badly as I wanted more of that."

"I was afraid that I would chase you away," she says, her voice trembling.

"No. Of course not. Because I needed it. But I didn't yet know how to do anything but take. That was all I wanted to do. Take it and use it to heal the broken places inside of me. But… When I fell, and I lost everything, the only thing that was left was you."

It's like a revelation. A slow-turning epiphany. "My foundation was always that pain. My foundation was always the way that my father shaped me. The way that my mother hurt me. The way that their violence played out in front of me. It is what made me into the man that I am. But when I lost all of that the only thing that remained was you. It was the first thing. And now… That's why I'm different, Cassandra. My Cassandra. Because I am built now upon a foundation of loving you. Of you loving me. And it's changed everything. Everything that was ever possible, everything that I've ever known about myself. You've changed it."

Her eyes fill with tears, and then they overflow. "Dragos," she whispers. And she flings her arms around me, kissing me deep and hard.

We've made love countless times. We've been rough, and we've been soft.

Fast and slow. But it has never been like this. It has never been filled with an overflow of the love between us, which is now spoken, which is now acknowledged, out in the open between us.

And as she kisses me, I know that I will never be the same again.

"I'm the virgin," I say as she begins to undress me, her hands on my body.

"You can't use that on me twice," she says, shaky.

"But it's true. Because I never understood what this was. I didn't understand what it was for. All this passion. I don't know what I thought I had found when I found you. Some new sort of pleasure, a new kind of sensual torment, but it isn't that. Of course it's not. It was always love. And I've never experienced anything like it before. I've never experienced anything like this. My Cassandra."

I pick her up, and I carry her up the stairs. I take her into my bedroom, and as I lay her down on the bed I whisper against her mouth. "This is going to be our house now. This will be our room. You will not be banished to an attic. You can paint anywhere you like."

She laughs against my lips. "I thought that this was a form of madness. I thought that I was going to be in the attic forever if I didn't leave."

"And you might've been. You might've been, because it took all of that to reach me. To change me."

I strip that beautiful pink dress off of her, and I worship her body. Every action is one of love. But when I make my way back to her neck I bite her, because for us it will always have an edge. She growls at me, and bites my lower lip as she moves in for a kiss. We are a passionate fire. But now I know what to call it.

It really is like my first time.

Like every time before it was training for when I finally, finally knew what it meant to make love to my wife.

I lavish attention on her breasts, kiss my way down her stomach and bury my face between her thighs.

I will never tire of the taste of her.

I will never want anything but her.

And I make that promise to her as I bring her to climax, over and over again, teasing her with my tongue, my fingers.

By the time I finally bury myself inside of her tight, wet heat, it's like my fear goes away entirely.

I'm not afraid of the work. I'm not afraid of all that I don't understand.

In many ways, I was a wiser man when I knew nothing. I was more able to find my way to the truth.

Letting her love be my foundation. And it is now. It is. So I don't have to fear the darkness. I don't have to fear becoming a creature made by my father.

Because I am a man wholly and completely created by Cassandra.

My wife.

The love of my life.

She arches against me, my name on her lips. And then she looks at me, her hand on my face. *"Dragostea mea,"* she whispers.

And I am lost.

I spill myself inside of her, and cling to her after, the shock of my orgasm leaving me breathless. She leaves me breathless.

"I've never thought about why I do anything," I say. "Everything I've ever done has simply been another move on the chessboard. A bid for survival. But I'm not that man anymore. The choices that I make are not just about power, or survival. They are about loving you, and loving you well. They are about… Finding a way to do as much good in the world as my family ever did bad."

Because I want to be a man worthy of her love. And I know that there is penance to pay so that I become him.

She puts her hand on my face. "I need you to know that I loved you exactly as you were. But it was just so hard. Because I felt like I was losing myself. But I want you to know that I've loved every version of you. And I'm so grateful that this is the journey you've gone on. That this is the way you want to love me."

Because she would've taken me either way. Eventually. I do not take that unspoken truth lightly.

"I loved you the whole time," I say. "Perhaps that's why you couldn't leave me."

She nods. "I think so. But I'm glad that it happened this way. Because now…"

"Now we have found a way to live this love in a way that will not drive you mad?"

She lets her head fall back and she laughs. "Yes. Yes. But best of all, I get to know you. All of you. Not the fantasy of you that I created in my head. Because Dragos, the man that you are is a man so very worthy of love. You have taken the darkest things, and you put them in the light. You chose the light. Even when you didn't know why it was important."

"You make it sound as if choosing to love in a broken world, especially when you've seen just how broken it can be, is an act of astonishing bravery. I don't need to be brave. I only need to be yours."

She smiles at me. "How beautiful to know that we can have all this passion forever."

"I promise."

EPILOGUE

Cassandra

I WOULDN'T SAY that I'm stressed. But the gallery is coming up soon, and I'm rushing to finish up a final piece, because I'm not happy with how the collection is rounding out. I'm finally doing an exhibition of the paintings I did of Dragos when we separated. And more that I've done during our time together since. It's an evolution of our love. Because it was always there. I recognize that now. In the years since, it's clear to me that we always had it. We had to learn how to show it, so that we could be together always. Because marriage is long; it's different than a fling. Different than a one-night stand.

We've been living that gloriously in the time since. Several gallery shows, a great many triumphs for him in his business and two children after our world could've fallen apart, but instead was remade into something stronger than ever.

"And how is everything coming along?" Dragos comes in with our son on his hip, and our three-year-old daughter trailing behind him.

"Good," I say, though that's a lie, but I don't want to get into my hysteria now. Even though I could. Because he's always here for my temperamental nature, my temper and my passion.

Because he's always here for me.

And I've learned I can love so many things. Him, our children, my art. I contain so much more than I ever thought I could.

We contain the universe.

"Good. I think that you should take a break and eat something. You can take it in here if you like, the kids are well managed."

"You're very good to me. I appreciate it. And I greatly appreciate the neglect that you're enduring while I finish this up."

"Well, I know that you're going to support me as I embark on my next scheme."

"And what is that?"

"I'm aiming to give away about half a billion dollars."

"Really?"

"Yes. But we need to choose how. And I want to do it together."

"Why do you want to do that?"

"I hear there's no such thing as an ethical billionaire. So as our net worth rises, I'd like to do what I can to manage it."

I laugh. *I* said that to him once. I didn't realize he took it to heart. But then, he cares so deeply about doing all the right things now. After a lifetime of not being allowed to care about them, watching his love not only for me, not just for his children, but for the world around him grow has been one of the most glorious things.

"I thought I was mad, but I think you might be," I say.

"You're still painting in the attic," he points out.

"Maybe we're both mad. Certainly everyone around us thinks so."

Though my friends, my family have come around, especially since we had children. Especially since… Things between us have changed and for the better.

"Let me tell you a secret," he says. "I don't care what anyone else thinks. I only care about what you think." He leans in and kisses me.

I begin to think that I can take a break from the painting for a little bit.

"I feel the same."

Somehow we managed to take all that wild passion and turn it into a life.

I wouldn't have it any other way.

It isn't the perfect, neat life I dreamed of.

It's better. This life where I get to be fully myself. Where I get to be fully loved.

This life with Dragos Apostolis.

It was fate after all. We just had to do the work to make it last.

And we did.

Which is why I know we'll live happily ever after.

* * * * *

MILLS & BOON®

Coming next month

BUSINESS BETWEEN ENEMIES
Louise Fuller

My heart feels like a dead weight inside my chest.

I stare at the man standing with his back to me beside the window, panic slipping and sliding over my skin like suntan oil.

Only it's not just panic. It's something I can't, won't name, that flickers down my spine and over my skin, pulling everything so tight that it's suddenly hard to catch my breath. And I hate that even now he can do this to me. That he can make me shake, and on the inside too, before I even see his face.

My stomach clenches and unclenches, and my heart starts to pound painfully hard, and I can't stop either happening. This is his doing. Just being near him does things to my body, things I can't control. But I need to control them.

'What's he doing here?' I say hoarsely. Although I don't know why I ask that question, because I know the answer. But I can't accept it until I hear it said out loud.

'Mr. Valetti is the new co-CEO.'

Continue reading

BUSINESS BETWEEN ENEMIES
Louise Fuller

Available next month
millsandboon.co.uk

COMING SOON!

We really hope you enjoyed reading this book.
If you're looking for more romance
be sure to head to the shops when
new books are available on

Thursday 23rd October

To see which titles are coming soon, please visit
millsandboon.co.uk/nextmonth

MILLS & BOON

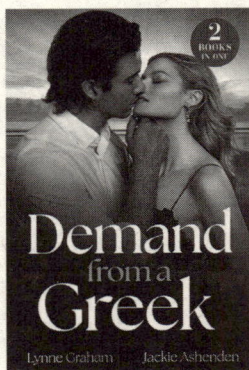

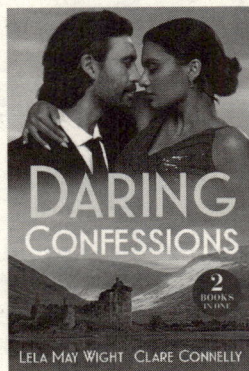

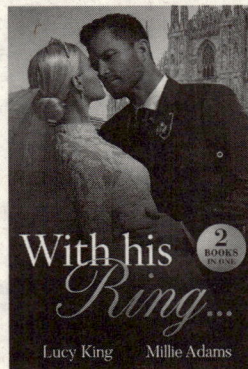

afterglow BOOKS

Afterglow Books is a trend-led, trope-filled list of books with diverse, authentic and relatable characters, a wide array of voices and representations, plus real world trials and tribulations. Featuring all the tropes you could possibly want (think small-town settings, fake relationships, grumpy vs sunshine, enemies to lovers) and all with a generous dose of spice in every story.

♪ @millsandboonuk
◎ @millsandboonuk
afterglowbooks.co.uk

#AfterglowBooks

For all the latest book news, exclusive content and giveaways scan the QR code below to sign up to the Afterglow newsletter:

SCAN ME

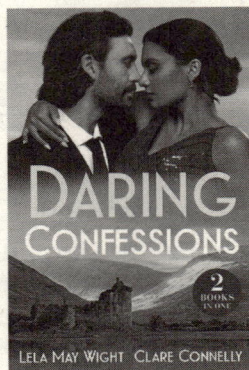

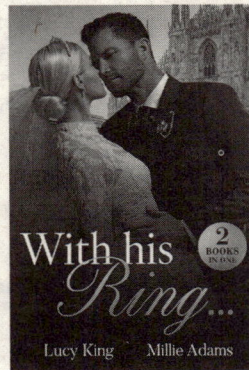

afterglow BOOKS

Afterglow Books is a trend-led, trope-filled list of books with diverse, authentic and relatable characters, a wide array of voices and representations, plus real world trials and tribulations. Featuring all the tropes you could possibly want (think small-town settings, fake relationships, grumpy vs sunshine, enemies to lovers) and all with a generous dose of spice in every story.

♪ @millsandboonuk
◎ @millsandboonuk
afterglowbooks.co.uk
#AfterglowBooks

For all the latest book news, exclusive content and giveaways scan the QR code below to sign up to the Afterglow newsletter:

SCAN ME